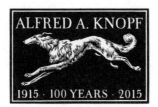

A Hand Reached Down to Guide Me

A Hand Reached Down to Guide Me

||||||

David Gates

Alfred A. Knopf
New York
2015

THIS IS A BORZOI BOOK
PUBLISHED BY ALFRED A. KNOPF

www.aaknopf.com

Knopf, Borzoi Books, and the colophon are registered trademarks of Penguin Random House, LLC.

The stories in this collection were previously published as follows: "George Lassos Moon" (*GQ*, December 2001), "Monsalvat" (*GQ*, December 2002), "Desecrators" (published as "Side Angle Side" in *GQ*, June 2003), "A Hand Reached Down to Guide Me" (*Granta*, January 2014), "A Secret Station" (*The New Yorker*, March 2005), "An Actor Prepares" (*The Paris Review*, Spring 2013), "Alcorian A-1949" (*The Paris Review*, Summer 2011), "The Curse of the Davenports" (*The Paris Review*, Summer 2013), "Locals" (*The Paris Review*, Fall 2014), "Round on Both Ends, High in the Middle" (*Ploughshares*, Fall 2004), "A Place Where Nothing Ever Happens" (published as "Where Nothing Ever Happens" in *Tin House*, Summer 2009)

Library of Congress Cataloging-in-Publication Data
Gates, David, [date]
[Short stories. Selections]
A hand reached down to guide me / David Gates. — First edition.
pages ; cm
"This is a Borzoi book."
ISBN 978-0-385-35153-9 (hardcover) — ISBN 978-0-385-35154-6 (eBook)
I. Title.
PS3557.A87A6 2015   813'.54—dc23   2014030241

Jacket photograph by Ed Panar
Jacket design by Chip Kidd

Manufactured in the United States of America
First Edition

In memory of Liam Rector

There is something at work in my soul, which I do not understand.

Mary Shelley, *Frankenstein*

Contents

A Hand Reached Down to Guide Me

Banishment

||||||

I

On the morning I was to be married for the second time, I found myself going to my knees in the shower and praying: that my ex-husband would find love again, that I would always love my new husband and that whatever pain I had caused in my life would be forgiven. Just one of those maudlin premenstrual moments; I suppose the wedding could have been better timed.

I washed and conditioned my hair, toweled off, blow-dried the fog from the mirror and laid out makeup on the ridge of the sink. The pictures from that afternoon show a bride who might still have passed for thirty.

In fact, I was thirty when I'd married my *first* husband, whom I'd met when we were both working for a Gannett paper in the Hudson Valley—not much of a job for a gal with a degree from Yale, but we can't all be Naomi Wolf. (She was in my year, and I suppose I have to admit to some envy.) He was twenty-seven and looked younger; they'd hired him mostly because he could speak Spanish, having spent two years with the Peace Corps in Peru. This was back in 1990, when somebody had finally noticed that Hispanics had come to Peekskill, Beacon and Poughkeepsie. I'd been at the paper for three years. When the editor brought him by my cubicle, with his flat stomach and male-model stubble, I thought: Maybe one time with him just because I can, if I can.

I stole him from a nice girl, a senior at SUNY New Paltz, fit enough to go rock-climbing and kayaking with him, fool enough to think her fetching round cheeks and her strong thighs and her blond hair entitled her to a happy life. Oh, I don't *really* know what she thought: there must have been something to her, because her favorite book was *The Bell Jar,* though I imagine she's moved on by now—haven't we all? We used to go out for beers, the three of us, and I enjoyed playing the treacherous older sister: confiding to her in the bathroom about the man I was seeing, then coming back to the table and running a bare toe down her boyfriend's shin. He told me, after she'd moved back to California, too heartbroken to go to her graduation, that she sometimes liked to slap his ass when he was on top of her—being a nice girl, she always asked first—and did I think that was weird. Poor babies: so scared of themselves and each other.

The man I'd been seeing was a writer at *Newsweek,* where I was a fact-checker—researchers, we were called, I suppose for the think-tankiness of it—hired straight out of college for twenty thousand a year. But of course with the prospect of moving up. The writer had graduated from some sweaty school like Penn State and had worked for the *Daily News,* so the Yale thing must have been part of my appeal, along with the prettiness and youngerness and wantonness things. He was married—shockeroo, right?—and years later, when he ended up in a wheelchair, the wife stayed with him. It's possible she loved him—I never met the lady.

I didn't start up with him, strictly speaking, until after I'd left *Newsweek,* where after four years I'd been getting nothing but the occasional shared byline: some writer, out of charity or laziness, would delegate me to do a phoner. And I'd had a seminar with Harold Bloom, for God's sake. So my writer got me a job at that loser paper—people knew his name back then—where I could write and report, review the occasional movie or concert, accumulate some clips while looking for something worthy of me. Because I still wanted to consider myself a New Yorker, I kept my walk-up on Eighty-Eighth off Amsterdam, reverse-commuting to Westchester an hour each way.

It turned out that my writer was mentoring another female researcher too; no wonder he'd been so willing to put in a word for me. A couple of evenings a week he'd come to my apartment straight from his office and give me a good mentoring, with a scarf tied around my ankles. He always had to leave by eight o'clock, which left me free to go out. I'd offer him my shower, but he was afraid to go home with wet hair.

I stayed faithful to my first husband for five years, which doesn't make much of a story, so I'm not going to string this out. The writer and his wife, though: Wouldn't *that* be a story? I asked my mother once, "Would you have stayed with Daddy if you hadn't had me?"

"That's like saying if you'd been born with flippers would I have aborted you."

"Yeah but if I'd been already been born . . ." I was twelve, with a steel-trap mind, though I picked up only the illogic, not the flippiness of saying this to a daughter about to get her first period.

"That's my point," she said.

Actually, she did leave my father, though not until I was out of the house. Whereas the writer's wife—I don't know, somebody goes, somebody stays, somebody latches on to somebody else, the thing with somebody else does or doesn't go on for a while: Am I missing something here? Sad old Harold Bloom—who never put a hand on *my* thigh, though he did call me "my dear," which is what he called every-one, male or female—made us read the *Paradiso*, where it turns out to be Love that's moving the sun and the other stars. That's the big kicker. I have to say, I'm not seeing it.

"So it looks like I'm moving up to Westchester," I told the writer. Now that we were no longer fucking, he'd begun taking me to P. J. Clarke's again; while the mentoring was intense, we'd met at a bar for alcoholics on Tenth Avenue, with fluorescent lights and signs all over the walls displaying the prices of drinks. I assume now that this was less about caution than about wickedness.

"At your age?" he said. "An extra five hundred square feet isn't worth a human life."

"Actually," I said, "I think I'm getting married."

"Oh," he said. "Huh. Well, I guess this was bound to happen, wasn't it?" He raised his snifter of Rémy. "Mazel tov. It's done wonders for *me*."

I grew up in Saddle River, New Jersey. Richard Nixon moved there a couple of years after I went off to Yale, and my mother claims she spotted him once, through the tinted glass in a black car, and gave him the finger, all of which I doubt. She'd gone to Smith, where she majored in English and made obsessive visits to Emily Dickinson's house. When I was in high school and college she was always going into the city for readings and off to Vermont or Provincetown to take classes with poets who picked up a living by humoring middle-aged ladies. I don't mean to make her sound silly; at least, as I found out, she became a bit of a pothead. I was sixteen when I caught her out behind the shed where my father kept the riding mower. "We won't tell your dad," she said—as if doing so had been thinkable—and passed the joint to me. My father was the executive vice president, whatever that is, of a company that manufactured speaker systems for movie theaters, which I suppose made both of them artistic people. He'd voted for Nixon the first time but not the second, or maybe it was second time but not the first—I know he didn't like McGovern, whichever one that was. When their marriage broke up, he took a lesser job in Philadelphia, while she stayed in Saddle River—all her friends were there—in a shabby one-bedroom condo.

Both of them showed up for my wedding—my first wedding, I mean. I hadn't seen them together since graduation, and neither had brought

a new partner. My mother called celibacy "taking early retirement"—
she was kidding herself: it wasn't that early—and the alimony payments her "pension." My father, God knows. But he'd always had a
little something on the side, and by then he'd probably had the sense
to lower whatever his standards had been. They sat next to each other
at our table, talking forehead-to-forehead. My father had put on weight
and had broken veins in his face, but he'd shaved his cheeks to a shine
and his suit fit him—no gap between the back of the coat and the shirt
collar, which was more than I could say for my new husband's suit. My
mother had frosted her hair, gotten a salon tan and taken a Valium.

"We were just talking about the Easter basket," my father said to
me. He raised his chin at my husband. "Here's something I bet she
didn't tell you."

"Is this going to be touching?" I said.

"This one year, I don't remember how old she was—"

"Seven," my mother said.

"Somewhere in there," he said. "Anyway, she got her grandmother,
Helen's mother this was, to take her to the drugstore and she spent her
allowance on an Easter basket for *us*. Which she then proceeded to
hide—*where* did she hide it?"

"The clothes hamper," my mother said.

"So she had us go all around the house—'warmer,' 'colder.' She was
the most loving little thing."

"That's a great story," my husband said.

I suppose I should be able to explain why I married such a *boy*, shouldn't
I? Technically he was both handsome and good in bed, so kind that one
time, early on, his guilt over the nice girl made him impotent with me,
and so besotted that it didn't happen again. And thirty seemed like an
appropriate age, as if you'd been holding out all that time for the right
man. I liked it that he didn't have that East Coast *thing:* he'd grown
up in New Mexico, near Albuquerque, and he thought Yale and Harvard were simply good schools, like Stanford and Berkeley. He gradu-

ated from the University of Wyoming. I don't want to give you the idea that he was a knuckle-dragger, despite the Peace Corps and the rock-climbing. He read Borges and Márquez, and he translated some of Neruda's love poems for me; no one, he claimed, had really gotten them right, though I doubt he did either. And he wasn't interested in having kids—for the record, here's exactly what he said. He said it was quote perfect just the two of us. I see now that this left him some wiggle room, if imperfection ever began to reveal itself. When I told him I'd rather stick my head in the oven, he probably thought it was just feminist talk from his feisty girlfriend.

We both knew I was a better writer, but while I bitched and moaned about having to cover an André Rieu concert, or the annual car show in Rhinebeck, he had what he thought was a book project: following around a young Dominican infielder who played for some minor-league team in Poughkeepsie. The manager gave him unlimited access—the dugout, the locker room, the bus, the budget motels. When he couldn't get any magazines to pay his way, he used up all his miles on a reporting trip to the D.R. But ultimately, he said, this was a story about America. Well, you see the sweet futility.

So our newlyweds rented a half town house in Croton: numbered parking spaces by our unit, a shared balcony divided by an iron railing. We bought a yard-sale sectional—don't think we didn't have our little joke about sectional intercourse—and bookcases from Ikea and a kilim from Pottery Barn that was too thin to stay in place on the parquet floor. We had—but what's the use of saying what we had?

On Saturdays he used to go over to the outdoor basketball court on our cul-de-sac. One of the neighbors had bought a pair of nets, and somebody would get on somebody's shoulders and hang them from the orange hoops. Women could play, if they showed up in even numbers. Afterward, we'd have his friends over for beers; he grilled on the balcony until the people on the other side of the railing complained.

He taught me to drive stick and I taught him to keep his fork in his left hand; I showed him Paris and he showed me Machu Picchu. We learned Italian together, with tapes and a book, though we owed so much on our credit cards from those two trips—his miles would've been a help—that we never made it to Florence. I was the teacher in bed, and the one time I found a girl for us—I met her at the gym—it was sweet to see that he didn't know the etiquette, though of course who does, and afterward he claimed not to want to again. Maybe he was afraid of hurting my feelings—he'd been scrupulous about looking only in *my* eyes—but I think I shocked him with some of our goings-on. A boy with boundaries!

Or maybe he just had better sense. I might have known this girl would make a pest of herself. I mean, a nineteen-year-old? Studying "communications" at a two-year college? But she was pretty, and eager, and I'd missed being with a girl, and she saved the *I'm in love with yous* until a couple of weeks later, when she begged me to meet her for coffee, just the two of us, and kissed me as I sat down. I finally had to block her number and her email and started going to a gym in Tarrytown.

His Dominican infielder: that's what we *should've* done. It might have opened up his girl side, not to be too graphic. He took me to a game once and we sat just behind the dugout near first base. He usually sat *in* the dugout, but he told me the players were superstitious about having a woman there. That's how gay baseball is. His infielder batted left-handed against the enemy's right-handed pitcher—my husband explained that he was a *switch-hitter,* which was too hilarious—so I had a good view of how his buttocks strained the fabric of his baseball pants as he bent forward, wagging his bat. When he scored a run and loped back to the dugout, his smile exposed a broken tooth. Picking out this boy to follow around couldn't have been a purely journalistic decision. This isn't a regret, exactly, though now that I'm in my fifties, I couldn't *pay* two boys to come to bed with me and play. Well one *could,* I'm sure, in some specialized corner of hell. Not all young women, it turns out, are such body Nazis; you have to wonder what's wrong with *them*. But I've become such a spectacle these days, with my still-handsome legs and not much else, that I mostly forgo the pleasure.

It was sometime after the debacle with the nineteen-year-old when my husband got a phone call at his desk, then came over to my cubicle with his poor-me look: his infielder had gotten caught selling cocaine. "I'm a shitty reporter," he said. "This was going on the whole fucking time, and I'm asking him like how do you place your feet to make the double play."

"But this is great," I said. "Now you've actually got a story."

"*You* go ahead and write it. I don't appreciate being lied to."

"Okay, but you can't waste time getting all humiliated. You need to go see him in jail. Like *now*. Before they deport him or something. Not to sound heartless about it."

"This wasn't the story."

"This was *always* the story," I said. "You just got it handed to you."

"Yeah, well I guess I'm not a realist," he said.

"Oh, baby," I said. "It's going to be a long life."

I'd been remarried for a year when I spotted him at the organic super-market outside Poughkeepsie, with my replacement. I'd heard they'd moved somewhere nearby, but I was passing through, needed to pick up olive oil and some decent coffee, and I figured what were the chances. He'd always hated shopping, but there he was pushing the cart, with green things up in the part you unfold to put a baby's legs through, while she was doing the hunting and gathering. That prayer of mine, about him finding love again—whatever it was he'd found with me, it had never been *that*.

The new wife might have been pregnant then, though she wasn't showing; their son must be a teenager now. I hear her on the radio all the time—maybe you do too. She's the one who does that two-minute spot every day on NPR: *A Word in Edgewise,* explaining what she calls the "always-surprising" origins of common words and phrases. The theme music is Tom Tom Club's "Wordy Rappinghood"—that's what she calls herself—and it runs on something like a hundred stations all over the country. Pictures on her website suggest she hasn't lost her looks, though who knows how recent they are. So in every way he traded up. And really, God bless him. Did you know that the word "maudlin"—but of course you do.

2

My husband was still feeling sorry for himself when my editor sent me to interview a once-almost-famous architect. The common council in Peekskill had approved his plan for converting a block of the old downtown into galleries and artists' lofts; as if this weren't enough booster appeal, he'd grown up in the Hudson Valley and had recently moved back after years in the city. Said to be an amateur musician, and a friend of Philip Roth's. Two thousand words, maybe three if he turned out to be a good talker. I'd never heard of this man—how many architects *has* anybody heard of?—but back in the seventies the *Times* had called him "a charter member of a loosely allied group of younger practitioners of quite wide diversity who are known as postmodernists." He was in his forties then, which I guess was the *Times*'s idea of younger, and had done "important" buildings in Düsseldorf, Turin, São Paulo, Shanghai and Cleveland. He'd gotten his degree from Columbia, and went back there to teach. Married to a viola player with the Steve Reich Ensemble. The most recent clip I could find was from 1989.

When I came into the coffee shop in Rhinebeck, a bell dinged above the door and a man at a corner table looked up from reading, lifted his chin, got to his feet and pulled out a chair for me. I'd said I'd be wearing a maroon silk blouse—actually rayon, but I thought I'd keep it simple for him—and carrying a leather shoulder bag. He'd told me to look for "a graying gentleman with a Mets cap"; I'm afraid my piece described him as "a tall, vigorous man, with hawklike features, whose restless energy belies his sixty-five years." (In time to come, he would wake me from a nap and say, "Mind if I belie you?" But let's not get ahead of our story.) He had broad hands, long fingers, no ring.

Before leaving home, I'd undone my top button and leaned into the mirror to check the effect: just enough to make a graying gentleman talkative. But after an initial up-and-down—what man can refrain?—he kept his eyes on my face or on the tabletop, drumming his fingers on a copy of *The New York Review of Books* (such an obvious prop that I didn't mention it in the piece) and massaging, with thumb and forefinger, the bridge of his not-all-that-hawklike nose.

I walked him through his influences: everything, he said, from Bauhaus to the outhouse—a line he'd used in one of the old interviews I'd read. How did he define postmodernism? He didn't, but *I* was welcome to have a go at it. When he and Philip Roth got together, did they talk about writing, or architecture, or both? "Now where on earth did you hear *that*?" he said. "I'm an *admirer*, of course, but—you're not thinking of Philip Glass?" Was he still teaching? Only by negative example. What did he do between projects? Well, he used not to *be* between projects, but these days he went to his workroom and painted. What were his paintings like? If I were to see them, I'd understand why he'd become an architect. *Could* I see them? No. What prompted him to leave New York? *Prompted?* That sounded rather Pavlovian. He'd had a weekend house here for . . . God, how many years? Let's just say it had gotten time to simplify. And of course he'd spent his childhood in this part of the world; he supposed I knew his father had taught at Bard during its glory years, which wasn't to say Leon wasn't doing a magnificent job. He'd always thought there was something strange and magical about the landscape—in fact, if you went back to the Hudson River School . . .

I got him off that as soon as I decently could—my editor hated what he called thumbsucking—and onto the project in Peekskill. "Yes, yes," he said. "Down to business. Good Lord, Peekskill, what can one say? It was a bit of a five-finger exercise—actually, don't quote me on that. Let's say it was a way of giving back to the community."

"Oh?" I said. "So are you giving them a hometown discount?"

That made him look at me.

"Aren't *you* devilish," he said. "Peekskill's a rat hole. Not without its dingy charms, but I hardly see it as the new SoHo. Is *that* the scoop you were looking for? Stir up a little small-town hoo-hah? Tell me something—am I right in thinking you're as bored with all this as I am? If you've got what you need, let's you and I go have a drink."

All these years later, I can't remember what I thought I was doing, if thinking came into it at all. He was intelligent, still handsome, obviously complicated, sufficiently knowing to discern that I was bored, though that probably required no great discernment. My husband would never have called Peekskill a rat hole, which is exactly what it was. I might have thought that an hour's worth of flirtation would do us both good. He seemed lonely—where *was* the wife?—but too civilized to embarrass himself. Not having been touched in weeks, not since the brooding about the baseball book started, I might simply have wanted to feel my power over a man.

So I followed his shiny new pickup truck—naturally I liked the pickup truck—to a cinder-block bar outside of town, with neon signs in the windows, a pool table and a single TV. "I thought this place might be noir enough for a hard-boiled newshound like you," he said. "Whiskey? Or do you want a *girl* drink?"

"Those are my choices?" I said.

"I certainly wouldn't recommend the wine list here. And I don't see you as a beer drinker."

"In that case," I said. He ordered us two Jack Daniel's.

"So is this your regular hang?" I said.

"Oh, just when I'm feeling particularly louche. All the bars in Dutchess County were like Duffy's Tavern when I was a kid—you don't know what that is. Okay, here's my favorite joke. 'Have you lived here all your life, old-timer?' '*Not yet.*'"

"That's your favorite?"

"Only because it's not funny. May I grill *you* for a change? You're young, obviously bright, and here you are. Writing for the *Hudson Valley Whosis.*"

"Is that a question? I might say here *you* are."

"Meaning why am I not in Barcelona or some goddamn place, campaigning for the Pritzker Prize? I know what I am at this point. I like just going up to my workroom, putting on some music and painting the hours away. And I like hearing the birds in the morning. What do *you* like? What *would* you like?"

"I don't know. To get through the day?"

"Aren't *you* a romantic." He emptied his glass—they were little ones—and raised two fingers. "Sorry, I don't mean to make light of it. It's hell to be young. But it does get better. Until it gets worse."

"How does it get better?"

"I suppose it's what Yeats said—find your work and choose your mate. Does anyone read Yeats anymore? Or maybe it's choose your work and find your mate. I see you've already got half of it covered." He touched a finger to my wedding band. "Or is this just a professional accessory, to keep the men at bay?"

"I'm not exactly beset," I said.

"Let me not believe that." The bartender set two more glasses down in front of him, and he pushed one over to me. "But. It's a principle of mine not to interfere with happy marriages."

"If *that's* a question," I said, "yes. Very. Your wife's a musician?"

"Well," he said, "you've got the musician part right."

"Oh," I said. "I'm sorry."

"Yeats didn't say anything about *keeping* your mate. Ah well, tales from the crypt."

"You have children?"

"A daughter. She's all grown up. Well, obviously. She fancies herself a cellist—electric cello. What they call noise music. She takes after her mother."

"*And* you," I said. "Do you see her?"

"That sounds like an accusation," he said. "She lives out in Oregon, in Portland, with her young lady. Whom I like. Actually, I try not to approve *too* much. I'm afraid she'll take up with some young man just to spite me. And what does *your* young man do?"

"He's got a book he's working on." At this point, it was still the line I was taking.

"Ah." He picked up his glass. "I can see it all. Well, here's to his book."

My husband was out playing hoops when I got home, so I opened a bottle of Dos Equis to account for the liquor on my breath and started transcribing. On the tape, the architect was talking about Thomas Cole's *The Voyage of Life,* about playing with a jazz trio at a restaurant in Poughkeepsie, about the music he put on while he painted: first "The Washington Post March"—"to nerve me up"—then something like the Schubert quartets, then maybe some Verdi highlights, building up to the big boys, Mahler or Wagner, before winding down with Miles Davis. "You must think I'm inventing all this to make myself sound interesting," he said. I typed that in, then remembered that my editor hated pieces that broke the fourth wall. I would have gone to see him play for a colorful on-scene lede, but since the piece was due the next day, I went with his how-it-all-began story.

"I was, I don't know, ten, eleven, something like that, my parents took me down to the city and we saw *The Palm Beach Story*—you've seen it, yes? I fell in love with that apartment where Claudette Colbert lived—that duplex with the balcony? Of course I also fell in love with Claudette Colbert. At any rate. After the movie I begged them to take me to 968 Park Avenue—never forgotten that address—so we could see the place and of course they had to tell me it was just a stage set—it didn't really exist anywhere. So I just began drawing pictures of it from memory, figuring out where the different rooms would be, so forth and so on."

Ever since, I wrote, *translating visionary spaces into the realm of the concrete and the practical has been*—but I'll spare you, and me, the rest. At least I'd never have to see this man again.

"He didn't give you much," my husband said when I showed him the first draft.

"It's a puff piece," I said. "Isn't that what we do? Should I have asked about his divorce?"

"He's divorced?"

"Stop the presses," I said.

"Okay, so you can't put that in, but I'm not seeing the human side."

"Like does he shop at Kmart?"

"*Something* like that, yeah. A little texture."

"This isn't *The New Yorker*."

"You do your best *wherever* you are," he said. "That's how you get *out* of wherever you are."

"I'm okay with where I am."

"You?" he said. "You're twice as unhappy as I am. You just didn't like the guy, so you're making him sound like a pompous ass. All this shit about Washington Irving—and what's the Hudson River School?"

"I'm quoting what he said. They're going to cut it anyway. Fine. I *didn't* like him much."

"Well, it comes through."

"What if I wanted it to?" I said.

"Then I guess it's a win-win. Except for anybody who has to read it. *He'll* probably like it—he seems like he's into hearing himself talk."

"It's not *that* bad, is it?"

"It's okay. It's not your best."

"You're right," I said. "It's not up there with Neil Diamond at the Mid-Hudson Civic Center. I can't believe this is my life."

"Then you need to do something about it," he said.

"So you don't think that if I whine loud enough, God will hear me?"

"It hasn't worked so far."

"I'm going to pretend you didn't say that," I said.

The architect called the day the piece came out, to say he thought it had turned out well—not to thank me, mind you, one didn't thank a professional for doing her job. But if I and my young man would care to—

"My husband?"

"How many young men do you *have*?" he said. "Listen, may I take you both to dinner? I'd have you come to the house, but I thought I should spare you the bachelor cookery. *And* whatever ghostly presences. Mexican suit you? There's a place up in this neck of the woods where they make their own tamales. If you're willing to come that far."

"My husband will be thrilled—he misses the food in Albuquerque. And he's spent a lot of time in Latin America."

"And you? Less than thrilled, I'm assuming."

"I'm happy to get out," I said.

"I know the feeling," he said. "Two of us happy, one of us thrilled—a couple of margaritas and they'll have to strap us into our chairs."

We met him at a place in Tivoli, with a southwestern-looking lizard on its hanging sign, where we drank margaritas out on the terrace. "Your wife tells me," he said, "that you're at work on a book."

"You need to stop telling everybody that," my husband said, then turned back to the man. "Not a real happy story."

"Well, but you'll go on to something else. Hell, I got fired off my first project—some car dealer wanted to put a beach house on this little narrow lot in Amagansett, and I came up with a design that looked like Oldenburg's clothespin. I suppose it was my little way of showing contempt. Anyhow. What sorts of things do you write about?"

"I don't know, just whatever interests me."

"And what interests you?"

"I can't really put it in a nutshell—stories about people, I guess."

"Well, then you'll never run short of material. So I take it you're in favor."

"Of?"

"People. Or do you think the jury's still out?"

"Are you asking me seriously?"

"Should we order?" I said.

"Now, see?" he said. "Our young lady has the right priorities. 'Grub first, then ethics.' I forget who said that—you don't happen to remember? It has sort of a thirties ring to it."

"I wouldn't know."

"No, why should you? Grub first, then obscure quotations. Anything on here appeal to you? I'm afraid this is more Tex than Mex. Not quite what you're used to."

"Actually, I haven't spent much time in Mexico," my husband said.

"Then maybe we'll squeak by. Why don't we just pick out a bunch of this and that and share? Do you both eat meat? One has to ask these days. We should have another round, too."

"He's even a worse asshole than you made him out to be," my husband said on the drive home. "He's into *you*, though. At first I thought he was gay."

"Why would you think he's into *me*? He talked to *you* the whole time."

"Yeah, exactly. Come on, I'm not stupid. Don't *you* be. And like how he kept talking about how old he was? It was so obvious."

"If you're right, that's really sad."

"You *know* I'm right. Are you teasing his cock or *what's* going on?"

"Are we really going to get into a thing about this? I just thought it would be interesting."

"As in, for a change?"

"I can't believe you're doing this," I said. "Listen, you want me to drive? Those margaritas were pretty strong."

"This is not a good man," he said. "And I have to tell you, it scares the shit out of me when you're *acting*."

The day after we'd had dinner, he called me at the paper, to thank me and my young man for coming out with him, then waited a week to call again. He happened to be on his way north from the city, and did I have time for a quick drink? I could hear my husband typing in the next cubicle. "That sounds fine," I said.

"Wonderful. You're welcome to bring your young man along, but I don't think he likes me much."

"Right," I said. "That's probably not necessary."

"Even better then. Five thirty too early for you?"

"I don't think so."

"And what's a good place? I don't really know this town."

The typing stopped. "It's hard to say just now."

"Surely there must be—ah. God, I'm a little slow today. You're not alone."

"Exactly."

"Okay, let me think. I passed an Applebee's coming in on Route Nine. You know where it is? We can go someplace from there."

"Right," I said. "Well, thanks."

"Copy desk giving you shit?" my husband said.

"No, just something I needed to find out about."

"It was that guy."

"For Christ's *sake*," I said. "Is *that* why you've been so weird?"

"I was going to ask you the same thing."

"This is too stupid to even discuss," I said. "Anyway—" I nodded over at the editor, who was talking on the phone.

"Then what time are you coming home?" he said.

"Not late," I said. "I was supposed to meet somebody for a quick drink. Probably seven, seven thirty? We could order in and maybe have a little date night after."

"Who are you meeting?"

"Andrea," I said. As soon as I said it, I realized it would have been more in character for me to resent being questioned. "I used to work with her at *Newsweek*? She's taking the train up."

"Mind if I come along?"

"It's going to be a lot of girl talk. But sure, if you want." Worst case, I could get away and call the man, then take my husband to a bar and keep checking my watch. *Andrea's such a flake*—that's what I'd say. How could he not believe in Andrea?

"No, on second thought I think I'll bag it."

"You weren't testing me, were you?"

"What would be the use?" he said.

The man was waiting outside the Applebee's in his truck, his window down, reading the *Times*. I'd put on a halter top that morning—it was such a hot day, and I hadn't thought I'd have to see anybody. Now I wished I'd had time to drive home and change. "Let's just go here," I said. "I shouldn't stay long."

"I suppose their liquor's the same as anybody else's," he said. "You'll have to provide the ambience." He opened his door, stood up on tiptoes and stretched his arms over his head. His T-shirt came up and exposed an inch of still-lean waistline, which might have been the idea. "It's certainly the last place anybody'd come looking for *you*."

"My husband doesn't *spy* on me. If that's what you mean."

"No, I can't imagine your putting up with that. Still, a booth might be in order."

"You're making this sound like something it isn't," I said.

"Good for you," he said. "You've spared us the preliminaries." He put a palm on my bare shoulder blade. Up to that point, I hadn't thought I was seriously considering this man. "Suppose we go in and talk about it."

When the waitress had set down our drinks and moved off, he said, "Since you're pressed for time—cheers, by the way. It's obvious that I've taken a shine to you, *and* it's obvious that I'm much too old, and of course you have your young man—my God, you look like you've just been shot. This is much more embarrassing for *me*."

"You don't seem that embarrassed," I said.

"I'm not, oddly enough. The *situation* is embarrassing, yes. But basically you're either going to tell me to go peddle my papers or you're not. Which should be clarifying. My position is just that I'd like some time with you."

"That would be difficult," I said.

"Hmm," he said. "I've heard stronger expressions of outrage."

"I'll bet you have."

"Oh sure, you can typecast me if you want to. You might take it as a compliment that I'm not trying to sneak up on you. Just one person to another."

"Except that I'm married."

"As was I."

"And I love my husband."

"I'd think the worse of you if you didn't. I'm not trying to make your life any harder." He picked up the glossy menu, with color photos of steaks. "God, this place is what hell's going to be like."

"Why would you think my life is hard?" I said.

" 'Getting through the day'? Isn't that what you said? Sounds like joy unbounded."

"So what would we do? If I *could* spend time with you? Apparently you're good at sitting around and drinking."

"Not much escapes *you*, does it?" he said. "I was thinking that what we did would be entirely up to us. We could start out just being kind to each other."

The day I'd interviewed him, it had been a muggy Sunday afternoon in July, and I'd gotten caught in traffic on the southbound Taconic, as if I were a weekender, heading back to my husband, drunk in my poor little Tercel, my overtanned left arm out the window—I hate air-conditioning—among the BMWs with their opaque glass, my clunky espadrilles slipping off the pedals. The cars ahead had come to a standstill, for no reason I could see, and I worked the things off; the toenails I'd painted that morning, to be a summer fun girl, looked childish.

The day I drove to Vermont to meet him, the maple trees were blazing. He'd wanted me to fly with him to Burlington—it was only half an hour from Newburgh—but I thought I might need to make a getaway, and there was the million-to-one chance of my husband's seeing the Tercel wherever I left it. In my purse, on the seat next to me, were the condoms I'd bought at a drugstore in Fair Haven—out of superstition, I'd waited to cross the state line—on the chance he proved not to be a gentleman, and a bottle of Astroglide to prove I wasn't a lady. It had been more than two months, just taking the train down to meet for early dinners in the city or to walk around the Whitney and the Modern. We saw a Mets game, and a trashy production of *Timon of Athens* in the park, which we took turns abusing over drinks in the Algonquin lobby. Nothing untoward, beyond the lies I'd had to tell my husband. So I'd given this due consideration.

"It's going to be peak weekend," he'd said on the phone. "Why don't you come up and see the leaves with me? My friend Craig's giving me the use of his house on Lake Champlain. He's going to Bordeaux for a month."

"God," I said. "I want his life. I want *your* life."

"I'd make that swap," he said. "But you'd better do the math before you sign on. Anyway, it's a big house. You wouldn't have to sleep anywhere you didn't want to."

"Have you been in bed with a senior citizen before?" he said that first night. "I'm probably good for about once, so we should make this count."

I continued living with my husband, so this was now called "having an affair." Nobody had cellphones back then, and I kept quarters in my wallet for those trips to 7-Eleven to pick up Beer Nuts or half-and-half or dish soap; it seemed we were always running out of something. The in-laws flew in from New Mexico for Thanksgiving and I cooked my first, and last, turkey. His mother said she was too young to be called Grandma (she was fifty-six), so maybe—when the time came—she could be Nana. "Just ignore her," my husband said as we were getting in bed. "Thirty-five's not old. We've still got plenty of time."

"Tell me you're not serious," I said. "I thought we were clear about this. Would you turn that out? It's hurting my eyes."

"Better?" he said. "That was a pretty long time ago. *I* sort of thought . . ."

"*What?*" I said. "Okay, let's hear all of it."

"This obviously isn't a good time."

"So what was your plan? Start working on me when I found my first gray hair?" Which I already had, though I hadn't showed it to him.

"You're being paranoid," he said. "Can't we even have a conversation?"

"Why don't you have your conversation with *Nana*," I said. "Maybe she's still ovulating."

Driving back to Croton after dropping his parents at LaGuardia, I told him there were things I needed to think over.

"Okay, I saw *this* one coming," he said. "Male or female?"

"Please," I said. "Are you a *child*?"

"If it's the old guy, I guess you got a little of both."

"It's not anybody," I said. "It's what I told you."

"Listen to her go," he said. "Just keep me up to date on your *thinking*."

I asked Andrea—yes, there really *was* an Andrea—if I could come down and sleep on her sofa for a while, just until I could figure things out. "Great," she said, "so I'm supposed to put you up until the millennium?" She'd left *Newsweek* to be a features editor at *Mirabella* and lived a few blocks from my old apartment. I went back to the reverse commute and the alternate-side parking; some nights, driving around looking for a space, it felt like I'd never left. I brought a suitcase full of clothes and a box of books, all anybody needed, and left the rest of my stuff hostage. The architect was after me to move into his house, but I'd told him what I'd told my husband (things that needed thinking over) and that I'd see him only on weekends. Every Saturday I'd drive up to Rhinebeck and spend hours in his bed, where, results aside, I liked how greedy he was for me; he humored my craziness by letting me hide my car in his garage. Then, come Sunday afternoon, I'd stop off and meet my husband for a miserable late lunch at the Croton Diner, our old spot. Of course I told him I'd just driven up from the city. I don't know why I put us through this. One time I forgot to put my ring back on—he always wore his—and he just looked at my hand and said nothing.

At Christmas, my husband went back to Albuquerque, where I imagine he and Nana had plenty to say to each other, and the morning after New Year's—his plane got in that afternoon—I drove up, bought boxes at U-Haul, rented a storage unit and packed the rest of my belongings. I left a letter for him on the kitchen counter, signed "In sadness." Exhibit A, I suppose, when I come before the Judgment Seat. The part of the letter that was true said that I didn't know where I'd eventually be going, and that I'd keep trying to make things as easy as possible at work.

The man—what do I call him at this stage? "My lover" is sick-making, and there doesn't seem to be a male equivalent of "mistress." (Wordy Rappinghood, help me out here!) At any rate, he'd gone to Portland to visit his daughter, and my mother was in Costa Rica, with a friend whose husband had just died, so I treated Andrea to a Christmas dinner at Café des Artistes; she was sentimental about being alone with nowhere to go. I couldn't really afford a second bottle of the seventy-dollar red wine, but one hadn't been enough, and it was good of her to listen to my back-and-forthings when she hadn't had a boyfriend—even in the loosest sense of the term—for three years, unable as she was to fake being either pretty or forward or biddable. *And* the waiter seemed to have low expectations of two single women, so I was determined to rack up an even more impressive total on which to tip him a fuck-you twenty-five percent.

"Why don't you pass along whichever one you decide you don't want," she said. "Kidding."

"I know how obnoxious I sound," I said. "I should just go back, shouldn't I? And chalk this other thing up to whatever."

"He *is* awfully old. But if you weren't happy . . ."

"Jesus," I said, "if *that's* the yardstick."

I drove up to Rhinebeck for New Year's Eve; he told me the boys were calling him pussy-simple because he'd backed out of a gig at some country club so we could spend the evening together.

"Listen," he said, "I bought us champagne, but how about a *drink* drink?"

"I hate champagne."

"Good—we'll give it to the poor." He got up and went to the kitchen, leaving me on the sofa hugging my bare knees, my bare feet on the soft leather cushions. A matching sofa faced this one, on the other side of a coffee table that had been an old wooden door in Guatemala, with plate glass over its carvings of droopy-necked birds. Two walls were all books; on another, he had a small painting by Richard Diebenkorn, whom I'd had to look up. The Diebenkorn, he said, was the one *truly* precious thing he'd been able to hang on to.

"I still think you're crazy," he said, handing me a glass of scotch with no ice. At home, he drank smoky single malt—he called it *"premier cru"*—with just a little water, to bring out the nose. It tasted like iodine, but I was getting used to it. "I'm rattling around in this big place by myself, and you want to rent some little studio where you don't have enough room to swing a cat. You can live here for nothing—costs the same to run this place whether it's just me or a whole seraglio. We could manage to stay out of each other's hair. *When* we wanted to."

"You realize I'm still married."

"Oh, well, *married,*" he said. "In that case, forget the whole thing. We don't want to call down Jove's lightning bolts."

"I just mean it's weird enough as it is, going in and seeing him every day."

"So quit going in. You don't want to be there anyway. 'The vibrant street life of downtown Peekskill'?"

"Now you're being a prick," I said. "I told you they wrote in 'vibrant.'"

"You could be doing your own work," he said. There was his insidiousness: a less clever man would have said *should* be. "Call me utopian, but it seems to me that solutions suggest themselves to all these problems."

"It looks easy to *you.*"

"That it does," he said. "Here, drink up. Do we really have to wait till the ball drops to hit the hay?"

In the morning, I made him take me to the loft above the carriage barn, which he called "my workshop of filthy creation." It smelled of coffee and turpentine, and his drafting board was shoved into a corner; a blank canvas stood on an easel. He'd been weird about his paintings, and I'd thought they might be sick and sinister—like Francis Bacon or somebody, not that this would have put me off—but they turned out to be bright generic abstractions, a little Klee here, a little Kandinsky there, a lot of Mondrian. "Here you have it," he said. "The inside of an utterly conventional mind. Are you still speaking to me?"

When I came back to work after the holiday, my husband was typing in his cubicle. I found the note I'd written him my under my keyboard, with a Post-it reading *You might want this for your memory book.* I took it to be his pissy way of giving me his blessing.

3

It was snowing the day I moved in, and when I pulled up to his house, he was shoveling a path from the front steps to the sidewalk, wearing his red plaid barn jacket—no gloves, no hat—and blowing out clouds of breath in the cold. I had signed on to live with an old man who might be prone to giving himself a heart attack. He helped carry in my suitcases and boxes: all I owned then was my clothes, my books and papers, some CDs—I didn't have to be told that I'd be listening to them with earphones—and my computer. I came to him with seven thousand dollars in the bank and six thousand in credit card debt.

I'd quit my regular job at the paper to kick in a column from time to time—who worried about health insurance back then?—and Andrea promised to hook me up with freelance work. A borderline kept woman, fine. But to live in a grown-up house, with a grown-up man? To be able to devote yourself to writing before it was too late? Otherwise I'd be like my mother in twenty years—a postsexual groupie going on about poets she'd "studied with" in some summer workshop. "Let's just say it's not your all-time most feminist move," Andrea said. "I mean, *I'd* grab it, not that anybody's offering. But you should probably think about making a splash sooner rather than later."

So how rich was he? It didn't occur to me to ask—how *would* you? To me it was magic money, like what your parents have when you're a child. Once in a while, early on, I'd look at a price on a menu or on an opera ticket and think I was in over my head, but you get used to not thinking. The house in Rhinebeck had been their weekend place, before what he called "the Great Awakening"; his wife had kept their loft on White Street. He'd inherited ten hilltop acres from his father, several towns to the south, on which he'd always meant to build someday, but his wife was a city girl, so they'd compromised on this place: a three-story house with a mansard roof, from which you could walk to the little shops and restaurants. Rhinebeck hadn't been unbearable back then, he said, but you could already see where it was headed. He wanted to take me to see the hilltop in the spring, after mud season, when you could get up the dirt road. The view, he said, was heartbreaking.

Of course he professed belief in the room-of-one's-own thing—after the seventies, what man didn't?—and he let me have my choice of places in which, he said, the soul might select her society then shut the door. (He didn't really say that; it's a little wink and nod to my mother. I don't know why I'm being so pissy.) How about the guest room on the second floor? The parlor off the living room? The finished room in the basement—more space, though not much daylight? Anywhere, really, except his daughter's old room: I could have the run of the house, since he went out to the carriage barn every morning at six thirty. I took what was once a maid's room, at the back of the top floor, with an arched ceiling and a dormer window looking out into the branches of a tree—which he said would eventually resume life as a maple. Together we moved the mission table from the parlor, up the broad stairs to the second floor, then, on its end, up the narrow stairs to the third. I asked if I could hang one of his paintings on my wall—he had none of them up in the house—and he told me to take my pick; that would *guarantee* he'd never intrude. He insisted on buying me an ergonomic desk chair in the city, and a narrow brass bed at an antique shop in town, for napping or—not to be grim, but these things *will* happen—in the event of a spat. I noted that he was imagining *me* as the one who'd have to go huffing out of the conjugal bed, but after all wasn't it *his* conjugal bed?

He said this was to be my home too, so we'd put out any favorite objects I'd brought and rearrange furniture to suit my taste. But his taste was better than mine. He did buy a new mattress for the conjugal bed, which he needn't have done: I wasn't that imaginative. *Her* dishes, *her* kitchen stuff—it was just dishes and kitchen stuff, though one blue spatterware bowl got on my nerves, I don't know why, and I put it out of sight on the top shelf of the cupboard. The glazed Chinese tea jars, the brass umbrella stand embossed with a comely lady in colonial costume and the pair of Staffordshire dogs might have been hers, or might just have been bric-a-brac that had come with the house. If he'd had pictures of her and their daughter on display, he must have put them away before I'd visited for the first time; how long before wasn't my business. I kept my own pictures in a plastic storage box in my room of one's own, along with old check registers, bank statements, tax returns and floppy disks.

I did my writing up there, or tried to, like the poor little second wife in *Rebecca*—the narrator with no name, which is a famous thing about *Rebecca*—behind the fancy desk in the morning room with no letters to write. Some days he'd bring lunch up to me: slices of sourdough bread, spread with goat cheese and tapenade. After I'd worked awhile, I'd take a book down to the window seat in the living room, where I must have made a pretty picture for him, my bare feet on the green velvet cushion, frowning away over Susan Sontag, Joan Didion, Elizabeth Hardwick—he took care to recommend what he surely thought of as women writers—and *The Art of the Personal Essay.* He had read my first attempt at a short story and told me my gift was for nonfiction.

In addition to whatever assignments I got from Andrea—not many, after I told her I wouldn't do celebrity pieces—I set myself a goal of writing a thousand words a day: just whatever happened to be on my

mind. Of course he encouraged me—"You'll see what it turns into"—
and I'll be charitable and assume he had no intention of exposing what
pitiful society my soul had selected. If you want to know my thoughts
about how Starbucks coffee shops and Barnes & Noble stores (top-
ics du jour back then) both favored the same snobby forest green, or
about how surprise parties betrayed contempt on the part of those who
gave them (an idea I'd adapted, to put it kindly, from Auden's essay on
Othello), you can find them in the files of the paper. My editor insisted
on accompanying my columns with a chip shot of my face, apparently
thinking it would lure a few readers—I was still enough of a looker—
though I doubt many of them made it past my first paragraphs. Most
of the time I got my ideas, if you can call them that, when I read that
somebody famous had died: I got lucky when Bella Abzug and Tammy
Wynette kicked off within a week of each other—you can imagine
what I made of that. I *will* still stand behind my piece about Edith Fore,
the old lady who did those TV ads for Lifecall America: of course I
called it "I've Fallen and I Can't Get Up." You should check that one
out if it's still around. But "Martha Gellhorn: In Papa's Shadow," in
which I tried to compare what little I knew about her life with my own
experience of having been married to a fellow writer? Oh right, who
was also outdoorsy and also knew Spanish? I'll give myself this much
credit: I sat there doing a word count every couple of sentences until I
hit four figures.

"Everything I think of is shit," I said.

He patted my head. "You have to work through it, is all. Or *with* it.
You know, 'Nothing to paint, nothing to paint with.' Just go as dark as
you want."

"It's not even *dark*," I said. "It's just fucking stupid."

"Then that's good information," he said. "'If the fool would persist
in his folly, dot dot dot.' I'm sorry to be quoting stuff at you. Why don't
we walk over and get you some ice cream."

"What, an affirmation of life?" I said.

"There," he said. "Now *that's* you. See how easy?"

Fed, flattered and fucked. I gained ten pounds that first year, and he didn't seem to mind. He was a man who never put on an ounce, though his jawline had started to give.

I see that I've been painting myself as the little creepmouse victim-wife in a gothic novel—the house really *did* have a mansard roof: Was I not supposed to notice?—what with the attic room, the sad little plastic storage box and so on, the overwhelming older husband. My crack about the conjugal bed. But really, given who he was, he didn't do one thing wrong. Yes, he paid the bills and picked up the check at restaurants, but he never slipped money into my wallet and he left it up to me to pay off my credit cards, or not. He even knew not to buy me a better car—at least not then. That crappy little Toyota parked by his handsome house for over a year and never a word out of him. He didn't nag me about my divorce—in those days it took a year in New York State after you'd filed for separation—which I'm sure was why I got it happening so soon. He did give me his lawyer's card, but only because I asked him for it. (The fee turned out to be suspiciously modest; I wouldn't swear that he hadn't supplemented it behind my back.) He did his own laundry, and sometimes mine. When he seduced me in the afternoon, he changed the sheets before bedtime.

If you're thinking, *Aha, so that's where the bitch earned her allowance,* no. If I could have any of this back—which I can't, and which is a weepy thing to say, and I promise not to hit the elegiac note too often—it would be those afternoons in bed. My first husband must have read somewhere that the woman had to come first and often, so he would slam away at me (it *was* impressive, for a while) or go after me with his tongue until my clit was sore. "How many was that?" he would say as I lay there catching my breath. But this man would take me at my word if I told him I just wanted to feel him let go. "Ah, God," he would say, plying the warm, wet washcloth he'd get up and bring us, "that was *so* irresponsible of me."

All of which might have been the most insidious campaign ever by a man to convince a woman that he wasn't a tyrant, and don't think I didn't suspect it—I wasn't the ninny I'm sure I sound like. But wasn't it on me whether or not I let myself be tyrannized, if he started showing his true face? And where *was* the line between tyrannized and taken care of? And if he pushed me to it, couldn't I find pleasure in tyrannizing back?

I just had to trust that we wouldn't get to such a place, or what was the point of my being here? Despite his money and his manner—and believe me, I could see why my husband had thought he was an asshole—wasn't this a good man? Or at least good enough to suspect he wasn't good *enough*. And wasn't I a good woman? Or couldn't I act as if I were?

A few weeks after moving in, I called my mother and asked if she'd like to come visit. I thought she needed to be reassured that I hadn't done a crazy thing, not that she was any judge. I picked her up at the train in the middle of the afternoon, showed her the town—she called it "charming enough"—and left silences in case she wanted to talk. Apparently not. We stopped off to get stuff for dinner—the wife had left behind *Cucina Paradiso: The Heavenly Food of Sicily,* and *pasta col tonno* seemed easy enough even for me—and when I parked in front of the house she didn't move to open her door. "This is it?" she said. "I guess you've come up in the world."

"It's not about that," I said. "I mean, sure. But he's really good to me."

"That's gracious of him."

"You're at least going to give him a chance, right?" I said. "It's not like he's Hugh Hefner in his smoking jacket."

"Baby, as long as you're happy. I *will* say, I never thought the boy was right for you." She looked into the backseat. "Do you need some help with those?"

"Oh, the cook will see to them—let's get you settled in. The butler will show you to the East Room."

"Don't kid your poor old mother. I'll be good." She opened her door. "You don't really have an East Room, do you?"

"For Christ's sake," I said.

At dinner, he kept filling her wineglass and got her talking about the workshop she'd taken years ago with Stanley Kunitz, and how

May Sarton, or maybe it was May Swenson, had once made a pass at her—*those* stories—and he told her about going to jazz clubs in New York as a young man and hearing Charlie Parker and Billie Holiday and how once, at a party in some loft, he'd sat in with so-and-so, playing somebody's borrowed bass. *Those* stories. Back in the living room, he opened more wine and put on Frank Sinatra. "I trust you like the Nelson Riddle era," he said to her. "We *can* go later, if you prefer the doo-be-doo-be-doo."

"No, this makes me very happy." The song was "I've Got the World on a String." "Someone's obviously briefed you."

"Random guess," he said. "There are times nobody else will do, right? When you're my age."

"I *am* your age."

"You're trying to butter me up," he said. "I'm not *that* well preserved. Pour you a bit more?"

"Oh, why not." She lifted her glass to him, leaned back and closed her eyes.

"You know, Mom," I said, "if you brought anything with you, you're not going to scandalize anybody."

Her eyes came open. "Oh, *God* no. I had to give that up—this stuff they have today is way too strong for an old lady. I'm sorry. If that was a hint—"

"Far from it," I said. "I know just what you mean."

"I suppose if I get cancer, it might be a different story," she said. "But for the time being." She took a long drink of her wine and closed her eyes again. "My God, that *voice.* It's hard to believe he's turned into such a terrible man. I remember when he used to be a Democrat."

"Happens to the best of us," he said.

After he went to bed, I turned down her covers in the guest room. "All right, I'm sold," she said. "I guess I've gotten to the age where I don't mind."

I went down the hall to the bedroom and found him under the covers reading *The Golden Bowl.* "Thank God," he said. "I'm about ready to give up on this. So, did I get decent notices?"

"Come on, you know she liked you." I took my hairbrush from the dresser and brought it over to the bed. I knew he liked to watch me.

"My well-practiced charm," he said. "She wasn't really a pot smoker, was she?"

"We were a very progressive family," I said.

"As were we," he said. "Except for us it was Henry Wallace. I'm glad you don't sit around smoking *pot* all day."

"I don't know," I said. "You might like me better if I was placid and stupid."

"I couldn't possibly." He ran a finger down my thigh. "She's wrong about Sinatra, by the way. He was always a shit, I don't care who he voted for. That damaged-soul-in-the-wee-small-hours crap—the fraudulence is the whole appeal." He patted the covers beside him. "Let's try not to be noisy tonight."

I never did figure out what had damaged him, assuming he was damaged. True, he liked to drink, but he *liked* liking to drink. (Having met my mother and heard my family stories, he must have figured out what damaged me, but I don't think he wasted any time worrying about it.) The stories he told about his parents never suggested they hadn't loved him, or each other. His father had been a professor and his mother a faculty wife, but supposedly the father had stayed out of bed with his students. Saul Bellow and Mary McCarthy and Ralph Ellison and F. W. Dupee—whoever that was—and Hannah Arendt used to come over for dinner. A painter named Stefan Hirsch, whom I also had to look up. He remembered seeing Eleanor Roosevelt, who would make the short trip from Hyde Park for international student conferences. I would have run screaming from all this, but instead of joining the marines—he was a CO during the Korean War—he made them proud by going off to study painting at the Art Students League, then to architecture school at Columbia. It was his brother, ten years younger, who disgraced the family, by becoming an investment banker.

He'd seemed so complicated when we'd first met—I think I said so—but you have to remember I was used to my husband. And now that I could pick up his allusions, most of them, and decode his ironies, he seemed to be a simple man who happened to know who F. W. Dupee was and had learned how to look at a Diebenkorn. When he took pleasure—in bed, at the opera, at a baseball game, reading *Bleak House* for the fiftieth time or a Trollope he'd somehow missed, playing his bass in that restaurant—he actually appeared to enjoy it. I hope I'm not being condescending; it's possible that I seemed uncomplicated to him too. I don't suppose we were any more or any less opaque to each other than any other two people, *or* to ourselves, though of course how would you ever know? Anyway—to go back to where all this started going off the rails, a couple of paragraphs ago—these days I miss the sex, meaning the traditional two-person, I-Thou sex, not that there was ever a lot of Thou when I was a party to it.

Well, I say this now. But when I'm tempted to get sentimental, I have to remind myself that back then it seemed pretty fraught. At his age, he wanted a woman who didn't want children—he'd already put in his time—but since he *had* once wanted children (or why would he have had one?) wasn't there something fishy about me? If you're a woman, you can't win that one: because I didn't want to be a mother, he couldn't trust me to mother *him*, however deep he burrowed his little peepee up into my birth canal. So no wonder he came to prefer the other venue, where he could hurt me—I was a good actress—and then be treated, literally, like shit. Okay, and now let's do me: this was not just a man old enough to be my father, but a man who had *been* a father—still *was* a father—so I needed him to fuck me and then to be turned over and punished. A grown-up dirty marriage, where grown-up dirty needs got met and afterward you smelled of mortality—except I can't use that; it's from *King Lear.* How about "smelled of subtext"?

Except it *did* smell of mortality. As we both knew: When I was forty-five, still more than fuckable if I didn't gain *another* ten pounds, he'd be seventy-five. When I was sixty, maybe still halfway viable, he'd be ninety, and even if he was still alive, no longer even Viagrable. Or *if* Viagrable, by some awful miracle, not a creature you'd want to see tottering at you with a gleam in his rheumy eye, a steely shaft clattering against his frangible pelvic bone. Didn't this argue that we should relish each moment while there was anything to relish? Or maybe "cherish" is a better, warmer word, since this is getting a little grim.

My father died that spring, of the heart attack I should've known was coming when I saw those veins in his face, and my husband-to-be—I'm getting ahead of the story, but in this sentence I need a new designation for him—offered to go to the funeral with me. It didn't seem like an ideal occasion for having him meet the family, such as the family was, nor did I want to show up with some other gray-haired man, suggesting that my heart either did or didn't belong to Daddy—unwholesome either way. He persisted just enough. At the last minute, my mother decided to stay away too—my father had had his own life, she told me on the phone, and she'd made peace with that, but she didn't want to see any of "those creatures."

My brother, though, flew in from Colorado; none of us had seen him since he'd gotten clean and saved. I was three when he was born: my mother told me he was an accident, which was indiscreet of her, and I passed it on to him, which was unkind of me. I'd wanted him dead until he was thirteen, when I made him my little drug buddy. He'd dropped out of UConn—it was a wonder he lasted two semesters—and shot heroin, first in Willimantic, then the Lower East Side, then Seattle, then nobody knew where. Somehow he'd ended up in Colorado Springs, where he was drug free, married and a so-called elder in some right-wing church. When he walked into the funeral home, I had the weird thought that it was my father, come back as he was when I was little: he had a businessman's haircut and a businessman's blue pinstriped suit, and black-framed glasses like the ones my father had worn before he'd gotten contacts. I ran up to hug him and felt him turn aside to avoid contact with my breasts.

None of my father's ladies showed up, if he'd still had any, and the only other mourners were two of his friends from work. One got up and spoke of his "community spirit"—I have no idea what that was about—and said he would be missed, not specifying by whom. My brother and I went on to the cemetery, in his rental car. He'd said yes to the offer of a "viewing" before the service—he hadn't seen my father since dropping out of college—but I'd been willing to take their word for it, until I saw the casket suspended above the grave on canvas straps, by which point it was too late.

"Was it okay looking at him?" I asked my brother as we walked back to his car.

"That wasn't *him,*" he said. "I don't even know why I did it. So, I'm guessing he didn't know the Lord."

"Probably not."

"That's fucked," he said. "Sorry—I don't use that language anymore. But it just *is.*"

"But don't you think he's at peace now?" I said.

"Probably we'd better not get into it," he said.

"You think he's in hell," I said.

"And you think I'm a pod person," he said. "Like somebody took me over, right? Well, somebody *did*. And praise Jesus for it. Okay? I said it out loud." He cast up his eyes at the top of a cedar tree, as if he'd never seen such a thing before. "It's all different now. I can't really tell you—it's like my eyes were washed." He sounded like he was thirteen again, in wonder after smoking his first joint.

"Are you okay to drive?" I said.

"You have to know, I pray for you every day," he said. "Then again, I prayed for *him*. Let's get out of here."

"Will you see Mom before you go back?"

"I've prayed about that too," he said. "But I think my family needs me home."

"Wait—you have *kids?*"

"Well. In a couple of months. A little boy, they're saying."

"That's great—I mean I'm happy for you. Does Mom know?"

"*You* can tell her. Let her know that this one's wanted."

———

But back to this man I was about to marry—I don't know if I'm really getting his appeal across to you. If he played music with men half his age—and there was no "if" about it—he didn't play rock and roll, and he hadn't bought a motorcycle. If he drank every day—and he did—he'd take care to feed the cat in the afternoon when he felt a big night coming on. (It took a while to get what he meant by "feed the cat." Repulsive, yes. But hilarious, no? Yet I never heard him say "cunt," though I said it often enough.) And he was never a mean drunk—okay, he did put my poor first husband through some shit when he took us to dinner that time, but I give him a pass for that. He called a perfume a scent, a chauffeur a driver—not that he'd ever had one—his studio a workroom, an author a writer. He claimed not to have watched television since Nixon resigned—I think I was thirteen—and this was probably more or less true, except that he didn't count baseball. He allowed the radio—by which he meant public radio—only while driving. He could always guess the Piano Puzzler on *Performance Today*. The news and talk shows he called "*bien-pensant* agitprop": the world, he said, was *not* ceaselessly fascinating, and all things need not be considered. When Bill Clinton's voice came on, he jabbed for the mute button; later, he'd do the same with Bush. After 9/11, he drew a design for a new World Trade Center and had me put it up on the Web: a giant replica of Scrooge McDuck's money bin. *That* would have stirred up a hoo-hah, if anyone had known his name anymore. But he convinced himself that this was why Bard College had given the commission for its new concert hall to Frank Gehry, so *fuck* Leon Botstein—if he wanted Gehry to be his fucking Albert Speer . . . and so on. Largely the single malt talking.

When I first moved in with him, he said, "Will you still goose me while you're changing my Depends?"

"Depends," I said.

"Well said." This was before people started saying "Well played." "But how about this? We'll buy them in bulk—so much Depends upon a red wheel barrow."

Okay, I haven't convinced you, and obviously the Frank Gehry thing doesn't show him to advantage. But even my mother was sold—and if you want to think I was bought, fine, but that's not how it felt.

The day my divorce became final—I'd been living with him for a little over a year—he took me to the Beekman Arms. "I hope you don't mind my being blunt," he said. "We don't need to have this conversation again, but you do realize that things could get a little unattractive in the homestretch."

"*You* don't know what's going to happen," I said. "I could get cancer, and you'd have to pretend you were still hot for me. No boobs, no hair . . ."

"Maybe I'd like you better—you know my peculiarities. Still, the odds are in my favor, no? So—how to put this—if and when you should feel the need for more congenial company, do try to hide it a little better than you did with Young Lochinvar. But I'd be forever grateful if you could see your way clear to sticking around for the last act, in whatever capacity—well, of course not *forever* grateful. Okay, there. How's that for a tender marriage proposal?"

I put my glass down. "That's what this is?"

"All right, I knew I was getting too poetic," he said. "I'd better just assume the position." He stood up, went down on one knee beside my chair and took my hand. The people at the next table looked, then looked away.

"Good Christ," I said. "We're really doing this?"

"I think we'd be fine," he said. "We could still pretend to be illicit— we'll get you a pair of those heart-shaped sunglasses. Do you need some time?"

I shook my head. "I'd just start to think."

"Never a good idea." He kissed my hand and went back to his chair. "This calls for champagne. Joke, joke. Here." He raised his glass of scotch. "To the loveliest widow in the Hudson Valley—in the far-distant future." He took a sip and reached down to rub his knee. "I'm really not coldhearted, you know."

"I know," I said. "I don't think I am either."

"Well," he said. "That part is *your* business."

So, a month later I was taking that shower, on the morning I was to be married for the second time, in the bath off the master bedroom, while he was getting dressed on the other side of the wall. I came out in a towel—he had the biggest, softest white towels, though maybe that was to his ex-wife's credit—with makeup and hair just right, as he was knotting his ironic bow tie. Not a clip-on: I was about to marry a man who knew how to do this. I saw him see me in the mirror. "Hmm," he said. "You know, they can't start without us." Was I not being prompted to pull out an end of his tie with my teeth? Grrr—c'mere, Tiger.

We had the wedding downstairs in the living room, with white orchids on the Guatemalan coffee table. I'd just wanted the two of us to go to the town clerk, but he insisted we invite some family—"to keep things on the up and up"—and find a Unitarian Universalist clergyperson to do a plain-Jane service: no scripture, no music, no e. e. cummings. His parents were long dead, but his brother, whom I'd never met, said he'd drive up from the city. His daughter told him she'd booked a flight from Portland, but she called the morning she was to leave and said she'd woken up with an ear infection and couldn't lift her head from the pillow. Okay, you did hear of this happening. My mother came up the night before and stayed at the house, and my brother flew in with his wife and their one-year-old. We had room for them too, and my mother claimed she wanted to reconnect with my brother, meet the wife and spend time with the grandchild she'd never seen. But he told me that he and his wife had prayed about sleeping under the same roof with a still-unmarried couple, and while he didn't judge, he needed to be a servant leader in his family and it was best for them to live their values. We offered to put them up at the Beekman Arms, but they'd booked a room at a Motel 6 and would drive over in the morning.

He showed up an hour before the ceremony—we'd just come downstairs, and I could feel still-premarital slime in the crotch of my underwear—with the bossy little big-breasted wife holding the kid, who was sucking his thumb. "Your brother's told me all about you," she said. "And this is Zacharias. He's a little shy. Well, congratulations." Did she not know you don't congratulate the bride? "I hope you'll be very happy." What a cunt. My brother brought her over to my mother, who did her kissy-cheek thing, then held him at arms' length as if in reverent examination. "*Look* at you," she said. "I don't know what to *say.*" No shit.

The groom's brother pulled up in a Lexus with a ski rack—he hoped he wasn't late; the traffic was a motherfucker—and left his cashmere overcoat on the bench in the hall; he'd told us he had to get up to Bromley that evening. When the U.U. minister came in right behind him, my brother's wife looked at her as if she'd never seen a butch lesbian before, clutched her one-year-old tighter, and the kid started to squall. Finally she had to take him upstairs, reluctant as she was to go where our bedroom might be, so we could get on with the show. Afterward, my new brother-in-law kissed me from inside his walrus mustache, clapped my husband on the shoulder and said, "You dog. Listen, gotta jet." We took the rest of them to lunch, and after we'd gotten the baby into a booster seat and ordered drinks—Diet Cokes for the Christians—my brother said, "Would you mind?" He reached for my hand and my mother's, his wife took my husband's and the baby's, my husband gave me a quick look and reached for my mother's hand, leaving me to take the baby's other hand, which felt soft and moist, between my thumb and forefinger. He pulled it away and began to wail as my brother said, "God our Father bless the bounty that we are about to receive in the name of Jesus Christ Our Lord amen. There, that wasn't so tough, right? Hon, maybe you should take him and see if . . ." The bounty—white wine for my mother, scotch for me and the bridegroom—arrived none too soon.

When we opened the gifts, theirs turned out to be a leather-bound Bible, the New King James Version, with a page in front they'd had calligraphized with our names; lines had been ruled below for the names of offspring.

And before we leave the wedding day behind, just one final word about my little moment that morning; I don't want to keep coming back to this as if it were some big motif, though I might be tempted to hit it one more time near the end, for the sake of symmetry. So probably every film critic in the world has already figured this out—originality has never been my strong suit, as I think we've seen—but in *Psycho,* in the shower scene, I think we're supposed to think that Janet Leigh is making atonement for stealing that money, as well as for being a slut in a slip, which for a woman-hater like Hitchcock is *really* the sin, and simply washing herself clean isn't sufficient. Only when the chocolate syrup goes swirling down the drain, and her open eye sees everything at last and yields up a tear—of contrition!—only *then* . . . et cetera et cetera. My point is, where was Mother when *I* needed her? To part the curtain, raise the knife and freeze me in a state of grace. Now *there's* a cadence, or am I flattering myself?

I'd been to Rio, Amsterdam, St. Kitts and wherever else a snotty Yale girl goes, as well as France and Peru with my first husband, but I'd never seen what you might call America: just New York, L.A., San Francisco, Washington, D.C., and Colonial Williamsburg. So for our honeymoon, which he called a wedding trip, we'd driven in his truck (and thank God for four-wheel drive) across days of increasingly desolate late-winter landscape, staying in grimmer and grimmer motels, until the Rocky Mountains appeared and we were in Montana, at a turn-of-the-century hot spring resort where I suspect he'd gone with his first wife. By day we skied trails in Yellowstone, just over the state line into Wyoming, and saw as many elk as a pair of newlyweds could wish for; by night we drank whiskey out of plastic cups while floating in water the temperature of our bodies, with snow falling on us. On the way back, we took a detour from Rapid City down to Mount Rushmore—"Would you mind indulging me?"—and he pointed above and beyond the presidents' heads, which were smaller than I'd expected, to where James Mason's *North by Northwest* house would have stood. "As you can see," he said, "it couldn't possibly have been there."

"Whoever thought it could?" I said.

"Nobody," he said. "I've probably seen too many movies."

Mud season had set in by the time we got back, but he couldn't wait to bring me up to his hilltop. He put the truck in four-wheel low, and we fishtailed up a dirt track, mud and snow and pebbles rattling under the floorboards. At the top, he got out, came around and helped me down, and we looked across the river at a rugged gray mountain on the other side. "What do you think?" he said.

I pulled the hood of my parka over my head against the cold wind and put my hands in my pockets. "It's impressive that you own all this," I said.

"Do you think you could live here?"

"It's a little short on amenities," I said.

"Amenities we can do," he said. "Just draw up the plans and add money. *You* don't want to live in a Charles Addams house the rest of your life. Hell, even the rest of *my* life."

"I *like* your house."

"You'll like this better, trust me. I'll show you what I've got, and we can fine-tune it together."

"Can we get back in the truck?" I said.

He put an arm around my shoulders. "Come on."

As we inched down the hill, heater blasting, I said, "You've wanted this a long time."

"All my life." He put on his old-timer voice. *"Not yet."*

They began excavating on the hilltop as soon as they could get their machines up the track, and by late April they'd poured the foundation, dug for the septic and the drainage field and started drilling the well. Next year at this time, he said, we'd be in there. He'd sat me down in his workroom to go over the plans with me, and what he'd designed turned out to be more or less the James Mason house, right down to the triangular braces under what I would have called the deck.

"Of course Wright would never have used those," he said. "You've seen Fallingwater."

"You don't mean *Niagara*?" I said. "That's not Hitchcock."

"Dear God," he said. He jumped up and went to the bookshelf.

His plan seemed fine, what did I know. Flat roof, two stories and a basement, balcony all around the inside, looking down into the living room, with rooms off it, something like the high-end motel where we'd stayed outside Chicago—a Radisson or something, with a pool down in the atrium—which of course I didn't say. Workroom for him, workroom for me, wall of windows facing west.

"For me to die in and you to inherit," he said. "We'll call it Viduity Manor."

"I'm getting sick of this motif," I said. "Maybe you should give it a rest?"

"Eventually, of course. Why do you think I'm running it into the ground?" He shook his head. "Maybe that's not the happiest metaphor."

I met my new husband's old wife at an opening—mobiles by a woman who'd been a friend of theirs—somewhere in the borderland of Chelsea and Hell's Kitchen. He was in what you might call rare form, if it had been rare, most of the way down the Taconic—"Hellsea! Do I have a genius for marketing?"—but on the West Side Highway he gave the finger to a driver who cut us off, which I'd never seen him do; now I realize that he knew she'd be there. He asked me what I'd like from the bar, then started pushing through the crowd. A wiry middle-aged woman in black jeans and a black silk top, her short black hair moussed up into flames, came over to me. "Quite the wingding," she said. "I know who you are."

"I'm afraid you've got the advantage." But of course I knew.

"I used to," she said. "You're lovely. You should last him the rest of the way. I see he's in no hurry to get over here." I looked toward the bar in time to catch him turning away. "One can hardly blame him. How's life in Lord Weary's Castle?"

"We're doing well," I said. "Thanks for asking."

"So you're feisty too. You'll need to be. Oh dear, am I being the bad fairy at the wedding? I do *like* him, still. But I think he's a task for younger strengths."

"He always speaks well of you."

"Aren't you sweet to say so." She looked over again. "I think he's nerved himself up to face the music. If you'll excuse me, I need to congratulate the belle of the ball."

He shouldered himself between a young man with a tattooed neck and a drag queen with a lorgnette and handed me a glass of white wine, some of which had spilled onto his wrist. "How was *that*?" he said.

"It was fine. She doesn't seem to bear you any ill will."

"Well, good," he said. "I hope that doesn't mean her memory's going."

"She reminded me of you. The way she talks."

"I suppose. We were together twenty-eight years. Twenty-seven."

"Was she the love of your life?" I said.

"Life is long," he said. "As you'll see."

The tree outside my window had leafed out when the daughter flew east to stay with her mother for a few days, then took the train up to spend a night and, presumably, to check out the new wife. I went with him to the station; probably I should have let them have time alone, but I wanted to be welcoming and he seemed grateful for a buffer. She was waiting outside with her bag: a slender girl, tall like her father, pale, with glaring red lipstick and straight black hair, a leotard under her long skirt. His truck had one of those extended cabs, and she insisted on climbing into the cramped seat in the back, sitting sideways, knees up, with her high-tops on the cushion.

"You're older than I thought," she said to me.

"Is that a good thing or a bad thing?"

"I don't know," she said. "I'm making conversation."

"You used to be a little more adept at it than *that,*" her father said.

"Well, we're not so civilized out in Portland. It's like, PBR and the Ducks."

"Is that a rock band?" he said.

"Are you trying to be funny?" she said. "PBR?"

"Your father says *you* play in a band," I said.

"I'm a fucking waitress."

"For now," he said to me. "But her band has been—"

"It's not a *band,*" she said.

"I thought you didn't like 'ensemble,'" he said.

"Can *I* try?" I looked back at her. "Listen, you don't want a step-mother and I don't want to *be* one. Maybe you and I can just—"

"Yeah, okay," she said. "Can we go back to generalities?"

"So how's Madeleine?" her father said.

"Queer," she said. "What else does anybody care about?"

"Okeydokey." Her father nodded at me. "*You* want to have another go?"

"No thanks," I said. "But I like her anyway. Anybody this angry *has* to have a heart of gold."

"Sorry I was pissy," she said when we pulled into the driveway. "This is just a little weird, being back here. Did you change shit around?"

"I don't think you'll see much difference." He got out, pulled the seat forward for her and took her bag.

"I don't know, I kind of wish you had. You need to trim the hedge." She got out and looked at me. "I bet you trim yours."

"I thought you weren't going to be pissy," he said.

"I do, actually," I said. "If we're talking about lady business. Do you?"

"Okay, I need to stop," she said. "I guess I can see why you guys liked each other. Can we go in and get this over with?"

When she went upstairs, he patted my ass. "Sorry about the trial by ordeal. You're doing fine."

"What did you do with all my shit?" she yelled down.

He went to the foot of the stairs. "You took it to New York," he called. "There's some of your stuff in the closet."

"Yeah, isn't *that* appropriate," she yelled.

"Give me patience." He shook his head. "Why on earth she needs to make me the bad guy . . ."

"Because she thinks she's a bad girl?"

"Even I know *that* much," he said. "I'd hoped Madeleine would've gotten her over this."

"Maybe she doesn't want to get over it."

"She's twenty-five, for Christ's sake. Why is she still being so teenager-y?"

I said, "You love her."

"Where *do* you get these insights," he said.

I heard the door shut upstairs, and she came stomping down. "I *knew* you had this." She held up a pink plastic-bound diary with a little gold padlock. "This is when I was eight. Did you and Mom read it?"

"Avidly," he said. "Your mother was going to set it to music. What is it, your memoirs?"

"I couldn't find the key," she said. "Do you have anything to cut this?"

"I'll look in my toolbox," he said. "As I recall, it could *use* a little cutting."

"How do you deal with him?" she said to me.

"We'll talk," I said.

That night he stuck to wine after dinner, but he'd been up since six and a couple of times I saw his eyes shut and then come open again. Finally he looked at his watch, braced a hand on the coffee table and got to his feet. "You gals probably want to have a little hen party," he said. "So if you'll excuse me." After he'd gone upstairs, I opened another bottle of red and she and I sat cross-legged on opposite ends of the sofa.

"So how is this for you?" I said.

"Better than I thought, to be honest. I mean, you seem to be good for him."

"I hope to be."

"Yeah, everybody *hopes* to be. Even him, I guess. Look, I don't mean anything against Dad, okay? I just don't feel like I ever knew him all that well."

"But you were away at school, right? For part of the time?"

"Yeah, whose idea was that?" She pointed a thumb at the ceiling. "I don't know, sorry, I feel like I'm planting the seed or something. Isn't that what the stepdaughter always does? This must be weird for you too. Like which of us is the third wheel."

"Maybe all of us," I said.

"Right, what a concept. Like a tricycle. Or like tricyclics. I can't believe I was so rude to you."

"You were funny, actually."

"So are *you* okay? Being with him? Not to be rude again, but he seems pretty old for you."

"We do fine," I said. "You're not asking me to be graphic, right?"

She put down her glass, stuck her fingers in her ears and went *La la la la la.*

"Are you happy with *your* person?" I said.

"You don't have to be such a priss," she said. "Yeah, she's great."

"That's what your father says."

"Sure, because he's hot for her—you know, I mean he *was.* I *thought.*" That pale skin made her blush easily. "Can I have just about that much more?"

"You don't have to be a priss either." I poured her another half glass, then more for myself. "People can be hot for more than one person."

"Yeah, tell me." She drank off what I'd just poured and held her glass up again. "So what were we talking about?"

"I've lost track," I said, picking up the bottle.

"Okay, I think I'm boring you." She put her hand over the glass. "I probably need to get to bed."

When her father took her to the train in the morning—I waved from the doorstep like a housewife—I went up and stripped her bed first thing, then came down and started putting stuff in the dishwasher. I held her wineglass for a few seconds, touched the lipstick smear with my tongue and tasted that sweet, chalky nothing-taste of lipstick before telling myself, *Five minutes from now you'll have forgotten you did this.*

He hadn't let her know he'd be putting the Rhinebeck house on the market; before bringing her up to the loft to show her the paintings he'd been working on, he'd taken the plans for the new house down from the wall.

"I feel a little funny that she doesn't know what's going on," I said when he got back from dropping her off.

"I don't think she has any great attachment to this place. Is there any coffee left?"

"That wasn't the impression I got."

"Well, whatever the case. There's time enough for her to come back and say her goodbyes if she wants to. Did you say there was coffee?"

"You were sneaky about it," I said. I heard the washer in the basement stop, then start the spin cycle.

"I just thought it best not to throw everything at her all at once."

"She isn't a child," I said.

"Are we talking about the same person?" he said. "All right, perhaps *I'm* the child. I didn't want to have to deal with any theatrics." He headed into the kitchen. "I'll go *make* some coffee."

"So you love her but you don't respect her."

He looked over his shoulder. "This isn't going to develop itself into our first fight, I hope? Shall we both go sulk now and gather up our energy for the reconciliation?"

"I need to go get the laundry," I said. "This isn't very real to you, is it?"

"So-so. Nothing to write home about. Suppose we depart from the script: you forget the laundry, I'll forget the coffee, we'll have a drink like civilized people and go upstairs."

"It's eleven in the morning," I said. "No, I *don't* want to go upstairs."

"It was a euphemism," he said.

"Yes, do you think I'm stupid?"

"What's put *you* in a mood? Were you two overbonding last night? I did think *she* looked a little blue around the gills."

"Maybe so. I've got a wicked headache." Which I did, now that I thought of it. "Is it going to fuck up the whole day to do the drink part?"

"What are days *for?*" he said. "I think my work of corruption is nearly complete."

I slept until five thirty in the afternoon, left him in bed and took a shower, then brought my book out onto the little back porch off the kitchen. I've forgotten what book, but let's say it was *Jane Eyre—Reader, I married him*—just because it wasn't. But I couldn't concentrate, so I watched a pair of chipmunks playing around the base of a tree: it must have been the tree whose branches I saw out my window. I hadn't written my thousand words today. Or my thousand words yesterday. It was still warm; the sun had just gone down behind the house on the other side of the back fence. So green out here: bushes I couldn't name, a small tree I knew to be a dogwood, a lumpy square of ground, overgrown with grass, that must have been where his wife grew her herbs. His wife, did I say? *I am Mrs. de Winter now.*

I prayed again, sitting out there—you must be thinking I'm not too tightly wrapped, unless you're a Jesus case like my brother, in which case you're thinking *Grace must be at work, even in this lost bitch's soul*—and this time I prayed that I would never hurt him. I probably thought this made me a good person, that's how fucking stupid I was. I didn't get any more specific than never hurting him, which was like lying to your shrink. I don't go all the way with my brother, who seemed to feel, oh, a little bummed out by, but basically okay with, my father being in hell for ever and ever and ever, I suppose because that was God's inscrutable will, which wasn't for him to scrute. But I do believe this much: sooner or later, and in my case I hope later, you'll have to look at exactly who you were and everything you did, and it's going to be a shitshow.

My husband came out, with his hair wet and a glass of single malt in each hand—and what happened after that? We went in and had dinner? Watched a movie? Had orgasms in each other's company, not to put it untenderly? Whatever it might have been, it was surely nothing we hadn't bargained for.

4

My husband's hilltop overlooked a wide part of the Hudson that the old-timers used to call Henry's Pond, and the Indians had called I forget what—he had a whole section of books on local lore. Downriver, a suspension bridge crossed a narrow bend; in the days before the bridge, people would holler across the narrows for the ferry to come. From the deck or through the glass wall of the living room, you could look a mile across the water at that rocky lump of mountain, in whose gray cliffs rattlesnakes supposedly nested.

The first settlement, at the narrows, was long gone; they'd built the present town in the early 1800s, a single street of brick and wooden buildings, intersected by Broadway, the old Route 9, which sixty miles south became the real Broadway. The businesses there now had, by ordinance, royal blue wooden signs with gold letters hanging over the sidewalk. Main Street led down to the Metro-North tracks and dead-ended at the water, where it looped around a green-painted iron tank, planted with geraniums every spring by the chamber of commerce. On weekends, out-of-towners swarmed the antique shops, the nouveau penny-candy store and the soi-disant organic bakery; my husband called it "Olde Quaintsburgh"—I'm inferring both the *e* and the *h*. I never told him that I'd once done a feature about it for a section of the paper called "Delightful Destinations."

We avoided the place, except for a sports bar where we'd go one night a week in the summer to watch baseball and eat linguine with sausage. We could have driven twenty miles to a mall with a multiplex, but he refused, as he put it, "to report for entertainment," so a couple of nights a week we'd watch a movie at home—*film* was another forbidden affection—first on VHS, later on DVD. The other nights we read: him with his Dickens or his P. G. Wodehouse or his books of Shakespeare criticism—after admiring *Shakespeare: The Invention of the Human,* he wanted to know all about Bloom's class—while I took down this or that from his shelves. He read all of Jane Austen aloud to me. Every week or two we'd drive to the city, to Lincoln Center or BAM, then a late supper at a place he knew on Seventy-First Street or a piece of cheesecake at Junior's, or simply a "civilized" dinner for two at places where waiters and bartenders pretended to remember him: Café Loup, Da Silvano, the Odeon. He bought me a black Audrey Hepburn dress for the opera; he wore an Armani tuxedo, which still fitted him after twenty years, and cowboy boots. Every Thursday night he played at the restaurant, with a pianist and a drummer. I'd go along sometimes to get out of the house, but it just sounded like a lot of notes to me, so I'd watch his long fingers for a while, spider-walking up and down the neck of his big bass, then open whatever book I'd brought and end up drinking too much. He was good about putting on a classic rock station during the drive home and letting me sing along.

The floors in the new house had come out of a barn in New Hampshire, pine boards a foot and a half wide that were oiled and buffed to a fare-thee-well—he had principles about polyurethane—and I wasn't to walk on them in what he called spike heels. Underneath were tubes for radiant heat; even in winter, the wood felt warm under my bare feet. Three walls of the living room were bookshelves, with just enough space for the Diebenkorn and a tarnished brass tuba—which mustn't be confused with a sousaphone, and which he said was the most beautiful object ever made by the hand of man, though he also applied this designation to an old automobile called a Cord, his Bang & Olufsen turntable, the Verrazano Bridge, the Japanese flag he hauled out every Fourth of July, and an egg slicer. We went down to ABC Carpet, where he dropped forty-five thousand dollars on antique rugs. I watched the salesman profiling him: the gray hair and trimmed beard—he'd begun growing it during the construction; I suppose the jawline had been bothering him too—and the jeans and blue denim shirt and the younger woman. After he'd presented his card and signed the slip, he shook hands not only with the salesman but also with the two underlings who'd pulled the rugs we'd chosen from the heavy piles and laid them out on the showroom floor.

For that much money, 187 children could have been operated on for cleft palate, with $120 left over. Did you know that one in ten such children will die before their first birthday? I found this out the other day, on operationsmile.org, and did the math. This was something I never knew to consider when I got out of my side of the bed, with its Dux mattress, and put my piggies down into that soft wool. I must be singling out the rugs to obsess over because they were on a human scale. Like the way we'd convey the magnitude of this or that calamity to the readers of *Newsweek: Every day, a town the size of TK,* the writer would write, and the researcher would look up places in the heartland with however many thousand people and pick one with a leafy name.

Beneath the showy part of the house was a basement with a laundry room, an exercise room, a music room (complete with baby grand piano) and a guest suite: bedroom, sitting room, bathroom, a coffeemaker, a microwave and a mini-fridge, with a private entrance giving onto the driveway. He called the guest quarters "the Bunker," or "the Black Hole of Calcutta," and, after Iraq, "Abu Ghraib." All those little *things* of his—not jokes, exactly; I don't know what the word would be—like calling Verdi "Mean Joe Green," or Lake George "Lago di Giorgio," or a futon a "futilitron," or pronouncing herpes "air-pess." When Target stores appeared, he called them "Tar-zhay" until everybody else started doing it. The house had no garage: he said it would clutter up the design, though of course our cars cluttered up the driveway, and in the winter we had to clear snow and scrape windshields.

When we moved in, he bought all new furniture, dishes, silver and whatnot. Except for the books—his father's library merged with his— he put most of the stuff from Rhinebeck in a storage unit, in case his daughter might want it someday. For all I know, it's still there.

She never paid her farewell visit to the old house—she told him it would be too sad—but she did come to see the new place. "Seriously?" she said as we got out of the car.

"Do I take that as a compliment?" he said.

"It looks like it's about to take off and fly."

"You hate it."

"*No,*" she said. "It's like where somebody famous would live. Actually I guess you *are* sort of famous."

"That was back when giants walked the earth," he said. "Nowadays I'm content to sit up here and watch the passing parade."

"Are you? I worry about you." She turned to me. "Is he?"

"What a thing to ask," he said. "'Is he a bitter old man?' What do you expect her to say to that?"

"I think your father's amazing," I said.

"See that?" he said. "Amazing. Now let me show you the inside. We're going to put you in the Holding Tank." He went around to get her bag.

"I'm assuming he means the basement," I said. "It's really comfortable."

"I don't know how you live with it," she said. "I mean I love him and everything."

"I guess we're a lot alike," I said.

"You and him? Or you and me?"

"Well—both. We both care about him."

"Yeah, that," she said. "Can we talk sometime?"

After he went up to bed, she helped me put away stuff from the dishwasher and pointed to a bottle of Rémy on a top shelf. "Would it be okay?"

"Pour me some too," I said. "Snifters are over in that cupboard."

I took an end of the sofa, thinking she'd join me, but she took her high-tops off, got into the leather armchair and put her stocking feet up. "So here we are again," she said.

"More or less," I said. "Is it strange seeing him in a new place?"

"I don't know, maybe less so. In a way. Could we have some music? If we put it on low?"

"What do you like?"

"You choose. Not jazz."

"I'm with you on that." I put on *Rumours,* since who didn't like *Rumours,* except probably my husband. "This okay?"

"I guess. What is it?"

"You're as bad as your father." I handed her the jewel case.

"Oh right," she said. "That's them? She's pretty. I mean, they're all pretty. Listen, I know I said I wanted to talk, but do you mind if we just kind of be here?"

"Of course not. I'm a little tired myself."

"Am I keeping you up?"

"No, I'm just— I don't know what I am."

She got out of the chair and picked up her sneakers. "I'm keeping you up." She pointed to the jewel case. "Can I take that down with me, for my Walkman? I want to hear it."

"No, stay," I said. "I'm enjoying it too."

"We both need to go to bed," she said. "I didn't even realize."

I missed saying goodbye to her in the morning, when her father drove her to the train. I hadn't been able to get to sleep, and around three in the morning I finally got up and drank more Rémy—and, I have to say, masturbated in my workroom—then didn't wake up until ten o'clock. I looked for the Fleetwood Mac CD on the shelves, then in the guest room. Maybe I'd given it to her and not remembered. Or had I meant to give it to her and she'd somehow known?

In good weather, I'd bring coffee out to the deck and read the *Times;* part of his morning routine was to trot down the half mile of driveway, get our copy from the box, then run back up and shower. Then I'd look out across the river and watch the light creep down the mountain as the rattlesnakes came out to take the sun. I'm just being imaginative here: of course it was too far to see them, and they might after all have been just a local legend, and the earth turns too slowly for anyone to detect the creeping of daylight. Once I believed I saw a tiny figure making its way up a cliff and had the insane thought that it was my first husband. When I was done dawdling, I'd get down to business. You *can* watch the creeping of the word count at the bottom of the screen. Three hundred fifty-three, three hundred fifty-eight. And then, when the sun got too strong, the deck too hot, I went inside to my new room of one's own. My husband's door would already be closed, the music in there already going.

My first idea was a book to be called *5 Blondes*. The figure 5, not spelled out: I think I had something in mind about women being commodified. Meditations on five women, real and imaginary: Marion Crane, Sylvia Plath, Blondie (not Deborah Harry, the one in the comic strip), Jayne Mansfield and myself. (Marilyn Monroe had been done to death, no pun intended.) I'd have to trust to my ingenuity to make it all hang together, though first I'd have to trust to my ingenuity to come up with things to think about them. Three of them came to bad ends, there was one thought, which they had deserved because of sexual transgression—wasn't that how the culture read their stories?—while Blondie and I went on and on, to no end at all. Blondie was drawn by an artist named Chic Young, and I planned to make much of the notion that Blondie looked both chic and young, despite the housedresses. Yet she was so stupid that only Dagwood would want her. She never had an affair—of course, what did you expect in a comic strip?—or even a flirtation. Not that Dagwood seemed to want her either, so I guess there was *her* punishment. Which left *me*—this was going to be the personal part. How I fit in was that I'd dyed my hair blond when I was sixteen, then let it grow back out.

Another try: *Medusa's Daughters* (a title I changed to *Daughters of Medusa* because it sounded more resonant), about images of angry-faced women. I had the Statue of Liberty, the woman on the Starbucks logo—both of them now look more blank than angry to me—and when *The Fellowship of the Ring* came out I added Cate Blanchett as Galadriel, with her face in psychedelic negative, ranting about how all would love her and despair. I was going to argue that repressed anger was the true solution to the mystery of the Mona Lisa's smile, but once I had that thought I couldn't take it any further.

Still another try: *Brides of Bluebeard* (which I changed to *Bluebeard's Brides* because it sounded less pretentious), about the old movies I'd seen with my husband in which women found themselves married to evil men. I'd read *The Runaway Bride,* by Elizabeth Kendall, and this was to be its sinister counterpart. Loretta Young in *The Stranger,* where Orson Welles is a Nazi who's managed to lose his accent, Grace Kelly in *Dial M* of course, *Gaslight, Rosemary's Baby* and borderline cases like *Rebecca* and *Suspicion* and *Jane Eyre*—all of which had Joan Fontaine, so maybe it should actually be about her? This book would have a personal part too, but I would've had to decide what I thought about my own marriage, and I'm *still* having trouble with that. (See above. See below.)

I should throw out my notes for these projects—God only knows how many thousands of words on floppy disks, the computers on which they were written being long dead—lest anybody should read them when *I'm* dead, but who might that be? My brother's home-schooled spawn? Anyway, I doubt I'll be feeling this shame on the other side: triteness will be the least of the sins for which I'll be called to account. "It's always rough going at first," my husband used to tell me. "You have to write *through* the self-loathing." I hated to hear myself complaining to him, but I think he liked it; he got to be supportive and wise, without being threatened by my actually accomplishing anything. This is the version in which he hates me for being a woman—and if that's too harsh a view of what was going on, I suppose it'll get straightened out for me when we're no longer seeing through a glass darkly. The other version is the one in which he knows he's a failure too. Peekskill had been his last commission, and what was he supposed to do—sit there designing imaginary museums and concert halls for the use of imaginary people? So day after day he went in and painted, and even I could tell his canvases were as trite as my own projects: he worked at them simply to be working. If I resented his finding some pleasure in that, and there's no "if" about it, then I guess that tells you what a bad wife I was, and what a crabbed spirit. I mean, no wonder the writing came to nothing. Apparently you need some joy in order to get anything off the ground, though I have to say that my husband's joy—that's what he called it, and he must have known—in giving himself over to his shapes and colors, with the music carrying him along, never made his results any better. There must have been a few hundred paintings in that storage unit, and that was back in my time.

During our first winter in the new house, we got snowed in for a day and a half and the power went off. "Why didn't I have them put in a fucking generator?" he said. "Christ, we can't even flush the toilets."

I had some life left in my laptop, so we got in bed, pulled the duvet over our shoulders and played solitaire together, taking turns. I reached under his pajama bottoms, under his briefs, and he said, "Your hand is cold." It was the first time he'd turned me down, which I'd thought neither of us was allowed to do. True, he was in a bad mood about the power—surely this needs no commentary—and my hand *was* cold. But. So I went under with my head and took him in my mouth, and our marriage was saved.

After I'd made him come, he fell asleep and I took care of myself, trying to be quiet about it. He snored awhile, then started giving out these little cries—*uh, uh*—which must have sounded like mighty yells to him, and I shook his shoulder to wake him. "God—horrible." He rolled his head back and forth on the pillow. "Thank you. I guess my mind wanted to have a talk with me. Do you suppose it shuts up when you die?"

"That would be the hope," I said.

"Some hope," he said. "We're fucked every which way, aren't we."

"Why would you expect *me* to be the expert?" I said.

"Oh, I'm just complaining into the void," he said. "It hits me every once in a while, that's all. I thought you might know the feeling."

"Are we having a moment?" I said.

"Okay, you're not inclined," he said. "Distasteful subject—whatever the subject *was*. Did we think to bring that bottle in here?"

———

We didn't know anybody in town—the New Yorkers who had weekend places socialized with one another and the locals were, what can one say, locals—but his friends would come up from the city, marvel at the house and sometimes stay for a night or two: musicians or artists or writers or academics. These were men his age, but not all of them showed up with younger wives or girlfriends, and not all the women his age were bitches to me. One of those women, a poet who was still friendly with his ex-wife, told me he looked ten years younger. "You must be a pistol," she said. "I wish Milt could borrow you for a week." (This was her husband, a gray-haired sculptor who wore bib overalls under his suit jacket, apparently to hide his weight.) "I bet he'd come back a giant refreshed." But when a married English professor brought his grad-student protégée for a weekend, she got drunk, took it into her head that I was flirting with her mentor and came after me in the kitchen. "If *you* want his bad breath in your face, it's fine with me. *And* his three-inch cock. Just do me a favor and drive me to the train."

The summer after we moved in, a friend of his stayed for two months in Spandau—yet another name for the basement—to work on his novel; a condo was going up across the street from his apartment in Brooklyn, and construction started at eight every morning. If he came up here, my husband told him, he wouldn't be underfoot—that is, he would be under*foot,* but. The novelist kept his own hours, ate dinner with us a night or two a week; other nights he'd take us out to the sports bar or go wherever by himself. One morning, I went downstairs to do laundry and met a woman coming out of his door, wearing a bar-length skirt. Fat knees, pretty face. I thought I recognized her from the convenience store in town, but maybe not. She introduced herself as a friend of the novelist's—she must have thought that knowing his name made it okay for her to be here—and went out the private entrance. I heard a car start up, stepped outside and watched a little sky-blue Kia—a good name for *her,* I thought—go down the driveway. I didn't tell my husband, because I couldn't decide what attitude to take. One possibility: that Kia might have sketchy friends among the locals and that he'd better change the codes on the security system. Another: that she was just some poor girl who'd wanted to get laid, and the novelist was handsome in what you'd now call the George Clooney mode. (He had a longtime girlfriend, whom I'd met, but she'd gone to Europe for a couple of months.) And still another: Why put my husband on alert, not that it really crossed my mind to sneak down there myself. Or if it ever *had* formed itself into a thought, well, you could just let thoughts come and go, and at this point my husband still fucked me like a man with a younger wife he wouldn't be able to fuck forever.

First thing after waking up was best for him, before he'd—crude joke coming up—pissed away his opportunity. But morning light wasn't, shall we say, his element. As much as he kept himself cardiologically fit, the skin was loose at his belly and buttocks, though his pubic hair, for some reason, was still black and the lines on his face still attractive in a daddy way. This was a man who could remember the attack on Pearl Harbor, when he'd been ten years old. Skin tags began to appear on his forehead, but I don't suppose he ever thought of them and, in fairness, I never suggested he have them removed. I did order light-blocking shades for the bedroom, which I assumed would flatter me, too, in years to come—years that, to be honest, wouldn't be long in coming. But in any marriage, one trains oneself not to look, and what must *he* have trained himself not to notice? My too-broad forehead and too-pointy chin? Maybe my feet, with the second toe longer than the big one—an ape foot. Or my areolas, the size of fifty-cent pieces, which I suppose might have looked like Mommy watching him. The things I could do something about, I did my best to remedy. Down in the basement, on the treadmill and the elliptical and the Smith machine, I could get through a movie in two days.

Of course wasn't it the *person* you were supposed to be fucking? And wasn't the expression supposed to be "making love to," or, airy-fairier still, "making love with"? He once said, "I never thought this would happen for me again," and I didn't ask what *this* was, exactly. Maybe he just meant bedding a woman with a still reasonably firm body. Certainly mine presented fewer obstacles than his for our souls to pass through, on their X-ray flights toward spiritual union. Sorry to sound so cruel, but now that I've crossed over into unwantable myself, I'm afraid I don't see much *besides* cruelty. Remind me what the compensations were supposed to be?

Anyhow, he wasn't without vanity. At first I was impressed that he did his own laundry—what a male feminist. Eventually I figured out that he was privately bleaching away the yellow stains on his briefs, and this also helped explain why he slept in pajamas; I'd assumed it was a generational thing. He'd warned me he was a light sleeper, that he might get up during the night to read in another room. But I'd hear the toilet flush and found the saw palmetto pills in his sock drawer. For a while, he was able to hide the Viagra too; he'd slip the pill into his pocket an hour before he had to put up or shut up. So when I'm called to account, as I surely will be, for my own deceptions and evasions, let's remember that I wasn't the only one harboring little secrets. The bad version is that we spent years hiding from each other in that beautiful house. A happier way to look at it is that this is what marriage *is*—mutual accommodation, tolerance and forgiveness. Or is there a distinction?

A computer infested with miscarried books—they never made it to stillborn—a husband whose body was beginning to bother me and whose mind was running out of fascinations—and more to the point, I suppose, a body and a mind of my own that I was beginning to despise. Now what would you expect me to do? Yes, thank you: find yet another man to fasten on to. The George Clooney in the basement was long gone, back to his apartment and his girlfriend; when his book came out, it had an acknowledgment to us for giving him "refuge in my hour of darkness" and got a mostly good review in the Sunday *Times*. (Poor Kia, pseudonymized again, had unwittingly sat, or rather bent over, for her portrait, though I don't suppose she ever knew it.) But the world was full of men who liked to think they were in their hour of darkness and that a woman could grant them refuge. A woman, that is, whom they didn't already have, preferably younger than themselves, and younger than the woman they *did* have. If I was no longer twenty and toothsome, weren't there still men who'd be perfectly glad to use me and whom I'd be perfectly glad to use? You know—that perfect gladness. It was just a matter of getting out of the house and hopping a train to the city. Instead, I had enough originality to take up smoking weed again.

I'd shied away from it ever since my first husband and I had shared a slender joint one of his basketball buddies gave us for a wedding present; he'd had to reason me out of going to the emergency room. But one night when the pianist and the drummer had come to the house to work out some new songs, my new husband brought them upstairs afterward, got out whiskey and glasses and put on a record by somebody named Bill Evans. (Yes, I understand now that everyone's supposed to know who Bill Evans was.) "Oh fine," the pianist said, "make me feel like shit. Anybody want some of this?" My husband put up his hand and said, "But feel free." When the wooden pipe came to me I said, "Maybe just one." I could tell what my husband's look meant: one hit would make me dangerous and sexy and I'd get fucked tonight; any more would frighten him. Not that this wasn't a temptation, but just the one did it for me: I was able to get through the first few minutes of panic—the whiskey must have helped—and found myself in a remote yet easeful state where the music sounded like the best thing I'd ever heard. "Is this *jazz*?" I said after a while. It was probably still that first song. "Indeed it is," the pianist said. "Don't tell me we've made a believer out of you."

Had my husband betrayed to his friends the secret that jazz made no sense to me? But I mustn't start worrying about *that*. "It's like a garden," I said. "Actually, that's crazy."

"No, no, you're exactly right," the pianist said. "Earth and flowers."

While that wasn't what I'd meant, it made me see that different people had different minds and that this was all right.

"Can I pour you a little more?" my husband said. It was so obvious that he wanted to bring me down from this place he couldn't get to.

"I'm okay," I said, meaning both that I had enough in my glass and that I was handling this. And I did get fucked that night, like the high and wicked girl I was. Turn out the *light,* baby.

The next day I got the pianist's number out of my husband's book. "Could we sort of keep this between us?" I said.

"We *did* make you a believer," he said. "I don't know, it puts me in a funny position. I thought I was picking up a little disapproval. I don't want to cause dissension on the home front."

"You wouldn't," I said. "If anything, you'd be helping out. Sort of like a marital aid."

"Thanks for putting *that* picture in my head," he said. "I guess he's a lucky man. This is really just between us?"

You're wondering why I didn't have an affair with the pianist, since it amounted to that anyway, and of course he'd called my husband a lucky man. But really, I wasn't the fuck-dolly you must think I am. Here, I'll count up my partners. Collaborators. Whatever word you like. I make it an even dozen, up to that point: we've got the two husbands, the *Newsweek* writer, the man before him—my only bar pickup, so handsome that I preemptively gave him a wrong phone number in the morning—and that girl from the gym, then the starter partners, two during high school, both male, five at college, two male and three female. And I'd engaged in the usual half-dozen different activities and passivities. So what would you say? About average for an American woman of my age and background? A hair above? A hair below? At any rate, neither maidenly nor unselective, and never out of control.

In the early afternoons, then, when I'd finished my thousand words, I'd take my one little hit—what I got from the pianist was far more fearsome than what I'd smoked at my mother's knee—and amuse myself, not that "amuse" is the word, for the three or four hours, just about the right length of time, before my husband appeared, summoning me sometimes to a seduction, more often to the first drink of the day.

In good weather, I'd take a walk, staying on the roads so I wouldn't get lost, though I'd sometimes think I'd gotten lost, or recline on the deck in a lounge chair, looking out at the river and the mountain and listening to music on my headphones. I could never get back to whatever peculiar pleasure I'd found in that one jazz record that night—a *garden,* for God's sake?—much as I felt I owed it to my husband to try. I only wanted to hear what I'd gotten high to as a teenager: the Pointer Sisters, Fleetwood Mac, Donna Summer, Carly Simon—all that sexy sheen. When I had to stay indoors, I listened while playing computer solitaire. Only once did I make the mistake of trying to read over what I'd written in the morning: I was too high to follow from the beginning of a sentence to the end, but the falseness and glibness revealed itself so plainly that I couldn't bring myself to write the next day. Maybe by this time you know the tone I'm talking about?

One stoned afternoon on the deck, I saw a UPS truck coming up the driveway—my husband was expecting stuff from Pearl Paint—and I ran into the house to hide in my workroom. I heard a chime so angelic that I had to try to find the note with my own voice; by then I'd forgotten someone must be at the door, and why I'd come in here. I lay down on the bed—the narrow brass bed I'd insisted on bringing from the house in Rhinebeck—and kept singing. Hours later, when we were sitting on the deck, having our first drink and watching the sun go down behind the mountain, my husband said, "I heard you in there this afternoon. You sounded so happy."

For our fifth anniversary, he took us back to the same hot spring in Montana—this time we flew—and from there we were to go on to Portland, stay overnight with his daughter and her partner, then back with a stopover in Cleveland, where he wanted to show me a library he'd designed in 1971, now ruined by a new wing, done by a young architect who'd once studied with him. There must have been some method of bringing weed on an airplane—wrap it in layers of plastic and hide it in your underwear?—but with all the new security I was afraid to try. Anyway, much as I might've liked it out in that hot pool with snow falling, I didn't want to be high around my husband, and how would I get away from him? It was just as well: the first night at the resort, he pissed our bed in his sleep.

"I don't know what happened," he said. "I was *dreaming* that I was pissing and I just—Jesus Christ. Maybe I had too much to drink. How can you go on *living* with me?"

"It could happen to anybody," I said. "Let's just get some towels and then—"

"Right, and then what? Jesus, it went right through to the mattress. Am I dying, is that what's happening?"

"Of course you're not dying," I said. "You had an accident."

"That's what they say to children." He sat down on the edge of the bed and covered his face with his hands.

"If you're seriously worried about this," I said, "you should see a doctor when we get back."

"Who's going to tell me what? 'Welcome to old age'?"

"You're only seventy-two," I said. "Why don't you to take a shower and change into your sweatpants."

"And that strikes you as not old?"

I sat down next to him and put an arm around his shoulders, which seemed to be the thing to do, little as I wanted to. He stood up again. "I've done you a disservice," he said. "I don't intend to drag on for twenty more years like this."

"Now you *are* being a child," I said.

He was on one knee, pawing through his suitcase, and I looked away so as not to see his wet pajama bottoms. "That's a new tone," he said. "I thought I knew all your little ways. I guess we're entering into unexplored territory."

"Right," I said, "you're the first person who ever got drunk and wet the bed. You should donate your body to medical science."

"Better," he said. "Now *that's* you. Ah—here they are. I did have a lot to drink, didn't I? Maybe we should try to forget this gruesome episode? Assuming I don't put on a repeat performance?"

"You'll be telling this on yourself when you're ninety," I said. "Adventures of your misspent youth."

"Don't jolly me along *too* much." He opened the bathroom door. "But I do appreciate your making the effort."

His daughter was going to put us up at her house, but after what happened in Montana, he called her to say we'd decided to stay at a hotel: *I* was used to his snoring, he said, but lately it had gotten so bad that he was afraid of keeping them awake. She must have thought I was being a princess about their foldout, or just being weird.

Madeleine turned out to be a short redhead about my age, with milky skin like the daughter's, smiley crow's-feet like mine (though mine weren't smiley) and breasts that swung free under a man's plaid flannel shirt; you could see why an old man might be hot for her. Why a young woman might too. At the door, she went up on her toes to kiss his cheek. "I love the beard," she said. "Very manlike." She gave me her hand.

"So where's your friend?" he said.

"Getting stuff for dinner. I expected her back by now."

"We were going to take you out."

"I'll let you guys argue about that," she said. "I think she's got something special up her sleeve."

"As do you," he said. "God, it's good to see you."

She threw up her little hands. "Why, Hopsie, you ought to be kept in a cage." The two of them seemed to be amused by this. "Let's go sit. Can I get you some tea or something? Now *you*," she said to my husband, "you probably want the something."

"I think tea, actually. It's a bit early."

She looked at me. "What have you done to this man?"

"We're still on East Coast time," I said.

"I thought that was three hours *later*," she said. "Sorry, I shouldn't be pushing drinks."

She was putting the tea ball into a round blue-and-gold teapot that must have been a Hall—my mother had collected them—when I heard the kitchen door open, a voice I knew calling "A little *help?*" and I found myself on my feet and through the archway, with Madeleine behind me.

"Let me," I said, and picked up a bright yellow canvas bag with "Nature's Way" printed in red; she had two more bags on the doorstep, all bulging, one with stalks of celery sticking out.

"Oh my," Madeleine said. "Did we overdo?"

"Did *we*? No, *we* are blameless. As always." She kicked the door shut with the sole of her boot, put down a bag and saw me. "You got here," she said. "Big change of plans—I'm going to make Flemish soup with winter vegetables. I read about it in the store. I think I wrote it down." She unwrapped her scarf and I could see her cheeks were red.

"You must be freezing," Madeleine said. "I just made some tea."

"Yeah, I don't drink that shit."

"Since when?"

Her father had appeared in the archway. "Hey," she said. She reached into one of the bags and held up a bottle of Rémy by the neck. "See? I made a stop just for you guys."

"Well," he said. "Since you went to the trouble."

"And?" she said to me. "Do *you* care about my trouble?"

"You didn't make a stop in addition to your stop, did you?" Madeleine said.

"Why?" she said. "Do I seem cerebral? No, what am I trying to say? Cel-e-bra-tory. That's a hard word."

"Oh, honey," Madeleine said. "Why don't you let me put stuff away and you can go sit with your father."

"I think I need to get to the bathroom." She headed down the hall, meandering rubber-legged to one side, her shoulder displacing a poster of Patti Smith.

"What's all *this?*" her father said.

"I'm not sure," Madeleine said. "This isn't her usual."

"Is she just drunk?" I said.

"Well," Madeleine said. "This *is* Portland. I better go in and see about her."

The house was small enough so we could hear vomiting. My husband got up and went to the kitchen; he came out with a glass of Rémy for each of us. "Cheers," he said. "She does have a flair for the dramatic. Poor Madeleine."

"What about *her*?"

"I imagine she'll pay for it tomorrow."

I heard more vomiting, then water running. "Should I go in?" I said.

"They'd probably rather you didn't. This isn't quite the jolly visit you had in mind."

"Probably not what she had in mind, either."

"That would be the charitable view," he said.

I heard the bathroom door open, then the two of them moving toward their bedroom. We finished our glasses, and he got up and poured us more. "May we always have the wind at our back," he said. "To get us the hell out of here."

Madeleine came in and sat on the sofa. "God, I am so sorry about this. I don't even know what to say to you. She has some friends I wish she didn't see."

"So is this a regular occurrence?" he said.

"*No.* That's the thing. I don't know, maybe it was you coming here—I mean, please don't think I'm blaming *you*. You know she loves you. It's just so out of character."

"How is she?" I said.

"I think she might sleep. She feels *terrible* about this. As far as I can tell. When do you have to leave?"

"Early," he said. "Unfortunately." Our plane didn't leave till two.

"Crap," she said. "Well, whatever."

"I'm just sorry you have to deal with this," he said.

"Should we go in and say goodbye?" I said.

"I think maybe not?" she said. "We'll all be in touch."

When we got home and I went through the mail, I found a birth announcement from my brother and his wife—what was this, number three?—and an invitation to Andrea's wedding, forwarded from the old address in Rhinebeck. To a Thomas Somebody, at St. Some-body's Church in Belmont, Massachusetts, June something. Below the engraving, in her handwriting: *Please please please come. Miss you. Much loves, Andy. P.S. bring the huz!*

Of course I'd neglected her, along with my other friends—that's what the "Miss you" was about. She'd stopped offering me pieces when *Mirabella* went under and she'd gone on to *Marie Claire,* and then I think to *Vogue,* and now she was someplace else. She'd come up to Rhinebeck for a weekend, back during the living-in-sin era; then the three of us had dinner in the city, and after that I'd taken the train down to meet her for lunch a couple of times. The huz had said she depressed him.

"Why, because she's not pretty?" I'd said.

"I wouldn't mind *that* so much. You bring enough pretty for two. It's more, what would you call it, the non-pretty *syndrome.*"

"You mean she tries too hard."

"Ah," he said, and kissed his fingertips at me. Back then it still made me wonder—these little things that seemed faggy. I imagine you've wondered too, but it was just him.

True, when Andrea was around men the voice went up, the hands were always going, fluttering, playing with her hair or—the worst—tugging her blouse down, since she was a little overweight, and she would make her eyes go wide and ask them questions and then say *"Really?"* But when you were one-on-one, she sat still and you could talk. Okay, I can't defend "Much loves," and certainly not from a grown woman, I don't care *how* long she'd been working at those magazines. At Yale she'd done a paper taking down Lionel Trilling's takedown of *Ethan Frome,* on which her professor—not Harold Bloom, but not nobody—had written: *Against my better judgment, you have persuaded me about this lady.* So what sort of creature must Thomas be? Either he was someone who had come to *see* her—knowing men, I wasn't hopeful—or he was as graceless and overweight and desperate as she was, which you'd suspect from a back-to-the-hometown church wedding in June.

———

This was the spring when I gave up and went back to work. Ever since Portland—I want to forget Cleveland, where my husband drank too much again and slept on the floor beside the bed as a precaution—I'd been writing a paragraph and deleting it, then a sentence, then a phrase, and getting out my one-hitter by ten in the morning, which made it a long day until the late-afternoon drink. I was too ashamed to call Andrea, or the *Newsweek* editor—at that point, though I didn't know it, he must have been burning through his long-term disability—and I couldn't think of anyone else. Good job of keeping up your connections. The only thing I could find anywhere nearby was a job as the so-called managing editor of a free want-ad paper in Kingston, organizing the stuff that came in—cars, sporting equipment and musical instruments with photos; sad personals without—and coming up with filler: quotes, maxims, fun facts, quizzes with the answers upside down, a joke column called "Strictly for Laffs," with a line drawing of a toothy goon laffing. I knew not to tell the so-called publisher—a printer who also did flyers for local supermarkets—that I'd worked at *Newsweek,* and Yale became UConn. I accounted for the years since I'd written my column by killing off my brother and sister-in-law (yes, in a car crash) and having to take care of their children. I suppose he gave me the job because no one else with any qualifications could afford to work for so little. It was an hour each way, but at least I no longer had to trust the Tercel; my husband had bought me a red Subaru, girly but with all-wheel drive. The radio was all about Iraq—this was 2003—but I'd usually catch *A Word in Edgewise* around the time I was driving over the Kingston-Rhinecliff Bridge, and I would read malign significance into the expressions whose always-surprising origins she'd chosen to explain: *letting the cat out of the bag, going haywire, a pretty kettle of fish, taken down a peg.* On the weekends I smoked when I dared, but my husband took time from his painting so we could be together. He brought me on expeditions that had a volkish vibe right out of *Lolita:* to Lago di Giorgio, where we ordered prime rib at log restaurants—he did; I had the salad bar—and wandered through the outlet stores, which had nothing either of us wanted; to musty-smelling country motels, which he chose for the campiness of their neon signs, where we played miniature golf among fat tourists and their fat children; to state parks where we picnicked at picnic tables, saw lakes and trees. I thought his sense of irony had gone critical; I should have realized he was running out of money.

We only went down to the city a couple of times that spring, when the Met put on an opera he was sure wouldn't be set in a disco or a Las Vegas casino; lately he'd only wanted to see tenors in tight pants and open shirts, sopranos in big dresses, soldiers with helmets and breastplates. Instead of getting us drinks in the lobby—they *were* overpriced—he brought airplane bottles of Dewar's, and we downed them on the sly during the intermissions, while looking at the costumes in glass cases. "Some brave soul," he said, "needs to grab a whip and drive the moneychangers from the temple." One night, we got stuck in traffic on the West Side Highway, even though it was eleven o'clock, and he said, "I hate the future." "I don't think it's exactly the future anymore," I told him. "All right, fine," he said, "I hate the present. Isn't that what you've been waiting to hear?"

I'd broken the news to him about the job only after I'd been hired, and then only after the first drink. "Ah," he'd said. "The first move in the Great Extrication. I can't say I didn't see it coming. For what it's worth, I've enjoyed our little idyll. Next thing we know, you'll be making *friends*."

"*You* have friends," I said. "Anyway, it's not about that."

"I *did* have friends." It was true that no one had visited us lately. "No, you're right, you're too young for all this." He swept his hand across the landscape, taking in the river, the mountain, a boat moving downstream, its sail pink in the afternoon light. "It must look like death itself to you."

"I'm not going anywhere," I said. "I was just losing my mind trying to be, I don't know. What I'm obviously not. I feel like I'm disappointing you."

"Let's say it's not what I'd envisioned for you. But I suppose that wasn't my business, was it?"

"It's not like you held a gun to my head," I said. "A normal person would have died for a chance like that."

"And you're sure you're not just going through a rough patch?"

"On the way to what?"

"On the *way*," he said. "Oh well. At your age, you have a different view of things. Will they be paying you decently?"

"No," I said.

"Then it's not *entirely* without dignity. Are they giving you insurance at least?" He'd dropped his coverage—not a good idea for a man who'd just turned seventy-three—because the premiums had gone up to six hundred a month. He'd been worried enough to visit a walk-in clinic when we got back from Montana, but he wouldn't go see the urologist to whom they'd referred him.

"Well, the drugstore next door gives flu shots," I said. "They have a sign about it."

"Oh," he said. "But it'll pay for your gasoline? And you'll continue to have a roof over your head. Assuming we're still . . . what would one call it?"

"You're making this into some big catastrophe," I said. "Nothing's going to change—I mean, *you* don't want it to, do you?"

"As long as you don't," he said. "Probably longer."

My mother's birthday was in May, and although she'd told me that seventy was nothing to celebrate, my husband offered to take her to dinner in the city and have us all stay at the Carlyle.

"I thought we were broke," I said.

"Bent," he said. "No worse than a forty-five degree angle. What would *you* do, put her on a bus back to New Jersey?"

"We could have her here."

"And stick her in the cellar?"

"It's a *beautiful* room," I said. "I mean, you designed it."

"For functionality, yes. I suppose we could give her *our* room. *She* doesn't piss the bed, does she? Should you invite your brother, just for form's sake?"

"He'd never come."

"How quickly they catch on, these young people. You will have covered your bases. You see, I'm looking out for you."

But he did come. He couldn't afford to bring the family, not that I'd asked him to, so the wife—praise Jesus!—stayed home with the baby and the two little ones. "Well," my mother said when I told her, "that was very thoughtful of you." She seemed content with what reconnecting she'd already done, and, having seen one grandchild, could handle the disappointment of not seeing more—just my interpretation. I had to work, so my husband drove to LaGuardia to pick him up, then out to Saddle River to get my mother on the way back. When I got home, I found the menfolk out on the deck, my husband with a glass of whiskey, my brother with a can of Diet Coke. My mother was in taking a nap. My brother got up—he was wearing a short-sleeved white shirt with a black tie—and took my hands to keep me at arms' length. "This is some house," he said. "I was just getting the story on it. That somebody'd see a movie and then haul off and build the thing— that blows me away."

"Maybe it just shows I don't have much imagination," my husband said.

"Did you remember to pick up the cake?" I said.

"I did. Mission accomplished. As our president would say."

My brother sat down and looked out across the river. "So what do they call that mountain over there?"

"You're right," my husband said. "We don't need to get back into that. As I said, you have to excuse an opinionated old man."

"I better get started on dinner," I said. "Can I bring you something? There's cheese, crackers, olives . . ."

"I don't want to get filled up," my brother said.

"I'm fine, thanks," my husband said. "I might come in and replenish. How are you doing with yours?"

"Still working away," my brother said.

In the kitchen, I said, "So how badly did you two get into it?"

"We managed to step back from the brink," he said. "I keep forgetting there really *are* people like that."

"This is where we live," I said. "You should come over to Kingston with me sometime."

"No," he said, "*this* is where we live. Thank God. Maybe our lesbian Unitarian could come and exorcise the place once he's out of here."

At dinner, my brother reached out his hands to me and my mother. I took his and reached for my husband's, but my mother said, "I'm sorry, but it's bad enough being this old without having to humor *you*. And your *pushiness*. Which is all this is."

My brother turned red. You had to feel sorry for him. A little. "I didn't mean to—you know, I just don't see that it hurts anybody to give a word of thanks."

"Well, why don't we all join hands and say the Lord's Prayer backward and see if we can get the Devil here?" She turned to me. "Isn't that what he thinks we do?"

"I really don't want to get in the middle of this," I said.

"Okay," my brother said. "Let's not ruin your birthday."

"May I propose a toast?" my husband said. "To a lovely lady, in honor of an occasion I know she'd rather not have mentioned, but which we all celebrate. Many happy returns."

"You're very sweet," she said. "I shouldn't have caused a scene."

My brother put his napkin in his lap. "No, I shouldn't have been so—what you said, pushy. I guess it's just being around people who, I don't know, people who are used to—"

"We understand," I said.

"I, for one," my mother said, "am going to *drink* your toast." She picked up her wineglass, drained what was left, said, "Cheers," and held the glass out to my husband. "How about one of those happy returns?"

We gave her our bedroom and I took my brother up to my study and turned down the covers on the brass bed. "She scared me tonight," he said.

"She was a little rough with you," I said. "Probably she's just tired. I know she's been stressing about turning seventy."

"No, that thing about the Devil. That doesn't just pop into a person's mind."

"Come on, she was *joking*."

He shook his head. "There was something going on. I could feel it in the room."

"Please don't get weird with me." I remembered that my husband had said something about an exorcism. "I'm sorry, I know you believe what you believe."

"You felt it too," he said. "Don't lie."

"What I *felt*," I said, "was that you and Mom were doing your usual. You were probably scaring *her*."

"What, with big bad Jesus? *Somebody* got scared when I was about to pray. That wasn't, like, even her voice."

"God, you seriously think this."

"We need to pray." He went down on his knees and tried to pull me down with him.

I jerked my hand away. "I can't watch this. It's like seeing you shoot up. I'm going to bed."

Down in the basement, I washed my face, brushed my teeth and went in to my husband. He looked up from his book. "You were right," he said. "It's perfectly tolerable down here. I have now officially stopped feeling sorry for any of our houseguests."

I sat down on the bed; he put a hand on my back and began to stroke up and down. "He's completely insane," I said.

"He *is* a curiosity. I suppose he's normal enough out there in America. Well, I'll have an opportunity for further study when I drive him back to the airport."

"I think he's terrified all the time."

"I thought you said he was insane. You need to make up your mind."

After he went to sleep, I lay there and prayed that if something evil *had* entered the house, we would be delivered from it—and wasn't that what the Lord's Prayer said? I might as well have stayed up there and got down on my knees with my crazy brother. My pillbox of buds was in the room where he was staying; I prayed that he might go through my desk and discover it, as if *that* were how the evil had gotten in. I prayed for the sound of a toilet flushing. I heard only the lowing and the clattering of a train passing through, down along the river.

Oh my—*that* was a little gothic-y. Let's get a grip before we have my mother sucking cocks in hell.

She stayed for another couple of days, I assume so she wouldn't have to ride back with my brother. For much of the trip to LaGuardia, he and my husband had apparently chatted about the best cars to drive in those Colorado winters and his job at CompUSA, steering clear of Jesus and the war. "He says in ten years we're all going to be walking around with computer chips in our foreheads," my husband told me. "He seems a little conflicted about it, working where he does—as am I. When the Antichrist gets here, I want that young man on *my* team." My mother and I went to hear his trio play at the restaurant, and she pleased him by requesting "I've Got the World on a String." "Why don't you come up and sing it?" he said. "What's your key?" "Good lord, no," she said. "I can't sing a note." He persisted—the place was practically empty, she was among friends—and she finally got up and proved it. She came back to the table blushing like a proud little girl. She still talks about it.

After my brother scared me about the Devil—all right, after I scared myself—I put the buds away in the freezer, inside a box of frozen green beans I'd bought for just this purpose. Hardly food that would tempt a hungry hubby. Now I looked forward to that drink when I got home from work, but I have to confess I'd begun to enjoy my job. I must have been the first managing editor to get Samuel Beckett into *The Pennypincher*—"What goes by the name of love is banishment, with now and then a postcard from the homeland"—or to pass along, thanks to my old researcher skills, the Fun Fact that when a hydrogen bomb explodes, it momentarily creates every element in the universe. I was sure the publisher would freak out, but I don't suppose he ever read the filler—who did? I understood that *The Pennypincher*'s new edgy sensibility wasn't a triumph I could share with my husband, but I was so lost at this point that I felt sorry for myself about it.

In June I drove over for Andrea's wedding, without the huz, who had a wedding of his own that afternoon, playing cocktail music until the real band started up; he said he couldn't in good conscience deny the boys a chance to make two-fifty apiece—read that as you will. Andrea, I saw, had lost some weight, and the groom—an only-once-divorced theater publicist, with an eight-year-old son as his best man—had just a little gray hair at the temples. Lightly worn, Andrea called him. "I'm sorry your husband couldn't make it," he told me. "An architect *and* a musician. He must be very creative. And you're a writer."

"Yes, we're a nest of singing birds," I said. "Andrea looks lovely."

"Doesn't she? You know, when we're back from Hawaii, we should all have dinner. You still come down to the city, don't you?"

"Not as often as we used to—but sure."

"Superb. Sounds like a plan. We'll get you back in circulation."

At the reception, Andrea had seated me next to the groom's son; luckily, he spent the dinner talking to her mother, on the other side of him, who showed him how to fold a dollar bill into a shirt with a collar. A couple across the table, apparently old friends of the groom, tried to include me in a conversation about *The Sopranos*—which I'd never seen, so I had to go into interviewer mode. After the cake, Andrea came over and pulled up an empty chair.

"I think you scored," I told her. "He seems very nice."

"Older men, right?" She pumped a fist. "Listen, we have to talk about that job of yours. What are you *doing*?"

"What I can, apparently."

"This cannot be allowed to continue," she said. "I'll be back in three weeks, and you are to *call* me."

"I doubt there's much you can do. I fucked myself living in the boonies."

"What happened to your book?"

"You didn't see the review in the *Times*?"

"Somebody's being difficult," she said. "It's so out of character."

"This is your wedding," I said. "Let's get on to something upbeat. Where are you guys going to live?"

"No," she said. "You call me."

His daughter had phoned to apologize, to both of us, as soon as we were back—it had been a terrible week, which was no excuse, she fucked up *everything,* Madeleine was furious at her (which I doubted), she was furious at *herself,* she never got to see us and now we'd probably never want to see *her,* and *now* she was being all *abject,* which she realized was unattractive . . .

"What a performance," he said after they'd hung up. "I hope Madeleine can keep her from rending her garments. Otherwise she'll be hitting the thrift stores again."

"Why do you have such contempt for her?"

"I wouldn't call it that. Just fatherly skepticism. There *is* a history here. She's basically a good girl."

"She was humiliated."

"And appropriately so, wouldn't you say?"

"I think we should have her come here for a few days," I said. "I mean when this has blown over a little. The two of you need to spend more time together."

"Aren't *you* a saint. Then again, you'll be safe at work all day."

"I think you're afraid of her."

"I'm just not sure I have the energy for it. Would you like some coffee?" He started for the kitchen, then turned around. "You're right," he said.

She only got a week's vacation, but she agreed to come east over the Fourth of July, stay with us for two nights, then have a night with her mother before flying back. Her father drove to LaGuardia to get her; I'd made a big chicken-and-avocado salad, with goat cheese, olives and vinaigrette, and I was on the deck with my earphones, on my third drink, watching the sun go down, when I finally heard them coming up the driveway. She set her bag down and I hugged her; I could feel the clasp of her bra under her T-shirt and realized I was working my thumb under it. I moved the thumb away, she hugged me tighter, then let me go.

"And no welcome for me?" my husband said.

I kissed him on the lips, medium light. "You must've had a trek," I said.

"I'd forgotten that every drudge in New York would be trying to escape tonight. Well, one shouldn't call them drudges. Fellow Americans. How many drinks are you ahead of us?"

I held up two fingers. It depended on how you counted.

"We'll be up with you in no time."

"Dinner's ready whenever you want it," I said.

"First things first," my husband said. "I think I speak for both of us." He went over to the marble-topped iron table where I'd set glasses, bottles and the ice bucket.

"How was your flight?" I said.

"I never know the answer to that," she said.

"Late," my husband said.

"Well, you're here," I said. "Okay, I'm being inane. I'm *glad* you're here. Your father's glad too—he's being grumpy."

"I need to go put my shit away," she said. "Am I down in whatever it is?"

"*Not yet*," he said. "Old joke."

After dinner, I noticed him nodding in his chair; he woke himself up by spilling his drink on his pants leg. "Christ Jesus," he said, jumping to his feet. He took the empty glass off the cushion and set it on the floor. "I guess that's all for the old man." He ran his hand along his thigh and looked at it. "Hell. I'll see you ladies in the morning." We watched him go up the stairs, his hand on the banister.

"He's tired," I said.

"He's old and drunk," she said. "It kind of breaks my heart. I don't know, I guess he's seen me in worse shape. You too—I mean, you have too."

"We all have our moments," I said.

"Yeah, but that was a pretty sick display," she said. "I mean back in Portland." We arranged ourselves on the sofa, as we had that first time, cross-legged at opposite ends.

"Listen," I said. "I've got some dope. Do you want any?"

She shook her head. "I stopped with that after—oh. You don't mean *dope* dope. Yeah, I could."

I went to the freezer and brought back my stash and my one-hitter, a metal tube made to look like a cigarette.

"This thing's *cold,*" she said.

"Here." I took it and breathed onto it in my cupped hands, then loaded it for her. "You want to sit over closer?"

She came and sat cross-legged beside me, our knees touching. "This isn't very comfortable," she said.

"What if we did this?" I uncrossed my legs and stretched them out while I took her shoulders and moved her to sit with her back against my chest.

"God, how sketchy is this?" she said. "If he comes back down, he's going to *really* think we've bonded." I put the one-hitter between her lips and lit a match.

"Nice," she said, after breathing out the smoke. I felt her head relax onto my breasts. I put my nose in her hair—it smelled of the drugstore shampoo I'd put in the downstairs bathroom—and she twisted her head up to look at me. "Aren't you doing any?"

"It's for you," I said. "Sometimes it makes me a little paranoid."

"Come on." She put it between my lips. "I won't let that happen."

When I began to feel it, I straightened up and said, "Music?"

"I don't need it," she said. "If you want."

"I'll go put something on, okay?" But the movements involved in getting up seemed too complicated. "Maybe not," I said after a while.

"Yeah, don't." She edged back, pushing her narrow hips between my thighs, and I spread them wider.

"Are you okay about this?" I said.

"Aren't you?" she said. "We can be close. I mean without doing anything."

"I think I *am* sort of doing something." I could feel myself getting wet.

"Oh." She breathed out. "Thank *God*. Can I just kiss you?"

She twisted herself around to be on top of me and my mouth was grinding into hers. "We need to go downstairs," I said. "Can we?"

Afterward, she lay on her back with her hands over her eyes. "I just want you to know," she said, "this is the weirdest thing I've ever done. I can't even imagine what it's like for you."

"It wasn't like *you* did it," I said. "I mean, we both did." I sat up and reached down for my clothes. "God, I really, really don't want to do this, but he doesn't sleep that well, and if he finds me not there, you know? Are you going to be okay if I go up?"

"I guess so," she said. "You probably need to go process. Is this the first time you . . ."

"Actually no. Did I seem like it?"

"I wasn't even thinking about that."

"Is this going to fuck up your thing with Madeleine?"

"I don't know," she said. "You better go."

"Kiss good night," I said.

"Isn't that a little mooshy?" She raised her head to give me a peck, then lay back down and covered her eyes again. "So is one of us going to say it?"

"What would we say?"

"Nothing. I'm just being crazy now."

"Oh." I put on my T-shirt, found my socks. "That *really* would be a first. For me."

She propped up on one elbow to face me, her long breasts touching the mattress. "What about my dad?"

"I'm just not very expressive," I said. "I mean, I *do*. I just—"

"Okay, this is a little too much, all right?"

"We *are* in deep shit, aren't we?" I got up, pulled on my jeans and stuffed my underpants in the pocket. "Was that enough of a confession?"

"Madeleine always says I have no filter," she said. "You *really* better go. Tomorrow's going to be one strange day."

The next day was the Fourth, and my husband draped his Japanese flag over the railing of the deck; it used to piss people off in Rhinebeck, but no one could see it up here. He told us *he* would make breakfast and set out bowls and a box of Cheerios; he was in high ironic mode. You'd think he would have seen it all over us, but he was so far away.

He took her for a father-daughter expedition—"No interlopers allowed," he told me—up to Hyde Park, to see the Roosevelt mansion, and also Val-Kill, where Eleanor used to fuck Lorena Hickok, though he didn't mention that as a reason for going. He did try to do everything right with her, as I hope she knows. In the afternoon, he listened to a ball game on the radio while showing her his latest paintings and letting her try to do his portrait in charcoal: in high school, she'd wanted to be an artist. His Mets beat the Reds seven to two, so that was good. As always, he refused to watch what he called "the fury of aerial bombardment," though from the deck we could have seen the fireworks displays from towns up and down the river. Instead, he'd planned a double feature for us: *The Parallax View* to be followed by *The Manchurian Candidate*. It wasn't a strange day, particularly. They'd stopped to buy steaks at the organic supermarket in Poughkeepsie—you remember the one—which he grilled for us like a real husband and father. "Dig in," he said. "Grub first, then ethics. I forget who said that." I'd been noticing that he was starting to repeat himself. While we ate, he and I made her talk about her music, as if we were Mom and Dad. Proud, but concerned, but proud. He fell asleep during *The Parallax View;* I stopped it and she and I helped him up to bed. "Let's not watch the rest," she whispered as we came back downstairs.

"I've seen it," I said. "I can tell you how it ends."

She put both arms around my waist. "Yeah, we both know how it ends," she said. "I don't care, do you?"

We put her on the train the next day, to go stay with her mother before her flight on Sunday afternoon. I packed a bag on Sunday morning, while he was in working, enough stuff to last me, and left a note: *Had to go to the city. Will explain later.* That would be quite the explanation. I waited where she'd said, at the corner of Sixth Avenue and Eleventh Street, in front of Ray's Pizza, and she got out of a taxi with all her things. "I can't believe we're really doing this," she said. "So now what?"

5

The other day I went with Andrea to a memorial for the *Newsweek* writer, who'd somehow managed to make it to seventy-six, because who wouldn't be curious. The family funeral and the cremation had been a month ago, but, this being New York, it had taken time to line up the venue and the speakers. We sat in the back of St. Mark's Church-in-the-Bowery and people told stories about old days I hadn't been around for at a magazine that no longer existed. Crashing a cover when Frank Sinatra died, then heading out to a dive near the Lexington Avenue subway at six in the morning. The headline they'd rejected for the writer's Linda Lovelace obit. The Friday night when he got a stupid edit and stomped a metal wastebasket flat. The still older days at 444—the address on Madison, before the move to Fifty-Seventh Street—drinking at a bar called the Cowboy with people called Ax and Shew. A middle-aged woman, all put together, got up and told about the note he'd put in an interoffice envelope after she'd written her first takeout: *A star is born.* I didn't recognize her as my onetime rival, until Andrea whispered her name. It seemed brazen of her to be up there speaking in front of the wife, who sat in the front row waiting her turn. It was as if we were already in a place where we no longer saw through a glass darkly, but he'd probably taken his secrets to the urn.

The wife spoke last. She looked like somebody's grandmother, which I guess she must have been, since a boy in a blue blazer was sitting there with what looked to be the family. Even in his last years, she said, he'd never stopped keeping up with the new books, and he'd given her the encouragement to sit down and write her memoir of growing up in Washington during the Kennedy years—which, she said, peering over her glasses to milk the laugh, was still in search of a publisher.

When the reminiscences were over, and his daughter—a cabaret singer who'd come in from Chicago—had sung "Bridge over Troubled Water," I went up to the star-is-born woman and said, "How many of us do you suppose there were?"

"I'm sorry?" she said. "Do we know each other?"

I live in the city now, where I've had the good luck to find a studio I could afford in the West Village, and every day I walk to the subway past a gated cul-de-sac where E. E. Cummings and Djuna Barnes and somebody else used to live. I work for a women's magazine, in ad sales—at *Newsweek* we used to call it the business side, as if a business had any other side. I'm the assistant to the director, meaning that I make myself useful, answer the phone and the emails—one no longer says "Girl Friday." I had the Yale degree, however many years out of date, I'd worked at *Newsweek* and so on, but mostly Andrea had interceded, and had told me how to finesse the lost years: everyone understands a failed marriage, as long as you don't present yourself as a woman who's belatedly ambitious. They let me write—without pay; what year do you think this is?—for the blog, about books and movies that wouldn't make it into the magazine proper: my choice, as long as it's something womansy. So I, too, have become a keeper-up-with. I'm known—not that I'm known—for being hard to please, and the editor of the blog, a young woman whose ambition isn't yet belated, finds this "refreshing once in a while." If I learned one thing from my husband, meaning my second husband, it was finicking. Yes, I see the wavy red line under that word, and no, I don't mean *being finicky,* which is a habit of mind: he actually taught me to finick. As you see.

Andrea's husband told her he was gay a year after they got married, but you must have known that, and so must she. She still sees the little boy, so there's that. She's been a better friend to me than I've been to her: she not only got me my job but let me stay with her when I needed someplace to go—not to diminish her generosity, but by that time she had room in her apartment. She's set me up with men she knows, age appropriate—what else could I expect?—and not all of them grotesque. The now-ex-husband gets her theater tickets, and she's always offering to take me to this or that, and I go sometimes to keep her company. I've become a person who's seen *Kinky Boots* and *The Book of Mormon.*

As to *my* husband—it didn't kill him, I'll say that. He's in his eighties, still in his house; he's got some sort of nurse-companion. Which, after all, is what I would have been by now. He and I don't speak, and why would we. The pianist he used to play with visits him from time to time, if you're wondering where I get my news. I say "used to" because he's got arthritis in his hands and sold his bass for enough money to buy him a few more months' help; I suspect that the banker brother, who must now be retired, kicks in a little. Before leaving the house that day, I'd hunted up the card with his lawyer's number, but it was a Sunday and I didn't get around to making the call till Tuesday. He would never have disappeared for so long without letting me know he was all right. He would never have disappeared. Just add it to my total for when the reckoning comes. I told the lawyer only that I'd gone, wasn't coming back and wanted nothing; he could deal with it from there.

She and I had agreed that no one should know we were together, not for now; I believe the word "hurtful" was used. And how could anyone find out? I would still be here on the East Coast, she would tell Madeleine she'd gone to visit friends in Seattle—they'd promised to back her up—and this would give us time to figure out how to explain to the principals that this was the right thing for all of us, and then when everybody was used to the situation, it might not be right away, but maybe someday we could actually all be together again and—well, God knows *what*. We probably thought we were innocent. It only took a few days for the knock at the door to come—we had credit cards, the Subaru had license plates—as we must have wanted it to.

We stayed together for six months. She was a child, as you've seen: moody, scattered her clothes all over the place, stopped washing her hair. She always had to have music—she said silence made her anxious, but what *didn't?*—and she wouldn't use earphones for some reason having to do with, I don't know, the air in the room? She still had the copy of *Rumours* she'd appropriated, but most of her CDs were hand-lettered in marker pen: electronic noises, some with a beat, some without. I couldn't read with that racket going, and she *didn't* read, except on her laptop. We used it to play chess—click on Human vs. Human—and she complained that I wasn't good enough to make it interesting. Of course she found out where to get heroin, and one night she laid out some for both of us—she gave me what she said was a safe amount for a newbie. I vomited while she held my hair away from the toilet, humming to herself. When she took off her fetching high-tops, her feet smelled.

Reader, she dumped me.

We rented a motel room by the week, a few blocks from a beach on the Outer Cape. "Now we really *can* be out," she said. Her father's daughter. We couldn't think where else to go—you're supposed to head west to start a new life, but west was where Portland was—and what did the place matter anyway? I'd add "as long as we were together," but I don't want to play the throbbing violin here. By November it had gotten cold, and we bought a ceramic space heater to plug in by the bed. She was young and perky enough to get a job at Starbucks in Hyannis—she could do perky when she had to—and took the Subaru six mornings a week. I worked at a drugstore in a strip mall that was close enough to walk to, just one more lady in a blue frock. Between the two of us, we made enough. I really *could* play the throbbing violin about those first couple of months, but it's nobody's business: only hers and mine. When she finally left, Madeleine wouldn't take her back, and I could never have returned to the house on the hilltop. We both gave up our lives for nothing. Which sounds akin to some holy undertaking, like saints renouncing the world and moving toward the pure empty light, except I suppose that what we did to other people wasn't so saintlike. But at some point isn't that on them, how much they decide to suffer? Something else we'll understand when we all see face-to-face. *Now I know in part; but then shall I know, even as also I am known.*

No, my brother hasn't swooped in and body-snatched me, if that's where you thought this was going, me with my little desperation prayer episodes and him with the Lord at the ready. He knows I'm a lost soul—I mean, we took acid together—and I think he secretly respects that. But when he heard I was living alone on Cape Cod, he emailed to invite me to Colorado for Christmas and asked if I needed money. The Lord, he said, had blessed them with a little extra this year, which was probably a lie. And he included a link to a passage that he said had been a comfort to him: 1 Corinthians 13, *Though I speak with the tongues of men and of angels* and so on. I thought it would be another sales pitch for Jesus, but He didn't even get a mention—just general wisdom, and a little bleak at that. Apparently if you didn't have love you weren't shit, that's what I took away from it: you weren't shit and you didn't *have* shit and you didn't *know* shit and you get the rest of the picture when you're dead—the glass darkly thing. Like, where do *I* sign up to be a servant leader?

Comforting as it may or may not be to know that this life is just a prologue, I feel like I'm living in an epilogue, and given my state of health (tip-top, thanks for asking), it could be a long one. When I'm out in public, at the theater, say, in the lobby at intermission, each handsome young man and lovely young woman seems to be lit with a spotlight, while I'm invisible. O for the tongues of men and angels, to dilate on the unfairness! The long-awaited diatribe from the author of *5 Blondes.* Ah well. I just saw that my first husband has a piece in *Outside* magazine, about rock-climbing in the Shawangunks—I give him props for plugging away at the sweet futility—and the photo on the contributors' page shows a man whose tanned face belies however many years it belies. He must be getting fan mail. From the girlies, and I hope from the boys too; I still think I was right about him. And I wish him a few months of joy too, even a few minutes, whatever that might cost him. *Or* his new wife, no longer new. A first wife's bad-fairy blessing.

In case you're waiting for the where-are-they-now, she's turned forty, not dead, not famous—a regular Everywoman. I gather you can find her on Facebook. I can't imagine that she ever sees her father, having stolen his wife (or vice versa), but that was years ago, he's old, and they loved each other and whatnot.

I don't know what all this is supposed to add up to: it seems to be about damaged and selfish people, the waste of money that could have helped somebody, the waste of gifts that could have given somebody pleasure—am I leaving out anything? I'm sorry to end without some note of redemption. See you after the shitshow, I guess.

When we left the church, Andrea wanted to go for drinks with a couple of the *Newsweek* people, and we ended up at a bar on Lafayette Street, in a dark back room with upholstered chairs and dim lamps on little round tables. Outside, it was still the middle of the afternoon.

I remembered one of the women: she'd worked in the makeup department, and I used to sit with her fitting stories on the page after the writers had gone home. Cut a word to bring up a line, add a word to make a last line full, if need be put on tight bands—who even knows what tight bands are anymore? When the magazine offered its second round of buyouts, she'd gone back to school and was now teaching third and fourth grade in Newark. Often, she said, she had to buy her kids pencils. She said taking the buyout was the best decision she'd ever made. I drank two martinis, excused myself—Andrea was lining up another woman to write a piece for her about sex trafficking—and walked back, drunk, to the West Village in the afternoon sun, through crowds of young people. This was a day that offered every temptation to get maudlin, but I had a book to finish reading, and a piece to write about it. As I passed the gated cul-de-sac where the distinguished dead had lived, I saw a drunken young woman screeching at her drunken young man and trying to pull him up off the sidewalk. They were in a miserable moment of their lives, and it occurred to me to pray for them, but really, why these two out of the multitudes who were suffering?

My brother says he knows the moment when his old life ended and his new life began: when he heard his own voice asking *What is God's will for me?* and yanked the piece of rubber tubing from around his arm. Fine: he's constructed the narrative he needed. I won't say he's lucky, but if I'm going to bring my own story to an end—look how little of it is left—while making it seem to have some sort of shape, I'll need to fasten on some more or less random moment and claim that right *there* was the point before which and after which. My plan had been to bring it around in a circle, back to that stagy little prayer in the shower, but how bogus would *that* have been? So let's go with the day I packed up the rest of my stuff in that half town house where I'd left my first husband, to put it in storage while I made up my mind whether or not to move into the beautiful house I would share with the man who would be my second husband, the beautiful house we would leave for the more beautiful house, the house he'd wanted for himself, the house in which I would leave *him:* the maddest thing I've ever done, the most willful, the most necessary. Anyway, it was the morning of January 2, and my husband would be getting in from New Mexico at five o'clock. It had snowed the night before; they hadn't yet plowed the parking lot or shoveled the walks, and I didn't have my boots. I put clothes in suitcases, then went through the books one last time—that *Dubliners* had been mine, *One Hundred Years of Solitude* definitely his, *Lolita* probably mine but I could always get another copy. Then I remembered the print of van Gogh's *Starry Night*. He'd said it was his favorite painting, and he'd given me the print for my birthday—oh, not

some cheesy poster, but a "framed canvas art print"—and naturally I'd
put on a show about how it was my favorite too, but my God. I'd had
him hang it in the bedroom—better that than having it out where visitors could see it. I went in and looked at the thing: Could you imagine
hanging this next to a Diebenkorn? So I left it for him, in all generosity. And there's my moment, okay? Not that I could have turned back
at that point.

So I carried the boxes and suitcases out, loaded them into the trunk
and the backseat, put the note and key on the counter, let the door lock
behind me, then drove fishtailing through the snow in my little car,
with its bald tires, my feet wet, fiddling with the vents to blow warm
air onto my hands, into the life to come.

Late one afternoon, when it was too cold to walk to the beach anymore, she and I drove there in the Subaru—I'd be putting it in the
paper in another month, as soon as the lawyer could get the title from
him—and parked in the lot that had cost a dollar an hour back during the summer. The gate was up, the booth was empty and there
was only one other car. We walked down, through heavy sand, then
over hard sand, to where shallow waves washed in from the bay—we
couldn't afford the ocean side. Far down the beach, a man with a dog;
otherwise we were alone. She had her hands in the pouch of her sweatshirt, her hood up; strands of black hair blew around her chin. "Somehow this has lost its allure," she said.

"We could go south," I said.

"We *are* going south," she said. "Ha ha."

I saw a piece of dull green sea glass among the shells, dead crabs and
Styrofoam cups. I squatted down and handed it to her. She held it up to
the sky, then dropped it back in the sand.

"I've already got a lifetime supply of this. What are we even *doing,*
you know?"

"Maybe we should think more about moving to Boston," I said.
"You said there was a music scene."

"What would *you* do?"

"I don't know. I'm just throwing it out as something."

"You used to be this great writer," she said.

"When was *that*?"

"It's the first thing he said about you."

Now that the man was closer, I could see he had on a nylon track-suit, that his dog was a chocolate Lab. He kept stopping to toss a tennis ball into the waves and wipe his hand on his pants; the dog, wet all over, kept bringing it back, dropping it on the sand and dancing back from it.

"Your father lives in his own universe," I said. "Are you worried that I'm going to be dead weight?"

"That's not what I'm saying." She looked over at the dog. "This is amazing. Isn't it going to get hypothermia or something?"

"Are you kidding?" I said. "They live for this."

"I need to meet that dog." She walked over to the man; I thought I'd better come along. "Is it a boy?"

"As you see," the man said.

"Doesn't he get cold?"

"Yeah, you'd think," the man said. "He never seems to mind."

"Can I pet him?" She put out her hand; the dog picked up the ball, dropped it and danced back.

"I'm afraid Joey's a little obsessed right now." He reached down and threw the ball into the waves; the dog leaped in after it.

"I wish I was that single-minded." She turned to me. "I want to go back, okay?"

I started the car and turned on the heater, but it blew cold air and I turned it off again. She reached in her bag and brought out *Rumours*. "Here, this'll cheer us up. We can drive around and get warm, do you want to?"

"You miss your life," I said.

"I don't know," she said. "Don't you miss yours?"

And I said, in old-timer voice, *"Not yet."*

An Actor Prepares

||||||

Last summer, on a plane back from Frankfurt, I happened to look up at an overhead screen while trying to learn my lines in *Twelfth Night,* and for a second I thought I saw myself in a promotional video for Singapore Airlines, among a crowd at JFK two weeks earlier. They couldn't possibly have produced this so fast, could they? But there was the distressed-leather jacket, the mirrored sunglasses, the gray hair—silver, let's call it—and the Profile: ah, still a handsome devil. (I'd been going to see a twenty-eight-year-old German woman I'd met in New York, who said if I came over she'd figure out something to tell her boyfriend.) Just this afternoon I told an old friend—someone I've known for years, at any rate—that this was the moment I knew I had to quit acting. I'd studied myself on tape however many hundreds of times and never had I been so convincing: Who wouldn't cast this guy as the old lech on his last go-round?

My father was a film editor—to begin this at the beginning—who'd worked with Stanley Donen and William Wyler, and I really *was* a handsome devil when I was in my twenties; I might have made it as a B-list male ingénue, saved my money and lived on a beach the rest of my life. But when I was thirteen, my parents took me on a trip to the East Coast, where we saw Nicol Williamson's *Hamlet* on Broadway. My father, to his credit, or not, never tried to talk me out of moving to New York; he even paid for my first year at the Circle in the Square Theatre School. I put in my time as Mortimer Brewster and Professor Harold Hill back in the days of dinner theaters, and I played Bernardos and Franciscos at this or that Shakespeare festival. One summer I was so broke I took the bus to Massachusetts to work as an "interpreter" at Plimoth Plantation, speaking Pilgrimese ("How are you faring this day?") and affecting puzzlement when tourists—we were to refer to them as "strange visitors"—tried to get me to break character. I'm proud to say that I never appeared in *The Fantasticks*, either on the road or down on Sullivan Street, though I took TV work when I could get it: a blind date in an episode of *Kate & Allie* and a corrupt lawyer in *Law & Order*. I was understudy to the guy who played A Gent when they brought back *The Cradle Will Rock*; he never missed a night, so I never got to do that first-act number with Patti LuPone. Fifteen years ago, all this amounted to enough of a résumé to get a job at a SUNY branch, teaching what they were pleased to call theater arts; I took the train up to Westchester three mornings a week, a reverse commute among people who seemed to be domestic workers.

Kenny Donnelly was at Circle in the Square at the same time as me, and he always tried to throw work my way. You might have called him a friend too. Last spring I was picking up extra money doing radio commercials while he was finishing a five-month run at Cherry Lane with his adaptation of *The London Merchant; or, the History of George Barnwell:* sort of a *Sweeney Todd* meets *Rocky Horror,* with Rick Calloway—who'd been his partner, off and on, for years—as Sarah Millwood. Kenny had invited me to audition for the murdered uncle, but I'd assumed the show would close in two days.

He comped me for one of the final performances—he'd been right, the uncle was a great part—and took me out for drinks after. Would I be interested in coming up to Vermont in July? The community theater he'd organized was doing *Twelfth Night* this year, and he needed a couple of professionals to glue it together. Two months in Arcadia: he'd put me up, feed me, and I could have my choice of Orsino or Feste; he'd take whichever I didn't want, and we'd let the amateurs have fun with Malvolio and Sir Andrew and Sir Toby. Barbara Antonelli—I'd worked with Barbara, yes?—was coming up to do Maria, and a Shakespeare professor from the University of Vermont wanted to try Malvolio. For

Viola he planned to cast a drama teacher from the local high school; she had a vaguely look-alike brother who was willing to give Sebastian a whirl, although he'd never acted before. And he knew a college girl, a drama major whose father was a lawyer in town, who might be right for Olivia. A good little actress, he thought, quite apart from the fact that the father was on his board.

"I might be getting a little old for Orsino," I said.

"And I'm not?" Kenny said. "Aren't you sweet. Actually, I sort of like the idea of an Orsino who's past his sell-by date. But listen, what you will. As the man says."

I'd booked my trip to Germany for mid-June, but if I made all my connections I could get to Vermont the day before rehearsals started. Pathetic as it seems, I took it all seriously and quit getting high in the evenings. I watched Ben Kingsley in the Trevor Nunn film, and listened to the old Caedmon recording. We all know Shakespeare criticism is a rabbit hole, but I bought Marjorie Garber's book and found her *Twelfth Night* chapter helpful, if less so than A. C. Bradley's "Feste the Jester," written back in 1929. And I came upon this, from good old Granville-Barker in 1912: "Feste, I feel, is not a young man . . . There runs through all he says and does that vein of irony by which we may so often mark one of life's self-acknowledged failures. We gather that in those days, for a man of parts without character and with more wit than sense, there was a kindly refuge from the world's struggle as an allowed fool. Nowadays we no longer put them in livery."

My only hope of memorizing anymore was to read my scenes aloud, over and over, and I recorded myself so I could listen when I was running or doing errands. The day before I left for Europe, I was jogging through Central Park, yelling along with myself, when I came upon the statue of Hans Christian Andersen, that kindly giant pedophile in bronze, with his open storybook on one knee and a real live little girl on the other, being photographed by her parents: "Fie, thou dishonest Satan!" The daddy picked his daughter up, as I might have picked up a daughter of mine. Even on the plane back from Frankfurt, and then on the train up to Vermont, I kept force-feeding myself Feste, moving my lips as I read and listened. My part of death, no one so true did share it!

I stepped out onto the platform in Montpelier as the sun was going down on what must have been a hot day; the last time I'd felt the open air I'd been in Europe. Kenny lifted my suitcases into the trunk of his Saab and drove me through countryside that looked like Germany without the castles. (My little German adventure is a whole other story; but you've seen *The Blue Angel*.) At one point we passed an Adopt-a-Highway sign with the name of his theater. Kenny told me he'd bought up here when it was still affordable; David Mamet had a house a couple of towns away. "Let it be recorded," he said, "that I loathed the man *before* he turned Republican. You hungry? I'm a little peckish. Let's go drop in on the folklife."

We stopped at a bar in his town; the kitchen was closed, but the owner, whom Kenny introduced as Mike, went back and started the fryolator to cook us his special wings, while we drank Bud and watched the last innings of a ball game. Kenny got into a discussion with Mike about the Red Sox pitcher ("They're sitting fastball, for Christ's sake—why is he not going to his changeup?") and bought a round for everybody when the Sox won in the bottom of the ninth.

His house, a big old Vermont cape framed by maple trees, sat on a knoll, up a winding dirt drive. "Hell in the wintertime," he said. He helped me carry my bags to his guest cottage, which had once been the henhouse and still had a wooden cutout of a rooster on the door, with a hand-lettered sign that read NO TEASING. "Aren't *you* flagrant," I said.

"This is only for my very special out-of-town guests," he said. "The iron law of country life—don't shit where you sleep."

After he'd made sure the bathroom had soap and sniffed the towels for freshness, we walked up to the top of his hill and looked down at the lights in his six-over-six windows. You could smell the hay that had just been cut in his fields. He pointed up, and what do you know: the

Milky Way, with its million million stars. "They used to call that the Pathway of the Secret People," Kenny said.

"Who called it that?" I said.

"I don't know, the ancients? I read it somewhere. Anyhow, that always stuck with me. Yes, hmm, I wonder why. You know, I love this fucking place. I never had a home before. Do I swear like this when I'm sober?"

"It's amazing," I said.

"Yes, well, those near and dear to us have a different view. You can take the boy out of the city . . ."

"How *is* Rick? Is he coming up for this?"

"Oh. You *haven't* been getting around much. Rick. No, Rick is currently receding at the speed of light. The Big Bang. Followed by redshift. We are no longer receiving signals from that quadrant. Should I put this in layman's terms?"

"Shit. I'm sorry."

"He always did say this was the ass end of the universe—which one would've thought was high praise, coming from Rick. But I'm not going to start singing that old sweet song. In every other respect, life is very, very good. Life is adverbially good. I own a fucking hill, can you believe that? Your life is going to be adverbially good, I can tell. We're both going through some shit, okay? The key is— Jesus, am I babbling? Come along quietly now, Kenny. Look, I'm a sad old queen and you're a sad old whatever the hell you are. But is life not adverbially good? What say we go down and look at that scene where Malvolio comes in with his yellow stockings—I'm not sure how that's going to play. Given the talent involved. You're not tired, are you? Shit, of course you are. We can do this in the morning."

The next day, Kenny drove me to a first read-through at the theater, a converted barn with seats salvaged from an old movie house. I kissed cheeks with Barbara Antonelli—I hadn't seen her since we'd done *The Crucible* in Williamstown, what, twenty years ago?—and took a seat in the front row. I was waiting for Kenny to get up onstage and do his ladies-and-gentlemen-we're-going-to-have-a-show speech when a young woman in loose cotton pants came in and sat down, leaving a seat between us, slipped off her sandals and perched yoga style, the soles of her feet turned up. The light from the open door caught the side of her face, and you could see the faintest blond down: Was she beautiful, or only young? She caught me looking and said, "I'm Julia. I know who you are."

"That makes you special right there," I said. "You're our Olivia, yes? I'm your corrupter of words."

"I know, I've been so looking forward to working with you. I don't really know this play, though."

"I'm just trusting Kenny," I said.

"Me too, but— Can I say something? I don't think he really gets women."

"Well, I could refer you to any number of women who might call my own understanding into question."

"Oh yes, he told me you had a history."

"Bless his heart," I said. "And he said *you* have a future. Then again, he used to say that about me."

"So is this how you charm them all? Pretending like you're old?"

"It's called getting into character."

"I can't decide if I like you or not," she said.

"And does that work for you?" I said. "Frankness, straight up?"

"If I might interrupt?" Kenny called from the stage. I realized we'd been the only people talking. "We need to get things rolling here. Where's our Viola?"

"In the ladies'," Barbara said.

"Mother of Mercy," Kenny said. "Does anybody else have to go?"

I thought Kenny was a little hard on the schoolteacher who played Viola, a not especially boyish looking lady named Louise. He corrected her lines—"Not 'for what you are.' 'I see you what you are' "—and shot down her idea of giving a sickly smile after her line about patience on a monument smiling at grief. Bad idea, granted, but of course her real offense was not being Rick Calloway. It seemed to me that Julia would probably be okay. At least somebody had taught her to project, and looking at how she carried herself you could see she must have done some dance as well. She played Olivia as bored, spoiled and flirty— enough like Helena Bonham Carter to make me think she'd rented the video, too. In our first scene, where Feste says, "The lady bade take away the fool; therefore, I say again, take her away," and Olivia says, "Sir, I bade them take away *you*," she poked my nose, and Kenny yelled out, "No, no, no—you're still pissed at him. Again, please?" She looked at me and mouthed, *You see?* But then she did it over, with just the right pout.

Back at the house, Kenny brought gin, tonic, limes and a sweating ice bucket out to the screened porch. "A word in your ear?" he said. "I have to live in this town. Not that she's not a lovely girl, but surely you can find other amusements." He dropped a wedge of lime on top of the ice cubes in my glass. "Her parents are good friends."

"I should certainly hope so."

"Please," he said, "leave the badinage to those of us who know how to do it." He picked up the gin. "I would warn you that she drugs a bit, but I know that wouldn't discourage *you*."

"You're thinking of me back in my glory days." He began pouring. "Whoa, easy—when. Exactly what did you tell this young lady about me?"

"Only that you had an eye for the young ladies. And that she might consider resisting your autumnal charms." He topped off my glass with tonic. "Just between you and me and the wall, there's been a little trouble in that quarter."

"Then she needs to rein in her . . . What's the opposite of autumnal? Vernal?"

"Oh, you're good. She *is* very gifted."

"So what's this trouble?"

"Well, since you insist on *dragging* it out of me. One of her professors—I believe he lost his job over it. And her father got all involved. Not a chappie *I'd* want to cross. In fact, I think he ended up here because of some—well, there I go. He's a friend, what can I say?"

"Just so we're clear," I said, "are you forbidding this or promoting it? Sounds like you've gone out of your way to plant the seed. On both sides."

"Am I that much of a devil?" He began putting ice in his glass. "Not that I mind watching a good train wreck now and again. Just not here." He poured gin, no tonic, and clinked his glass against mine. "Pretty please?"

The next day, I turned down Julia's invitation to go swimming after rehearsal, at some locally legendary swimming hole, but that night most of the cast ended up at the bar in the town's Mexican restaurant, owned by the guy Kenny chose to play Sir Toby, who'd had some stage experience, God help us, in a road-company *Joseph and the Amazing Technicolor Dreamcoat*. On Fridays he provided the entertainment, with mic, stool and plug-in acoustic guitar, singing what he called "sixties and seventies"—blessedly, this was a Wednesday. I saw our Sir Andrew, a slender college boy with black-framed glasses, sitting at the end of the bar and beset by Julia, who was touching his upper arm with her fingertips, then her palm, then running the back of her hand down his cheek, then twirling his long hair around her index finger. She saw me watching and gave me her Olivia pout. I took a seat at a table, between Barbara Antonelli and the Viola woman—I've lost her name again— with her supposedly look-alike brother. Louise.

Barbara looked over at the bar. "I'd fight you for her," she said, "but she'll be forty before she knows she's gay. By which time I'll be dead." I looked to see if Louise had heard, but she was talking with the brother. "How did he drag *you* up here?"

"I wasn't doing much else," I said. "It's good to see you."

"Don't waste it on me," she said. "He put me up in this dreadful bed-and-breakfast. Who *are* these people? Could you get me another one? No salt this time. Will we even get through this?"

"One way or another." I looked around for a waitress.

"Aren't you the trouper. Oh, well. A year from now, we'll all be even older. How are you doing? You don't look that much the worse for wear."

"All on the inside," I said.

"And do you hear from that lovely ex-wife of yours?"

"Good Christ," I said. "Why don't you just reach over and slap me like a human being?"

Louise turned away from talking with her brother. "How do you think I'm doing so far?" she said to Barbara. "Honestly. I'm afraid I'm in over my head."

"Shakespeare," she said. "We're all in over our heads, dear."

"Not you," Louise said. "Or you."

The waitress was standing over us. "You're going to be fine," I said. "Another one of these? No salt? And I'll have a Bud. What can I get you guys?"

"We're good," Louise said. "Have you met Billy?"

"Not officially," Billy said. "You were great this afternoon."

"We'll see when I start having to remember my lines," I said.

"And what is it that you do in real life?" Barbara said to him.

"I was managing a Curves, in St. Johnsbury. We had to close a couple months ago."

"Curves. Now, is that a bar?"

"No, you know—Curves. It's like a women's fitness?"

"Oh. Of course. We have those. I was thinking it was one of those gentlemen's clubs." She turned to me. "When we get back to civilization, let's you and me make an expedition to this place in Midtown—aspiring actresses out the wazoo." She looked over at the bar again; Julia and her young man were gone.

The waitress set down my Bud and Barbara's margarita. "Can I get you folks anything to eat? Marty told me half price on everything."

"Isn't he a dear," Barbara said. "Can we drink now, think later?"

"Perfect. Kitchen doesn't close till ten."

"And on a weekday night," Barbara said. "I think we should all move up here."

"It's really not such a bad place," Louise said. "The winters can be a challenge. But I spent a winter in New York once, and *that* was a challenge."

"Did you," Barbara said. "Well, then, you know. What about we all settle in Vermont and help Kenny revive the drama."

"Did I hear my name?" Kenny sat down next to me. "They treating you right here?"

"Half price, can you imagine?" Barbara said. "Anything on the whole menu, from what I could gather. They didn't say about the drinks, though."

"Mother of Mercy," he said. "Okay, I'll take care of this."

"Kenny's a big man in this town," I said.

"I was. You degenerates are ruining my good name." He leaned closer to me and said, "Playing a little rough, aren't we?" He stood up. "Let me see if I can awaken our host's bounty."

We dropped Barbara at Blue Jay Way, a Victorian house painted San Francisco style, with a wooden sign out front that showed an officious-looking bird chirping on a twig. I got into the front seat, and Kenny said, "I expect *Barbara* to be snotty. Believe me, I know how pathetic this must seem to you."

"Come on, you know what my life is," I said. "And everybody here seems to like you."

"Well, yes, of course, *hello,* this is the new NPR Vermont—it's now a hate crime not to have David Sedaris on your iPod." There were no other cars out, but he put on his blinker to turn onto the street that led toward his house; only then did I spot a police cruiser with its lights off parked next to the drive-in bank. "Those fuckers," he said. "Pull you over for not having your hands at ten and two. When Rick and I started coming up here, somebody left a dead dog in the mailbox, little miniature poodle or something. Dressed it up in a baby's pink T-shirt. I'll never get over it. You know what they said? 'Call animal control.' And then Rick would piss and moan because I kept a shotgun under the bed."

"Jesus. Well, so things are better, no?"

"Any sane person would think so. Even *I* think so. But I have to tell you, back then they really got who you were. Like: a man who did dirty things to men. So now I'm our oh-so-charming gay theater guy.

I mean, who wrote *this* shit? Why am I doing fucking Shakespeare? Why am I not doing Genet?"

"Because Genet's terrible?" I said.

"Well, if you're going to be *rational* about it." He put on his blinker again and took the road that went past a pine-smelling sawmill, lit by a couple of bluish floodlights, then up a steep grade along a rocky stream. "I don't know, I just want to have my nice house on the hill, put on a nice little show for the nice people. This is what it's gotten down to."

"Listen, you're a good man," I said. "I'm going to do my best for you."

"*You're* a good man," he said. "I think I drank too much again."

"Daily, as we rehearse together," old Granville-Barker wrote of his production of *Twelfth Night,* "I learn more what it is and should be; the working together of the theater is a fine thing." I just wish you could have seen Julia as Olivia, in the scene where Malvolio comes in with his yellow stockings and she can't imagine what's gotten into him: she and Kenny worked out this business where she first had her hands over her mouth, then covered her eyes and watched Malvolio through her fingers, then let out a giggle—just one—despite herself. And meanwhile there was Barbara—always a joy to watch her—trying to keep a straight face as Maria. And even our Malvolio, who'd volunteered because he thought some "acting experience" might help his teaching: Kenny had him worming a finger under his cross-gartering as he said, "And some have greatness thrust upon them." I'm not saying this was magical—I remember what magical was—but I was standing next to Kenny in the wings and saw him nodding yes.

Julia and Sir Andrew didn't seem to be speaking. A couple of days after their little display at the Mexican restaurant, she and I were out front, watching the scene where he tells Sir Toby, "Your niece will not be seen; or if she be, it's four to one she'll none of me," and he gave us both a look. "Whoa, whoa," Kenny said, "why the stinkeye? Can we keep the fourth wall in place, people?" She put a hand next to my ear and whispered, "He needs to grow up."

The morning of the dress rehearsal, the Eye on the Sky weather forecast was calling for ninety degrees, so we set up fans on the stage. I was sweating under my Beckett greatcoat, and I could see Julia was suffering in the long black mourning dress she had to wear in the first act. The prompter, an English teacher who'd retired from the local high school, had nodded off by the time we got to the recognition scene; poor Sebastian looked right, looked left—his bewilderment was actually more credible than he'd been able to make it before—and then went into improv: "O Viola, is it really thee?" By the time I had to sing "O mistress mine," the guitar I'd borrowed from—now I've lost his name again, you know, Sir Toby—had gone out of tune. "Dress rehearsal is always a disaster," Kenny told us. "Go home, forget about it, and tonight we fucking kill."

After the performance, Julia's parents had the cast over to their house on the village green: your standard-issue New England Federal, three stories, white clapboards, black shutters, oval plaque reading BUILT 1814 beside the front door. In the backyard they'd strung up chili-pepper lights and set out crudités, earthenware bowls of whitish dips, plastic glasses, a Manhattan skyline of bottles. Malvolio, who'd just promised to be revenged on the whole pack of us, was tapping a microphone while Sir Toby tuned his guitar; they'd been working up a "special" song together. Sebastian, still wearing his soldier jacket with the frogging, was pouring wine for Viola, who'd changed into jeans and a peasant top. No sign of our Sir Andrew. Julia was still in costume too—the white dress she wore in the last act, cut to make the tops of her pale breasts bulge out—and splashing liquor from her glass as she put an arm around Barbara Antonelli. I started for her, but Kenny touched the back of my arm and brought me over to the mother—a puffy-faced woman my age, whose wooden beads rattled at her tanned bosom when I air-kissed her—and then the father. "Tom," he said, sticking out a hand. "You're quite the actor, aren't you? Even I could see that."

"Didn't I tell you?" Kenny said. "You'll excuse me, I need to go over and pay homage to La Antonelli."

"I shouldn't be admitting this," Tom said to me, "but I haven't seen a real Shakespeare since I was at Yale—well no, that's not true, we did see Julia when she was Puck, in sixth grade. Of course, as a father, the leading lady was the whole show."

"I've been very impressed," I said. "Kenny thinks the world of her."

"Well, we all think the world of Kenny. He does a lot for this community—a lot for this *family*. He won't tell you, but he's the one who got her into Middlebury. He knows one of the muckety-mucks. You'll never hear anybody say a word against Kenny Donnelly."

Julia came over and put an arm around her father. "Kenny says I was naughty." She reached out with the hand holding the glass and touched a finger to my nose—as she'd done in our first scene. (I'd sneaked a look at Kenny in the wings and saw him throw up his hands.) "I still think it worked."

I saw the father's face get red. "What was this?"

She kissed his fat cheek and said, "Just actor shit. Did you like me?"

"Hey, hey," he said. "Language." She took her arm away and touched my nose again.

"We tend to argue over the fine points," I said, keeping my eyes off her breasts. "I doubt people out there even notice this stuff."

"Don't you have to do what the director tells you?" he said.

"There's always some leeway," I said. "Your daughter's got good instincts."

"Well, I'm sure you know more about it than I do. I thought you were both excellent. You need to go a little easy, Punkin'. Don't forget you've got tennis in the morning." He turned away to hug Viola. "Louise, you were terrific. And how about our girl?"

"Is *he* pissed," she whispered in my ear. "He hates that I'm twenty-one." She finished her drink. "I'm getting more. Come with?"

Malvolio was speaking into the mic. "Is this on? Okay, Marty and I worked up a little number for the occasion . . ."

"Oh, fuck," Julia said. "Let's get away from this."

She took my hand, and as we moved to the back door I heard them singing in unison: "They're gonna put me in the theater . . ."

We made it into the kitchen, where she shut the screen door behind us, then the wooden door, then leaned her back against it and raised her face.

"Now that you've got me," I said, "what do you plan to do with me?" I went in for the kiss, and she turned her head.

"Make you wait," she said. "Like you've been doing." She flicked her middle finger off her thumb and hit my fly. "I have to get something. Meet me out front, okay?"

"You know, people saw us leave."

She was already starting down the hall that led to the foyer, which had a fanlight above the front door. "We're both adults," she said. "Especially you."

She went upstairs, and I found a bathroom off the hall. I hooked the door behind me and washed my face with cold water. You need to get out of this, I said to the mirror. Just the obligatory drunken line: it was as good as done. I waited for her out on the wide stone doorstep and traced the date on the plaque with my index finger, that song from childhood in my head: "Along with Colonel Jackson down the mighty Mississip." She opened the door, still in the dress, thrust a pipe into my mouth and held a lighter over the bowl. Anybody could have seen us from the sidewalk, over the white picket fence. When I exhaled, she kissed me lightly on the lips and said, "Now one more."

"You *are* crazy," I said.

This time the smoke hit my lungs so sharply I had to cough it out. "Good," she said. "That should do it." We kissed full on: so wide and hard I felt I was biting through into the back of her head. She pulled away, breasts rising and falling. "You're a bastard, you know that? Come."

I followed her to a Lincoln Navigator parked at the curb. "Where are you taking me?"

"I want to see the famous henhouse. I'll let you pretend I'm one of Kenny's boys. I bet that's what you're really into."

"You have a most inventive mind." My voice sounded far away, and

I couldn't remember who Colonel Jackson was. "This is some strong shit," I said.

"Door's unlocked," she said. "You need me to open it for you?"

"I'm fine." This was a car door. It was not beyond me to open it.

I settled into the leather seat, thoughts coming too fast to focus on. She turned on air-conditioning, then music—some kind of music I didn't know how to go about recognizing, except I knew the speakers must be amazing because you could hear all the way to the bottom. "What is this?" I said.

"Bob Dylan?" she said. And sure enough, it rearranged itself into— what was it? The one about *threw the bums a dime, didn't you,* the famous one. "Isn't that your age group? My dad had it in."

"I thought it was an oratorio," I said. A word I didn't know how I knew.

"Wow," she said. "Okay, I want to be where you are."

She pulled over—or had we been moving?—and took her pipe out of the, whatever you call the thing between the seats.

Then we were on some road and the whole inside of the car was flashing blue. "Shit," she said, and the music was gone: big silence. "Just don't say anything, okay?"

Her window was down and a cop was standing there, shining a flashlight. "License, registration?"

"For real?" she said. "We were just out for a drive."

"Yeah, your dad called." He sniffed. "Been smoking that good shit tonight?" He shined the light between the seats. "What's that? Give it here."

She handed him the pipe.

"What else? Am I going to have to search the car?"

"It's not hers," I said. "I had it."

"Aren't you the gentleman. And you're who?"

"He's in the play," Julia said. "He's a friend of Kenny's."

"I bet he is. See some ID?"

I got my wallet out. "I don't know what you need," I said. "I have this."

He shined his light on my Equity card. "The hell is this, insurance?"

"You can *get* insurance," I said.

" 'Performing for You.' Beautiful. How about a license."

"He lives in New York, for Christ's sake," Julia said. "Nobody drives in New York."

"I wouldn't know. So, Julia. Do you have any idea why I stopped you tonight?"

"You said. My father called."

"I guess you didn't notice the stop sign back there. How many moving violations have you had in the last year?"

I looked around. We were out in the middle of the country somewhere. Blue flashes kept lighting up a collapsing barn. "Listen," I said. "There's nobody here. Can it be that *I* was driving?"

"What are you, simple? How did you *think* it was gonna be?" he said. "Get out of the car."

"You're not going to hurt him?" Julia said.

He shook his head. "Everything's a drama, right? You got your cell? Why don't you call your folks to come out here, get their car and drive you home."

"See, that's your problem, you never look on the bright side," Kenny said as he drove me to the train. "You were getting too old to be a matinee idol anyway. Now, if they ever bring back *Golden Boy* . . . Are you hurting? I have some Percocet."

"I fucked up your show," I said. They'd broken my nose when they handcuffed me behind my back and shoved my face into the side of the cop car. Kenny came to get me in the morning and told me they were dropping all charges—possession, grand theft auto, resisting arrest—in return for my getting out of Vermont. Just a hundred-dollar fine for failure to carry a license. Apparently he *was* a big man in this town.

"Don't give yourself airs," he said. "Rick's coming up. He's going to take over Feste. We'll miss Wednesday and Friday, and then he thinks we'll be ready to roll."

"How did this come about?"

"Pleading? Contrition? I'm an actor too, don't forget. Actually, I think he was missing me."

"Will he be able to do it?"

"We'll see, won't we?"

"Shit. Maybe I did you a favor."

"One more favor like that and they *will* run me out of town. You need a keeper."

"Listen, if you know of any."

"Not of your persuasion," he said. "I don't know, I guess not of my persuasion either." He looked at his watch. "We're early. I'm still mad at you, by the way. You want to grab a drink?"

You'd think my Vermont adventure would have put me off the country life, but all this summer I've been renting a small house overlooking a lake in Dutchess County, where you can go out on the deck at night and sit and look up at the Milky Way. Which, yes, you can only do for so long. It was this or get the Profile restored, and I thought I might as well spend the money on myself, if you see what I mean. The trees have already begun to turn; tomorrow I have to give this place up and go back to the city.

Barbara came by this afternoon—she has a cottage in Katonah—and we sat out on the deck in the sunshine. She told me Rick and Kenny were on the outs again, though of course with those two . . . Anyhow, Kenny was in Chicago for six months, to put together the Lyric Opera's production of *The Balcony*—who knew they'd made that into an opera? *Twelfth Night,* she said, had gone swimmingly. Rick had camped it up as only Rick could do, faking the parts he was sketchy on, and the audience loved him—not to say they hadn't loved me. This was when I told her about my little bullshit epiphany in the Frankfurt airport.

"I can't hear this," she said. "You're just feeling sorry for yourself. Use it."

"Actually, I'm happy to be out of it all."

She put her glass down. "You are, aren't you? You prick. I always thought you'd go down with the ship. This isn't about our little friend, I trust? You have to come to my gentleman's club. You could still pass for a gentleman if you got your face fixed."

"Just tell me when," I said.

I made sure she got out of the driveway all right—we'd both been drinking the summer's last gin and tonics, and this house sits right on a blind curve—and then walked out the sliding doors to the deck again. The air was getting chilly; going to need that jacket. The sun hung just above the trees, soon to turn the lake and sky orange, soon to be gone. And then the stars. You don't imagine, do you, that anyone's watching us, our love scenes and death scenes, and thinking, *I see you what you are.* But this has nothing to do with anything: I have my clothes to pack for tomorrow, the books I brought, the DVDs, computer, have to clean the bathroom, wash the last dishes, just a million million little things.

The Curse of the Davenports

||||||

Every Christmas Eve, my father used to drive us down to Uncle Wayne and Aunt Phyllis's house: a two-bedroom box in a subdivision backed up against the Connecticut Turnpike. They didn't have kids, but they tethered an inflatable snowman in the yard: their cramped living room, with twin plaid recliners, velour couch and a braided rug, smelled of cigarettes and their fat cocker spaniel. I remember asking my mother, as we were loading gifts into the trunk for them and Grandpa Davenport, how come we always had to go *there*. "I know," she said, "but it's only once a year. Be thankful you're not the Christ Child." She nodded at the life-sized crèche on our neighbors' lawn and said, "What a dump."

Yet here I was at forty-three, divorced and living in Wayne's house. He'd had to put Phyllis in a home—she no longer recognized him or knew her own name—and he'd driven to Arizona in pursuit of a brassy-haired widow he'd met at Mohegan Sun. "Just pay the lights and the cable and we're good," he told me. "Somebody might as well be in there." So spoke the voice of Christian charity. *Surely,* I emailed my mother, *an unseen hand is at work.* She wrote back: *God is not mocked,* followed by a frowny face.

I'd come back to Connecticut just once after college, to stand with my mother and Wayne—Phyllis was already a liability in public—at the veterans' cemetery in Middletown. My mother sold our house in West Hartford, bought a condo in Santa Barbara and told me she wanted her ashes scattered in the Pacific: better to end up among the sharks and the oil slicks than among the military.

I was a graduate student when Sarah came to Berkeley as an assistant professor, with witch-black hair and Katharine Hepburn cheekbones, and we reinvented the traditional academic scandal; a few of her colleagues even came to our wedding, when she was already pregnant with Seth, the flower of our unprotection. What a bad boy I was, and what a bad girl I made her be. We had a cottage in Oakland, with the old Sears, Roebuck gingerbread; during Seth's naptime, we'd open our bedroom window to let in the scent of eucalyptus and edify the neighbors. If I'm sentimentalizing those days, bear with me. When Seth was eight, I started taking him to A's games, and nobody gave us shit for not standing during the national anthem. My thesis ("Cattle Are Actors: Archetype and Artifice in *Red River*") never landed me a job out there—who in the Bay Area *didn't* want to teach film?—but I made some money copyediting and reviewed movies for a free weekly, in a column I called Be Generous, Mr. Spade. My takedown of *Titanic* got more letters than any other piece in 1997.

Still, when Sarah got an offer from Yale, what could I say? They even sweetened the deal with a gig of sorts for me, teaching composition alongside the TAs, and the weekly wanted me to keep sending in reviews. Like the good sport I think I hoped to be, I amused our acquaintances with a theory that New Haven wasn't actually part of Connecticut, but a free city like Danzig or Trieste—no, better, West Berlin stuck in the middle of East Germany. A realtor showed us a turreted stone palazzo in what might eventually become a safe neighborhood, where we could live like *New York Review of Books* dissidents under house arrest.

But Sarah had seen enough smashed car windows in Oakland, and those genteel towns up the shoreline called out to her: the Congregational churches, the white-clapboard colonials, the maple trees and, God help us, the occasional American flag. Besides—cue the screechy shower music—Seth was starting high school. She found us a Federal house in Guilford, only a couple of exits from Clinton, where Wayne still lived, with foot-wide honey-colored floorboards. "Just promise me we'll never own a Volvo," I said, and we never did.

So how long would *you* give it? I handed my freshmen bad grades and they handed me bad evaluations, much as the daughters of Eve bruised the Serpent's head while he bruised their heels. I quit my column after I'd overheard Sarah at a party telling one of her new colleagues that it was "a wonderful outlet for him." We had her department chair and his partner over, and, many drinks into the evening, I'm afraid I went off on how the money boys had run the fucking school ever since Cotton Mather grabbed his ankles and bent over for old Elihu Yale. When the gents took their leave, Sarah asked me if I'd lost my mind. In fact, I *was* seeing a shrink by then. You see where this was heading. Picnic-lightning version: TA, Gene Tierney overbite.

Sarah kept the house and the Saab; I kept my old Toyota, took Seth on alternate weekends and wrote her a check every month. She could have made sure my contract didn't get renewed, but the Gene Tierney episode had given her a taste for the moral high ground, if that's not too mean to say. Had it not been for Wayne's kindness (pride, fall) I might have stayed at my weekly rates refuge up near the Wilbur Cross until Seth finished high school. And when Wayne came back . . . but this is a sentence God alone could finish.

By now you must be wondering about this God talk, so let's get Him covered. My grandfather—a Swamp-Yankee Nobodaddy who was always roaring *Well, by God* this and *Well, by Jesus* that—became convicted, as he put it, of a sense of sin when I was in fourth grade. God must have been lying in wait for him all his life. I remember Thanksgiving dinners when Gramp would rise and freestyle a King Jamesian grace, his palms heavenward. I'd look over at my mother, who would make her thumb the lower jaw of a nattering mouth. My father never saw these transactions: his eyes were closed—in embarrassment, I first assumed. He was a VP at Pratt & Whitney and paid to stash Gramp in a trailer near Wayne and Phyllis. But by God's grace, he too was convicted of sin—though afterward he still didn't mind working for a defense contractor—when he was about the age I am now. My mother called it "the Curse of the Davenports." This was the one thing I couldn't talk about with my shrink—unlike, say, my sexual imaginings and my issues with women. To his credit, he got the joke when I said my only issue with women had been Seth. But this kindly rationalist wouldn't have understood my God dread, not that it rose to the level of dread. And enough about that.

I moved into Wayne's house last October; now it was almost summer again and still no word of his coming back. From what I could gather, the widow was playing him against a richer, feebler retiree, but even if he crapped out with her, she couldn't be the only hot senior in the Sunbelt. I put the welcome mat, which still read THE DAVENPORTS, out in the garage, where he had his machine shop and kept his restored Plymouth Duster under a tarp. Every few weeks I got the key from its peg in the kitchen, took the tarp off and ran the Duster up to Killingworth and back; they fall to shit fast, he told me, if you let them sit. I slept alone on the driver's side of the king-sized bed that took up most of Wayne's bedroom, Gene Tierney having long since bestowed the sweets of her unhappiness on another married man. And I kept the photographs of Aunt Phyllis and the Mohegan Sun Goddess side by side on the nightstand, just as he'd left them. I'd promised myself not to put them in the drawer until I'd attained his perfect sanity.

Sarah would be dropping Seth off for Memorial Day weekend, so Friday afternoon I mowed the lawn before the rain could start, washed dishes that had been piled in the sink and stood in line at Stop & Shop among carts overloaded with hot dogs and soda. I'd suggested to Seth that we take a road trip to, oh, wherever. Since he had his learner's permit, we could split the driving. But he said he'd rather just hang out, and maybe Kendra could come over? Not what I'd had in mind, but what *had* I had in mind? I'd asked Sarah about this new girlfriend, and she'd said, Well, *I'd* probably like her, which I understood was not an endorsement. But in order to put my best foot forward, I worked out a mnemonic involving Ken Russell and Sandra Dee. The name wasn't her fault.

I put the groceries away and jammed the plastic bags up the skirt of a knitted old lady hanging next to the refrigerator: one of Phyllis's homemaking touches that I'd kept for the kitschy fun of it, along with the rooster clock and the pegboard with the legend ALL "KEYED UP." As I minced garlic and listened to *Marketplace,* the sky boomed right in front of me, over the turnpike—had it been the Promised End, it would've come from the direction of New York City—and rain started rattling in the gutters. Usually Sarah dropped Seth at the corner of Bayberry Drive: walking the last block or so, he said, made the "passage" easier. But surely in such a downpour she'd bring him to the house.

I heard a car pull up to the kitchen door and Seth burst in with Sarah behind him, black hair pasted to her head, man's white shirt pasted to her body.

"Come on in," I said. "Let me get you a towel."

"Don't bother. I just thought you might have that check."

"Hell," I said. "I put it in the mail this morning. You should have it Tuesday." And so she should, if I went out and mailed it tonight. "You have time for a drink?"

"I've got to get back," she said. "I'm having people over. I thought you'd stopped."

"Pretty much."

"He really has," Seth said.

"Oh," she said. "Well. Everything you know is wrong and now *that's* wrong."

The wet shirt showed brassiere that showed nipple. Had she put on a little weight? "I thought we weren't using civilians for cover," I said. "So who all is coming over?"

"No one you know."

"One assumes *that*," I said.

"Well," she said, "enjoy your weekend." You see what I was saying about the moral high ground.

As she backed out of the driveway, Seth said, "You guys need to stop." He sat on the step stool and began taking off his wet running shoes. "How come you're listening to *this* shit?" *Marketplace* was playing "We're in the Money," betokening a gladsome day in the stock market. He peeled off a sock and threw it at the radio. "Like we're supposed to be all happy for the rich people?"

"I just keep it on for company," I said. "Does that sound pathetic?"

He got up and picked the wet sock off the counter. "Sorry. I need to work on impulse control."

"No, turn it off, would you? I hate it too." The jocular shills for capitalism left off in mid-banter. No sound but the rain. "You getting hungry?" I said. "I'm making pasta *à la usuelle.*"

"I guess."

"Oh, hey, and I got us some movies." I pointed a thumb at the stack of DVDs; I'd put *Fail-Safe* in the middle, but sticking out, as if forcing a card.

"Is there anything that's not black and white?"

"Now *there's* a hanging curve," I said. "But yeah, come to think of it. You've never seen *The Boys from Brazil,* right?" This was my second choice: Olivier, Gregory Peck *and* James Mason all at their over-the-hill worst.

"So what is it, subtitles?"

"I wouldn't do that to you again," I said. "It's about Nazis. Actually, if you'd rather, the Mets are on in a minute." I'd driven him down to Shea for a few games when we first came east and he was still in his baseball phase.

"I know I'm being a pain in the ass, okay? Can I just go lay down for a little bit?"

"Are you all right?" I said.

"Yeah. I just need to have the passage, you know?"

If I only had a picture of what he looked like at that moment: his shaved head, because he said any hairstyle was a *style;* his crooked nose, broken by a pitch when he was in ninth grade, and which he refused to have fixed because that was part of his life. So much for the theory—favored by wife and shrink alike—that what was wrong with me was an inability to love.

During a rain delay after the first inning, they killed time by giving the scores, and I thought one might amuse Seth: Mariners nothing, Marlins nothing. His class had been reading *The Old Man and the Sea.*

I eased down the hall and stood outside the spare room, across from Wayne's bedroom. I'd allowed Seth to tape a poster of the Dalai Lama to the hollow-core door—that bare arm could have used some toning, not that I was beach-ready myself—and I heard him in there talking on his cell. Okay, time to crack a cold one. Seth's door opened during the top of the eighth, the bathroom door closed, the toilet flushed and his door closed again. After the postgame show I still wasn't sleepy, which was why the Good Lord made Tylenol PM. I read synopses of failed movies in *Halliwell's Film Guide,* under the two ladies' unjudging eyes, until beer and antihistamine took me down.

When I came to the next morning, it was hot and stuffy in the bedroom; I opened the sash and raised the shade just enough to let fresh air in. Seth's door was still closed and the Dalai Lama was still giving me that look: *I'm all about compassion, but you smell.* I made coffee, brought my laptop out to the slab Wayne had poured for a patio and toweled off a lawn chair. Beyond the concrete, a lumpy patch of grass that used to be Phyllis's garden; beyond that, a chain-link fence woven with strips of green plastic, then a stand of trees, then the turnpike. What Wayne said about how you stop hearing it after a while? Not true.

My mother had sent an email at 3:00 a.m. California time: *Are you going up there on Monday?*

Sorry, I typed. *Slow on the uptake this morning. Clarify?*

She answered within a minute. Had she been up all night? *Hello?* she wrote. *Mem Day? I can't stand to think of nobody visiting him.*

I'd never been back to the grave; as far as I knew, neither had she. *For serious?* I typed. *Do we really think he's been hanging out in his casket all these years?* I changed *his casket* to *Middletown, Conn.*

Another minute, not a second more. *Could you just go?*

At least this might give me something to do with Seth on Monday. But longer range, I'd better see what sort of a fare I could get to L.A. I was due for a visit anyway, and didn't this come under the heading of Sudden Personality Change?

I knocked on Seth's door so he wouldn't sleep the day away, then opened it a crack and saw a dark-haired girl sitting on his bed, knees up, barefoot with black-painted toenails, a book open on her chest. Pretty little round face, a bruise below one eye. Her skirt let me see too far up her pale thighs.

"Sorry," I said. "So you must be . . ."

"Kendra?" she said.

"Right, Seth told me you might be coming over. I just didn't expect—I'm Seth's dad. I mean, obviously."

"He went out for his run," she said. "Is it okay for me to be here?"

"You're certainly *welcome.* You just took me by surprise."

"We tried to be quiet," she said. "You *look* like Seth. Yeah, well duh." She dog-eared the page, set the book aside and hugged her knees, from which I intuited—I know this sounds crazy—that she let Seth fuck her.

"I always thought he looked like his mother," I said.

"Yeah, but not so much," she said. "Anyway she doesn't like me. Listen, before he comes in? You know he worries about you, right?"

"That's just him," I said. "But I'm glad he talks to you."

"Doesn't he to *you*? Sorry, that sounded bad. I didn't mean it like, you don't communicate." She took a breath. "I talk too much, that's a big problem I have."

"No, I appreciate your saying something," I said. "Listen, it's good to have you here."

"You don't really know that," she said. "But thanks. I like your house."

"Actually, it's not really—"

"I know, Seth told me, but it just feels like it's a *home,* you know? Like my aunt's house, I mean they're real poor and everything, like my cousins have to share a bedroom, but it's like, I don't know, I don't even know what I'm *basing* that on." She shook her head. "You don't have to keep listening to me. Is it okay if I just stay here till he gets back?"

I was pouring more coffee when Seth came in the kitchen door, his tank top sweated through. I pointed back outside, mindful of Wayne's thin walls, and shut the door behind us. "I wasn't prepared to find your friend here," I said. "When did *she* arrive on the scene?"

"I don't know, you were asleep. I just told her, if things got weird she could come here. Could you not call her *your friend*? She has a name."

"I know. She had to introduce herself. Now what's the deal?"

"Okay, so her mom's seeing this guy. Who's like married? And the guy's wife keeps calling their house, and so last night Kendra picks up the phone and the wife is like, 'You're going to die.' Like, 'I know who you are and you're going to die.'"

"And where was her mother?"

"I don't know, I guess with the guy?"

"So I take it the father's not in the picture."

"Kendra thinks he's in Wyoming or something," Seth said. "She said not to tell you *any* of this."

"Has she tried to reach her mother?"

"Like fifty times," he said.

"So her mother doesn't know where *she* is. Did she call the police?"

"Are you kidding? Her mom would beat the shit out of her."

"Jesus," I said. "Here, can we sit a minute?" I took the top step; Seth sat on the concrete. "How did she even get here?"

"Yeah, I knew you'd ask that."

"You didn't take my car keys?"

"It was only over to—"

"Good Christ," I said. "You know you can't be driving without an adult. When *was* this?"

"I don't know, late."

"And so she slept in your room," I said.

"Yeah well it's not like she *slept* very much."

"Okay," I said. "You realize this isn't cool, right?"

"So what was I supposed to *do*? Listen, can she just stay here until she gets ahold of her aunt?"

"Absolutely not."

"That's fucked up," he said. "What about when *you* didn't have any-place to go? Sorry I said 'fuck.'"

"How old is she? Is she even sixteen?"

"She's *going* to be."

"Sweet," I said. "Well, we're not getting in the middle of *this*. She needs to keep trying her mother—at least let her know she's safe."

"You don't get it." He unfolded himself and stood up. "Look, she's freaking out. I have to go talk to her."

I waited until I heard his door close in the house, then took out my cell and got Sarah's voice mail. "Call when you get this, okay? Everybody's fine, but we've got sort of a situation here with the girlfriend."

When she called back, I was in Wayne's recliner watching the day game; the kids were still holed up, doing whatever. "What's going on?" she said. "I assume the girlfriend in question is Seth's wounded bird. Or is it one of *your* projects?"

I muted the TV. "Let me go outside."

"She's not *there,* is she?"

I shut the kitchen door behind me and sat on the step. "Apparently she got some crank call, and she just showed up." Better, I thought, not to go into the when and the how. "Nobody seems to know where her mother is. Obviously this isn't tenable."

"So you haven't heard from the mother? You will."

"Wait—this is a thing?"

"Welcome to my life," she said. "Seth told *me* she was visiting her aunt this weekend. I assumed you'd be spared."

"Look, I hate to ask you, but would it be at all possible to bring them over there?" I said. "This could look pretty sketchy, him and me and a fifteen-year-old."

"Fourteen-year-old," she said.

"*He* told *me*— Jesus. What the hell is he *doing*?"

"Learning to lie, for one thing. I can't imagine where he picked *that* up."

"Okay, can we *not* right now?" I said. "So you've dealt with the mother?"

"Well. Let's say I've *encountered* the mother. The girl turned up here—this was *last* weekend—eleven thirty at night, mother's off somewhere, she's afraid to be home alone, blah blah blah, she's in tears, so I let her stay in the guest room. Anyway, the next day *mama* bird shows up at the door and she's accusing me of kidnapping. I think she's a cokehead."

"Shit," I said. "I bless the day God brought us to Connecticut."

"Is that *really* where you want this conversation to go?" she said. "I could start blessing a day or two myself."

"Sorry," I said.

"No, I should've given you a heads-up. I guess you'd better bring them over. You know, I did have *plans* this weekend. Actually, maybe I'd better be the one to drive her."

"Yeah, good thought. When could you get here?"

"I don't know, an hour? I have to make some calls."

"I hate to put it off on *you*."

"I know you think I'm a bitch," she said. "That's why I'm going to be gracious about this."

I went back in and knocked on Seth's door.

"Change of plans," I said. "Your mom's coming to pick you guys up."

He stuck his head out. "How come?"

"We just thought it was a better idea," I said. "Your friend's mother is going to be looking for her."

"Listen, we need to talk to you." He opened the door for me. The girl was still sitting on his bed. "Kendra can't go back there."

"I understand that it's a difficult situation," I said.

"You didn't *tell* him?" the girl said.

"Seth's mom filled me in a little," I said. "If there's anything we can do to help—"

"So I guess you're not going to let me stay here."

"We can't," I said. "I'm sorry. We don't have any right to just—"

"*That's* brilliant," Seth said. "You don't know how fucked up this is. Mom's just going to send her home. That's everybody's big answer."

The girl put her hands over her ears, elbows to her chest. "You're *fighting*."

"I'm not letting this happen," Seth said.

"It's okay," she told him. "I can try my aunt again."

"Look, I have to run a quick errand," I said. Of course I'd forgotten about putting that check in the mail. "You guys get together whatever you need and we'll talk when your mother gets here."

"And everybody goes away happy," Seth said.

"I could do with a hair less sarcasm," I said. "May I have my keys?"

"I put them back in the kitchen," he said. "I wasn't being sarcastic. I was trying to tell you something."

And I suppose he was. Though I didn't realize it until I'd gotten back, searched the house, finally thought to look in the garage and—shower music—there was the tarp lying on the concrete.

I came to the door when the Saab pulled in. "They're gone," I said. "I had to go out for a minute and apparently they took Wayne's car."

"Are you serious? You left them *alone*?"

"Well, naturally if I'd had any idea—"

"You know what he's like. He's probably taking her to Mexico or something."

"I would doubt he has a plan," I said. "It was obviously a spur-of-the-moment thing."

"Did you try his cell?"

"I left him a message to get the hell back here."

"I'm sure *that* was a help." She reached into her purse, poked at her phone, then said, "Sweetie, it's me. Call the minute you get this, okay?" She turned to me. "Can they track you if your phone's off?"

"You're not thinking of getting the cops involved?"

"He stole your uncle's *car*. Can he even drive that thing? And he's got that stupid little bitch with him."

"Come on in and let's think this through a minute," I said. I led her into the kitchen and on to the living room. "Here, why don't you sit down. Can I get you anything?"

She examined the seat of Wayne's recliner, brushed at it and sat. "So this is where you live."

"Yeah, I know," I said. "What a dump."

She tapped a fingernail on one of the metal shades of the pole lamp. "You don't see *these* every day."

"*I* do. Seltzer?"

"This can't be happening," she said. "You don't think they would've gone to *my* place?"

I shook my head. "He's afraid you'll turn the girl over to her mother."

"Oh God, the *mother*. Well, this is the end of *that* little romance. He can hate me forever."

"I don't disagree," I said. "I *do* feel bad for the girl."

"She's going to eat his life." She took her phone out again. "Okay, now that we've done our thinking."

"I'll make the call," I said. "Let's just give it another fifteen minutes."

"And do what? Talk about old times?" She raked her hair away from her cheek and behind her ear—I noticed some strands of white—and then touched her pinkie to her cheekbone, as if to make sure it was still Hepburnesque. Such a creaturely gesture.

"It's an idea," I said. "Look, this probably isn't the moment, but I'm well aware that I fucked up."

"Did you," she said. "Sort of an inadvertency?"

"Fine, okay, I said my little piece. But can we wait this out together?"

"I guess I'm here," she said. "Did you say you had seltzer?"

I got up. "Put something in it if you want."

"Not just now," she said. "Do you have lime? I don't know, maybe this will all just . . . do you think?"

"At this point," I said, "I'd make a promise to God."

She said, "Do it."

And here's the thing: I was out in the kitchen slicing the lime and formulating my prayer—*Dear God* seemed childish, *O God* operatic—when my cellphone rang.

I ran back to the living room and angled it between our ears. "Look, I'm not going to say where I am, okay?" Seth's tinny voice. "But I didn't want you to get all worried."

"What do you think you're *doing*?" I said. "Your mother's here."

"We didn't go real far, okay? Kendra's aunt's coming to get her so I need to wait with her."

"Where's her aunt?"

"New Jersey? She's like on her way."

"Well look, if that's the case, why don't we pick you up and you can wait here?"

"Because I don't trust you guys?"

"Let me talk to him." Sarah took the phone. "Seth, listen to me, please? If you'll tell us where you are, I *promise* you—yes, okay, but you're not going to drive anywhere else, right? We'll just come pick you up and—" She shook her head and closed the phone. "Well," she said, "they're *somewhere*. I don't know, probably some mall? At least they're off the road. Supposedly. He said he'd call back. They could definitely trace his phone."

"Do *you* want to do that?"

"Not really." She flumped down on one end of the couch. "So I guess your prayers got answered. I hope you didn't promise your firstborn."

I sat down at the other end. "Do we know anything about this aunt?"

"Another of life's winners, I'm sure. How long does it take to get here from New Jersey?"

"I don't know. Holiday weekend? Look, I say we trust him."

"He's a *kid*, for God's sake."

"He thinks he's doing the right thing," I said. "You want him never to trust *us*?"

"Oh God," she said. "I don't know. You'd better be right."

"Yeah, when have you ever known *me* to show poor judgment?" I said. "I made a funny."

"I think I *will* have something." She bent to untie her track shoes. She was wearing that same shirt and I saw between her breasts. The weight she'd gained had made them fuller. "Since you brought it up," she said, "what *were* you thinking? When you decided to fuck her."

"How sorry I'd be."

"Then you *did* get some pleasure out of it. You see how well I know you?" She drew her feet up under her to sit sidesaddle.

"Gin and tonic? We do have lime."

"And gin," she said. "Why am I not surprised."

I brought the drinks in and sat closer to her on the couch. "No touching," she said. "I can't believe I'm drinking with you in the middle of the day." She drained half her glass in the first swallow.

"Look at *you*," I said.

"Maybe you had the right idea all along," she said. "Just fuck everything."

"We should probably go slow," I said. "This could be a long day."

"That's exactly why," she said. She drank the rest and rattled the ice. "One more. Is it irresponsible?"

"I doubt anybody would judge us," I said. "Considering."

"Oh no, we've been model parents," she said. "And I teach at Yale—actually, *you* teach at Yale. It's the get-out-of-Yale-for-free card. See, I can make a funny too."

I poured us each another gin and tonic and sat next to her again. She offered her glass to clink. "Old times?" she said. "Better days?"

"Can't have both," I said. "Can't have either."

"Come on, your life doesn't look so bad." She took a good gulp. "You're a man with a pole lamp. There must be *scads* of women just dying to get their hands on that."

"If I didn't know you," I said, "I'd think you were getting bawdy." Her hair had strayed down to her cheek again, and I reached out and smoothed it back.

"You *must* be out of options." She took my hand and placed it on my thigh. "An old biddy like me? Or was that just a reflex?" She drained the rest of the glass and sank back on the cushion. Her phone went off in her purse; she got up and checked the number. "I knew it." She touched a finger to her lips. "Really?" she said into the phone. "No, she hasn't been *here*. No, Seth is up in his room. Listen, I'm in the middle of something. If we hear anything I'll be sure to call you." She put the phone back in her purse and sat down on the couch again. "There. I guess I'm officially on the team. I could use just one more little one."

"Hell," I said. "What's another bad idea at this point?" I brought our glasses out to the kitchen.

"*Little*," she called.

When I sat down next to her again, I thought she'd undone a button, but I could have been wrong. She tasted her drink and said, "I didn't mean wimpy. You know, this is all very strange."

"For me too."

"Oh," she said, "the *sincere* look. Your little TA girl didn't even have a fighting chance. So what all did you do with her?"

"I don't suppose you want to talk about something else."

"Not ever," she said. "Did you make her get the butter?" I took her glass out of her hand. "*I'm* not drunk," she said. "I'm showing interest in what interests *you*. It's one of those how-to-talk-to-a-man things."

"For fuck's sake," I said. "Would it make you feel better if you just hit me?"

"Well I don't *know*," she said. "Nothing else seems to be working."

I turned my head, pointed to my cheek. Of course she wouldn't. But her hand came up, I winced my eyes shut and the slap rocked my head. I put my hand to my cheek and she slapped the other side. "One to grow on," she said.

"That fucking hurt," I said.

"Good," she said. "To tell you the truth, it really didn't do that much for me."

"Can we try something else?" I brushed the back of my hand down her breast and hit nipple.

"Don't," she said. "You're not funny."

"I wouldn't say either of us is keeping this light."

"You made those things too strong," she said. "I just *hit* you."

"Babe," I said. She closed her eyes and shook her head. I smoothed her hair again, and her cheek was wet. I put my hand around the back of her head and drew it into my shoulder.

"No." She sat up and rubbed into her eye socket with the heel of her hand. "He's going to call any second."

"So?" I said. "We're here."

"This must just be idle curiosity," she said. "See if she's picked up any new tricks."

"Have you?"

"Surely you can't be jealous," she said. "Don't tell me *that* was the key to your heart. The things we learn. Well, good. I like a level playing field." She got up and went in her purse. "I was *not* going to do this." I got up and pressed into her as she bent over. "Put out your hand."

I opened my palm: a silver-wrapped condom. "Really," I said. "Boy Scouts' motto. So who *was* in your plans this weekend?"

"New rules," she said. "Did you think this was the good old days?"

Whenever my father worked late, my mother and I had movie night. She was the one who explained to me why the man in *Notorious* got upset when he saw the wine bottle and pointed out when the lady in *The Maltese Falcon* was lying. We didn't let my father know that she'd always give me a glass of wine, at first with water, later without. Once, when I was ten or eleven, we watched *The Awful Truth,* and she said the ending, where the little mechanical boy in lederhosen finally follows the little mechanical girl into the clock, was the filthiest scene ever shot. I understood the principle even then—and went on believing that less was more until I saw actual pornography—so I'm honoring it now.

Sarah sat up, pulled the sheet over her breasts and picked up her watch from the nightstand. I was still on my back. "It's been three hours," she said.

"Sure, we could talk about that," I said. "The silence *was* getting loud."

"Meaning you're not concerned."

"Not much to say about it, until we know something. Whereas."

She set the watch back down. "Who are the ladies?"

"My aunt," I said. "And that's Wayne's new flame."

"Ah," she said. "The *other* family tradition."

"I told you the situation."

She felt around on the floor and came up with her shirt. "I'm chilly," she said. "Can we shut that window? Yes, you told me. Your aunt's the one he's got in storage?"

I got up, naked, and walked to the window. Daylight was still coming in under the shade, and I knew how I must look from behind; when I reached up, I saw the flesh of my arm swinging. "I'm not much of a trophy these days," I said. "Just so you know, you're the only one who's been here."

"Aren't you sweet," she said. "I feel like a bride again. Listen, can we agree that we're not telling Seth about this? It's just going to play into all his fantasies."

"So it's like nothing happened?"

"Nothing *did* happen."

"Oh, then it's like *Waiting for Godot.* Nothing happened twice?"

"Okay," she said, "that was an indulgence."

"I finally got a smile out of you," I said.

"I just hope *you're* not entertaining any fantasies. Is your phone still on?"

"We would've heard it," I said. "I *think.*"

"Could you check?"

I picked my phone up from the floor. "Zip," I said. "You want the bathroom first?"

"I can't believe I let this happen," she said. "This was your shirt, by the way. I'll wash it and get it back to you."

"No, you look good in it." I put my hand under the shirt and touched her belly. "It's going to be okay," I said. "We just have to hang on until he calls. I'm glad we're doing this together."

She wormed away, sat up and mimicked playing a violin. "Do you ever listen to yourself?"

"Ceaselessly," I said. "Are you always going to hate me?"

"I'll have to think about that one. Right now you're not my favorite person. Right now *I'm* not my favorite person."

When I got out of the shower, Sarah was on the couch with my phone to her ear. "Just as soon as we can get there," she said. She closed the phone and said, "Clinton Crossing. Main entrance. Apparently the aunt actually showed up and took the girl. He must be the luckiest little shit alive."

"Let me get some clothes on," I said. "I'll drive Wayne's car back here. What do we do with *him*?"

"How about grounded till he goes to college?"

"No, I mean do you want to take him home to Guilford?"

"It's still your weekend," she said. "I've had my fill of miracles for today."

But this is a story God alone could finish. Our guy must think he's in *The Awful Truth,* where they get back together after their escapades, no damage done. Our gal doesn't seem to want to be in *that* movie, except there she was with her knees on his shoulders and coming back for seconds. I emailed her that night to ask if we could talk. It took her two days to write back: *Not just now.* And if an unseen hand *had* reached down just as I was about to humble myself and pray, what was the big miracle? A kid got away with driving for a few miles, and a couple with unfinished business wound up in bed.

I took a redeye to LAX, dozing in and out of Dramamine sleep, rented a car and drove up to Santa Barbara. Insert praise of the Creator for a June morning in California. Let there be palm trees. From my mother's balcony, you could look down the street and see, between two oceanfront mansions, just about that much of the Pacific. "Was it wicked to make Bloody Marys?" she said as she set them down on the glass-topped table.

"We're good," I said. "They're a vegetable."

"Speaking of which"—she raised her glass—"to Phyllis. Poor thing, she's well out of it. You know, I'm still not clear what's supposed to happen when your uncle gets back. Will you two keep bachelors' hall?"

"I doubt *that,*" I said. "As Dad used to say, God will provide."

"Dear heart—the weapons industry did the providing. Not that I turned my nose up at it. As you see." She swept her hand like a queen to indicate her balcony and her slice of ocean. "Thank you for going along with my little whim, by the way. Every once in a while it just hits me what a terrible wife I was to him. I've calmed down."

"I'm glad we went up there, actually. Seth brought along one of those Tibetan prayer flags."

"Oh my. Did you hear a whirring noise underground?"

"He's a better person than I am," I said.

"Give him time," she said. "I know—I'm getting grim in my old age. But the evidence does start to pile up. You remember that horrible woman next door? Who made her husband put up the crèche every year? She told us that the couple across the street was living in sin, and your father said, 'Who isn't?'"

"That was Dad," I said.

She said, "He was such a good man. I think I used to wish he was dead."

"Well." I raised my glass. "Cheers. We've got a beautiful day."

"They're all beautiful days here." Her glass stayed on the table. "Bought and paid for."

Well, all right. I was out a thousand dollars I didn't have, if you figured in the car and whatnot, but nothing here seemed to cry out for intervention. No piles of newspapers, no dishes in the sink, no empty bottles visible, flowers on the dining table. Her book club was reading . . . I forget what, you can make something up if you want. Her remorse—who doesn't have it?—seemed manageable, and she was past the place where she could have done anything to mitigate it. If she was undeserving of mercy and bereft of grace—who isn't?—at least now she knew the shape of her story. Whereas.

A Place Where Nothing Ever Happens

||||||

Lily has figured out this much: open the downstairs windows at night to let the cool air in, then close them in the morning and the house stays cool all day. Didn't her father always say she had a splendid mind? While Portia, her older sister, only had a good head on her shoulders. The upstairs windows you always keep open, because of the heat-rises axiom. No, higher than an axiom: a law. No, higher still than a law: a truth. Unless truth and law rule side by side. Upon a throne of adamant. Is this not a splendid thought? She should really be writing this stuff down.

She's in Connecticut, house-sitting for the Hagertys the first three weeks of August, with the use of their second car, and sleeping in their dead daughter's bedroom. This is their weekend-and-summer getaway, but Marian Hagerty hates the look of air conditioners in the windows, so in August they fly to Main-à-Dieu, on the easternmost coast of Cape Breton, in a chartered seaplane, to watch the fishing-boat races. Joe Hagerty had hired Lily's father straight out of Harvard Law—a charity case, he liked to say. This got a laugh at her father's memorial. Everyone there knew Skip Kiernan had turned down Harry Blackmun's offer of a clerkship.

The Hagertys' daughter, Elena, had gone to Dalton while Lily was at Brearley, but the summer Lily turned nine, the Kiernans rented a house near Joe and Marian's—they hadn't yet bought their own getaway—and her father drove her over one day to play tennis with Elena on the Hagertys' clay court. (Portia, who was twelve, chose to go to the lake with their mother.) Elena, long hair flying, had Lily panting and sweating in the first few volleys. Lily remembers, years later, doing coke with her in the bathroom at Portia's wedding, and Elena, now with boy-length hair, possibly coming on to her. A kiss on the lips? With just the most petite dart of the tip of Elena's tongue? She had on an electric blue dress with spaghetti straps, and when she leaned forward over the countertop, Lily saw the nipples of her small breasts. Elena's been dead for five years now, and Lily's found not a trace of her in her old room: nothing in the dresser drawers but flowered paper lining the bottoms, nothing in the closet but satin-padded hangers. Are the Hagertys really so sure the dead don't mind?

In these three weeks, she will swim every day; the Hagertys' Subaru Forester has a sticker for the recreation area at the lake. She will eat better, keep her cellphone off, go online only once a day—just in case anybody responds to the résumés she sent out—and not smoke the weed she's brought. She will read *The Custom of the Country* (the others were so good), reread *Mansfield Park* (the only one that's still not too girly), try again to push beyond the beginning of *Adam Bede,* and leaven all this with whatever she may choose, on a whim, from the Hagertys' shelves. Won't *that* be something, to have a whim. As distinct from an impulse. And every night, eleven o'clock sharp, in bed, lights out, with a movie on her laptop and a glass of something. She's brought only a half dozen of the old usuals along, since Marian told her the video store in town was owned by "film buffs." This got Lily picturing gay boys with toned bodies, whom she could go look at every day in their tight T-shirts. Who says the pastoral is dead?

Portia had tried to talk her out of coming here—a bad time to isolate, she'd said. She's also confided that when she's alone she sometimes hears their father speaking to her. But Lily needed to get away from her one-bedroom in Brooklyn Heights, which she'd rented on the now-exploded theory that neighborhood trumps space. And also, let's admit it, to get away from Dagon, whom she'd lately been feeding Rice Krispies, and whose litter box she'd been finding herself unable to clean and refill. Renaldo, the intern she's kept in touch with since being laid off, agreed to stay with him in return for the three weeks of air-conditioning and a shorter subway ride. On the morning she gave

Renaldo her keys, she finally bought cat food and changed the litter, which proved that she *could* do it.

And then there was this. On the Fourth of July, after a party where the revelers got high to watch the fireworks from a roof garden in Tribeca, she'd shared a taxi back to Brooklyn with Portia's married boyfriend—Portia being otherwise occupied—and kissed him when he dropped her off at her building, tongues involved, then hands under the clothes. He's been emailing her ever since, and while she's been emailing back, she's managed to avoid seeing him again. So really, doesn't this speak well of her?

It's after midnight when she gets here: a bus to Torrington, then a taxi along miles of dark country roads. Inside, the house is hot and stuffy; she sets her bags down in the kitchen and goes around opening windows. On the counter, under the keys to the Subaru, she finds a note from Marian Hagerty that goes to the tune of *You may go down the lane*, whatever whatever, but don't go into Mr. McGregor's garden. Lily is not to drink the wines in the cellar, each laid down by Joe to be opened at such and such a time. ("Not that you would, of course.") She is not to have parties—"a friend or two is perfectly fine"—or overnight guests. If she uses the court, she is to wear only tennis shoes: i.e., bare-assed and breasts bouncing? Oh well, poor Marian. The once-scandalous second wife, suddenly in her sixties, bereft of her child and having to deal with Joe, now eighty-four and still playing doubles, with neighbors' young wives as his partners.

Up in Elena's bedroom, thank God, there's a big floor fan; Lily puts it on the highest speed, opens a window and goes back downstairs for her duffel and her wheeled suitcase. She takes her orange plastic box of weed out of the zippered compartment and puts it in the freezer, between a pint of Häagen-Dazs vanilla and a bottle of Stoli. Any one of these three things could lead to the other two. But she goes to bed without. Isn't that what she's *been* doing?

In the morning, she makes coffee in the Hagertys' French press and takes it out to the shady porch ("Please do not leave food on the veranda—we get the occasional raccoon") along with a bowl of the muesli she found in the cupboard. The box says both "no sugar added" and "not a low-calorie food": mixed signals, as if from a man!

Driving into town along the shore of the lake, she spots a farm stand: a rustic wagon that holds an array of tomatoes, squashes, ears of corn. Then a bar called Tony's, with a green canvas awning. The town is a two-block main street without parking meters; she finds the video store, the organic market and the wine shop, where she is to ask for Victor. A tiny hair salon, so wittily called Delilah's. In the wine shop, she buys a seventy-five-dollar bottle of sherry—yes! inspired!— for movie time. The younger, more handsome of the two men, the one with the curly hair, must be Victor. Oh, just a guess.

On the way back, she slows down for a better look at this Tony's, although bars are *not* in the plan, then stops at the farm stand and buys zucchini, yellow summer squash and a fat tomato. It's when she opens the kitchen door that she makes her discovery: she'd closed the down-stairs windows so nobody could get in, and now it's actually cool in here. Not a word of *this* in Marian Hagerty's note!

She puts on her black bikini and checks herself: today is a good day. She and Portia had been issued the wrong bodies, back in the ante-cedent life. Lily has the ectomorphic mind—even the ectomorphic name—while portly sounding Portia stole the show, slinky-limbed, in the one ballet recital they did together. After that, Lily begged to take tap instead—all those old musicals their father made them watch— then refused to go when she learned the students had to wear tights: you could see the flesh shaking even on *Ruby Keeler*'s thighs, for Pete's sake, when she tapped in *42nd Street*.

At the lake, she spreads one of the Hagertys' towels on the grass and takes her sweet time unbuttoning her shirt, sliding her jeans off, arching her back. From behind her sunglasses, she looks around her: all moms and kids, which is just as well. No, truly. The water's warm at the surface, icy when you dive down. When she comes out, her body feels cool at the core, and lying down in the sun she's so calmed it's disturbing.

She eats a dinner of brown rice with zucchini and garlic, sliced tomato on the side. Then she goes up to Elena's room, pulls down the shade, slips panties off one leg and thinks up Garrett in the taxi, her hand down the front of his jeans, her other hand down the back, then thinks up reaching into Elena's blue dress—it's vacation!—and touches her own breast with her free hand, then brings Garrett back in to play with her and Elena: even alone, you can't know who's watching. She makes herself come, twice, in Elena's bed. Outside it's still daylight.

When they went through her father's things, Lily took a white shirt with a Brooks Brothers label and his razor, with which she now shaves her legs. In the back of his closet, she found the framed photo of the Shelley Memorial at Oxford that used to hang above the desk in his study; when he got sober, he'd replaced it with a photo of their cottage in Dennis Port. ("What's your favorite sport?" her father would ask them, turning his head to the backseat, and they would shout back, "Dennis Port!") When she was little, she would go into the study to look at it: a statue of a beautiful naked drowned man lying on his side; you could sort of see his junk. Neither her mother nor Portia had wanted the thing, so Lily hung it over her nonworking fireplace in Brooklyn. Sometimes she thinks it's bringing her bad luck. But didn't she already have that?

Except during the couple of years before he went to Silver Hill, Skip Kiernan had continually reread Shakespeare, Johnson and Wordsworth; their subliminally channeled cadences, he believed, had saved some corporate criminals from doing serious time. He used to pay both his daughters ten cents a line to memorize poems and recite them while he sat in his leather armchair with his drink. Portia stopped because it was babyish, but one night Lily made five dollars on Emily Dickinson. When Lily finally found a full-time job, copyediting at an upmarket bridal magazine, her father offered her ten thousand dollars, on top of her tuition, to quit and go get what he called "your Ph.D." Behind Matt's back. So now Matt's out of the picture, she's lost the job anyway and she's just turned thirty-three. Should it be "Woe is me" or "Woe am I"?

Lily was in Amsterdam with Matt when Elena was shot by bandits in Malaysia, where she'd gone to work with Catholic Charities. "They had all that trouble with her," Lily's father said, "finally she gets her act together, and now this. Don't *you* go doing good in the world."

"Yeah," Lily said, "what are the odds."

The next morning she goes into the video store on the chance they might have *Gold Diggers of 1933,* which she was stupid not to have brought.

"I knew it," the man at the counter says. "No. I'm sorry, we should." His short blond hair's just starting to go gray, and he's got lines at the corners of his eyes and the beginnings of man breasts under the knit shirt.

"Oh, it was just a whim," she says. "I'm afraid if I start browsing, I'll never get out of here." Already she's spotted *Carnival of Souls.*

"That wouldn't break my heart," he says. Straight for sure, just unappealing. "If you find yourself jonesing for something, here's the number." He hands her a card. "Ask for Evan."

Well, it's a day for whims, isn't it? Walking past the hair salon, she sees that both chairs are empty—and there's your gay boy. Maybe. He's got a shaved head, and he's wearing a Hawaiian shirt. "Don't be bashful," he says when she sticks her head in. "Come. Sit." A boom box on the glass shelf is playing the Robert Plant–Alison Krauss CD that everybody's sick of back in the city. "First let me get a look at the lay of the land, and then we'll shampoo you."

He's got strong fingers—she can feel her scalp move on her skull—and he's rough with the towel. She's still not sure about him. "So," he says, walking her back to the chair, "what are we doing today?"

"Something we may end up regretting," she says.

———

On the drive home—why *not* call it that?—she keeps pulling down the visor to check herself in the makeup mirror. The sky's getting dark to the west; when she gets out of the car she hears faraway thunder. Excuse enough to bag the swim. She allows herself a few minutes in the bathroom to turn her head from side to side in front of the mirror; she hadn't realized her ears were so big. She takes a shower, puts on her father's big white shirt, then goes out to the porch, lies in the hammock and tries to stop touching her hair and get serious about *Mansfield Park*. Maria has fled with Henry Crawford—and Mary Crawford has proved so deficient in moral sense that she merely calls it "folly"! When the storm hits, she closes the book to watch: hailstones bouncing off the lawn, big trees waving like feather dusters—isn't that good? Better write that one down.

After eating dinner she turns her cellphone on and finds a new message, from Garrett. *You're not answering your email. Call me. Contact me.* What time is it, eight o'clock? A couple of hits now and it'll wear off by movie time. She goes to the freezer and pinches just that much off a bud. It's cool in the living room, where the original wood paneling has been cured in a couple of centuries of smoke from the original walk-in fireplace. She presses her nose into the wall, wishing to exchange molecules with that aroma, then lies back on the long leather sofa with her head propped up and starts her iPod—a mix Renaldo made for her, which sounds cold and clattery. The second song takes a much longer time to go by than the first, and when she's somewhere in the middle of the next one she can't remember back to the first song—oh, good, this is good. If you could be like this all the time, you'd never worry about the years flying by, because even an hour is just so full. Too full, actually.

She wakes up on the sofa in full morning light. She'd considered going up to the bedroom, but it would've been hot and she would've had to deal with the fan and, let's admit it, she'd been afraid Elena might be up there. One of the big buds is gone, and half the bottle of sherry. She starts coffee; that should take care of the headache, though Satan's whispering, *How's about a little drinkie?* She eats a handful of raisins and—though it's way off schedule—goes upstairs to get into her bikini.

The lake water feels so cold she just stands there up to her knees, hugging herself. She looks around: at this time of morning there's nobody here to see her punk out. Just a thin little girl whose fat mommy is yelling, "That doesn't work for me!" What has the little girl done?

Back at the house, she finds rackets and some cans of balls in the mudroom and goes out to the tennis court. She hits a half-dozen balls over the net, then walks over, barefoot on the hot clay, and hits them back. Okay, clearly, she can't put this off any longer. She goes back inside and turns on her cell.

"Hey, I was about to give up on you," Garrett says. "Listen, some friends of mine invited me up to Kent this weekend. That's not too far from you, right?"

"Don't you get enough action with my sister?" she says. "*And* your wife?"

"Correct me if I'm wrong, but somehow I got the idea that you and I both sort of take things on a case-by-case basis."

"You're making me wet," she says.

"Okay, you're pissed at me. I'll give you a call when I get up there tomorrow night."

"You really like yourself, don't you?"

"I'll pass on that one," he says. "How about you?"

Lily and Matt had broken up a year before Portia's marriage ended—which was counterintuitive, because shouldn't the less traditional couple be revealed to have the stronger foundation, or was this counter-counterintuitive? She'd moved into Matt's low-tide-smelling factory loft in Greenpoint, where he used to live with Melanie, his previous girlfriend. One night the bass player in his band said, "Thanks, Mel," as Lily passed him a platter of couscous and lamb; when she brought it up later, Matt said it wasn't his fault. That was when she got the idea to fuck the bass player.

He was a tall, lanky specimen, like all bass players, named Rob. *Called* Rob, strictly speaking. This would be a one-shot deal, off in its own space: wear a halter top to a gig, brush the girls against his arm, email him to consult about a gift for Matt's birthday, meet him at Sam Ash, go for a drink afterward. Portia herself couldn't have done it more efficiently.

When Lily refused to go to his place a second time, Rob quit the band and moved back to Chapel Hill, which wasn't at all the spirit of the thing. And then she began to email him—not only men were allowed to send mixed signals!—and of course Matt got into her email, and so on.

By the time Portia found out about her husband's girlfriend in Bilbao, Lily was able to give her refuge in Brooklyn Heights, on the foldout she'd been so prescient to buy. Every night they drank a bottle of Sancerre apiece and watched one of the old movies their father had loved; Portia always sobbed at the happy endings, then kept sobbing, even after Lily had clicked over to CNN.

"I felt like Daddy was watching with us," she said one night, when *Swing Time* was over and Larry King had Ed Asner on, talking about his autistic son.

"I'm curious," Lily said. "What kind of stuff does he say? You know, when he's speaking to you?"

"He just says—I don't want to say." She began to cry again. "He says, 'I'm taking care of you now.'"

"I wish he'd spread it around a little," Lily said.

"I don't know," Portia said. "He's not doing *that* good of a job."

Portia had never liked getting high when they were teenagers, but Lily asked around and found some weed sneaky enough not to panic her at first. But they overdid anyway, and after vomiting (Lily used the sink and let Portia have the toilet) they lay spooned on the bathroom floor the rest of the night. "Don't take this the wrong way, okay?" Portia said in the morning, when they finally felt okay to go to bed. "But that was the most fun I've ever had with you."

Portia had met Garrett when some of her friends brought some of their friends to the housewarming at her new apartment. Lily had disliked him—the leather jacket plus the soul patch *plus* the wedding ring. She overheard him telling Portia that he'd rather read Edith Wharton than Henry James—clever fellow—and then he whispered something and flicked her earlobe with his tongue.

"But what's in it for you?" Lily asked her a couple of weeks later.

"Nothing," Portia said. "I mean, the obvious. What you used to call it—uninhabited sex? I just don't really trust him."

"Why would you?"

"I don't mean it like *that*. I mean, of course not. I mean, I think he could get really angry?"

"Oh, honey," Lily said. "So does the wife know?"

Portia refilled her glass and passed the bottle to Lily. "Who knows what that's about. Why are you trying to make me feel bad? I don't go off on *you*. And *your* weird stuff. Actually, he reminds me of you."

Portia had promised to drive up with Lily to spend the Fourth with their mother in Dennis Port, just the three of them, and they would take the Hobie Cat out and scatter the ashes. Lily had already reserved a rental car. Then Portia called to say that Garrett had invited them both to watch fireworks.

"Great, so Mom's going to be alone on the Fourth."

"This can't wait one day? Anyhow, the Rosenmans are going to be having their usual bash. She'll be fine with it."

"Are *you* going to be fine with it?"

"Listen, I just need to do this, okay?" Portia said. "I thought you were supposed to be the great mind."

But surely only the mind of Omniscience could have foreseen that Portia would go into the bedroom with the host, a lean man in his sixties with a trimmed white beard, and his plump young wife. And that she herself would let this Garrett tell her these were "cool people," that Portia would be okay, and that they could share a cab back to Brooklyn.

On Thursday night the parking lot at Tony's is full—weekenders getting an early start. She's chosen her black tank top, nothing under it, and taken out her contacts in favor of her black-rimmed glasses, to make herself look more violable. There's a lone pool table with a faux-Tiffany lamp above it and three televisions over the bar, the sound off, playing what look to be two different baseball games. Lily takes a stool at the end of the bar with an empty stool next to it. The bartender looks like—it takes her a second—the gink who sings "Shuffle Off to Buffalo" with Ruby Keeler! Whose name she happens to know is Clarence Nordstrom.

She orders a gin and tonic and begins watching the Red Sox and Cleveland. The batter in the whiter uniform has pants that come down to his feet like pajama bottoms, but so tight you can see his kneecaps. When she was thirteen and had hit a home run in softball at summer camp, her father took her down to Philadelphia, where the Phillies lost a doubleheader to Atlanta. He'd said, "Only the Braves deserve the pair," and refused to tell her why that was funny. She can't really taste the gin, which is either why you should never order gin and tonic or why you should always. She turns to check out the room—stools that swivel! the best!—and some guy's already coming toward her, as if she's the drop of blood in a cubic mile of ocean.

"I almost didn't recognize you with the hair," he says. "Looks good, actually." His eyes go to her breasts. "Evan."

"Evan, right." The video store. "Lily. Actually, it should be Portia." Oh my: Clarence Nordstrom does pour a good one. "At least it's not Elena, right?"

His eyebrows come in toward his nose. "What's wrong with Elena?"

"Now that," she says, "is genuinely funny. I'm liking you already." She leans forward—okay, embarrassing, but—and fiddles with the hem of her jeans long enough for him to see what there is to see. Then she straightens up and looks him in the eyes, which is easier than you'd think: you look *at* the eyes. "What are you drinking, *Evan*?"

"Let me." He raises a finger and Clarence Nordstrom is there. "Another one for the young lady," he says, "and I'll have . . ." He looks at the bottles behind the bar. "Knob Creek rocks?"

"*Grazie*," she says. "So *Evan*. Is this a place where nothing ever happens?"

"Apparently not," he says. Oh, now surely he's in the right age demographic to have listened to Talking Heads. She thinks to check his ring finger. No. But he's *been* married, you can just tell. The bartender sets the drinks down. "So tell me something, is that what you do?" she says. "Work at the video store?"

"Actually, during the year I teach media studies." He raises his glass. "Success to crime. What do you do?"

"Work for a magazine nobody's ever heard of," she says. "I mean I used to."

He does his eyebrow thing again; it's imaginable that someone might find it fetching. "And you live in the city?"

"You're remarkable," she says.

"I'm not." He takes a sip and she sees he's already down to ice cubes.

"Oh. Well, maybe I'm just setting the bar low tonight."

"Then you're just up here visiting?"

"Tell you what," she says. "Why don't we finish up the due diligence, and then I have some very expensive sherry back at the house." She'll decide later if weed will scandalize him.

"Really," he says. "Whatever the catch is, it must be a doozy."

"Oh, I *like* a man who says 'doozy.'" She fishes out her lime wedge, sets it on the bar and rocks it with her fingertip. "Do you know 'Wynken, Blynken and Nod'?" She leans forward again—those pesky jeans! "What's the trouble, do you not want to?"

"Oh no, believe me," he says. "Just, I should probably tell you I've sort of been seeing somebody. Does that bother you?"

"Ah," she says. "So *you're* the one with the doozy. No, actually this makes me very happy. I mean, as long as she's not waiting outside with a gun." She drains her glass. "It *is* a she?"

His mouth comes open. "What the fuck?"

"That's better. You were starting to lose me when you were being so nice. I have to go use the doozy." She gets off her stool and stands up just fine.

———

"Daddy used to say he was a high-functioning workaholic," Portia said at the memorial, and got the laugh. "But today I wanted to tell you some things you *didn't* know." Their father had asked them both to speak, along with Joe Hagerty, but Lily froze while trying to write something. It was Portia who'd pulled herself together to get up there and wing it from a half-page of notes, who'd dealt with the Harvard Club and even hired the fucking bagpiper.

Lily had been waiting in the cottage when they'd brought him home to die. They'd taken him off the plane on a stretcher, but her mother said he'd sat up straight in his seat all the way from New York. High on the morphine and the five-hundred-dollar-an-ounce hydroponic Lily found for him—a last-minute appeal to Matt—he asked her to read him "Wynken, Blynken and Nod," probably for some drifty Rosebud reason. She had to go online to find it, and now she can remember only something about rocking in the misty sea, and that the original title was "Dutch Lullaby."

And then she'd missed the main event because she had to be at work. She'd run through her vacation time—a stupid trip down to Chapel Hill—and the magazine would give her only two weeks of family leave, plus her personal day. When they must already have been planning to lay her off! That Tuesday night, while her car was warming up in the driveway, she promised her father she'd be back on Friday, very late. According to Portia, he'd tried to wait for her—he'd made it till three that afternoon—but the fact remained.

Their father, Portia told his friends and colleagues, had taken them to see Dexter Gordon at the Blue Note and Pavarotti at the Met and Nureyev at ABT, taught them to sail and to change a tire. Every Wednesday had been movie night, eight o'clock sharp. "When I was little," she said, "I believed that Fred Astaire could actually dance on the ceiling. I believed my father could too. And Daddy, I always will." Well: after that, one hardly needed "Amazing Grace."

When she finally gets poor Evan out of Tony's bar, Lily keeps his head-lights in her rearview mirror, though what's she going to do if he takes it into his head to peel off? He pulls up next to her in the driveway, and she sees him turn his cell off before getting out of his car.

"You know, I go by here all the time," he says. "I always wondered what it was like inside. How old is this house?"

"Old." She takes him by the hand. "Come."

She has to put the candle over on the dresser so the fan doesn't blow it out, and in this light he's really not unthinkable. After he gets off the first time she has to persuade him that no, she *likes* getting (as he puts it) turned over, and then she has to talk him through it. So it was smart to have said nothing about weed. This time he groans as if wounded. Sweet man. The due diligence had revealed that he *was* divorced and that, surprise surprise, the wife got the house.

After his breathing smooths out, with a growl at the end of every outbreath, she eases out of bed and goes down to the kitchen. She takes one hit—just one, or she'll never get to sleep—and settles onto the sofa, gets to work with her fingers, then has a superstitious thought: she mustn't come while thinking up Elena—or else in that white instant when she's bodiless she'll find Elena there, waiting to snatch her through into the world of the dead! Okay well now she *has* to, just to prove the thought wrong. When she returns to herself, still breathing hard, she understands what a crazy risk she's just taken.

She goes back upstairs, lies down so they're not touching and feels herself start to drift. Poor, sweet man. But then it's daylight and he's all over her again.

"What time is it, baby?" She rolls out from under him. Maybe she can get out of this one with hands and the Astroglide she was so prescient to pack—or how about her hands cupped around his hands? This always got Matt.

When he catches his breath again, he says, "You're pretty incredible."

She's wiping up with last night's tank top, which is a lost cause anyway. "So are you going to have some 'splainin' to do?"

"Do we have to talk about it right this second?"

"I'm not trying to *steal* you." She lies back down, pressing the girls into his arm. "Just borrow you a little more."

"Shit," he says, "I forgot I have to open up this morning."

"Haven't you already?" She remembers he'd done that same little thing last night, with the eyebrows. "I'll make us some coffee."

She gets out of bed and puts on a T-shirt, which comes down just far enough to cover and still give him glimpses, then goes down to the kitchen. Spooning coffee into the French press, she hears the toilet flush upstairs. She puts water on to boil and goes into the half bath off the living room.

When she comes out, he's sitting on an arm of the sofa, fully dressed, even his loafers. "So we have to talk about tonight," she says. "What time can you come over?"

"I actually can't tonight."

"Oh," she says. "Now let me guess."

He's turning red—sweet to see. "I could see you Sunday night."

"That's going to be too late," she says. "Why don't we have our coffee out on the porch."

"You going back to the city?"

"Oh, you sound so hopeful," she says. "Has something happened to my incredibleness?"

"I told you the situation," he says.

She darts over to the front door and leans her back against it. "What if I don't move?"

"Please don't fuck with me," he says.

Clearly he means the "please" to sound ominous, but she can hear the "please comma" beneath it. He doesn't seem like a hitter. "If you don't come back tonight," she says, "you're going to jerk off to me the rest of your life."

"Shit," he says. "I fuckin' *knew* you were crazy. Let's not make this a big drag for both of us, okay?"

So he has some wit after all. And some woman, surely, has loved him. Maybe his wife, for a while. And maybe his new lady is beginning to love him too, the lady she's gotten him to betray.

When Lily had come by to pick her up in the rented Ford Explorer, two days after the Fourth, Portia opened the passenger door, stuck her suitcase in and said, "I don't really want to talk, okay?" She made her seat go back and slept for most of the drive to Dennis Port. Lily set the cruise control between seventy and seventy-five—the golden mean!—and they passed through one public radio listening area into another, like Venn diagrams. Lily learned that since the solstice they'd been losing two minutes of sunlight every day, and that seven people had been killed in two suicide bombings—she didn't catch where—and that Terry Gross's nervous fake laugh was getting worse. As they were going over the Bourne Bridge, Portia opened her eyes and said, "I can feel you over there judging me. So what did Garrett have to say?"

"Why should he get to say anything?" Lily said. "Me either, for that matter."

"Oh, you're so Zen," Portia said. "Fuck you. Fuck *me,* actually. So who did *he* go off with?"

"Nobody," Lily said. "Actually, he was nice enough to drop me at my place."

"Really. Are we talking about the same person?" Portia looked over at Lily. "Oh. And were you nice enough to invite him up?"

"Come on, I have *some* boundaries," Lily said. "So does he, apparently."

Portia settled back in her seat. "I need to get my head around this."

They found their mother out on the deck with a canvas on her easel. "No, don't look," Janet said. "How was the traffic? I always hated the drive up here." Their father's favorite car game had been for them all to take turns improvising verses to "I Know an Old Lady Who Swallowed a Fly"; once he'd rhymed "swallowed your father" and "Why did she bother?" Their mother hadn't spoken again until they got there. "Listen, I've got tuna steaks marinating. What do you think, should we just go out and do this while we've still got some daylight?"

"How far out are we going?" Portia said. "I don't like those clouds."

"As far as I'm concerned, we can *wade* out and do it," Janet said. "I doubt he's going to know the difference."

"You don't know what he knows," Lily said.

"Do you think he's *hovering*? You're not back on pot, are you?"

"Mom, we have to respect his wishes," Portia said.

"Oh, well far be it from me," Janet said. "I know how much *my* wishes always counted."

"I think you did all right for yourself, Mother," Lily said.

"Can we not get into this now?" Portia said.

"No, I like it that she thinks," Janet said. "It's a very attractive quality. Or would it be an *attribute*? Whatever it was your father had."

"Please?" Portia said.

"I'm sorry, am I ruining the occasion?" Janet walked back over behind her canvas. "This is vile." She took it off the easel and dropped it facedown on the decking. "I hope he *is* hovering, actually. Just to sweeten up his eternal reward."

How's this for prescience? Of course Lily will turn her cellphone on, and of course Garrett will call, and of course she will give him directions. And again she will fuck a man in a dead girl's bed. Two in two days? She's unstoppable!

She rolls back over against Garrett, fingers creeping around in his chest hair; you always come when it's the bad boy. The fan's still roaring, drying her sweat, giving her chills. "So," she says, "I think I'm going to go for sixteen men on a dead man's chest. Or is the pirate thing over with?"

"Hmm, I'm picturing that," he says. "Looks a little gay."

"Have you ever done two women?"

"Why? Is that a thing that interests you?"

"Did you and Portia do that?" she says.

He takes her hand away and sits up against the headboard. "I don't think I need to answer these questions."

"I forgot," she says. "You go case by case. Is it hot to fuck sisters?"

"What about you? Is it hot to fuck somebody who fucked your sister?"

She puts her legs over the side and stands up. "Do you really have to leave so soon?"

He grabs her arm and yanks her back onto the bed.

"What are you going to do?" she says. "Rape me?"

He lets go of her arm. He reaches down, finds his T-shirt and pulls it over his head. Stands up and steps into his briefs. "Question." Picks up his shirt. "Is Portia going to know about this?"

Lily makes no move to get up again. "Come on, wouldn't you rather just improvise?" she says. "It should be more exciting for you. Test your little"—she flitters her fingers—"*ganglions.* You can watch her face for signs. If you're looking for your pants, they're over by the door."

From the bedroom window, she watches his car back out of the driveway; her arm still hurts where he grabbed it. Already eight o'clock, and getting dark. Two minutes less light every day. She's got three hours to fill just to get to movie time—and she's already run through everything she's brought except *Royal Wedding,* which she really doesn't want to watch. And then? And after that? She hasn't had her swim today, could that be what's wrong? The recreation area closes at sunset, but that shouldn't stop a girl who's already figured out so much.

She leaves her underwear on the floor, pulls on her jeans and gets her father's white shirt out of the closet, goes downstairs and tucks the one-hitter and her lighter into the pocket. She's halfway to the lake before she looks down and sees she's driving barefoot. Since the gate's closed, she passes on to the far side, where it's privately owned and narrow paved drives have signs arching above them: Lochbrae, Breezy Shores, Pinewoods. She turns into a lane with a small sign simply reading Private and parks on the dirt, out of sight of the road, then reaches into her pocket.

When she gets out of the car, the white shirt seems to glow in the dimness, so she takes it off, her jeans too, and walks, naked, through the trees, on merciful pine needles, to where she can see water, a dock, a cottage with lights on. She looks right, looks left, then leaves the cover of the pines and tiptoes toward the grassy bank. These people won't spot her: she's been gifted with invisibility. Only the dead can see her nakedness, and haven't they been watching all along? She steps onto the moss at the edge of the bank—its softness feels green—and into the weeds and water. Her feet sink to the ankles in muck. It'll be warmer once she gets in. She wades till the water's up to mid-thigh, leans forward and launches herself.

It's as close to flying as we get in this world: breast-stroking through this uncanny element midway between earth and air, your legs extended behind you, your feet touching nothing. She swims out until she's breathing hard, turns, treads water and looks back. The lights are on in the cottages, and here and there on the shore she can see tiny people clustering around the flames of outdoor grills. The stars are coming out, and the voices from far across the water are pinpricks in the silence. Her heart's slowing again, she's catching her breath. She treads water, floats awhile on her back, then treads water, then floats awhile. You could do this forever—or until you see the way that leads on from here, or until the dead speak to you at last.

Alcorian A-1949

||||||

The man who built this house—Royall Brown, 1750–1797—is buried in the graveyard up across the road, along with his wife, his son and his son's wife and children. I've outlived him, at least in the sense that he was forty-seven and I'm now sixty-one. He built it in 1790, so I've occupied his house longer, too—unless you believe the lady we bought it from, who told Deborah she used to hear his ghost. Bring your drink out to the porch. You can see his headstone up there, the one with the top carved in the shape of wings.

The year we moved here, Deborah did a rubbing and had it framed for my fortieth birthday, his epitaph in forward-slanting script: *Dear Christian Friend, as here you stand / Thy Flesh is dust, thy Time is Sand.* We were ironists but we weren't—does that contextualize it for you? He the still-promising composer and sometime pianist who had studied with Morton Feldman; she the once-promising mezzo, pregnant with a last-chance child who was to be raised in clean air, among woods and white clapboard houses, where the wicked cease to trouble. Royall Brown's epitaph sang to me, as words sometimes will even now, in a darksome, twisty melody, which I put through the grinder—inversion, retrograde, retrograde inversion—and set for baritone and cello. You've heard that old Library of Congress recording of Golden P. Harris singing "I'll Lead a Christian Life"? Well of course you haven't, but that was the mood I wanted, though if you were to hear my piece—and there's an *if*—it would just sound like good old dentist's-chair serialism. Wasn't I the shit back then? I must still have it on reel-to-reel somewhere, performed by colleagues at a faculty recital.

Mrs. Gartner, who'd heard the ghost, lived on here after her husband died, despite macular degeneration and incipient dementia. When she finally fell and lay at the foot of the stairs for a day and a night, her granddaughter got her into Merrivale, the nursing home here in town—so her friends could still visit, in theory—and put the house on the market. But the lady signed the papers herself, God bless her, in the solarium, a lighted magnifying glass in her other hand, with the grand-daughter standing beside her wheelchair. Then she clutched Deborah's wrist and said, "You won't forget me now?" Deborah and I took the girl to lunch afterward, though I shouldn't say "girl"; she looked to be in her mid-twenties. She told us her grandparents had raised her—no explanation given—and that she'd lived in the house from when she was six until she went off to UNH. She had chopped-off black hair, black nail polish and black tights that showed white flesh through their ladders. Her name was Jessamyn. I'll omit all that the male gaze reg-istered, but isn't it always a question of would you or wouldn't you? Deborah (though she'd seen me looking and surely knew I would) told her to stop by anytime she came to see her grandmother. But we never heard from her.

Deborah took to visiting Mrs. Gartner once a week. Mrs. Gartner would ask if hummingbirds still visited the feeders she'd put up—of course Deborah said they did—and if the swallows still made nests in the corner of the porch, which was true. She would bring roses from the garden (the old lady could smell them, at least) and stewed rhubarb from the plant in the side yard. Deborah got stories about the Gartners' courtship—he used to bring her blueberries he'd picked, in a Maxwell House coffee can—but she could never find out how they had come to raise the granddaughter. "Children can be such a disappointment": that was all the old lady would say. A few times, at her request, Debo-rah went over to sing, in what the nurses were instructed to call the living room, and she roped me in to accompany her, on an old Chicker-ing upright. For conservatory types, we were convincing enough: I'd worked my way through Buffalo playing lounges, and Deborah could sing "My Old Flame" or "Someone to Watch Over Me" without sound-ing like a lieder-trilling twit. After Sophia was born, Deborah brought her along a couple of times, but Mrs. Gartner got "agitated," as the nurses put it, when Deborah took the baby away, thinking it was *her* baby.

Demented though she may have been, Mrs. Gartner had kept her mouth shut about Royall Brown until after we'd closed on the house. Deborah asked her how she'd known it was *his* ghost, and she said, "Why, who else would care?" Before Mr. Gartner's heart attack, he'd been trying to talk her into moving to Florida.

Deborah began hearing Royall Brown, too: a floor creaking somewhere as we lay in bed, a door slamming, a thump outside, the faintest ping from my piano down in the living room. Never anything that might not have been a gust of wind, or the house settling, or an apple falling from one of the old trees I never got around to pruning—we used to talk about buying a cider press—or a wasp lighting on a piano string. Or, in the fullness of time, Sophia sneaking out to buy drugs. Deborah once saw a patch of fog over his grave in the shape of a man, but it dissipated by the time I could get out to the porch. His presence, she told me, felt "disapproving." I made my will a couple of months ago, and it specifies that my body be cremated, so I won't be joining the cast of characters up across the road. Or my own mother and father, buried in the town in Massachusetts where I grew up, seventy miles from here as the spirit flies. And I doubt that my own spirit—if I have such a thing, if I *am* such a thing—will be mooning around the house, rattling windows and wringing its see-through hands over, say, having failed to love when it was still possible.

Deborah had clearly worked up her farewell aria with some care: she would never have a career now, she told me, but at least she might have a life (this was a false ending), and (here comes the final cadence) she never wanted to see this place again. Come Judgment Day, they'll confront me with a pie chart, showing just what percentage of me wanted this. So I've left the house to Sophia—who, when the time comes, might be more sentimental than she is now and unwilling to sell off her childhood home, from which she ran away for good at sixteen. She's twenty-two, has apparently straightened herself out and lives with a boy in Berlin; if I'm accurately intuiting my own trajectory, she'll inherit this place when she's about thirty. By which time I will have done my important work—you understand that's a joke, yes?—and the world (if I'm accurately intuiting *its* trajectory) will be shot to hell too, and she might be glad of a refuge—for however long such a refuge will last—twenty miles off the nearest interstate, where you can still sit and drink on the porch of a white clapboard house.

I hadn't seen Sophia for three years when she paid me a visit last month before flying to Germany, bringing the boyfriend as a buffer. Since my time, she'd had a piece of metal, like a tiny dumbbell, installed in her eyebrow, to show the world she'd been wounded. They sat together on the sofa and turned down my offer of a gin and tonic. "I'm trying to picture what your life is like now," she said.

"I can help you with that," I said. "First you picture a hand coming out from under the piano lid."

"I guess you were always funny," she said.

"Until I wasn't."

"I've let that go," she said.

The boyfriend had wandered over to the piano. He played a scale with his right hand—I watched the thumb spider up under the fingers—and then grabbed a two-handed diminished chord. The only kind of chord of which my piano is now capable, one might say, if one were still funny. "This is an amazing instrument," he said.

"Well then," I said. "Oblige us."

"I don't really play."

"Oh, bullshit," Sophia said. "Eric's band is going to Scandinavia next month."

"Ah," I said. "Well, give my regards to Norway."

He went back and sat on the sofa. She got up and said, "We're going out on the porch for a little, okay?"

"*I* can go out," he said.

"No, you sit."

"If you change your mind," I said, "the gin's in the freezer."

I followed her out; she sat down in an Adirondack chair and tucked her feet under her. I lowered myself into the chair next to her, bracing on its arms like an old man. "Why are you being a prick to him?" she said.

"I thought I was being self-ironic. I guess I'm not used to being around people anymore."

"Is that supposed to make me feel sorry for you?" she said. "This was Mom's idea, you know?"

"I'm just glad you came. And I had wanted to meet your friend."

"Well, now you can check that off."

"Since you're here, I should probably show you a couple of things. This house is going to be yours someday, so—"

"Oh," she said. "Lucky me. What, are you making plans for an early exit?"

"Okay," I said. "Believe me, if I were in your shoes? I'm sure I'd feel the same way. I just want to do what little I can at this point."

"What am I supposed to say? 'I'm sorry I was such a handful'? How about this? When *I'm* getting ready to check out, I'll forgive you."

"I thought you said you'd let it go."

"So I guess I was lying," she said. "I studied under the master, right?" She stood up. "We're going."

"Could I just make one thing clear?" I said.

She opened the door to the living room and looked back at me. "What?"

What indeed?

"No, nothing," I said. "I'll let you have the last word."

By the time Mrs. Gartner died, Deborah had been living in Cambridge for a year. But she'd kept in touch with a couple who live on our road—my road—and who no longer keep in touch with *me*, you'll be surprised to hear. She called me the night before the funeral to say she was renting a car and coming up. "I just wanted to forewarn you," she said. "I promised her."

"Now you've shamed me into it," I said.

"*That* would be something to see," she said. "Your shame."

"Oh, it's on permanent display," I said. "It's become one of the local attractions."

"Good you still have your sense of humor," she said. "It must be getting quite a workout these days."

You see? I *always* let them have the last word.

It was the third week in August, still hot, though while driving to the church I noticed a red leaf on a maple tree. I took a seat in the back, next to Deborah—how could one not? She gave my hand a quick squeeze. Could it possibly be? Might I possibly want it? I spotted the granddaughter in the front row, sitting with a white-haired couple and an old lady with a walker. Jessamyn (I remembered the name) had to be forty now, though she still had that chopped-off hair, with a new tinge of maroon. I saw that her cheeks had gotten pudgy, suggesting she might be both appetitive and attainable—ah, this was just one of those reflexive thoughts that still intrude, as a corpse's hair and fingernails are said to keep growing. I'd given up pursuing students, belatedly you'll say, after a collegial talking-to from my department chairman, and—since I have no secrets from you—after taking a young woman to bed and being unable to follow through. Still, back in May, at the end-of-the-semester party, I drank too much—that is, I drank—and kissed one of my students good night, on the mouth, though I knew she'd been aiming for my cheek. The next day, to try to head off another complaint, I emailed her an apology for what I called "an excess of good cheer," and she wrote back that she'd been "amused": the midpoint, I took it, between "offended" and "saddened."

After the service, I walked out with Deborah and touched a hand to the back of her arm as we went down the steps. "There's Marcia and Walter," she said. This was the couple I was telling you about. "I should go say hello."

But Jessamyn was walking up to us, patting sweat from her forehead with a bandanna handkerchief that looked out of keeping with her black dress. "I don't know if you remember me," she said. I saw she wasn't wearing a ring.

"Of course," Deborah said. "How are you holding up?"

"Well," she said, "it's not like I wasn't expecting it. Actually, I have a favor to ask? I wonder if I could come out this afternoon and see the house one more time."

"I'm probably not the one to ask anymore," Deborah said.

Jessamyn looked at her, then at me. "Oh. I guess I stepped in something." I remembered her fetchingly harsh little voice.

"That would be fine," I said. "We were going to grab some lunch, but maybe three, three thirty?"

"That works. I've still got all this to deal with." She looked over her shoulder at the white-haired couple getting the walker lady into the front seat of a minivan. "Thanks." I took care not to eye her as she walked away.

Deborah said, "Aren't we amicable."

"*Would* you like some lunch?" I said. "Let's say hello to Walter and Marcia, and then we can go over to the Pine Grove."

"I think I'm just going to run along," she said. "I'm sure you'll have your hands full." False ending. "Anyhow, I don't want to weigh down your afternoon with any *more* nostalgia."

Sooner or later I'd been bound to get a DWI; I suppose I was lucky it happened while Deborah was still in the picture. After teaching a theory class one evening—this would have been February of last year—I went to a bar in the South End with my students, then headed up 93 listening to *Hope in the Night,* where gentle June Hunt gets callers to invite Jesus Christ into their hearts. Somehow I made it as far as Manchester before getting pulled over. For the rest of the term, Deborah drove me down to Concord once a week to catch the bus to Boston; only when they reinstated my license did she announce she was leaving. After she moved I had to unplug the phone at night, since the sainted Deborah—and I'm not saying she didn't *deserve* Walter and Marcia's sympathy—had developed a little problem herself. One night I forgot; I let the machine pick up and I heard her say, "You're just up there waiting to die." One of these days I need to set *that* shit, don't you think? Just mezzo and snare drum—you hear the six-eight rhythm? "March from an Unwritten Opera" we could call it. Might end up becoming my little out-of-context keeper, my *"Treulich gefuhrt"*—"Here Comes the Bride," to you—or my Ride of the Valkyries. *Kill the wabbit! Kill the wabbit!*

For my community service, I chose to go over to Merrivale one afternoon a week and play for—I almost said pray for—the moribunds. Mrs. Gartner was now in her nineties, and she'd had a stroke on top of everything else, but the nurses thought she still responded to music, so they rolled her out, hands strapped to the arms of her wheelchair, like the statue of the Great Emancipator. The first afternoon, I tried them on the usual American songbook shit, but Deborah was in no mood to come in and sing with me, and who knows the words anymore to "Mountain Greenery" or "A Fine Romance"? Finally a lady in a flowered top and a white neck brace asked for "Sweet Caroline." It's one of those songs you've heard a million times, and I managed to get through it by ear. I didn't know anything beyond "Where it began," but the lady had the "Warm, touching warm" part, and a few of them came in on the *dum dum dum:* apparently this was a phenomenon at Fenway. So when I got home, I went online and ordered something called the *Wedding and Love Fake Book*—somebody else had a sense of humor, no?— with 450 songs: "My Cherie Amour," "Baby I'm-a Want You," "Danny's Song" (that's the one that goes "Even though we ain't got money"), "Time in a Bottle." And I paid the guy who tunes my piano to come from Hanover and try to get the one at Merrivale halfway playable. I've got my license back now, but I keep going there, partly to give my weeks more of a shape, partly to bring myself low. The nurses tell me I'm the favorite of all the people who come in, except for a woman who brings her Labrador retriever around.

During the school year I still drive down to teach, though now I put up at a motel and go back the next day. Otherwise, I'm here. I get up, drink coffee and—in order to irritate myself, I suppose—put on New Hampshire Public Radio and listen to the *Morning Diddle Diddle*

Dum. (Did all those Baroque composers have Asperger's?) Then I go to the piano and work at working, until disgust tolls fancy's knell. In the afternoon, the obligatory walk in the woods, or perhaps a trip to town for pie and coffee at the Pine Grove, where I'm known for my geniality. Every Tuesday I drive to Hanover to give a piano lesson to a no-hoper high-school boy, and on the way back I stop by the state liquor store in West Lebanon for a couple of handles of Tanqueray. After sunset, of course, I'm immobilized, as the undead are by day: this is when I drink, and the town cops know my car. Picture the door to the freezer inching open, the hand creeping in. So I sip the hours away, playing computer solitaire and listening to the radio. In the p.m., I switch to AM—my little way of bidding defiance to Time—crossing over into the wonder world of Jesus: *Hope in the Night;* Brother Stair, "The Last-Day Prophet" who sometimes bellows in the voice of God; and *Open Forum* with Harold Camping, who mikes his Bible so you can hear the pages turn, and who's calculated the Rapture for May of next year, and the end of time for October 21. I'd find this fixation hard to explain if there were anyone to whom I had to explain it. You don't suppose He's calling me, or that I'm seeking Him? And of course I worry about my work. When you lose a game of solitaire, a box pops up: *There are no more possible moves. What do you want to do now?* It's one of those ironies so obviously pointed at you that you can't take it seriously. As I tell my students, if you're not at a creative impasse, you're not paying attention.

I've already told you I studied with Morton Feldman, yes? Don't bother to check—you won't find me on Wikipedia's list of his "notable" students, though I see they've got Kyle Gann, as well they should, and even Elliott Sharp. Back in the eighties, I wrote the music for a Canadian horror movie you wouldn't have heard of—not that you've heard of Morton Feldman—which gave us the down payment for this house. I used to call it my big score; was that not witty? And ten years ago, or I guess more like fifteen, the Kronos was supposedly going to record a piece of mine, but of course by then they had Tan Dun—*there's* a son of a bitch who knows how to work it—as well as the Africans and whoever else.

Oh well. Even back when I was studying with Mort, I knew that whatever sang to him was never going to sing to me. He knew it, too. But once, when I was broke, he bought me dinner and when he died, a couple of years before we moved up here, I helped put together a tribute in Boston; wasn't I the shit back then? We recruited players from the BSO to do *For Samuel Beckett,* the last thing he ever wrote, and for a curtain raiser I'd worked up *Palais de mari,* his final piano piece. The chamber orchestra for the Beckett outnumbered the audience. You play Feldman with the sustain pedal mostly down, to make the notes after the notes, the echoes and harmonics, ring and shimmer and beat against one another inside the piano. A couple of minutes into it, I got lost in listening, fucked up a note, fucked up another—I doubt now that anybody noticed—and just got up and walked off. They must have thought I was too devastated to continue. So of course you're asking yourself, *Did he secretly have it in for this man?*

Mort once assigned us to write a piece for soprano and string quartet based on an item out of *The Buffalo News,* and ever since I've mostly stuck to setting other people's words—a sufficiently dinky arena for my dinky gift. This is going to sound like I'm bullshitting, but back in Buffalo I started writing a Watergate opera—this was long before *Nixon in China.* Then, around the time the Kronos deal was happening, or not happening, I thought I'd better take notice of hip-hop, as old hacks like Milhaud had felt they'd better take notice of jazz. Ah, *that* was the answer: sample a smidgen of Boulez or Golden P. Harris, whatever struck your fancy—this was where intuition came in—and sequence them to a dance beat, so people might actually listen to it, then put your text on top. In *Sprechstimme:* no more screwing around waiting for some melody to sing itself to you. I even bought a Roland 808, which I've still got up in the attic. And after I got over that, the answer was what? One's oh-so-personal vision?

At any rate, I'm now working toward working on a piece—a little *Gesamtkunstwerk,* you might say, since it'll involve some visuals in performance—that I'm calling *Alcorian A-1949.* This is how they've registered Ted Williams's frozen corpse at the Alcor Life Extension Foundation in Scottsdale, Arizona. Did I tell you I saw Ted Williams once? My father took me to Fenway when I was six, just so I could say I saw him. And now I've said it. How I got the idea, there's a man at the nursing home, Jimmy Condon, who used to be a great friend of the Gartners. Jimmy doesn't let them wheel him out much—he says it gets him down to see old people—but I bring him what he calls "reading matter." He likes fat paperbacks, mostly histories, and since he follows the Sox, I naturally thought of him when that biography of Ted Williams came out. The next time I went in, he handed it back. "Maybe you want to pass this along to somebody else," he said. "You know his son put him in the deep freeze? Ted Williams. Yes sir. And then they cut off his head and froze *that.*" He drew a finger across his throat. "But I'll tell you who was a hell of an athalete—Gene Conley. He'd pitch for the Sox and then turn right around and play for the Celtics. Two sports. Nobody can do that anymore."

That made me curious enough to read the book myself—if I'd known how depressing it got toward the end, I would never have inflicted it on Jimmy. Not just the head business, but fat old Ted Williams, stroked out, hooked to machines, disinheriting his daughter and still signing autographs on his deathbed for his son to sell. But how the man could blaspheme!

Virgin Mary All-Clapped-Up Mother of God!
Cocksucking fucken syphilitic Jesus!

I could hear him singing to me—and how often did that happen anymore? So my idea was, you have the singer up there—a soprano, since you don't want maleness to be an issue—and you see only this head, with white makeup like the Commendatore, and it's singing from this place beyond this life but not in the next life either. I'd prefer that the singer shave her head, but I suppose that would have to be negotiable. As I say, I've been working toward working on it.

I don't imagine you know the name Roberto Loomis, but they gave him an NEA a couple of years ago. He's got CDs out on Lovely Music, which he always has them send me, and I'll say this for him—his stuff is less unlistenable than mine. The reason I mention him, he was one of my students, back when he was Bob Loomis from somewhere in Idaho. At the time he came into my composition class, he was a death-metalhead who'd belatedly begun studying classical guitar; I got him listening to Glenn Branca and Rhys Chatham. He emailed me the other day, to say he was organizing a festival in February, in Cozumel, and did I have anything he might consider. Well now: to have one's work *considered*, and by Roberto Loomis no less. Was he looking to enhance his credibility by passing me off as a neglected master? Anything, please, but an act of kindness. At any rate, it's given me some incentive to get on with this Ted Williams piece. For which one is obliged to feel grateful. Which in turn must account for the nasty tone one hears oneself taking.

I had washed the dishes and mowed the lawn, and the sun hung low over the hill, an hour from touching the treetops, which would be sweet Nature's signal that the first drink might now be poured. I was sitting on the porch, going through *Ted Williams: The Biography of an American Hero* with a yellow highlighter, when a Mini Cooper with Rhode Island plates pulled into the dooryard. I got up to greet Jessamyn, and as she walked toward me I saw that she'd changed from her black dress into tight jeans, the tops of her thighs just touching, and a loose denim shirt. She turned around, as if to show me those womanly charms, and looked back at the graveyard. "Gran always used to say how she'd like to be buried up there," she said. "So now she gets to be shipped out to fucking Harrisburg."

"Is that where her family was from? Come on up and sit."

"His family. She hated those people. That was Gramp's sister—with the walker? I always thought she was a witch. Can I look in the barn first? We used to make hay forts in there."

"My daughter did the same thing," I said. "Great place to grow up. *I* always thought."

"If you can deal with a little weirdness," she said. "I mean, you know about our ghost."

"Your grandmother did say something about it."

"Oh, old what's-his-face? That was bullshit. No, there was this little girl who used to play with me. Gran wanted to think she was like my imaginary friend."

"I never heard of a little girl."

"Seriously? Well, maybe she—I don't know, what does anybody know about this stuff? You don't mind if I look in the house after? And then I'll get right out of your hair."

I went back to work, but Ted Williams wasn't singing to me today—hadn't been for weeks, really—and until he did there was no point in going inside to the piano. A breeze had come up, and every now and again I'd hear an apple hit the ground.

I heard her call hello and looked up—I'd forgotten anybody was here. This was a good sign, no? "I'm going to look around inside, okay?"

"Liberty Hall," I said. "I should warn you, it's going to look a little different."

"No worries. After seeing Gran in her box?"

I listened to her footsteps going from room to room, then up the stairs. She seemed to stay a long time in what used to be Sophia's bedroom. Then I heard her go back down to the living room and plink a single note on the piano.

She came out to the porch, sat down in an Adirondack chair, wiped her forehead with her bandanna, then let her head fall back. "This is all kind of an overload."

"What can I get you?" I said. "Coffee? Drink?"

"I think I have to go." She brought her head back up. "My partner's had the kids all day."

"Ah," I said. So there went that, not that there'd been any prospect of a *that*. "How old are your kids?"

"Four and six. We started late. Well, Tonya started late. I'm too old to start late."

"You don't look it. I mean, from *my* distant perspective."

"Yeah, Gran looked okay too. Check her in a couple of months." She took a phone out of her shirt pocket and fingered through pictures: two generic little blond girls on a beach somewhere.

"They're lovely," I said. "You know, if you ever wanted to bring them up and show them around. And your partner might like to see the place."

"She's heard enough at this point. I don't know, maybe when the kids are older. Right now they're all about Disney World."

"I remember *that* phase," I said. In fact, when Sophia was six we were bringing her to the Bang on a Can Festival.

"Right?" she said. I had to think for a second to realize this was the new term of agreement. "I'm trying to remember—weren't you a songwriter or something? I saw your piano. I wish I would've learned to play. Can I change my mind about the drink?"

"I was just about to get one for myself," I said. "Gin and tonic? We've got a *little* summer still to go, yes?"

In the refrigerator, I found a nearly full bottle of tonic—I generally don't bother with it—and a hard, shrunken lime. I got the Tanqueray out of the freezer, still two-thirds full, took a good pull at it, then quartered the lime and began pouring.

"Easy on the gin, okay?" she called. "No, actually, easy on the tonic."

When I came out she was going at her phone again. I set her glass on the arm of her chair and took the chair next to her. "If you can master that," I said, "we can have you playing Scarlatti in six months."

She pocketed the phone and picked up the glass. "That's classical, right?"

"See? You're catching on already." I raised my glass. "Here's how."

"Thanks. Cheers and whatnot." She took a sip. "God, I used to *live* out here in the summer. Gran even let me bring my sleeping bag. This is where I saw Sally the first time."

"That was the—?"

"It was like, she wasn't there, and then she was."

"That must've scared you."

"Not really." She took a long drink. "She was my first crush—how weird is that? She was right, exactly, there." Jessamyn pointed over to a spot underneath the swallows' mud nest, now empty till spring. "She had on this little blue dress with yellow—like violets or something. I remember I was playing tic-tac-toe against myself."

"Did other people see her?"

"Yeah, Tonya doesn't believe me either." She took another drink. "Jesus."

"I can get you more tonic." I could feel mine taking hold, too—and no wonder. I saw that I only had about that much left.

"No, it's good," she said. "This is the first time I've relaxed since they called about Gran."

"Make yourself at home," I said. "Be right back." I got up and went into the kitchen, ran water to cover the sound of the freezer opening and took another good pull to hold me until I could decently refill my glass.

When I sat down next to her again, she was looking up at the graveyard. "Poor Gran," she said. "I guess poor everybody." She turned to me. "She used to say you were good to her. You and your wife."

"*You* were good to her," I said.

"We had our issues." She picked up her glass and drank until the lip touched her nose. "Okay, I probably shouldn't tell you, but she wasn't just my first *crush*, okay?" She raised the empty glass as if to toast. "Go, *Jess.*" She set it down. "So now you're thinking, how do I get rid of this person."

"No, it's good to have you here."

"Yeah? Then you *must* be in Shit City," she said.

"What I was thinking, if a succubus appeared I wouldn't turn her down. If I'm understanding you correctly."

"I don't really know what that is," she said. "So how come your wife left?"

"Well, you know, different theories," I said. "I think the ghosts drove her out."

"I always push too much," she said.

"That's okay," I said. "I always drink too much and make moves on women." I got to my feet. "Present company excepted. I'm going to go re-up."

I took one more good pull from the bottle, put ice cubes into the peacock-feather bowl—Deborah had collected pressed glass—and brought it out to the porch, along with the gin and what was left of the tonic. "You mind keeping your lime?" I said. "Had to make a house rule: No using knives after the first cocktail."

I held the bottle up and she put her hand over her glass. "I think I'm good. I didn't freak you out, right? With the ghost stories? Actually I get the feeling there's nobody here anymore."

I poured gin, sending my ice cubes into a merry dance. "You and me both, my friend." I drank, then topped off. "*That* is the truest thing you've said all day."

"I used to drive by here sometimes when I was up visiting Gran," she said. "One time I saw this little girl on the porch, and she was like, swinging in that hammock you used to have up. Was that your daughter?"

"Jesus, I hope to Christ so. Listen, tell me something. Why didn't you ever stop in?"

"I didn't think your wife wanted me to. She didn't like me very much. When we had lunch that time?"

I heard myself say, "I'd always sort of hoped I'd see you."

"Yeah, well, I'm not a big fan of situations."

"Ah," I said. "Now this seems to be leading us into a very interesting place."

She took her phone out, looked at the screen, got her thumbs going again and put it back in her pocket.

"Here's the thing about situations, okay?" I said. "Having been in situations myself. What was once a *situation* can turn into—you see what I'm saying. It's good you and I can finally talk about this."

"I don't know what you think we're talking about," she said.

"Ah, deniability," I said. "I used to be the king of that. But I think we owe each other a little more, no? Or am I being too blunt?"

"Okay, well thanks for the drink and everything." She set her glass on the arm of the chair and got to her feet.

"You can't possibly go *now*," I said. I leaned forward and saw my hand around her wrist.

"What the fuck?" She yanked her arm away. "What kind of an asshole *are* you?"

"Oh," I said, "just a harmless old drunk, really. You don't need to leave."

"Do you have any idea the shit I had to go through? Just to have a life? And you put your hand on me?" She grabbed the bottle by its neck, the handle over her knuckles like the—hell, what's it called?—on, you know, a buccaneer's sword.

"Whoa," I said. "Easy. What say we just wind this back?" I stood up and reached to take the bottle away from her.

She stepped back and swung it against a porch post. It rang off the wood, but she swung it again, smashed it, splashing gin on her jeans and shirt, and held up the jagged, dripping glass that was left. "You don't even know what the shit you're dealing with," she said. She looked at it, then flung it onto the lawn and ran to her car.

I watched her out of sight around the corner and went inside to look in the freezer, though I knew damn well that had been the last of the gin. The whole night still ahead, with the state store closing in an hour.

I took back roads as far as I could, then went through the speed-trap towns with the cruise control locked in at twenty-five. I bought three handles of Tanqueray, as if I were a party giver, opened one in the parking lot and poured a used Styrofoam coffee cup full. I kept it between my thighs the whole way back. But I had the secret of invisibility that night: I could have steered head-on into a van full of children and no one would have seen there was a problem to be addressed.

I pulled in the dooryard, banged into something, walked zigzag to the house and stood swaying in the living room, calling out to Mort till the strings of the piano rang. You see now how funny that is, right, yelling, "Mort! Mort!" to a dead man? I cried out for the little dead girl to come be *my* little dead girl, I went to my knees and asked Jesus Christ into my heart, I went out onto the porch and hollered across the road at Royall Brown, the Great Disapprover. In the silence—watch out for the false ending now—I heard an apple fall.

———

Have I been showing you a good enough time? Why don't you come on out, bring your drink, and we'll get old what's-his-face down here to do his little buck-and-wing to the tune of "Dear Christian Friend"— would that amuse?—and favor us with his views on how flesh is dust and so on. Or how about a private performance, first time anywhere, of my latest. Oh, I finished it—you didn't take all that poor-me shit too seriously, I hope—and sent it off to young what's-his-face. It's scored for string quartet, but I can approximate it on the piano, if you don't mind how half-assed it sounds, and at this point in the festivities, what's the difference? Ted Williams never did sing to me anymore, so I had to patch it together out of this and that—plagiarize it really. You'll hear a smidgen of *Eight Songs for a Mad King* in there, a smidgen of Stockhausen's *Momente,* a smidgen of "Time in a Bottle" (who says I lack the common touch?). And Feldman, of course—can't get away from him. That pair of four-note phrases, the second seeming to question the first, at the beginning of *Palais de mari*: didn't I work the variations on *that* sucker. Well, I *say* you'll hear this stuff, but it's all been through the grinder, so you'd have to know what you were listening for.

So here we go: five movements, five sets of variations on five lines of text, word for word from *Ted Williams: The Biography of an American Hero.*

1. The plan is to live on the big boat.
2. I made a mistake. I need a lawyer.
3. You know who did this to me? Jesus Christ did this to me!
4. You're the abortion I wanted—how do you say that to your son?
5. At the damn gate of the park, where we always meet.

Don't you like the little story it tells? I had to chuck out the stuff that inspired me in the first place—*Cocksucking fucken syphilitic Jesus* and whatnot. Let Roberto Loomis be the Rebel Angel and take up a flaming sword against the Disapprovers. According to the biography, some nurse said that Williams, on his deathbed, finally came to know Jesus was his savior. I thought the third movement was the place for the Wagnerian Jesus drama, then the death-metal family angst in four and finally, in five, the Meeting at the Gate—or the Parting at the Gate, however you want to read it—in pastoral quietude.

So I await my judgment: was I father enough to Roberto Loomis at least? As for you, whom I've been trying to sweet-talk this whole time, I get the feeling there's nobody here anymore. I will have done my important work: you have to picture the hand coming out from under the lid. I drank too much—that is, I drank—though Deborah (as I said) had developed a little problem herself. And I got lost in listening, for which one has to be grateful. Clearly I've worked up this farewell aria with some care, but—and here comes the final cadence—I'm going to let you have the last word. Wasn't I the shit back then?

Desecrators

||||||

While Fran was in the bathroom, Cal told Cammy one more time that he'd have his cell with him and that if anything at all— Okay, Daddy, *okay.* Fran came out with fresh lipstick. Cal slung his bag over his shoulder, kissed the lips lightly and he was out of there. In the lobby, Hector asked if he wanted a cab; he said no thanks and stepped out into sunshine. Hot for October. So at the Hertz place on Seventy-Seventh, he chose the convertible over the SUV—shit, let's go for piggy *and* slinky—and it arrived still dripping, long, low-slung, midnight blue.

He double-parked at the corner of Forty-Ninth and Tenth Avenue and got out his cell; better not to wait in front of Margaret's building, even though the boyfriend was off reporting a story. Or that was the boyfriend's story. Cal's story was a Milton conference in Princeton, which he would tell Fran was so tedious he couldn't even write the piece of mockery he'd had in mind. Margaret must've had a story too. They'd fucked the first time on Tuesday afternoon, her place, the boyfriend ninety-nine-point-nine percent certain not to come home early. So a weekend had been a must. *This* weekend had been a must.

She came around the corner wearing sunglasses and a Dodgers cap, bag over her shoulder, cigarette pack rolled into the sleeve of her white T-shirt. Cal got out and said, "Welcome to my midlife Chrysler."

"*I'm* impressed," she said.

"With the car?" he said. "Or the jeu d'esprit?"

"The car," she said. "I told you I was a simple girl."

He put her bag in, slammed the trunk, then looked her over good. "We like the nips," he said.

"What, these?" She looked down, grabbed a handful of T-shirt on each side and pulled it tighter. "Externals," she said. "Can we have the top down?"

"I won't say the obvious," he said. She reached for her door handle, but he thumbed the button on the key ring, the headlights flashed and the locks snapped shut. "You haven't greeted me properly."

She looked behind her, said, "Yeah, fuck it," stepped to him, took hold of his ass and pulled him into her. Her tongue on the roof of his mouth, right back to the soft palate. Fingernails in his neck.

"Jesus," he said. "Who taught *you* the password?"

"Come on, you're easy to read." But she was breathing hard too. "Like Nancy Drew." She stepped back. "Okay, so Nancy gets accepted to art school, goes into class with her pencil and stuff, and there's Ned Nickerson sitting there on the podium with all his clothes off and his dick standing straight up. So what did she do?"

Cal thought, then nodded. "Got it."

"I put the dick in to throw you off," she said.

"I won't say the obvious," he said. "No, actually I won't say *that*."

Cal had been circling Margaret all year—*and* getting signals back: he wasn't *that* much of an asshole. She was the best of the writers he'd inherited. His first week, she covered a drive-through Christmas-lights festival in Pennsylvania. He asked her out for coffee and said it was a waste for her to keep writing for the Bottom Feeder section. Sure, she'd said: that was why she did it.

Naturally he'd gone back and read the stuff she'd done for *Lingua Franca* and *Nerve*. The *Nerve* piece was just a riff about an ex-boyfriend and gave away nothing about her own sexual stuff. But her name for the guy—Dick Minim—came from what, the *Rambler*? (He looked it up: the *Idler*.) So how could you not want to do her? According to Nancy, the managing editor, she had a history with married men but had lately moved in with some guy her own age. "So I gather you're into Johnson," he'd said as the waiter set down their coffees. "What girl isn't?" she'd said.

―――

He looked over at her profile, chin out like Mussolini, as she lit a cigarette: American Spirits in the yellow. "You mind? I'm down to three a day."

"Do it," he said.

"I promised myself that if I couldn't keep it to three I'd just quit."

"And that's working?"

"So far. This is the first day. It would be nice not to end up like my father." She blew smoke up and away. "Actually, you know what this car could use? One of those crown things on the dashboard. With the air freshener?"

"Yeah, speaking of fresh, do you know yet what you're giving us for next week?"

She blew out smoke again. "Not really. Maybe the Christian board games. That or toilet-paper tots. You know, on the wrappers?"

"Yes," he said. "That. Now that *is* unwholesome. That little girl with the eyes? Done deal."

"So," she said, "you're not at all freaked out about this, right?" Another drag of cigarette.

"Why, are you?"

"So-so. You know, I'm theoretically in this appropriate relationship."

"I think I've just been called old," he said.

"And of course these things always end so well," she said. "So why did the blonde go to Mass?"

"Hmmm," he said. "Mass as in, not Massachusetts. Okay."

"Because she heard they had a guy there who was hung like that." Cupped her hands, spread her arms.

They stopped at the first service area so she could pee and check out the crap in the gift shop. People coming out: three white boys with backward caps and baggy jeans ending mid-shin; a fat woman in skin-tight burgundy pants, with a foot-tall cup of soda, dragging her scrawny daughter by the hand; an ex-Marine-looking geezer with white crew cut and I ♥ MY GRANDCHILDREN T-shirt. "This is so

Fellini." She put both hands around his upper arm. "Thank you for bringing me."

"Sheer self-interest," he said. A pudgy couple came rolling toward them, holding hands, in matching plaid Bermudas: he in a bulging knit shirt, she in a bulging Old Navy T-shirt. "That, on the other hand, has to be true love."

"You are completely evil," she said. "I want your cock in my mouth."

"Here and now?" he said. "Or just on principle?"

Their cabin was to have a deck overlooking the lake. The view was prominent in the pictures on the website: green trees and blue water in some; in others, skiers kicking up a spray of snow. The guy on the phone told Cal this would be the best weekend for the leaves, and sure enough. As they drove north, the colors came on and it got too cold to keep the top down. Cal got a joint out of his cigarette case.

She guided him off the Northway onto the state road, then onto the county road, then onto the dirt road, then onto the dirt road they wanted, which ended at a log building with an OFFICE sign and antlers over the door. Inside, a grandfather clock was going *Gonk gonk gonk gonk.* The guy behind the counter—the same one as on the phone?—handed across a map of the trails and two key cards, imprinted with pine trees.

"We get stuff walking out of the rooms all the time," he said. "Even up here in the boonies." He had this fucked-up ear—looked like it had been burned off. "This you folks' first time?"

"Second, actually," Cal said. Margaret kicked his ankle.

"Well. Good to have you back."

"We've been looking forward to it," Cal said.

They drove up to their cabin, from which no other cabin could be seen: another selling point. Cal set their bags on the doorstep and stuck his card in the slot.

"I *love* this," Margaret said. Gleaming log walls and a white chenille bedspread on a queen-size brass bed; a blue-enameled woodstove, quarter-split birch chunks in the woodbox. Smell of actual woodsmoke.

Cal opened the sliding door and they walked out onto the deck:

good, okay, a still-green meadow sloping down to the blue lake. On the far shore, a red, yellow and orange forest, and slim white birch trunks in among the evergreens. Behind all this, an isosceles mountain. "Check it out," he said. "An Adirondack."

"What do you think happened to him?" she said.

"To?"

"Didn't you see his ear?"

"Oh. Can't imagine. Listen, I think I left the wherewithal in the car. Why don't you start getting us settled in. This place needs the woman's touch."

"As soon as I unpack," she said, "I'll go out and pick a frisson of hysteria."

Cal got behind the wheel, shut the door and took out his phone. It said *Searching* . . . then locked in. He looked out the windshield at this tree, then that tree, then that tree: Which one was the signal tower in disguise? He tried the apartment, got the machine, tried the cell.

"God, it took you forever," Fran said. "What's it like?"

"Oh, you know. Oxonian. Faux Oxonian."

"Did *Il Pesce* show up?" Stanley Fish was supposed to be on one of the panels.

"Haven't seen him yet. People are still getting here."

"He always makes me think of Cammy's fish." Cal had given her that mounted fish toy that writhes and sings "Take Me to the River." A terrible lesson: never get high to go Christmas shopping. "God, speaking of which," she said, "we're right in front of Citarella? And I'm looking at this very dead and unhappy sea bass."

"Ah. So is Cammy with you?"

"Yes, everything's under control. Would you like to speak to her? She's clamoring."

Cammy's voice: "I am not, I'm just— Daddy? Hi. We're going to watch *Amadeus* again."

"Ah," he said. At least it had better music than *Shakespeare in Love.* "That should be fun. And Mommy's okay?"

Margaret rapped a knuckle on the glass.

"Jumping Jesus," he said. "Sorry, sweet, something just . . ." He held up his index finger. "No problems, right? I know you can't really talk."

"I don't think so. But are you coming back tomorrow?" Margaret hefted a breast.

"Monday, actually," he said. He did a Groucho Marx with his eyes at Margaret. "Listen, I should get going. You have my cell, so if you need me for *any reason*. Anyway. Enjoy that movie. May I have Mommy back for a second?"

"So," Fran said, "are you reassured?"

"About?"

"Oh, please."

"I'm not *re*assured, no," he said. "This is just—you know, a weekend like all weekends." Well, Hector and Antoine both knew to hold any packages for Fran until he was home, and they'd told the new guy who was on midnight to eight. "You guys take care of each other okay? I'd better go justify God's ways to man."

He pushed End and opened the door.

"Listen," Margaret said, "my cell's not working and I was supposed to call Morgan at, like, two o'clock."

"God, covering your ass," he said. "The curse of Adam." He handed her the phone, reached across, opened the glove compartment and took out the cigarette case. "I've been obsessing about that. Like they've figured out that they're naked, but they're so new at it that they can't just act like it's okay. And God is totally fucking with them." He pointed a finger that trembled in wrath. "'And who *tooooold* you you were naked, hmm?'"

"Why are you obsessing about *that*?" Margaret said.

"Trying to reread Milton," he said. "For this alleged piece. Which reminds me—I found out the story behind the ear."

"Really." She snapped the phone shut. "Do tell."

"Seems our friend used to run this honeymoon resort in the Poconos, and he was a bit of a Norman Bates? So when God found out that he was bugging the rooms—"

"Oh, fuck you, Cal."

"He sent His fire down from heaven—"

"Not funny."

"Ah," he said. "If her readers could hear her now."

In graduate school, Cal had played with a band called the Desecrators, whose specialty was covering Dylan songs and changing the pronouns. They'd begin sets with "Knockin' on Heaven's Door" ("Take this badge off of him / He can't use it anymore") and close with "He and He." Fran had majored in piano, though she'd soon given up on a concert career. She was amazed that Cal could just play with nothing written down; he was amazed that a real person could sit at a piano and out would come, say, a Chopin nocturne. He taught her to play eight-ball and to walk on the street with a can of beer in a paper bag, and he put her onto Dawn Powell years before Tim Page made a big deal out of it. He used to know Tim Page, actually, through a painter friend. And he gave her coke for the first time. The coke turned out to be not such a good idea.

When he finally got Fran to marry him, he quit the Ph.D. program and stopped playing music, like some Jane Austen lady who'd hooked a husband and no longer needed her accomplishments. He sold his guitars to come up with the two months plus a month's security plus the fee on a three-bedroom at West End and 102nd. She got pregnant, sort of not accidentally, and they tossed a coin for whose study would be the baby's room; she won, but gave it up anyway. Her piano students and the occasional accompanist gig hadn't been bringing in much; he was writing a column he called Manufacturing Contempt for a weekly that people picked up for the listings and escort-service ads, plus stuff on the side for *The Georgia Review*. His template was Edmund Wilson. When Cammy was three, the weekly hired him as an editor, just in time for him to use his benefits for Fran's first rehab. Now he'd taken over as number two at this online magazine, which had begun to break even; he could also write as little or as much as he wanted for a buck a word on top of his salary. He'd just bought a painting from the painter friend. His template now was James Wolcott. He could twist the knife, there was that to be said.

They took off their clothes, got under the covers and started a fresh joint. It was low-rent to relight a roach, like a cartoon bum smoking a cigarette butt impaled on a pin. Fran's deal as opposed to Margaret's was not to show her body unless they were quote being sexual: that was hotter in the long run, though this with Margaret was also hotter. The inside of Fran's cunt was slickly muscular, Margaret's more mooshy—even rubbered up, you could feel it—though you'd expect the opposite, for some reason he couldn't articulate. Fran came louder, but Margaret more, with these fluttering contractions up inside. When he judged that she'd come enough, he started up the hill himself, got snagged thinking about the Hill Difficulty in *The Pilgrim's Progress,* then broke through into the world of light.

After a long enough time for it not to seem coldhearted, he rolled away, slid the condom off and wrapped it in bedside Kleenex. Then back shoulder to shoulder, thinking up the first thing to say. Any first thing said must of necessity be stupid, yet sooner or later one or the other of them would have to break the silence. Would it not be Christlike to take the stupidity upon himself?

"So would you have contempt for me," he said, "if this turned out to make me a better husband?"

"*What?*" she said. "Oh." She rolled onto her side, away from him. "Sorry, I'd been forgetting the context. Do you want your Zagat rating? Morgan's in better shape than you, but you're a little better as a fuck. More calculating, you know? Like trying to figure me out. It makes you seem mean."

"Huh," he said. "I would've thought solicitous."

"No, mean is good," she said.

"But at any rate," he said, "not a mercy fuck."

"I doubt that mercy comes into this." She rolled onto her back and looked up at the ceiling. "I feel sorry for that man."

"That man," Cal said. "Oh—right. The guy."

They started yet another joint and settled back on their pillows. But they'd smoked so much by now that it just wasn't doing it. She reached over. Handled him awhile, then got her mouth down.

"Hmm," he said. "This may be a lit-tle premature. Given that I'm no longer twenty-one. No longer *forty*-one."

She popped him out, still limp—he imagined the sound of a festive champagne cork—and said, "I don't believe in the soft bigotry of low expectations."

By the time they got out of bed, the sun had gone down. Cal stepped onto the deck, T-shirted and barefoot, and discovered the moon, full, its never-to-be-deciphered pattern of marks, not quite a face going *Ooh* but not quite not. Sharp chill on his arms: you could feel all of winter compacted inside it, like a Zip file.

Back inside, he sat on the bed and picked up his socks. "So tomorrow?" he called. "Up with the lark, yes? We should look at the trails."

"I *knew* it." She came out of the bathroom. "Shit. Okay." She sat down next to him on the bed and he unfolded the map. "I was thinking this one." He pointed to a trail called Moose Meadow, 5.5 kilometers, marked with a blue square. *A green circle means an easy trail. A blue square indicates a moderately difficult trail. A black diamond advertises the most difficult trail Ridgeline Lodge has to offer.* There was a mind behind this: perhaps the mind of the ear man? Look at how they varied the verbs.

"Have you ever *seen* a moose?" he said.

"Of course not. Nobody has. Have you ever seen anybody die?"

He looked at her. She was looking at the map. "*There's* a question," he said. "Not actually. I saw what was supposedly the Danny Pearl video."

"Do tell," she said.

They drove back toward the town looking for somewhere to eat. The sad little strip by the Northway had a McDonald's, a Dunkin' Donuts and a Ponderosa. "*This* is grim," she said.

"I should've asked our guy." He pointed to the Ponderosa. "Okay, now when I'm president, every one of these will be required to have an Italian place next door called L'Allegro."

They passed under the Northway. (So was she not impressed with the jeu d'esprit?) On the other side, a Stewart's and darkness beyond. "Okay, this is hopeless," she said. "Why don't we just go in here and sort of forage."

"There must be some quaintee oldee innee," he said. "I'll give our guy a jingle." He pulled into the Stewart's and got out his cell.

"Don't, okay?" she said. "I hate to think of him putting a phone up against that ear. Look, I'll get some treats and we'll have a picnic in our room."

"Okay," he said. "You've obviously got a vision of this."

Back at the cabin, she shooed him onto the deck. The moon had gone higher up and gotten smaller. As he tried to find a face in it, he heard the yodeling witch-laughter of coyotes, echoing off lake and mountains. He opened the sliding door. "You need to come hear."

Margaret stepped outside, listened and said, "Is that what I think it is? It's *horrible.* Soup's on."

She'd laid out a feast on top of the dresser: Beer Nuts, Nabs, a Hershey's Special Dark chocolate bar, a Slim Jim still in its wrapper, a rectangular bar of yellow cheese, out of its package, on a paper napkin. The pair of plastic glasses from the bathroom, poured full of Bloody Mary–looking stuff.

"Well well." He picked up the Slim Jim. "Protein suppositories. What'll they think of next." He tried to bite open the top.

"What are you *doing?*" She touched his hand. "I just thought you'd be amused. I don't want you sick. This is the low-sodium V8, incidentally." She put both arms around his waist. Side of her head against his breastbone. "So are we the two most awful people who ever lived or died?" She took a long breath, let it out. "I want this just to be exactly the way it is, you know? Even a little bit depressing."

"Aren't *you* the connoisseur," he said. "Connoisseuse."

She slid a hand inside the back of his pants, under the briefs. Dry finger at his asshole. "What would you think if I broke up with Morgan?"

"Is that in the cards?" He tightened himself.

"Isn't everything *always* in the cards?"

"Well. I guess initially I'd be sad for you."

"Okay," she said. "B plus. B." Took her hand out. "B minus." She headed for the bathroom. "I need to wash my hands. You notice their soap, by the way?"

"Should I have?"

"Cashmere Bouquet. It's so grotesque. That man with his ear, putting out the Cashmere Bouquet."

"Presumably they've got *bonne à toute faire*," he said. "I think he's more the concept guy. Or is that a pricky thing to say?"

She said, "I won't say the obvious."

He picked up his watch off the night table: ten of seven. Daylight at the bottom of the window shades. Sunday morning. Margaret was still asleep. On her stomach, head to the side, lips parted, bent arm guarding the head. Each exhale a growl down in her chest, thinning to *Sssh* as it came up and out. He considered the face: here we had what was agreed to be loveliness. But one was also supposed to intuit the pilgrim soul in there. He closed his eyes and kissed the cheek, as if a real person were kissing another person.

When he woke up again she was sitting on the bed taking off a shoe.

"It's so incredible here," she said. "I told the cleaning woman to go away so you could sleep." She dropped the shoe on the floor and started on number two. "Actually, I think it's his wife. I was down talking to him and I noticed he had a ring on."

"Wait, you were down *talking* with him? What does he talk about?"

"I don't know. He seems kind."

"Hey, anything's possible," Cal said. "So what should we do about breakfast?"

"First things first?" She reached down and started rubbing through the covers. "Or are you really hungry?" Stopped.

"I am, to tell you the truth."

She took her hand away.

"What?" he said.

"Nothing. Let's eat, then we can have the hiking segment and get *that* done."

He looked at her. "What."

She sat up and started putting her shoes back on. "I guess we *should* hike a little. Otherwise we could have just fucked at my place. *And* had a decent meal."

"Come on, I liked our picnic," he said.

"Well, now you get to have more of it."

She got up and started taking things out of the paper bag again, then froze. "Do you hear that?" Jet going over.

"What, the airplane?"

"I guess it's nothing," she said. "I always think, you know, it's starting. That would be the worst, to be caught up here."

"Yeah, wouldn't *that* surprise the nearest and dearest," he said. "'Um, sweetie? Where exactly were you when I was getting vaporized?'"

"I just have this fantasy of all these burned people who didn't die right away, just all walking north in this big mass." She shook Beer Nuts into her palm. "So what's the worst joke you know? Like the most offensive."

"I'd have to think," he said. "Okay. What sits on a wall and bleeds?"

"And *bleeds*?" she said, chewing.

"Humpty Cunt."

"Oh." She swallowed. "Well. That came readily to mind."

"What's the most offensive one *you* know?"

She shook her head. "I don't really like that word."

"Huh," he said. "Hitting limits left and right here."

He got up and went into the bathroom, closed the door to piss. Margaret—another of her peculiarities, possibly endearing—went the whole hog, not just closing the door but running the water.

When he came out, she was back in bed, covers up to her chin. The old surprise-surprise. "I *will* think this is romantic," she said.

"So," he said, "you want to fuck?"

"Oh sure." She sat up against the headboard, her clothes on. "My *cunt*," she said, "is just *dripping* for it."

When he got out of the shower, she was gone. And the half joint gone from the ashtray. Well, was this not her little interlude too? He should've made it crazier for her: pot didn't cut it these days. Handcuffs? Coke, for sure.

Somebody banged on the door, then the lock clicking, and there stood the ear guy, Margaret behind him.

"You folks are checking out," he said. "I told the lady."

"We're actually booked for tonight too," Cal said. "If you look in your—"

"You heard what I said. Fifteen minutes, that's when I'm calling the trooper."

"What the fuck—"

"The lady'll tell you about it."

"Suppose *you* tell me about it. The fuck exactly is this?"

"What the fuck this exactly *is*," the ear guy said, "is just what I said." He looked at his watch. "Fifteen minutes I call the trooper and give him your plate number. Right? We straight on that?" He stepped aside to let Margaret into the cabin. "I won't charge you the extra day. *That* oughta be a load off your mind." He walked off leaving the door open.

Margaret was cramming stuff into her bag.

"So," Cal said. "Will *the lady* be good enough to tell me what the fuck happened?"

She didn't turn around. "He's a total asshole."

"And here I thought he was one of nature's gentlemen. So what happened?"

"Let's just go," she said. "Before he really has us busted."

"What did you do, smoke up in *front* of him?"

She grabbed the bag and went into the bathroom. He heard something clunk into the tub.

"Hey," he called. "I asked you something."

She came out and stood in the bathroom doorway. " 'I asked you something'?" she said. "Who the fuck *are* you? I told him I'd get high with him if he wanted. Okay?"

"Are you insane?" he said. "What, you came *on* to him?"

"And now would you fucking get out of my sight? Out of my field of vision?"

When he took a step toward her, she drew back her hand to hit him.

"Okay, we need to get out of here," he said.

As they drove past the office, he saw a lanky woman in a pink uniform standing on the steps, watching them go.

"Here, I'll tell you a story," she said as they passed the exit for Warrensburg. "Will *that* put you in a better mood?"

"I'm sure," he said. They hadn't spoken since she'd told him to drop her where she could get a bus and he'd said that seemed appropriate.

"You're not very encouraging," she said. She lit another cigarette. "Okay, when my father was in the hospital? He was in so much pain that he told my mother, if she didn't bring him these pills he had? That he was going to get God to send her to hell. He was going to, like, intercede with God. So when he was actually, *finally* going out, after, you know, months of this, my mother and I were each holding one of his hands, and he was whimpering. As if he was, like, coming."

"How long ago was this?" he said.

She shook her head. "And I had this thing where I couldn't stop giggling. And my mother slapped me. And right then, like that second, he went *Haa* and you could feel it in the room—everything, I don't know, *shimmered,* and you could just feel it go."

"How old were you?" he said.

Shook her head again. "This is *my* story." She took a drag of cigarette. "I don't need your editorial guidance."

———

He walked from Hertz up to Ninety-Sixth and Broadway; it seemed important that he get across Ninety-Sixth before taking out his cell. "Listen, I'm around the corner," he said. "I got Miltoned out. You want me to pick anything up?"

"Oh, *good*," Fran said. "Good good good. I mean, not good that you're Miltoned *out*, but you know, good that you're *back*. I was just in the middle of playing the piano and we were *just* about to call Flor de Mayo. This is amazing, you couldn't *possibly* have timed this better."

Cammy's voice: "Is that Daddy?"

"I see," he said. "Well. Good."

"Yes, it's Daddy. She's pumping her fist. She's not really, but that's the mood, or I guess that's the *vibe*. I can't quite put my finger on what the mood is."

He took the elevator up and stood for a moment at the door, hearing the piano inside. It was that Schubert Impromptu—she'd never been able to get that *Nude Descending a Staircase* cascade of notes quite clean. One time he'd caught her listening to the Mitsuko Uchida recording, weeping. "Well," he'd said, "you're a lot better looking." She'd said, "Fuck you, too." When his key touched the lock he saw a pinprick of spark, betraying the hot energy bound in all things.

In the living room, Fran sat at the piano, backlit by sunset. Her calves below the piano bench, right leg forward left leg back, butt spread fetchingly, her chin up like an inspired Lisztian virtuoso's, her hair hanging straight down and shimmying like a hula skirt. He sneaked the door shut, stood listening, then eased down to sit, knees up, against the wall in the foyer.

When she finished, he began to clap.

She turned around: "Oh, come come come. None of that. You'll turn a girl's head."

"So where's the Caminator?" he said.

She pointed with a thumb down the hall. "Denned up. Like a wolf cub. Like a flower, like a fire, like a fresh footfall in a long-forgotten snow."

He rapped a knuckle on Cammy's door.

"Daddy," she said. She looked toward the living room. "I've been counting. That was the seventeenth *time*."

"For what?"

"That she's *played* that."

"Babe, why didn't you call me? Has there been, you know, behavior?"

"Not really. Just a lot of the piano."

"Did she get any sleep?"

"It's okay," Cammy said. "It wasn't all that bad."

"Well. I'm back now. I wish you'd called me."

"So Daddy?" she said. "Can you help me with geometry?"

He sat at Cammy's computer; she knelt, a hand on his knee. *If two sides and the included angle of one triangle are congruent to two sides and the included angle of a second triangle, the two triangles are congruent.* "I don't get why they even need to *have* this," she said. "I mean, Duh-*uh*. All you have missing is the last side. Figure it *out*."

"Right, I see what you mean," he said. "Listen, let me go get a feel for things, and then I'll come back and we'll swarm all over this puppy."

He went to the kitchen and opened a beer.

"So," Fran called. "Did you have your father-daughter moment?" He came into the living room; she was still sitting at the piano. "I am *fine*, by the way, thank you very much for asking. Oh God, I sound so *critical*. What can I play for you? I've been on a total run with Schubert. As I imagine you've been told. Now what would you most like?" He'd had this said to him last night in a different context. "It doesn't have to be Schubert. Tell you the truth, I think I'm *done* with Schubert."

"Anything," he said. "Maybe something on the austere side. Not a heartbreaker."

"Oh, that is *you*," she said. "Well. You in *one* mode. God, I hope I don't sound as critical as I *sound*. Well. Austere. Yes. We have just the thing. Almost just the thing."

She began to play, from memory, the first of the Two-Part Inventions. He listened to the two lines of notes snaking around each other. Amazing, still, in the general what-a-piece-of-work-is-man sort of way, even if no longer something to love a person for.

Margaret kicked in her Bottom Feeder piece on Tuesday, attached to an email saying it was her last, and to send whatever checks she had coming care of Sylvia Moss—was that the mother?—at an address in Jupiter, Florida. It was unpublishable and unfixable. It started out with her on the bus from Albany and a TV up front blaring game shows and then to how the planet was done for—okay, no argument there—and human life was a virus. (Wasn't that in *Naked Lunch*?) She said it would be better to get shot trying to kill the president than to die "the slow death of consent"—an arresting phrase, but what did it mean, exactly? She said the whole ride long she pictured New York nuked before she could get there, then how sorry she was to see that it wasn't. Then she had stuff in there about cancer—how did that connect to anything? Where would you even begin?

George Lassos Moon

||||||

Aunt Lissa's saying something very serious, and bad Carl's playing with the metal creamer thing. He thumbs the lid up, lets it drop. Tiny clank. Aunt Lissa says, "Are you following?"

"Absolutely."

"Give me strength." Big sigh. "All right, enough said. What'll it be? I don't imagine you've been eating."

"Coffee," he says, which makes him sound blown away (like he's *not*) because he's got a cup right in front of him. He just means he's fine.

"You've got to eat a *little* something."

"Let me look in the Book of Life." He lifts the menu from the metal rack. "Pray *Jee*-zus that mah name be written thar." Inside they've got a color picture of a hot dog with gleaming highlights. "This is incredible," he says.

"Why am I doing this?" Aunt Lissa says.

"You're an enabler," he says. "That's a joke." He'd better start marking them as such.

"Carl. You do understand what's going on, yes? Could you look at me?"

He sees in Aunt Lissa's eyeglasses a miniature glimpse of his own face. Boy, he is never taking drugs again, except down drugs. "You mean do I know I got arrested?" he says. He rubs his fingers back and forth across the stubble on his jaw, and it sounds exactly, *exactly*, like sawing wood. He's even going to get off the Paxil, which makes like an empty space underneath your consciousness.

"Thank heaven for little mercies." She looks at her watch. A man's watch. "I still don't quite— You were visiting somebody here?"

"Long story." He thumbs up the lid of the creamer again. Lets it down without a sound.

"I don't want to know, do I?" She checks the watch again. "Now, what about your job? Do you need to call them? I assume this is a working day."

"Hey, works for me," he says. "Joke."

"All right. I've done my duty," she says. "I guess I should tell you, I called Elaine. I had no idea you two were . . ."

"Right," he says. "Actually, you know what I actually want? I actually want waffles." He holds his palms six inches apart to show her the squareness.

"Is there anything you *would* like to talk about?"

He picks up his fork and drags the tines across the paper napkin. "Okay, what movie?"

"What movie *what*?"

He nods. "Think about it."

"You know," she says, "since your hearing isn't until Friday? Why don't we go down to the farm for a couple of days. I'm sure Henry would like to see you."

"What, are you on the pipe?" He wouldn't mind just staying right here. He looks down at his feet under the table: wet running shoes in a puddle of snowmelt. He'd patched them with Shoe Goo where the soles were separating from the uppers: so much for this, what's the word, this *canard* that he doesn't take care of himself. This *duck*.

"He *is* your brother," Aunt Lissa says.

The waffles arrive, and Carl mooshes the ball of butter with his fork. "You never guessed my movie."

"I'm afraid I'm not following," she says.

He sucks the fork clean, drags the tines across his napkin again and holds it up so she can see the marks.

"Wait," she says. "This *is* ringing a bell."

"Should." He puts the napkin in his lap. "You took me to see it. Film series they used to have?"

She claps her hands. "Of course." Shakes her head. "What could I have been thinking of? You were all of what?" She watches him pour syrup. "If I could have just a bite," she says, "I'd be your friend for life."

When they get to the car, Aunt Lissa paws in her purse, then looks in the window. "I *knew* I left the keys in the switch," she says. "Is your side locked?"

"You don't have a spare?"

"Actually, I— Oh, *damn it*. It's under the hood, and of course you can't— Oh. This is *so* exasperating. Well, there's a gas station." He looks where she's looking. Sunoco: sky blue, sun yellow. "Maybe they have one of those things you stick through the window. Don't ever get old."

"Yeah, I wouldn't worry."

"Pooh. Just because— I don't know. We don't have time for this discussion now."

"Good," he says. "You want me to go over?"

"It's nice of you, dear. But I think I'd better."

Aunt Lissa's driving him down the Thruway into the snow country. It's the pea-soup Volvo Uncle Martin bought the year he died, and she still steers strong handed, chin jutting. She'd looked older when she showed up at the jail, but now she's settled back into Aunt Lissa.

Drunk driving. Which is the most incredible joke in the world because he was only drinking to try to ease down off the other shit. In fact, hadn't he gotten stopped right along here somewhere, near the exit for Coxsackie? He had Hot Country Radio going because the Best of the Sixties, Seventies and Eighties had started playing *Here come old flattop*, which was *not* a helpful song when you just wanted words that hooked up to something. At one point he caught himself watching for the place where his parents died, except that was on the Connecticut Turnpike, near exit 63. Meanwhile he was working on a theory that if he could make it as far as Kingston he'd be okay. He had a bottle of Old Crow between his thighs, sticking up like a peepee, or a tepee— you know, as in "sticking up like a tent pole"—which he put there precisely *because* it was a joke. Here, let's spell it out: being drunk fucks up your sexual performance. When the cop pulled him over, he turned the radio off but decided that hiding the bottle would look furtive. The cop said, "And do you know how fast you were going, Carl?" And Carl said, "I think I got carried away by the radio," which was *not* a surreal saying but just the very, very traditional association of uptempo songs with driving fast. He pointed at the radio as evidence. The cop said, "You were going twenty miles an hour."

Black trees are sticking up out of the white hillsides. Sky seems white, too. He closes one eye and looks from hills to sky, then back again. Maybe what it is, the sky's a darker white? Aunt Lissa's telling him, again, the story of how she and Uncle Martin came to buy the place in Germantown. The house just *spoke to her,* that's her formulation, so they stopped and an old woman came to the door. "We were admiring your house and just decided to stop and tell you so." And the old woman said, "Well, it happens to be for sale, and my son's coming tomorrow to put a sign up." They bought the house, Henry bought the hill.

Carl thinks Aunt Lissa might in fact have turned *into* that old woman, but maybe that's just to scare himself. As a kid, he used to scare himself for real by thinking that his mother, to keep from dying, had magically turned herself into Aunt Lissa on the Connecticut Turnpike when she saw that his father was steering them across the divider. Since his mother and Aunt Lissa were sisters, it seemed believable. He would watch Aunt Lissa's face and see his mother in there, coming and going.

They take the exit for Catskill and Cairo and pass an abandoned cinder-block store with plywood in the windows and a Henry Craig Realty sign. "Hammerin' Hank," Carl says to Aunt Lissa. "Now, that has to make a brother proud." Zero reaction.

She takes him to Walmart, where he picks out a three-pack of Fruit of the Loom briefs, three black Fruit of the Loom pocket tees, a gray hooded sweatshirt (90-10 cotton-polyester, which is incredible for just some mystery brand), a package of white socks and a pair of Wrangler blue jeans. The darker blue to last him longer. Aunt Lissa says she'll treat him but he says, No, no, he has money, like flipping his cigarette away before the firing squad.

Coming around the last corner, he tries to see if he can tell independently what it was about the house that *spoke to her*. It'll be a test of his—let's say this exactly—his *congruence*. He squints and says in his mind, *Okay, now what exactly is the charming feature here?* Like, *There are x number of bunnies hidden in this picture, can you find them?* Could it be the wooden filigree along the porch? No, because "form follows function" is a major theme in world aesthetics, and Aunt Lissa takes the train down for shows at the Modern. Yet olden fanciness is also one of her themes; she gardens with heirloom varieties. See, this is the kind of shit he needs to be able to sort out again.

She parks by the kitchen door, then reaches under and yanks the hood release. "Fool me twice, shame on me. Could you get the groceries?" She lifts the hood and pulls a magnetic Hide-a-Key box off the engine block. "Voilà." Closes the hood and tucks the box up under the front bumper. "Bingo. You don't think anybody would look there, do you?"

"*I* wouldn't," he says.

Up the hill behind Aunt Lissa's house, Henry's lights are on and white smoke snake-charms out of his metal chimney. Can you actually own a *hill*? Half a hill, really, but it's like the moon in that no one sees the side that's turned away. Down low in the sky, there's an orange light that tints the snow. He takes the grocery bags, follows Aunt Lissa onto the screened-in porch and stands shivering while she rattles a key in the storm door. "We never used to lock up," she says. If this were a movie scene, you'd cut right here.

He closes the door behind him and rubs his feet on the hairy brown mat. That old-refrigerator smell of an empty house in winter. Aunt Lissa clomps in her flopping rubber boots to the thermostat and the house goes bump; then she clomps into the kitchen. Carl hears water running. The *foomp* of a lighted burner.

She comes back in, rubbing the knuckles of one hand, then the other. "It should warm up soon," she says. "I keep the downstairs at fifty." She pulls a chair over to the register. "Water's on for tea."

"You have coffee?"

"Instant."

He makes a cross with his index fingers.

"It's terrible for you anyway." She sits down, still wearing her coat. "Supposed to be a full moon tonight. I hope it doesn't cloud over again."

"'When the moon is in the sky,'" he sings, "'tell me what am I, to do?' So what movie?" He thinks he hears a car, gets up and goes to the window. A Grand Cherokee's pulling up behind the Volvo, headlights beaming, its grille a toothy smile. "Huh. Looks like a small businessman."

"Be nice."

The headlights go out, the car door opens. "Yep," he says. "Big as life and twice as natural."

Aunt Lissa turns on the porch light. There's Henry wiping his feet.

"I saw you drive in, so I thought I'd stop down," Henry says. "Carl?"

"Yo, mah buvva," Carl says. "You keepin' it real, yo?" Henry cocks his head. "You know, like real estate."

"I'm not up on my jive talk." Henry turns to Aunt Lissa. "Why don't you come on up to the house while it's getting warm in here? Connie's making soup."

"Yum," Aunt Lissa says. "We might stop up later. How about some tea? I just put water on."

Henry twists the sleeve of his leather jacket. "So how'd it go?"

"Well, I suppose it was fine," Aunt Lissa says. "I don't have a lot in my experience to compare it to."

"Hell, I should've done this."

"But you had your closing. It was perfectly fine."

Henry looks at Carl. "So what were *you* doing up this way?"

Carl looks at the tabletop. Honey oak with flamelike grain. "I don't know, long story."

"Aren't they all. The hell happened to your face?"

Carl shakes his head.

"Christ," Henry says. "Shouldn't he be back in detox?"

"I hate to do it," Aunt Lissa says.

"He goes up in front of a judge in this kind of shape, they'll do it *for* you."

"I think what Carl needs most is just to get some rest," she says.

"*I* think what Carl needs most," Carl says, "is a good old pop of Demerol. Speaking as Carl."

He knows Henry heard this because something jumps in that fat throat. "They're probably going to want him in some kind of a program."

"Hey, *Teletubbies*," Carl says. "Believe it or not that's an incredibly cool show."

"This is funny to you?" Henry says.

Aunt Lissa gets up, so whatever the noise is that's been going on for a while now must be the whistling teakettle. Good that it's *something*. "Now, what's anybody's pleasure?" she says. "We have Earl Grey, plain old Lipton's, chamomile . . . green tea?" Sad: back when she used to read him *The Tale of Peter Rabbit,* she said camo-*myle.*

"Actually I better hit it back up the hill." Henry looks out the window. "Supposed to snow again."

"Sorry, this is kind of getting to me," Carl says and goes into the kitchen, where steam's whistling out of the little pisshole. He takes the kettle off the burner and the noise stops.

"Lissa," he hears Henry say, "are you sure you're up to this?" Or maybe he said "listen."

"Oh, for heaven's sake," she says.

He hears the door close, and Aunt Lissa comes into the kitchen. "You had to show off for him."

"He's a dick. Pardon the expression." Carl hears the Cherokee start up.

"I know the expression," she says. "Now help me put this stuff away."

"Is that a denial?" he says.

"You," she says, "are wicked."

How all this current shit started, he'd gotten involved with a person in the city who was also originally from Albany—okay, Schenectady— and when they'd been together a couple of days, she'd thought up this idea. Rent a car, both get as much cash as possible from their cash machines (this was like a Saturday night), buy whatever they could find, drive upstate to her parents' house, her parents being in Florida, and sell it at a major markup to all these people she still knew. This was a very young person: cigarette smoker, chopped-off hair bleached white. Tiny stud in her left nostril like a blackhead and seven gold rings around her left ear, nothing in her right, so when she tried out for modeling jobs she could give them two different looks.

She was temping at the place he worked, filling in for somebody's assistant. Carl at this point was sort of not living at home anymore, big troubles in Our Marriage (Elaine's formulation), staying with people, carrying his laptop and a duffel bag with clothes and DVDs. What was weird, he didn't *feel* weird. This was thanks to the Paxil, which he was now getting through two doctors at two drugstores, because the one doctor had said 40 milligrams was "rather a lot." And he was using again on top of it, but not big-time, and mostly to help him write: he'd been posting stuff about *42nd Street* on what was really a very serious website.

any dickhead can see that dorothy brock (bebe daniels) is the same person as peggy sawyer (ruby keeler), but the scrim of gender may prevent said dickhead from discerning that julian marsh (warner baxter) is also mutatis mutandis a projection of the "sweet" sawyer's nut-cutting inner self, the very name suggesting she'd "saw off" your "peg" to "get a leg up," it being no accident that brock's "broken" (note further pun) leg is sawyer's big "break."

He told the temp with the rings in her ear that there were all too few outlaws on the seventeenth floor, and said Albany was their shared shame. Then she was bold enough to show up at the Christmas party when she'd only worked there a week. He said could he get her a drink—he was on like number three—and she said, "So how much of an outlaw are *you*?" He held up his left hand, worked his wedding band off and said, "Observe me closely." He pinched it between thumb and forefinger, showed her both sides, put it in his mouth and swallowed. It scraped going down, but no worse than swallowing, say, a hard candy. And it would, in theory, be recoverable. He chased it with a last swallow, put his glass down and pulled his cheeks open with his forefingers. She looked in his glass, then looked at him. "How did you do that? Let me see your hands."

Anyhow, you'll never guess what happened: they ended up using most of the shit themselves. They pretty much stayed in her parents' bed, watching cable, DVDs on Carl's laptop and a video called *Barely 18* that her father kept duct-taped up inside his radial saw. And *Monday Night Football,* which is how they figured out it was now Monday, or *had* been. Carl called his supervisor's voice mail and said he had the flu. This Kerri—he'd briefly thought the *i* was a turn-on—called whoever's voice mail it was and said she had food poisoning. Carl pointed out how stupid this was because she'd have to come up with something else tomorrow. And she said, "It would've been nice if you'd said that before."

They'd gotten like two of their eight hundred dollars back when they had this fight—*literally* a fight, where she was hitting him and he hurt her wrists trying to hold her and she told him, "Get the fuck out, just get the fuck out." She'd dug it that it took him forever to come— the Paxil plus the other shit made an orgasm just too high to climb up to—and then she stopped digging it. "I don't like you, I don't *know* you." She hit first, remember that. He grabbed her wrists with both hands, found he didn't have a third hand to hit her with, then tried to get both her wrists in one hand to free up the other, and she broke loose and hit again, "Get out get out," in the middle of the night, middle of the afternoon, actually.

So he got in his car and made it onto the main drag, just barely, where he pulled into some non-Dunkin' donut place, like an indie donut, guided the car between yellow lines and closed his eyes: it looked like all these flash cameras going off. No chance he could drive all the way back down to the city like this. Had to get something to take the edge off, and he had no idea where you went in Albany anymore. Sure, Aunt Lissa would put him up, but he was in no shape to deal with her: she was in the sort of space where she'd be "hurt" if he'd "come to town and didn't call." He had an incredibly scary thought that it was her sitting in the car next to his, but when he nerved himself to look it was just one of those Winnie-the-Pooh pictures.

He went in and bought a fat old sugar donut, which he thought might weight him down, take him earthward, but he had to spit the mouthful into a napkin. In all fairness, maybe it really did taste nasty. At least there must be a liquor store open, unless it was already Sunday again.

Morning sun on snow. Clean blue sky.

Carl's sitting at the kitchen table looking out the window. Aunt Lissa's gone to town for the paper and left him with what she biblically called "tea with milk and honey," though it's hard to trust its dimensionality: it appears to be a flat khaki disk fitted into the cup. Halfway up the hill, Henry's house is hanging there and snow clings along the tops of the tree branches in simplified versions of their shapes, and dead apples, like dog-toy balls, hang from the leafless tree. Some of the apples have a curve of snow on top, like a phase of the moon.

When he hears Aunt Lissa's car, he gets up and turns the radio back on. The good-morning classical music had been sounding too much like thoughts racing. What we've got now is some sprightly guitar piece. Almost certainly not a harp.

She sets the *Times* before him like the dainty dish before the king. "Voilà," she says. "Glorious morning out." She drapes her coat over the back of a chair. "Now, what would you like? I can fix pancakes, we have oatmeal . . ."

He shakes his head, holds up a hand.

"Toast? You can't not eat."

"Let me guess. Is breakfast the most important meal, do you think?"

"Stop."

"What about the importance of dietary fiber?" That was when he remembered about the ring. Long gone. Must be.

"You're welcome to sit here and make witticisms to yourself," she says. "I've got to work on my presentation." Aunt Lissa's reading group is doing *To the Lighthouse* next week.

"Don't we all," he says.

He manages to hold back from retching until he hears her on the stairs, then gags up nothing and feels sweat popping out of his face. After a while, he stands up and sees how that feels. He scrunches up a slice of bread in his fist to make a bolus and eats it just for something solid. Then pops his Paxil and puts his mouth under the faucet. The cop got a hard-on, of course, when he found the Paxil—"And what've we got here, Carl?"—but they had to give it back. Actually, he really needs just to get off absolutely everything and purify, purify, purify. On the other hand, don't the laws of physics suggest that all this not-unhappiness will have to be paid for by an equal and opposite period of negative happiness, an equal distance below the baseline? Lately he's big on the idea of being nice to the right people on the way up because you're going to meet them again coming down, "people" meaning entities in your mind.

He goes back up to the guest room to lie down again. For a night-stand, she's put a lamp on a small mission bookshelf that she's stocked with light reading. He picks out *Try and Stop Me,* by Bennett Cerf, and stacks the two pillows against the headboard. The idea is what, that Bennett Cerf has so many stories you better not try to stop him? Carl's studying a cartoon of Dorothy Parker hurling a giant pen like a javelin when Aunt Lissa knocks on his open door.

"I was going through some pictures the last time I came down here." She holds up an envelope. "I was going to get these copied for you, and then of course I forgot all about it. Don't ever get old."

"Yeah, you warned me about that." He claps hands, then holds them out, meaning *Throw it.* She comes over and reaches it out to him.

He flips through with Aunt Lissa in his peripheral vision. The one of him as a baby, held by his mother wearing a black dress and pearl necklace, his father in a tuxedo, grinning like Mr. Skeleton, his fingers making a V behind her head. The one of Uncle Martin pitching to him in the backyard in Albany, when he was like eleven and had Henry's old Hank Aaron bat, with "Hank" in quotes. The one of him at six, in that red flannel cowboy shirt with the white pinstripes and slant pockets. Chubby cheeks. Little heartbreaker.

"*These* cover the waterfront," he says.

"Now, you can't have them until I make copies."

"I don't know where I'd even keep them right now."

"Well, they'll be here. You know, it's *such* a glorious day. You really should go out and get some fresh air."

Outside, the cold makes his face sting, but he can feel no difference to his body thanks to Uncle Martin's old Eddie Bauer coat. Maybe she'll give it to him: a hoodie under a denim jacket doesn't really cut it. He walks as far as the corner, to the house with the sign on the lawn that says STOP THE DREDGING. This is about the Hudson River.

Walking back to Aunt Lissa's he sees something else that could have spoken to her: the vine that—losing the word here—*ornates?* That ornates the porch in summertime and is now this brown wire-like arrangement clinging to the chalky posts. Does green somehow seep back up into it, or could a whole new vine grow quickly enough to replace itself every year? Both seem impossible, yet one must be true. But he remembers the name: Dutchman's pipe. Now there's something that hangs together: when he was a kid, Uncle Martin used to have this expression for a hopeful patch of blue among the clouds, *Enough to make a Dutchman a pair of britches.* It gave you the idea of big people living in the sky.

When the phone rings, he's back looking at *Try and Stop Me.* He can't really follow the anecdotes, but he's into the cartoons. In one, captioned "Mankiewicz en riposte," a smirking man removes a cigarette from his mouth and blows a cloud of smoke with an arrow in it at a quailing man. Now are we talking Joe or Herman? Carl knows this Hollywood shit cold.

Aunt Lissa calls, "Carl? For you." He gets up off the bed, pads out into the hall with socks sliding on the glossy floor and looks down the stairs at her looking up. "Elaine."

The phone on the kitchen wall is still the only one in the house. Aunt Lissa's going to break her neck some night coming down those stairs. Because of the socks, he's extra careful himself.

"Carl. Hi. I just wanted to make sure you were okay."

"Oh yeah. You know, thanks."

"Lissa called me yesterday. Apparently she didn't know that we, you know . . ."

"Right," he says.

"I hope you didn't mind that I told her."

"No, no. God no." He picks up Aunt Lissa's egg timer. Such an amazing touch, giving the Wicked Witch red sand. "So," he says. Like, *To what do we owe the pleasure?*

"I really didn't call because I want anything," she says.

"Right." He sees something move out the side window. Just a gray squirrel across the snow.

"So are you using again? Or just drinking?"

"Neither one. You know, to any degree." He would actually like to steal this egg timer. Whip it out at parties. He puts it back, sand side down.

"Well, so how come they busted you?"

"Oh, you know. Just a stupid thing. Open container."

"I heard it was a little more than that."

"Well, you know. They throw in the kitchen sink to make it sound really dire."

"Did I tell you somebody called about the guitar? He wanted to know if you'd take less."

"Like how much?"

"He didn't really say. I've got his number here."

"Look, why don't you just call him, get whatever you can get and keep the money, you know?"

"Okay, look," she says, "let's not worry about the money for now."

But Carl heard that *for now,* don't think he didn't.

———

He wakes up to the smell of something yummy. It's like a famous smell, but he can't come up with the name. Not coriander—something more household. He goes down to the kitchen.

"You must've needed that nap," Aunt Lissa says. Something's hissing in the skillet. Onion! She gets under it with the spatula. Louder hissing. "I thought I'd make a quiche to take up. Connie asked us for around seven."

"Cool."

"I know it's not the most comfortable thing for you."

"You figured that out," he says.

"I must say, they *have* been wonderful."

"In all fairness," he says.

She pokes a fingernail through the plastic that covers a bouquet of parsley on a Styrofoam tray and plows it open. A nosegay? "You know, I often think we made a mistake keeping Henry at Mount Hermon after the accident. If we'd brought him back to Albany to finish high school, maybe you two would've had a better chance at . . ." She takes the parsley over to the sink.

"Bonding?" he says.

"It's easy to make light of it."

"Yeah, I guess I'm just a merry Andrew," he says. "Like a merry widow."

She turns the water on and begins washing the parsley.

"God, I'm sorry," he says. "I didn't mean anything by that."

"I do all right," she says.

He watches her dry the parsley in a dish towel.

"So when I get this in the oven," she says, "what do you say we try on that suit? You'll want to look as respectable as we both know you really are."

"Now that hurts," he says.

Up in her bedroom, she opens the closet door and pushes jingling hangers to the side. "I gave his suits to Goodwill, but he kept this one here just in case." She holds up a gray suit with fat lapels.

"I hear these are coming back," Carl says.

"Never you mind. Let's see the jacket on you."

Carl pulls it on. Tight in his armpits and across the shoulders, sleeves too short.

She lifts the pants up to his front. "They've obviously mistaken me for a much shorter man," he says.

"Maybe I can let the cuffs down," she says. "We'll make this work."

By seven o'clock it's already down in the zeros, but Aunt Lissa insists they walk up the hill. Carl puts on the Eddie Bauer, Aunt Lissa hands him the quiche to carry and they step out into the cold. She doesn't know he found that vodka under the kitchen sink, so he keeps his distance. Sky's so incredibly clear there looks to be nothing between you and the stars, as if "the atmosphere" were an old-school theory like phlogiston.

"Jim!" he says when Henry opens the door. "They didn't tell me *you* were here. It was *grand* of you to come."

Henry says, "Let's not let the cold in, shall we?"

"Where do I put this?" Carl says.

"What is it?"

"I thought I'd make a quiche," Aunt Lissa says.

"Christ, you didn't have to do that." Henry holds out his hands. "Should it go in the oven?"

"Wouldn't hurt just to warm it up," Aunt Lissa says.

She takes one end of the couch, Carl the other. Over on the sideboard, glass decanters with silver tags like good doggies: scotch, rye, brandy. At different levels, but all the same amber.

Connie comes in from the kitchen, wearing black leggings as if she were a slim person, and a big sweater that comes way down. "Lissa, that was so nice of you. Carl? Good to see you too." She bends down to give Lissa a kiss, and Carl can't help but see her movieolas swing forward.

"Now what can I get everybody? Tea? Hot chocolate?"

"I wouldn't mind just a touch of that port you had the other night," Aunt Lissa says. "And I bet Carl would take you up on the hot chocolate."

"Yeah, let's go crazy," Carl says. That vodka could use a booster, but he can bide his time. Shit, if he gets a second alone in here, he can tip up a decanter.

"Carl, you haven't changed a bit," Connie says.

"Me either," Carl says. She gets a look on her face like, *What?*

They eat while watching *Who Wants to Be a Millionaire;* Connie says she's "totally hooked on it." It's a new one on Carl, but he likes the part where the host guy and the person are sitting across from each other in the middle of space and the damned-soul voices are going, "Ah, ah, ah." There's a question asking if Mata Hari was a spy during (a) World War I, (b) World War II, (c) the Vietnam War or (d) the Gulf War? The person says, (b) World War II, and Aunt Lissa says it amazes her what people don't know. Henry says it amazes him what people *do* know, like when they get into those questions about rock bands. Connie wants to know, what exactly *is* trivia? Because to one person it may be trivial, but. When the show's over, Henry gets out the cards for gin rummy and asks what would anybody like. A touch more of that port for Aunt Lissa, Diet Coke for Connie, same for Carl. Henry gets himself a glassful of ice and pours in scotch. Carl is absolutely fine with this. If nothing else, he'll eventually get another crack at that vodka. He fans his cards out and holds them up to his face for a sneaky smell of them.

At ten o'clock, Henry puts on the news. Big fire in Albany, hoses arching icy rooster tails in the dark and a young woman talking into a microphone and blowing out white breath. "The apparent cause?" she says. "A faulty heating unit."

"A faulty crack pipe," Henry says.

"Now, you don't know that," Connie says.

"I know that part of *town*."

She gets up. "I better put that stuff in the dishwasher."

Aunt Lissa gets up too. "Let me give you a hand."

Now there's a thing about the dredging, people in parkas holding signs. "Those GE fuckers have got the yahoos stirred up," Henry says. "The money they spend buying ads, they could have cleaned *up* the fucking PCBs."

"Wait, so you think they *should* dig up the river?" Carl had assumed Henry was a Republican.

"What do you, just let sleeping dogs lie? That philosophy hasn't gotten *you* too far. You go to court tomorrow, right? I guess if you manage not to lose your shit in front of the judge, they'll let you off with a fine. Yank your license, of course."

"I don't plan to lose my shit," Carl says.

"They're going to want cash, probably. How much you have?"

"Couple hundred." That was before the clothes.

"It's going to be more than that. So you were going to do what? Hit *her* up?" Henry tosses his head in the direction of the kitchen. "Look, call my office. Here." Lifts a hip as if to fart, digs out his wallet, hands Carl a card. "Or call my cell. I might be out showing. That's got all my numbers. Let me know how much, and I'll drive up there."

"You're kidding. Well. Thanks." Carl looks at the card, then reaches up under his sweatshirt and puts it in his T-shirt pocket.

"So I'm assuming you don't need to be here past tomorrow. Correct?"

"I honestly haven't been thinking."

"Well, why don't you honestly get cracking and *do* a little thinking. I mean, I know you're the one damaged soul in God's green universe."

Carl gives him the finger, but Aunt Lissa's coming in from the kitchen and he converts it to scratching his nose. "We should think about getting down the hill," she says to Henry. "We need to be there by ten."

Henry gets up. "Well, let me run you down."

"The air'll do us good. Do *me* good, anyway. That last glass of port was one too many."

"Then you should definitely let me drive you."

"Oh, pooh," she says. She crooks her elbow at Carl. "I've got my protector here."

When they get outside, the moon's up: big, round, alarming. Carl says, "George Lassos Moon. You remember she draws the picture?"

Aunt Lissa stops walking. "This looks a little slippery through here," she says. "Could I have your arm till we get past this part?"

Carl raises an elbow and feels her hands clamp around the puffy sleeve. He takes a couple of baby steps: now she's got *him* worried. "So what movie?" he says. "Easy one."

"I'm sorry, dear," she says. "I've had enough for one night."

The morning sun's on their right as Aunt Lissa drives them up to Albany. Carl's pulled the visor over, but he can't face too far left because he had a couple of pulls at that vodka bottle when she went up to brush her teeth after breakfast; he's opened his window a crack to let out fumes. He also shook his Paxils into an envelope and poured the vial full; only a shot, but it could come in handy. Another blinding day. The Eddie Bauer is draped over his seat back. The pavement's wet and Aunt Lissa has to keep squirting fluid and using the wipers to clear the salt spatter.

"I wonder," she says. "Do you remember much about when you first came to live with us?"

"Yeah, I thought it was weird that all my stuff was there but it was in the wrong room," he says, at the windshield. "That incredible wallpaper. The bucking broncos?"

"Now that," she says, "was Martin's idea," and he knows the whole rest word for word. *I remember he came* "I remember he came back from the store with the rolls under his arm, and he said," *Now this is what* "'Now this is what a six-year-old boy would like.'" Aunt Lissa's spin on this deal has always been that she and Martin just picked up where his parents left off, as if it deeply made no difference who anybody was.

"You know," Carl says, "I don't think I ever even said I appreciated what you guys did."

She does another wiper thing. "You can't be serious. I still have that lovely letter you wrote the day you graduated from high school."

"That," he says. "Yeah. But I guess the point is, here I am again."

"This too shall pass," she says. "I'm just glad I'm still able to help."

"What, the son you never had?" He says this as an experiment, to see how it would feel to do a one-eighty and be mean.

"I imagine there's something of that." Aunt Lissa shakes her head. "Do you want to *really* talk?"

"Probably not," he says.

Sign for the New Baltimore Travel Plaza.

"I need to use the restroom," she says. "Shall we get you some coffee? They have a Starbucks now."

"I thought it was bad for you."

"You *told* me I was an enabler," she says. "You know, you still make the mistake of thinking you can see everyone and no one can see you. It was cute when you were six."

He shades his eyes and looks out his window below the visor. A farmhouse with a metal chimney goes by.

"Have you thought about what you're going to do?" she says.

"I guess take a bus back down to the city." He needs to make some calls and see who he might be able to stay with.

"I mean in the longer term."

"Oh. Yeah, I thought I'd run for Congress. Mah fellamericans . . ."

"Give me strength," she says. "Isn't there a chance that you and Elaine . . . I don't know. I've barely met Elaine." She swings left to pass a station wagon, a golden retriever pacing behind the dog gate, then into the right lane again.

"Well, I *would* say you could come up and stay with me until things get straightened out. It's not that you're not welcome."

"But what would Henry say, right?"

"Henry can say whatever he damn well pleases. I suppose he'd be right."

In the service area, she parks next to a Sidekick with skis on the roof rack. A leg sticks out the driver's window: sheathed in metallic blue, the foot in some robot sneaker. It's a pretty woman with iridescent blue sunglasses and big blond kinky hair, tipping a flat silver flask into her mouth. She sees him looking and lifts the flask as if to toast. Outlaw recognition? Or does she mean to scandalize, mistaking him for what he must look like, in his suit and tie?

Aunt Lissa, getting out of the car, misses the whole thing. "Aren't you coming in?"

"I'll just hang."

He watches her go inside, then gets out of the car. He pries the cap off the pill vial, raises it to toast, says "Cheers" to the woman and drains the fucker. In goes her leg and up goes her window. He walks around to the front of Aunt Lissa's car, squats, feels behind the bumper and plucks away the little metal box. Then he walks over to the Sidekick and circles his fist counterclockwise. The woman puts her window halfway down.

"How about I race you to New York?" he says. "Loser buys the first round."

"I'm waiting for my friend," she says. "Anyway, aren't you going north?"

"So I'll race you to what? Lake Placid."

She puts up her window.

"Bitch," he says. But again just experimentally, like pretending to be somebody who'd hit on a woman and then call her a bitch.

He gets into the driver's seat, his bottom warmed by Aunt Lissa's leftover heat, and sticks the key in the ignition. If he were to drive away, she'd be fine here: all she'd need to do is go back inside and call Henry. Who of course would make her call the police—no, call the police himself, so you'd want to get off at the next exit and take back roads south, as far as Poughkeepsie maybe, where you could be a good boy and leave her car at the train station.

He backs out of the parking space. Experimentally. Drives a few feet toward the entrance ramp, stops, puts it in Park and races the engine while giving the wheel little turns, playing with how it would feel to do this. Probably incredible.

A Secret Station

||||||

At a decent interval after his seventy-first birthday, Martine sat him down: she was leaving him, moving to New York. To be with a man he presumed she'd met at that conference—last fall, had it been?—from which she'd returned two days late, after supposedly seeing friends and taking in the new production of *Così* at the Met. She would come up a couple of days a week to teach the rest of her classes, then figure out what next. She would ask for nothing in their settlement. Well, no blame to her: if she lived to be ninety, as more and more people were doing, she had half her life ahead. "The one thing I swore not to do," she said, "was to be trite and ask you to understand." Oh? Had she not also sworn to forsake all others? But he couldn't very well get on his high horse about that.

When the spring semester ended, he went in and told Jack Stephenson that he was retiring. Jack had been urging this for years—"You could get back into research," he would say or, "You and Martine could travel"—but now he said, "Are you sure this is the time?"

"What's this?" He sniffed. "The sweet scent of compassion?"

Jack shook his head. "I just don't want to have to replace you with some twerp out of Johns Hopkins." This was Jack giving himself airs: Who from Johns Hopkins would come to a state university so far from civilization, with a hospital that looked like a parking garage?

"You'll bear up," he said. "With what you've been paying me, you can hire *two* twerps."

"There's that." Jack frowned at the computer screen on his desk. "One second. Let me deal with this idiocy." He hammered at the keyboard with his index fingers, stopped, nodded and clicked the mouse.

"Sometimes I wish I were back tapping old ladies' knees with a rubber hammer." He took a deep breath, held it, let it out. "Since we're being frank, I have to tell you, I do have some concerns. I know it hasn't been an easy year. Do you really want another change in your life just now?"

"Aren't *you* the soul of delicacy. They ought to have made you dean long ago."

"Whoa." Jack raised a hand as if to protect his face. "I'm not your enemy, Don."

"It's a moot point anyway," he said. "I've decided to become a Doctor Without Borders."

"You can't be serious." In fairness to Jack, Martine hadn't gotten this joke, either. "Well, I mean, of course there's nothing worthier. But, my God, you've been in the classroom for what? Longer than *I've* been here."

"I do like the way you put things."

"Don. With all due respect, I'm not quite seeing you as Mother Teresa. Couldn't you assuage your conscience by volunteering at a clinic once a week?"

"The still, small voice," he said.

Jack looked at him over the top of his half-glasses. "You *have* lost your fucking mind. Okay, look, here's what we're going to do. We're going to keep your office as is. You go off and think this over, and when you're ready to—"

He held up both hands. "Will it save time if I tell you I'm not interested in what *you're* going to do?"

Jack took off his glasses and laid them on his desk. "Don, are you talking to someone?"

"A higher power?"

"I can suggest a very good—"

"You'll have to excuse me. I hear that still, small voice calling."

"Always smarter than everyone," Jack said. "I've never doubted that you could dance rings around me. But, just as your friend—and if I'm out of line here you can tell me—isn't it possible that you're well out of this thing?"

"I suspect 'marriage' is the word you're looking for," he said. "If you don't mind, I'll be dancing off."

They'd planned the trip back in November, at Red Fish Blue Fish, the one decent restaurant in town. Dinner was on Martine: the English Department had just made her a full professor. It helped to think that at this point she hadn't fully decided to leave. Paris, Amsterdam, Prague, then on to Rome—to visit his daughter and her husband—and finally to Crete for the first three weeks of July.

"Can people still go to Jim Morrison's grave?" Martine had said. "In Père Lachaise?"

"I have no idea," he said. "He was the singer, was he not? I wouldn't have thought he came up to your idea of a poet."

"He didn't," she said. "He was just the most beautiful man who ever lived. Present company excepted." She broke off a morsel of bread and dipped it into the saucer of olive oil. "So, will Claudia be her usual intransigent self?"

"You've met Claudia *once*. In ten years."

"QED," she said.

"At any rate, we'll only be there for two days."

"I guess I shouldn't complain," she said. "I *am* a home wrecker. Wasn't that the draw for you in the first place?"

Before leaving for the airport, he flushed away all but one of his last Viagra samples; then he flew across the Atlantic next to Martine's empty seat. In Paris, he swallowed the last pill and, for the first time in his life, picked up a prostitute: a tall, broad-shouldered young woman made taller than him by spike heels that had her on tiptoes. "So you know," she said as she took his hand, "I am not a *twahn-nee.*" What a world: Did they now have trainees? He instructed her in what he liked but found that he no longer liked what he liked. In Amsterdam, he drank a bottle of wine with dinner, had a brandy afterward, and went to a coffeehouse and smoked marijuana, which he hadn't tried since a party on the night Robert Kennedy announced that he was running for president. That had been pleasant and silly; this overwhelmed him. He couldn't imagine what was happening to him—could it have been laced with something? When he managed to get back to his hotel, he spent what he believed to be hours lying on his side on the white sex-agonal tiles of the bathroom floor, unable to raise himself to do his vomiting in the toilet. In the morning, he put the bathmat and the towel he'd cleaned up with in a plastic valet-service bag and took a taxi to the airport. Instead of continuing on to Prague and Rome, much less Crete, he flew back to New York, paying fifteen hundred dollars to change his ticket. In a Portosan off the bicycle path along the Hudson, he feasted on a street boy—artfully unshaven, hair artfully mussed—who must have been able to tell he'd never done this before. The boy let loose in his mouth, then beat him, took his wallet and kicked him with the snakeskin cowboy boots that had been the pretext for their conversation. In the emergency room at St. Vincent's, he told the young woman doctor that he was a doctor, too; she slipped him an envelope with a few Percodans to hold him over until he could get to an oral surgeon.

Back upstate, he arranged to rent the main house to Karen Fried-man, a neurology resident who'd been his most promising student two years—no, three years—earlier, and her partner, as the expres-sion went, a dumpy older woman named Gloria, who managed the Staples store at the mall out on the bypass. He put the Volvo away in the barn and covered it with a blue plastic tarpaulin. (Martine used to say the car made her feel like a "doctor's-wife impersonator," which was why she'd picked it out.) He drove his Jeep up the hill behind the house to the cabin that he and Nathan had built the summer Nathan turned sixteen: their last father-son project. A couple of years ago, a contractor had installed a woodstove and a composting privy. Elec-tricity came through a series of hundred-foot orange cords, the first plugged into the outlet down on the back porch, the last connected to a power strip for the computer, coffeemaker, microwave, mini-fridge and a combination radio/compact-disc player. The cabin had served as a guesthouse and a—what term wouldn't be pretentious?—a place to do his taxes. He stacked split cordwood between the trees around the cabin, making a meandering wall with a gap by the front door. On a tree along the steep path down to the house, he hung a clapperless bell and a large eyebolt so visitors could give warning.

Jimmy Huggins, whose office had been across the hall from his, took over the reconstruction of his mouth. The choice was between implants (now the "gold standard," Jimmy said) and bridges, which would involve grinding down undamaged teeth on either side of the extractions. In the meantime, since they knew him at the family-owned pharmacy on University Avenue, he phoned in a Percodan prescription to the Rite Aid in the mall, using the name Kaspar Hauser.

He had brought a single carton of books up from his library: Anthony Powell, Simenon (to see if he could get his French back), Patrick O'Brian, the Oxford Shakespeare. He hadn't read Shakespeare since Princeton—half a century ago—and how could you stand before God without having tasted the best His world had to offer? (He now allowed himself God thoughts: intellectual integrity was no longer worth the vigilance.) Sitting in the Morris chair, he worked through *Lear* again, but *Othello* turned out to be a bit close to home.

He filled gallon plastic jugs, ten at a time, at the kitchen sink and carried them up in the Jeep. He had a blue enameled basin, a handsome thing Martine had bought, for doing dishes, rinsing with mouthwash (brushing was still uncomfortable), shaving and washing above the waist. Saturday night was bath night, as in his childhood; after the girls went into town, for a movie or for dinner with whoever their friends were, he walked down to the house, filled the claw-foot tub that Martine had restored and poured in their perfumed bath salts. If they knew, so be it: he was turning into a strange old man. Percodan was no longer doing the trick, so Kaspar Hauser had been put on Dilaudid. He moved his bowels in the privy—because of the drugs, he supposed, he'd had to resort to laxatives—but pissed on the ground, like Adam. Sometimes he would unplug the power strip, fling the end of the orange cord out the window and let the cabin float free.

He had given thought to the possibility of AIDS and decided that it was unlikely. His mouth had been bloodied only afterward, but he had swallowed the boy's semen, not knowing what else to do and not wanting to seem, well, unaccepting. So he drew a sample from his arm and sent it to the lab. The negative result, of course, meant nothing: he would have to take another sample in six months or so. He made a note on the December 31 page of his appointment book: *Draw blood.*

One Saturday night, early in the fall, he went upstairs after his bath, the towel around his waist, smelling of roses and remote on Dilaudid, his old man's dugs swinging. In the master bedroom, he took a pair of Gloria's black lace underwear from the top drawer of what had been his dresser. They were so large that the scalloped rim slipped down to his buttocks. He tried to imagine himself inhabiting the bulky, penis-free body that would fill them up—"panties" was the word—but couldn't quite cross over. He lay down on the bed and turned on his side. He'd got so lanky that his knees banged together. He put a pillow between them and reached into the panties to handle himself, to make his disgrace definitive, but the poor thing was dead and per- haps *this* made his disgrace definitive. The curtains were open, the shades up, and he saw the leaves of the maple tree suddenly brighten to orange. Headlights: the girls coming home. He would let himself be caught, and that disgrace would set him free. But it was only someone passing by.

His first wife had been a nurse: this was back when such arrangements were countenanced. Wide hips, full breasts, a fondness for musicals and Dave Brubeck. She thought he looked like Brubeck, and in those days, before Martine had urged laser eye surgery on him, he might well have. Angela had had a bad habit (he'd never called it to her atten- tion) of prefacing statements with "Truth to tell." He could no longer remember what they'd talked about, late in the night. She had stopped working when she began to show and stayed home to raise Nathan, then Claudia. Another age of the world. And, years later, the younger woman, the son hanging up the phone, the weeping daughter telling him she would never have a family. How could all this—"tedium" was the word for it—have given any of them either pain or joy?

He had saved lives. At first he'd tried to keep count—could he ever have been that young?—but these were lives that any doctor could have saved. Once, when he was still in practice, he was on emergency-room duty and they brought in a teenage girl: some fool woman, a hairdresser of all things, had thought she knew how to perform an abortion—it was that long ago—and afterward he had put the girl on the Pill. Half a year later she came to him in his office, pregnant again; insanely, he had given in, risking not just the loss of his license but, in those days, a charge of murder. When the girl came to him one more time, he turned her away, and that same night—or so he'd taken to telling the story; it was really the following night—she died in the ER, of an overdose of Nembutal. Well, any doctor of his generation had such stories. She was a homely, overweight girl named Cheryl—Robinson, she had told him, but it was actually something else—with pimples on her forehead. She smelled. He had looked into it a little afterward; he *had* been that young. The parents were divorced; the mother had a boyfriend and what was then called a drinking problem, and she'd taken out an order of protection against the father. All three, apparently, had beaten the girl. Cheryl Robinson had been sixteen, ten years older than Claudia. And now Claudia was old enough to be Cheryl Robinson's mother. Although she had chosen to be no one's mother.

The night after the girl died, he had told Angela that he'd had enough of practice and meant to teach full-time. And he suggested that they adopt a child. "This *is* a turnaround," she said, and poured herself more wine. "So why did I get my tubes tied?" The next day—and it really *was* the next day—he made a date to get together with the receptionist who'd been flirting with him. Since she, too, was married, there would be no complications.

Martine had been his sixth adventure, if that was the word: of this he had kept count. He'd been seated next to her at a dinner party after she'd arrived at the university as the new specialist in the Victorians. Did she not find them a little stodgy? "Everybody thinks that," she'd said. "The Victorians were hot hot hot. Of course, it was all encoded. You should come in when I teach 'Dover Beach.'"

"I warn you," he said, "I'm a hard sell." He saw Angela looking at them from across the table.

"I'll sell you," she said.

He sat in the back of her classroom among the undergraduates, who had stared at him when he came in, and listened as she lectured. "'Begin, and cease, and then again begin, / With tremulous cadence slow'? I mean, what does this *sound* like, boys and girls?" Her black T-shirt fit so snugly that he could see the nipples of her small, unbound breasts.

"Intriguing," he said afterward, when they'd ordered their drinks. "But weren't you taking things somewhat out of context?"

"What *is* context?" She took off her narrow black-framed glasses and cleaned the lenses with the bottom of her T-shirt.

"Ah. Am I guilty of old thinking?"

"It's charming," she said. "It's *so* old it's transgressive."

"Then that's a good thing, yes?"

"I have an idea you don't transgress enough."

"You might be surprised," he said.

She put the glasses back on, and her face seemed prettier again. "Oh, I don't mean *that*. Of course, you do have a reputation."

"Have I?"

"Or else I wouldn't be here with you. I *like* a woman-hater every once in a while. It might be fun to take your cherry."

"Well," he said. "If you think you're man enough."

There had been an ice storm the night before he was to go in for the last, most difficult extractions; he scraped away frost to look out the window and saw the bare trees silvery with sunlight. Apparently he had brought wood in last night, a kindness for which he was grateful to himself. He opened the draft and built up a fire. His skin felt raw, as if he had a low-grade fever.

He swallowed a Dilaudid with his coffee and turned on the radio, to a secret station he had found: "music" that was simply noises and drumbeats, about guns and money and women, and where even an old man, provided he was by himself, was allowed to listen in on all the rich obscenity. Bitches on their knees, black men chanting about what the bitches must do.

He heard the bell ring and turned the radio off. When he opened the door, he felt the cruel air and saw Karen, in her black leather jacket.

"It's cozy in here," she said, stepping inside. She unwrapped her red scarf, unzipped the jacket. A pretty and delicate young woman— a gamine, she would once have been called—with short black hair.

"Could I get you some coffee?"

"Maybe I'd better take it along? We should allow some extra time because of the roads. If fact, can we take your Jeep down to my car? The path is all ice."

"I still don't think it's necessary for anyone to drive me."

"They're going to put you under," she said. "This is not discussable."

He'd tried to research the interaction of Dilaudid and Pentothal. Not ideal, but probably all right. "Why don't I drive us there at least," he said. Her little Japanese putt-putt had only rear-wheel drive. "And you can drink your coffee. Can you drive a standard shift? Assuming it becomes necessary."

"All dykes can drive standard," she said. "It's in our DNA."

At the stop sign, he put on his turn signal to take the shortcut and crept down Breakneck Hill Road in first gear, steering from one patch of sand to another. His quietude was deepening now; the ice had bent the trees on either side, making the road a tunnel. When they came to the curve, he felt the Jeep become a heavy object gliding down, its back end sweeping to the left, and heard Karen yell "Shit!" But then the tires bit into sand, he cut the wheel and the Jeep straightened out and resumed its crawl. In his old life, his heart would have begun pounding now in a delayed adrenaline reaction. He looked over and saw Karen using a Kleenex to mop coffee off the leg of her jeans.

In the waiting room, she sat next to him, a paperback copy of *The*

Man Who Mistook His Wife for a Hat in her lap. "You know, I never got around to reading that," he said.

"This is what made me want to go into neurology," she said. "I have to say, I'm loathing it this time. All this bogus *compassion*. And his bogus beard."

"Since when have you been so fierce?"

"Sorry," she said. "I'm just in a shitty mood. Let's worry about *you*."

"Ah, that's a young man's game. And what are you in a shitty mood about?"

"About half the time," she said. "See? You're not the only one who can be evasive."

As instructed, he had gone without breakfast; coming up out of the anesthesia, he vomited bile. On the drive back out of town, Karen pulled into the quilted-metal diner on the bypass and helped him up the three steps. Really no need: they were dotted with ice-melting pellets, and he felt remarkably normal, considering the morning he'd had.

Karen ate an omelette while he drank coffee and studied the map of Greece on his place mat: a country in the shape of a splatter. Islands called the Sporades? He had never heard of them. Must this not be where "sporadic" came from?

"You sure you don't want some rice pudding?" she said. "You wouldn't have to chew. You should eat something."

He shook his head.

"Here, at least take my jelly. You need to get your blood sugar up. We have apple or—let's see. Grape."

"Ah. The Puritan or the Mediterranean. *This* will tell you something about me." He peeled back the seal on the tiny oblong tub and picked up his spoon. "Out, vile jelly!" It tasted sweet, but not particularly of apple. He swallowed without letting it linger in his mouth; he still didn't dare feel with his tongue where the teeth had been. "Martine and I were going to spend the summer in Crete."

"Do you know this is the first time I've heard you say her name?"

He put down his spoon. "Do *you* know," he said, "that you have a gift for making yourself offensive?"

"Donald, why are you being so ugly to me?"

"Perhaps that's *my* gift," he said.

Back in the passenger seat, the inside of the Jeep looked familiar but reversed, like a mirror world. Karen waited for a Sleepy's truck to pass, then pulled into traffic. "Listen, I want you to stay down at the house tonight. Gloria and I can take the guest room." She meant Claudia's room; Nathan's had been redone as a study for Martine.

"Absolutely not," he said.

"Then I'll bring a sleeping bag up."

"This is foolish. I— Watch out!"

"I see him." She hit the horn as a minivan seemed to be nosing into them from the left lane. "You don't even have a phone up there."

"For what purpose?" he said.

"I'll let you think about that." She shifted down to pass the Sleepy's truck. "God, I want one of these," she said. "It makes me feel like a real lezzie."

"Do you consider yourself not a real lesbian?"

"Well." She looked in the rearview mirror and swung back in front of the truck. "I've been with men. It's not the same."

"*I've* been with men," he said, "if it comes to that."

"You?"

"Well. *A* man. I found it pretty much the same."

"When was this?"

"Oh, back when I was willing to try anything." He had told Karen only that he'd been beaten and robbed.

"So," she said, "this must explain why our bath salts keep running low. I was picturing you splashing around with some loose woman."

"That's a distasteful picture." What they'd done to his mouth was beginning to hurt. "Listen, I need to fill this prescription they gave me. I don't suppose you'd go into Rite Aid for me?" Little chance that they might accuse Kaspar Hauser of impersonating Donald Blakey to fill a prescription for codeine, but nevertheless.

"Of course." She put on the turn signal. "So who would have thought. No wonder we get along so well. Both galloping bisexuals."

"Hardly that," he said. "Unless you mean off into the sunset."

She pulled into the parking lot and began prowling for a space. "Now I'm supposed to tell you that you're not old," she said. "Aren't we tired of this dance?" She glanced over at the Staples store. "You know, it used to be that all I had to do was see this place and I'd feel myself blushing."

"That's a lovely stage," he said.

"Stage," she said. "That's a lovely word."

Neither Nathan nor Claudia had come to his wedding; he'd thought they'd perhaps have been tempted by an August weekend on the Vineyard. At Martine's insistence, he invited them for Thanksgiving that year; it was Claudia's first semester at Bryn Mawr and Nathan's junior year at UC Santa Cruz. Martine had reserved a fresh-killed turkey and made the dressing with truffles that had just come in at the market on University Avenue. The wine was a Riesling she had discovered at Vin Ordinaire and was now having a vogue among the faculty.

He and Nathan had spent the morning in the woods. Nathan felled five trees with the chainsaw, and they took turns cutting them up and splitting the logs with the maul. As the weak sun rose higher, Nathan took off his denim jacket, then his plaid shirt. He was broad across the chest and shoulders, narrow at the waist and hips; as he raised the maul high and brought it down again and again, sweat darkened his black T-shirt in an inverted triangle between his shoulder blades. It had been clear since Nathan was in seventh grade that he would never go to medical school. Now, as he looked at his son's strong body, this seemed perfectly right.

Late in the afternoon, the kids came downstairs flushed and red-eyed. Nathan, he saw, had not changed out of his blue jeans and sweaty T-shirt; you could smell his rank odor through the scent of roasting turkey. Claudia slouched next to him at the far end of the sofa. Martine opened a second bottle of wine—they'd killed the first before the kids made their appearance—and brought out a tray of roasted chestnuts. She held it out to Claudia, who shook her head. Nathan took a handful and asked if they could see what was on TV. Martine gave him a look that would have quelled one of her students but handed him the clicker and went to take the bird out of the oven. He started going at the shell of a chestnut with his teeth, staring between his knees at a football game. Claudia had got hold of the scalpel they'd used as a letter opener when they were kids and sat slicing parallel cuts into the flesh of a green olive.

Martine came back in with a third bottle of wine. She broke the cork, tried again and finally had to force it down into the bottle with one leg of the nutcracker. "Ten minutes, boys and girls. Claudia? Would you care for more wine?"

"Would I *care* for it? I mean, what does that even *mean?*"

"Somebody's losing her shit," Nathan said. "Listen, can me and Claud carve the turkey?"

"I suppose," Martine said. "I'm a little impaired myself. I'll show you where we keep the knives."

"Same place as always, right?" Nathan stood up. "In the knife thing? Come on, Claud. Bring your scalpel. You can give it a hysterectomy."

They went into the kitchen. Martine said, "I wish I had some."

"Some what?" he said.

"Couldn't you smell it on them? Maybe they'd share a little."

"They're probably just ill at ease," he said. "I suspect Nathan has experimented some, as all—"

He heard a putt-putting noise out in the kitchen, guessed what it was and burst through the door to see Nathan wielding the chainsaw and Claudia, index fingers pressed into her ears, laughing. Nathan revved the saw to a deafening snarl, white smoke belched into the room, then the giant turkey twisted on the platter and flew apart, splattering meat and stuffing onto the wall Martine had redone in blue milk paint.

Now the saw was idling again, and Martine was standing in the doorway. She walked over to the counter, set her wineglass down and said, "You know, you're absolutely fucking right. We should just make this a performance piece." She picked up a severed drumstick and hurled it at the window, breaking a pane of the original glass whose waves and bubbles Angela had particularly admired. Nathan stared at her, then shut the saw down. "Wait a second, wait a second," she said. "I've still got its *dick*." She reached into the garbage and came up with the turkey's neck, which she'd boiled along with the giblets to make the gravy, squeezed it in her fist and jammed it against the front of her black velveteen slacks. "Get down and suck it," she said to her husband.

Claudia said, "I'm afraid." She began to weep. "Daddy?"

Martine let the turkey neck drop and put an arm around her shoulder. The greasy hand left a mark on Claudia's silk blouse. "Sweetie, we're *all* afraid," she said. "Can we just agree that I'm shit and make this a good day for your father?"

After they'd all pitched in to clean up the mess, they called Domino's and played Scrabble: Martine and Nathan against him and Claudia. He put on *Sketches of Spain,* and the others sat on the sofa and smoked some of Nathan's marijuana. He sat in his leather armchair and put his hand up when the cigarette came around to him, then watched the three of them get quiet. At one point he thought he saw Martine put a hand on Nathan's thigh, but by then he'd been sipping Cognac for hours.

The next day, he and Martine drove them to the train. They all decided that they must do this again over Christmas. Martine hugged Claudia, whose hands hesitated and then rested on the back of Martine's coat. But something must have been said on the way to New York. Or perhaps visiting their mother had restored their sense of perspective. At any rate, he next saw Nathan and Claudia only at their college graduations and their weddings, from all of which Martine absented herself.

At Claudia's wedding, in the cloisters at Bryn Mawr, he saw that Angela had cut her hair and dyed the ends—there was a term for this. She'd gotten a desk job with UNICEF after burning out at Calvary Hospital. They sat with Nathan between them, and he noticed that she wasn't wearing a ring; Claudia had told him that the marriage to the real-estate broker was in trouble.

He watched Claudia and Giancarlo perform their waltz; the groom was the better dancer, as Fred Astaire was said to be better than Ginger Rogers, though wasn't there now a revisionist view? He instructed himself to curb his mistrust; it came of having watched all those old movies in which American girls were pestered by European hand-kissers. This Giancarlo seemed solid enough: a visiting professor of economics at Wharton. What he'd wanted with an American college girl, however serious-minded—of course her dress put that on display for all the men to see.

The band struck up "I Won't Dance," which argued some wit, he thought. The floor filled up. He held out his hand to Angela and she came to him, a kindness he did not deserve.

"Do you think they'll be happy?" he said.

"They're going to live in Rome," she said. "What's not to be happy?"

"And how are *you*?" He put his right hand on her waist (he could feel a stiff undergarment) and fox-trotted her toward the middle of the floor, the tips of her breasts brushing his jacket front.

"Truth to tell"—she showed teeth in what must have been meant as a smile—"I'm much better alone."

It had been dark for hours when he heard the bell ring down the path. *Damn* that woman. He was sipping Talisker, for the taste, really, and reading *A Dance to the Music of Time.* He got up and opened the door: not Karen but Gloria, wearing a backpack and carrying a sausagelike nylon bag. "No," he said.

"Karen said you'd give me an argument. She got called in to the hospital."

"That's never good," he said. "You're welcome to come in for a *drink*."

"Except you're blocking the door. It's cold out here."

"Forgive me." He stepped aside. "I just didn't want there to be a misunderstanding."

She set the sleeping bag down, wriggled out of her backpack and unzipped her down vest.

He fetched another glass.

"Here, I can get that." She took it from his hand and poured herself a couple of fingers, then added a dribble of water from the jug. "My husband used to drink Macallan."

"I didn't realize you'd been married. Have my chair."

"I'm okay." She sat on the floor, her back against his bed. "Yeah, five years. Amazing, huh? My wedding dress was a size six."

He poured himself another finger and sat back down in the Morris chair. He couldn't decide whether he liked her throaty voice.

"So how's the mouth?" she said. "Karen tells me they went in with earthmovers."

"I don't think there's going to be a problem."

"Meaning there *is* a problem?"

The pain was still there, but at such a distance that it didn't seem to apply to him. "I mean that it's fine," he said.

"So are we going to fight about this?"

"About?"

"Me staying."

"I don't believe I have the energy," he said. "If you do stay, could I ask that you simply keep quiet? Without offense. I just don't feel up to carrying on a conversation."

"Don't worry about me, I have thick skin. Thick everything." She put a hand to her belly and made the flesh shake.

He looked away. "Make yourself comfortable, if that's possible. There are books here."

"I brought mine." She reached for her backpack. "Just tell me when it's lights-out."

After a while, he felt the room begin to cool, and as if she felt it too—well, she did, of course—she got up and fed the stove. He clicked on Deal to start another game. The drugs he'd taken at six thirty were wearing off, and he took another codeine for the pain, another Dilaudid—because he was addicted, he supposed, though this was hardly the desperate condition they wanted you to believe—and an Ambien to get to sleep. If he wasn't careful, one of these mornings he would fail to wake up. (If he continued to be careful, then it would be some other morning.) He lost, clicked on Deal again, studied the array, then moved a red two onto a black three and dragged the king into the empty space.

He seemed to think someone had hold of his upper arm, guiding him toward what must be the bed. At one point someone had said, "Are you all right?" There had been a noise, some sort of disturbance. There was a connection among these things, or if not a connection, at least a sequence. But such considerations existed far outside him.

He opened his eyes and it was daylight, and wide Gloria had been replaced by narrow Karen, fitting a paper filter into the coffeemaker. His mouth was hurting; his back too, as if he'd thrown it out again. Could time possibly have gone backward, to that episode with the boy? But there was a rule against that. The cabin stank of whiskey. He closed his eyes and the negative afterimage of the window appeared, complete with the tree branches outside. He followed it, now here, now here, now here, until it faded, then opened his eyes and burned it in again.

He woke up the next time to the smell of coffee. He ran his tongue along his lower lip: it smarted, felt fat, and he tasted blood.

He woke up again and Karen was sitting on the bed.

"Say again?" she said.

"What time is it?"

"Ten thirty. So how much of this have you been taking?" She rattled the vial of Dilaudid in his face. "You scared the living shit out of Gloria."

"Where *is* Gloria?"

"Where she always is. Berating some stock boy." She got up and set the pills on the table. "Could you drink a little coffee?"

He turned on his side—what in God's name had he done to his back?—to fold the pillow double against the headboard and watched her fill a cup and pour in milk.

"Thank you." She had put sugar in, though somehow he hadn't seen her do it. "So. Am I being called to account for my sins?"

"I'm not the Puritan," she said. "You have a medical problem."

"Granting it's a problem. That's your assumption."

"I think Kaspar Hauser could validate my assumption. If we could reach him in the Black Forest."

"Ah, at least someone appreciates my little jokes."

"I'm surprised you haven't been busted," she said. "How stupid do you think people are?" She sat down on the bed again. "Apparently you passed out and fell into your keyboard. And I guess you smacked the floor pretty hard. Let me see you." She rested a finger on his lower lip and pulled it down gently. He hissed in. "Not terrible," she said. "I made some oatmeal. In the microwave." Point of information, evidently. "You haven't been eating."

"I need to take something," he said. "I hurt everywhere."

She shook her head. "Not on *my* watch. I don't doubt that you hurt. We're going to get you to someone who treats these things."

He worked his elbows to get himself sitting up. "Oh? By whose authority? I've had about enough of *you*, I can tell you that."

"You'll feel better," she said.

"You're damn right I will. I want you out of my house. The both of you. You *and* your fat lesbian whatever-she-is."

She looked at him and got up off the bed. "Good," she said. "A little honesty." She took her leather jacket off the peg. "I have to say, you were a wonderful teacher. Beyond that—I don't know, I guess I'm glad to know there *wasn't* anything beyond that." She wound the scarf around her neck and put the vials of pills into her jacket pocket. "You have an appointment for one forty-five. I'll give you some privacy to get yourself cleaned up."

Nathan flew in from Seattle to see him in the facility—to use the facile term—then back to attend to his Lexus dealership and to be present for his son's sixth-grade graduation. Claudia, coming in from Rome, missed Nathan by a day—the two of them hadn't seen each other for years—and stayed on, visiting for the half hour the rules allowed and sleeping out at the house, in her old room. She told him that the girls had moved their belongings away in a U-Haul. They'd been perfectly lovely to her, she said; the thin one had invited her to go out for coffee.

When he had gotten through the worst of it and they'd discharged him, Claudia took him to have his bridgework completed; on Thanksgiving night he was able to eat with her at Red Fish Blue Fish. She had the veal, and what she said was a good Pinot Grigio; he had the branzino, a fish once unknown, and was drinking mineral water for now. She was not going back to Italy, she told him. She and Giancarlo—but this probably wasn't the time.

"Come, come," he said. "I'm not such a delicate soul."

"No," she said. "No one's ever accused you of *that*."

"Ah. I take it you've been talking to your mother."

She nodded. "I'm going down when you're, you know—sometime over Christmas."

"When I can be trusted by myself? Well, that should be a pleasant visit."

"Why are you so hateful about her? Because she still loves you?"

"You're not becoming one of those truth tellers, I hope. I only meant that New York should be a welcome change from this outpost. Martine certainly found it so."

"She was a bitch," Claudia said.

"*I* was the bitch," he said. "As they say. I'm afraid I must have liked it." He took a sip of his water.

"Well, Daddy, look—you wouldn't consider coming with me? Mom says Joe Family might be there." This was her new name for Nathan.

"Thank you, no. I wouldn't have thought that you, of all people, would still entertain *that* fantasy."

She stared at him, the glass halfway to her mouth, then dropped her eyes. "I don't know why I keep being surprised."

"I'm sorry. As you say, I'm not a delicate soul."

She drained her glass and held it out to be filled. "Daddy, are you not even curious? About me and Giancarlo?"

"I was waiting for you to tell me." He lifted the half bottle, dripping, out of the thing—"humidor" wasn't the word—and wiped it with the towel, then poured some for her. "I had assumed you didn't want to talk about it."

"Fine, you're right," she said. "I don't want to talk about it." She took a sip. He noticed fine traceries around her eyes and a single hard line slicing from each side of her nose down to the corners of her mouth. These lines seemed to have been drawn onto the face of the true Claudia, who had always looked young for her age—disturbingly so. "I think I'm going to apply to law school," she said. "Given all that's going on here."

"Bind up the nation's wounds?" he said.

"You can't just throw up your hands."

"Spoken like a woman who's spent the last ten years in sunny Italy."

"Yeah. Well, that's over." She picked up her glass again. "I was hoping maybe I could stay with you. While I get things figured out?"

"And, meanwhile, keep an eye on me."

"Do you think you need that?"

"What a question," he said. "What am I supposed to say?"

"You could have said no. Should we talk about what *you're* going to do?"

"As a matter of fact," he said, "I've decided to go work in the inner city." He had been thinking about how to phrase the joke to make its meaning more precisely double, but this would do.

"Daddy, I think that would be wonderful for you. And the people you could help."

"The people I could help." He clinked his glass against hers. "Here's to them."

Without telling Claudia, he wrote out a new will and faxed it to his lawyer. It left her the house and five acres, which included the barn and the tennis court; the other forty acres, with the pond and the cabin, went to Nathan; the money, fifty-fifty, to Claudia and her mother, since Nathan had done so well. The Volvo should rightly have gone to Martine: he'd heard from Jack Stephenson that she had found only an adjunct position at Fordham, and she could've sold the car for the money or kept it for the irony. But now that she had true love, there was no need for either. He directed that the car be auctioned off and the proceeds donated to Doctors Without Borders. He left the Jeep to Karen Friedman.

Claudia was staying at the house with him for a few more days before going down to New York. Through Jack, she'd arranged for three LPNs to come out in eight-hour shifts while she was gone. He was back in the king-size sleigh bed he had shared with Martine, which marked the place where he had shared the old double bed with Angela. Each night after dinner, he and Karen—no, he and Claudia—would play three games of Scrabble in front of the fireplace; they'd become evenly matched. Then, after trying to put himself under by puzzling out Shakespeare, he would swallow the one sleeping aid she allowed him: L-tryptophan, from the health-food store. The liquor cabinet, of course, she had emptied. One morning, when she went out to get the mail, he telephoned Rite Aid but was informed that his prescriptions could no longer be honored.

It snowed the night before he was to drive her to the train; they were calling for a foot or more. That afternoon he'd gone out to the barn and uncovered the Volvo, the blue tarp spattered with the droppings of swallows. It started right up, like the good Swedish car it was, and he moved it out into the driveway to make loading her bags easier in the morning. He had thought of simply driving off, but to where, and what then?

That night he lay there trying to decode the scene in *The Winter's Tale* where the wife is pretending to be a statue—the silliest part of a particularly silly play—but then gave up, got out of bed and went to the window. Snowflakes were pouring straight down: he tried to follow this one, this one, this one, this one. White knife-edged crests had built up on the branches of the maple tree. Then he heard a roar that shook the house: only a section of accumulated snow sliding down the slate roof.

At some point he heard the plow come through and saw its yellow blinkers light up the window. He awoke to the sandy scraping of a shovel down below: Claudia clearing the walk. Daylight, and snow still falling. He smelled coffee. He had himself dressed when she clumped in, snow sticking to her green rubber boots. "I got a path dug out to the car," she said. "But shouldn't we take the Jeep? I don't know if the trains are even going to be running."

"I thought we ought to go in style," he said.

The snow was knee-high on either side of the path she'd made; he saw that she'd cut the sides down at an angle, just as he used to do it. When she was a child, still living here. He went out and started the Volvo, put the heat on full blast and came back inside. "Be warm in ten minutes," he said.

She poured him a cup of coffee and turned on the radio. "Let's see if we can get the weather."

"It'll be fine." He tapped his forehead with his index finger. "My own secret station."

"That's half your problem right there," she said.

"I'd call that a conservative estimate," he said.

They slung her bags into the trunk. A couple more inches had fallen since the plow had come through, and the smooth white of the road showed only a single pair of tire tracks.

At the stop sign, the tracks went straight ahead; Breakneck Hill Road was a virgin slope. He put on his turn signal.

Claudia looked over at him. "We're not going this way?"

"It'll save time," he said.

"We have lots of time," she said. "Do you want to get us killed?"

He jammed the shift lever into park. "Would you care to drive?"

"I'd care to *live*, Daddy. Do you even have snow tires?"

"I've been a doctor for forty years," he said. "Do you think I don't know what I'm doing?" He closed his eyes and listened to the *tick-tick-tick-tick*. "I'm sorry, Bunky." He switched the signal off. "We'll take the long way. It won't make that much difference." He pulled the lever back into drive and started the car forward; it fishtailed, then righted itself. Snow blew straight across the windshield, from left to right.

"I must be hearing things," she said. "You haven't called me that since—you know."

He glanced over to see if she was crying. No. "Is it all right if I call you that?"

"As you say, it won't make that much difference." She reached over and patted his leg. "Sorry, Daddy. I'm just . . . Do you promise to take care of yourself while I'm gone?"

"Aren't we leaving that to the professionals?"

"I told you, right? Mrs. So-and-so's going to meet us at the station and she'll follow you back to the house. Mrs. Chesler."

"Now there's something to look forward to." He had already taken his vow of silence: not a word to any of them. If they reported him, well, he was a strange old man.

"You've always had women looking after you. So now they're being paid."

"That's how it generally ends up," he said.

"And you're going to look into that volunteer work?"

"A Doctor Without Borders," he said. "Heal the sick, raise the dead."

"Always so modest."

"Yes, well," he said, "I can tell you a story about that." The wind had shifted now and was blowing snow straight at the windshield, like an attack from the stars. An attack *of* the stars. "This was back when I started out in practice," he said. "I had night duty in the emergency room and they brought in—"

"Daddy," she said, "I've heard this how many times?"

"Then I guess there's no need to drag it out," he said. "But you see where I'm going."

Round on Both Ends,
High in the Middle

||||||

A remote white moon was howling down with its man-in-the-moon face as she swung out across the double yellow line to pass an ass-dragging old van (whose driver turned out to be the hero of the story) and we came face-to-face with a Ford pickup. I had time to read the F-O-R-D and to register that the grille looked like a modernist grid of windows. The next thing was this feeling, a certainty rather, of floating up in silence (I'm not saying *I* floated up—this wasn't me anymore) and down below a car and a truck with their fronts mashed together and both hoods up as if they were chatting. Off on the shoulder, a guy getting out of a van. Moonlit view of the top of his cap, Red Sox B upside down, and his hands going to his face as he approached the truck. The driver of the truck hadn't had his seat belt on—blood-alcohol level of such and such—and had died instantly, which I now understand means fuck-all, having had an instant of my own. I've told this story so many times that it's become a story.

The guy from the van got her door open, pulled her out and walked her, his hand in her armpit, into frosted grass at the side of the road. Then he supposedly pried my door open with a tire iron. I wrote him a letter to thank him for my life, Dan somebody, from Barre, but I never heard back. She lived too. Is living still, for all I know, why would she not be, though she's made herself hard to find. At some point she came into my hospital room, one arm in a sling, and said she couldn't stay long. How was she going to explain this? Meaning to her husband. I said, Make a clean breast, don't you have pHisoHex? The morphine was making everything a medical pun. But I could imagine how this might seem real to her. I got off easy, as always: just a limp you wouldn't notice, even on rainy days. It takes months for my shoes to show the uneven wear.

We'd been coming back from our Saturday night in Burlington. I'd picked her up at the airport the night before—she'd told her husband a lie that she said wasn't my problem, or maybe she said it wasn't my business—and driven her down to my cabin. We'd seen each other only in the city, but we had a long weekend because of Columbus Day and I wanted to give her the full-on Vermont. So we'd gone to the Flynn and heard Leila Josefowicz with the VSO, playing the hell out of the Adams Violin Concerto. Two ladies in front of us chattered through the first movement about how awful it was. Subscribers feeling baited and switched—I could sympathize. On the other hand, the *Rite of Spring* première had been a long time ago. I finally said, *Would you mind shutting the fuck up?* Something I wouldn't have said had the ladies been gentlemen. As the truck came at us, I also had time to think of this: that my last act on earth had been uncharitable.

Not that it would have been my last act on earth in any event. After the concert we went to some Seattleoid restaurant: she had the pork loin with prune sauce and jicama, and I had a steak—how could they ruin that?—with wasabi mashed potatoes. I asked her how was the far pork. She said, Far pork? Ah, *oui, entendu.* We split a bottle of pretty much okay Washington State Shiraz. She asked if I'd thought Leila Josefowicz was hot. I said I had, but that the conductor was her husband and I was a great respecter of people's marriages; had she thought *he* was hot? So-so, she said, I like it that we can cop to this stuff. Do you not have this with your husband? I said. No, she said, he thought that was getting into the danger zone. Ah, I said, well, everybody has things they keep to themselves, do they not? Like what things, she said. Oh, I don't know, I said, like minor annoyances—do we need to be having this conversation?

I put down what I hoped was a working credit card, signed the slip and said, Shall we? It would be a long drive back to the cabin, down 89 to Montpelier and then over toward St. Johnsbury, but she didn't want to end the evening. As opposed to never wanting the evening to end, if you see the distinction. So we found a bar where a shaven-headed bouncer, pretending not to be a bouncer, said hello at the door. I couldn't understand what the place was about: too crowded to dance, too loud to talk, the music too blurry to decode. I said things into her ear, the point mostly being to brush her ear with my lips, and she shook her head, not a specific no but a general can't-hear-you, or a general you-don't-get-it. We seemed to have a better time in bed, and wasn't all this in the service of that? After three rounds of drinks, I helped her along the sidewalk to where we'd parked, first by her elbow, next with an arm around her waist. She kept her hands in the pockets of her jacket until I felt an arm slip around and a hand on my side, then the hand went away and back to her pocket. Either she was disgusted now to touch the old-guy softness, or, or, or. Oh my God, she said, look at the *moon.*

I drove while she manned the radio and found us a show called *The Bible Only Church of the Air,* where a woman preacher with a hillbilly accent kept soaring off her sermon into gibberish: *O hoola hoola shacka-lacka!* Do you think this actually means anything? she said. Yeah, I said, it means she's a schizophrenic. The station must have been beaming in from far away—as they do here late at night, from Chicago, Cleveland, Cincinnati, the baseball cities. It faded into static, and she said, Oh shit, I think she was just about to come.

When we got off of 89, she asked if she could drive the rest of the way. She seemed okay, and I wanted to please. Appease, I guess I mean. And can we have the thing open, she said, and blast the heater? The roof thing? I want that moon.

I'd met her at a bar party, one of those things where somebody sends around an email, the occasion being to celebrate somebody else's installation that had been written up in the *Times*—why not get it out there what kind of people we were? The bar was a good call, sparing everybody the installation itself. I liked her kinky blond hair, advertising wildness. And let me fine-tune that: I liked her need to advertise her wildness. I checked the left hand. Oh. But.

I asked how she knew Rachel, so on and so on, I won't walk you through it all. She was an actress, back to looking for auditions after a summer in Pennsylvania with a production of *The Tempest* that had played village greens all over the state. Tiki torches in bamboo holders, Martin Denny on a boom box: the director had wanted a Trader Vic's vibe to send up the postcolonial thing. And his theory of Miranda—she had been Miranda—was to bag the airy-fairyness and do her as Daisy Mae. She stopped chewing gum only to speak her lines, which actually worked because—I *knew* the play, right?

No, I said, I came into town on the last load of turnips.

Well, fuck you too, she said.

Now this *is* promising, I said. I pinched her ring between my thumb and forefinger. Let me ask, I said, did you take that off for verisimilitude?

She yanked back the hand and said, Who are you again?

Oh, I said, some aging longhair putting the moves on you.

I'd managed to figure out that much, she said.

Ooh, I said. Cruel.

Is that what you like? she said.

Actually, no, I said. I like 'em simple and loyal. Big chest if possible. I said this because she was on the small side, which was really what I liked.

Then it's good I'm married, she said. I don't think I'd quite do. In any respect.

Ah but *I'm* not, I said. This had been true for a year.

Oh, see, I automatically assumed you were, she said. Most men aren't this blatant if they can really follow through.

Whew, I said, I need to look at that one when it stops spinning. Get you a drink?

Good, *that'*ll piss my husband off, she said. That's him. The black T-shirt.

Huh, I said. Very Ted Hughes. So why does he let you go to parties if you're not allowed to drink with strangers?

You wouldn't get it if you're not married, she said. It's like normal life except you always go home with the same person.

Actually, I *was* married, I said.

She dropped her mouth open.

Fuck you too, I said. What are you drinking?

Eventually the husband came over to break it up, but I'd already gotten her email out of her, to send her a piece I'd read by some guy riffing about *The Tempest* and his woodstove and his marriage breaking up.

She emailed back to thank me, and I emailed back to ask how about lunch? No, no lunches, no can do, but she forwarded another group email about a screening, at another bar, this one in Williamsburg, of a video that had been shot during that summer production. And a note at the top: *Want to see me act up a storm?*

Since this isn't theater criticism and who cares anyway, let me just say it was mostly shitty actors with a decent Prospero, who was black, either to make you think complicated thoughts about colonialism or because he was the best guy they had, sort of a James Earl Jones being *aware* that he was being a James Earl Jones. I decided not to mind the rasta Caliban either: *I-man mistress showed I-man dee, and dy dog, and dy bush.* Her Daisy Mae shtick was so mannered you couldn't tell if she was good or not. She showed lots of leg, and a couple of times a panty flash. She did a toss-her-head thing, a twirl-her-hair-on-her-index-finger thing, a tug-down-the-back-of-her-skirt thing, the last of which might have been unconscious. While flirting with Ferdinand, who had Harry Potter glasses, she ran a finger down his arm, which I think I thought was good, and that bothered me since I was looking for weak points.

When I went up to her afterward, she said, God, you *too*. I can't believe I sent that out to all these people. Did you get a good look at my underwear? I think I need to get very drunk.

I greatly enjoyed your underwear, I said. I was assuming you'd calibrated every little glimpse.

I did *not*, she said. I was *exploited*. I mean, I *sort* of was. Will you make sure I get *very* drunk?

Why am *I* elected? I said. Did your husband stalk out when he saw your unmentionables?

He's in California, she said. Thank *God*. If you don't want to—

No no no, I said. Nothing would make me happier. Well *that's* not true. Should I spirit you out of here right now?

I can't not speak to people, she said. Can we in a little?

I brought two Jamesons and slipped one into her hand without interrupting her conversation with a tall henna redhead, whose arm she kept touching in what looked like supplication. I took a stool at the bar and watched her move from person to person, clapping her palm to her forehead, her palm to her mouth, shaking her head no. When she came back to me her glass was empty. Could you wait for me outside? she said.

She came out before I'd finished my cigarette. I'm parked over there, I said. So where shall we go?

Oh, you're such a smoothie, she said. She plucked my cigarette out of my mouth, took a drag and tossed it. How do you keep the fly bitches off your dick?

I stopped at a liquor store where you bought through a Plexiglas window, and we passed a bottle of Jameson as we drove back to my place in the Village. After we fucked, she wept, then went into the bathroom. She ran water, but I could hear her vomiting, then gargling. She came out and kissed me, tasting only of my Scope. We fucked again, neither of us could come, and she started putting on clothes. She refused to let me walk her to a taxi. I pulled on jeans anyway. She said, You really don't listen, then pushed me onto the bed. We fucked again. I walked her to a taxi, our hands in each other's hip pockets.

She'd gone to high school in one of those Greek-name noplaces in Ohio, where of course she'd played Marian the Librarian though she couldn't really sing—which wasn't true, because one night I heard her lilting wordlessly while brushing her hair to go home to her husband and I thought, *Man, you are in too fucking deep*—and what's-her-name in *Our Town*. Couldn't wait to get to NYU, and had made herself into such a New York person that she now talked about Ohio in order to seem exotic. What's round on both ends and high in the middle? she'd say, and nobody knew. She'd wanted to be a serious Shakespearean and went to study in London for a year, but she could never even work up a Brit accent that hung together. So now she supported her-self and Ted Hughes by doing commercials. In one, she was a satis-fied bank customer; in another, she and some actor threw snowballs at each other. I taped them off the television—she refused to give me copies—and during the months after I got out of the hospital I used to watch them to make myself feel like shit, which was no great achievement. I've still got them somewhere. No, that's a false note: they're in the bottom drawer of my file cabinet, five feet from where I'm sitting.

I was about to say I don't know where the time has gone since then, but of course I know, since I've taken to keeping a journal: time of get-ting up, time of hitting hay, progress on the porch I'm building onto the cabin, stuff done to keep money coming in, people who come to visit. (That last item is a joke. Though see the very end of this story.) My son, who's now in film school at UCLA, his mother having raised him right, will find the notebooks in that drawer when this place becomes his, or that's the plan. Nothing in them either to embarrass or enlighten him, just a record of how the days went. This isn't part of that: you might call this the story of how the days began. But we don't want to hit the woo-woo note too hard. I've also taken to smoking weed—can you tell?

We were lying in bed, in this very room, looking out at the bare tree-tops against the moonlit sky, when a string of yelping geese flew over, apparently heading south over into Plainfield.

My God, it sounds like *dogs*, she said.

'Tis new to thee, I said. Let's see if we can see them.

I got up, naked, and went to the window, and she came to me, naked. There, I said.

I pointed and cupped her rough-skinned buttock with my other hand. A wavering V, moving across the sky. Her flesh eased into my side, a breast against my rib cage. The cold air had made the nipple hard—you see I don't flatter myself.

That's them? she said. They're so high up. We must not be hearing them in real time. Do you ever have dreams where you fly?

Used to, I said.

So why do you think you stopped having them?

Now you're getting personal, I said. Okay, because I don't need to have them anymore, how's that? My every wish has come true.

You don't have to be ugly, she said. She moved away from me, got back in the bed and pulled the comforter up to her neck. I went and got in with her. This is a lot different for you than it is for me, she said.

Okay, I said. But that's, like, a universal truth, no?

I ventured a hand onto her coarse hairs. Sometimes you guess right: she did something with her hips to arch up against the hand. I ventured a finger down.

Mm, okay, she said. I'm going to pretend. Just do that. She writhed, then said, No. No, stop it, that was mean what you said. You still don't get it that I'm smart. Would you do that some more?

You feel good there, I said. We lucked out, didn't we?

Sssh, she said. Somebody will hear you.

Somebody's always hearing me, I said. That's the nature of my disease.

And you're so unique, she said. That's another selling point.

Fuck you, I said. I really do like you.

See, she said, I'm the same person as you. I'm only going to say that once.

This was our Friday night conversation, before our Saturday night conversation, the one where I asked her if we needed to be having this conversation. On Friday night she'd been drunk and travel weary—as opposed to Saturday night, when she was just drunk—and we'd sat up sipping the Jameson she'd bought, which diffused into your tongue like stinging honey. When I got back here, a month later, alone, in a walking cast, the bottle was still sitting on the night table, and the two snifters had penny-sized pools of amber.

———

At the time all this happened I'd hit the wall moneywise. In order to keep my job—at a men's magazine, if that's important—I'd rented a studio in the East Village, where I spent Tuesdays through Fridays and drove up here late Friday nights, sometimes getting in after daybreak. I'd taken over the entire mortgage on the cabin and was still covering the maintenance on the apartment where I'd lived with my ex-wife and my son. A six-hour drive, in the car with the sunroof, on which I was still making payments. But hitting the wall—what did that mean really? It was like one of my son's computer games, where you're *about* to hit a wall but then take an impossible left turn, the stones fly past on your right and now you're in another space skimming over a field of green, then leaping a trench to land on a hillock where a monster attacks you but you biff the monster away—*biff biff*—and he vanishes howling and then you're skirting another wall, in which a gate opens: you go through, everything drops away beneath you and you're flying over an ocean where fishes are sporting. To translate: I'd send away for a new credit card, and on it went.

These days I'm out of debt, like wise old Ben Franklin but not so fat and femmy, having lost twenty pounds and shaved my head. Studio in the East Village long gone, maintenance on the apartment off my back, thanks to my ex-wife's smart investing and, I have to say, her charity, and the cabin and its ten acres paid off in six more years. My son says he doesn't want the place, but we'll see about that. From this window, you can see his swing—or you could if it were daylight— still hanging from the big maple tree. I cut the seat from a pressure-treated two-by-six: it will outlast the ropes, already rotting, then me, then him. I used to push him and he'd fly out over the bed of daylilies, stretching to touch the toe of his sneaker to this one high branch. Blackberry brambles and tall grass now grow where I used to stand behind him, and the bare patch of earth is gone where his feet used to come down. The only thing worse would have been to keep clearing it all with the lawn mower every year—but we can't have *that* tone taking over, it's worse than the woo-woo. Let's get back to something like Ben Franklin being fat and femmy, that was good. I've cut up my credit cards, like the people on *The Dave Ramsey Show,* though I wrote the American Express number down so at Christmas I can still send shit from Harry & David. Okay, we like the word "shit."

The people on my Christmas list: now that would tell you something. My mother in the assisted-living place outside Washington. (Ah, but is there any other kind of living? I live assisted by whoever does those rotisserie chickens at the Price Chopper in St. Johnsbury.) The two editors who still give me work. My ex-wife and my son: gifts neither acknowledged nor returned. This is the year I crossed off my father, whom I ordered to be moved from the hospital in White Plains to the assisted-dying place, a mile from the Price Chopper. I visit on my shopping days, but he no longer knows me, and even if Royal Riviera pears could be mashed into the feeding tube, there's a limit, is there not? But I still send gifts to his nurses: the fat one, the other one, and the one with the nose stud. And to the doctor who put the titanium screw in my leg, then removed it. And to Dan somebody in Barre, whose card I always sign off on as "A Friend." He probably gets shit from his wife—looking down I saw moonlight glint off his wedding ring, although, as I say, it wasn't me—who probably thinks she knows what "Friend" means.

When I got out of the hospital I emailed my ex-wife and asked if we could have lunch sometime. She was actually the one who said, No, no lunches, no can do—I attributed that line to *my* Friend as an in-joke, though who was there to be amused? I emailed the Friend too, but it bounced back. All I'd said was *I hope you're well and that your life is good.* Now you'd swear *that* was harmless. I Googled her once—that "once" is another false note, but this late in the story we need a little hit of the elegiac—and didn't even find a Facebook page. So I assume—well, I don't know what to assume. The worst? The best? Her twentieth high school reunion was coming up, I found out that much, and they were looking for her and three other people. It would bring everything around nicely if I said I've had no Friends since, but there's no end of

Friends, though there is eventually. My latest just went home a couple of hours ago, because she has to be up at six thirty to get in and open her store. Another refugee from New York, except she's been here since the eighties. She's my age—strands of white, which I've decided to find fetching, in the single braid that goes down her back—but with a yoga body. Her store carries mystical books, herbal cosmetics, hoodoo powders she gets from a place in New Orleans. She will *not* stock crystals or dream catchers, which she calls wankery. If you know her, she'll sell you weed, which is how I got to know her. That sounds circular, but what I mean is she sells weed to the nurse with the nose stud, who introduced us. The first night she and I got high together, I asked if she'd ever had an out-of-body experience—I was getting ready to start telling my story—and she said, Is there any other kind?

Locals

||||||

When I was nineteen years old, I dropped out of the Berklee College of Music, where I'd been studying guitar—the one thing I'd ever been halfway good at—to tour with a band that wanted a screaming lead player, and when that all got too stupid, I moved back in with my parents in Connecticut, stayed in my room trying to get scales and modes and arpeggios up to speed and coming to realize that never in a million years. My father was at me to go to work for him and start regular college in the fall; he owned a chain of furniture stores, and a salesman had quit at the one in Westport. Then Mike, my hippie older brother, called from the hill town in western Mass where he was living in a cabin on a dairy farm, doing chores in exchange for rent, and said I should come hang out; it was a cool place, with a small lake and a bar where maybe I could get a job playing. This was the summer of 1975. Mike picked me up at the bus in Greenfield, and I remember driving with him up along the river and the train tracks, through Martin's Falls and Crowsfield, then taking the turn-off for Bozrah, over a concrete bridge built by the WPA, onto a narrow road up out of the valley, following a brook with whitewater tumbling over the boulders, then past the town hall and post office, the church with the square steeple, the general store and the white clapboard houses, and on to a farm at the top of a dirt road and getting out of his car into the quiet, looking off at the green humpbacked hills and smelling that good air. It made me think I'd had enough of the world, and I still think so.

Mike's pot was so strong it made me paranoid, and the bar at the lake turned out to be all shitkicker music, so there went those temptations. I helped out some at the farm and put up a handwritten notice at the general store: *Lawns Mowed, Leaves Raked, General Yard Work, Reliable Service,* with Mike's number repeated across the bottom where you could tear it off. He told me the locals did this shit for themselves, but I'd noticed that people with money were discovering the place: two and a half hours from Boston, four from New York. I spent forty dollars on a decent used mower, and if somebody called I'd bring it around in the trunk of Mike's old Ford Fairlane, which didn't look too professional. Still, there's a right and a wrong way to mow a lawn—my father taught me that—and I'd always rake up after, so the weekend people started asking if I also did handyman stuff: put up a new gutter, fix a leak around the chimney, replace cracked clapboards, paint the house. Sure, let's get together on a price. While I didn't really know what I was doing, it was all pretty intuitive, and Mike's farmer let me borrow tools and a ladder. When I got more calls than I could handle by myself, I talked Mike into coming to work for me. On account of my father, "businessman" always had a bad sound to me, but it turned out that's what I was.

My company still does lawns and landscaping, anywhere in a fifty-mile radius; we cut, split and deliver firewood, plow driveways in the winter. Our main business, though, is construction. I'll still put on a tool belt myself, but a lot of days I'll just be driving from one job site to another, making sure stuff's getting done right. At any given time I might have up to a dozen people working for me—master carpenter, plumber, electrician, a heavy-equipment operator who doubles as a mechanic, a girl to run the office and answer the phone, and a revolving cast of Asscrack Harrys for the grunt work. Though I'd rather do renovations and additions—I hate to see it getting too built up around here—if somebody comes in and buys five or ten acres and wants a nice log house, I won't turn away the business. I've probably done my own part in fucking up the look of things. I had to put up a metal barn on Watch Hill Road, where I've got my office, for all the equipment—backhoe, dozer, tractor and brush hog, plow trucks, a flatbed. I had them leave a row of trees so in the summer you can't see it when you go by.

Mike moved to Alaska twenty years ago; he said it was getting too suburban here, which I took to be aimed at me. He'd be sixty-eight, so he's probably still alive, but I didn't even know how to get in touch with him when our father died. My main guys now are Myron Stannard, Jesse Biggs and Johnny Iaconelli. Customers love to watch Myron when he's doing tree work: he's a rock star up there in the cherry picker, with an Asscrack Harry as his chainsaw tech to hand up a fresh saw when the one he's using starts to get dull. Jesse, who does the heavy equipment piece, moved up here from Hartford to get away from what he called "the crime"—like there was just one. He's the only black man in town. Both of them can bang nails and do whatever else, but Johnny's my master carpenter. He's not as old as the rest of us—he's got to be late forties—and he's been with me the shortest time. Myron warned me he could be hard to handle when he was drinking; still, he's the best around, and I'll take a drink myself. So will Jesse. They're artists, those three. I'm the one who knows how to run a business, though, and how to deal with the clientele; I get why get rich people have a boner for plank doors, woodstoves, Hoosier cabinets and eight-over-eight windows. I keep track of sources for salvaged wainscoting and hand-hewn beams, or I can take a drawknife to a beam from the sawmill and make it *look* hand hewn. I bought an old house myself, on a dirt road. I've got three albums with pictures of all my projects; mostly to show clients, but some nights I'll just take them out to look at them.

While my father lived long enough to know that at least one of his sons wasn't a fuckup, I think it hurt him when my wife and I split up without having kids. That would be a whole other story, not really to the point of this one. You'd think Bozrah was a town where you'd want to raise a family, but the select board closed the elementary school ten years ago to keep taxes down, and what kids there are get bused twenty miles down the valley. The ones who have anything on the ball get away as soon as they're finished with high school. Even Amber, the girl in my office, moved down to Greenfield for a while to go to community college. It's only the Asscrack Harrys and their fat girlfriends who stick around, living with their parents, or in the shitbox houses people were putting up before the five-acre zoning came in, or over in Egdon where you can still stick a trailer on a half-acre lot. So we've got fewer people than we did in 1975, except now there's an MIT professor, a Broadway actor and his boyfriend, a retired anchorman who used to do local news out of Boston, a Web designer, a mystery writer who supposedly sets her stuff in the area. What keeps this place from turning into a Lenox or a Stockbridge is that there's nothing here. The nearest supermarkets are in Greenfield and North Adams, forty-five minutes either way, and the same for the nearest hospital, which if you're retired could be a deal breaker right there. Since the general store closed you have to go over to Egdon for gasoline or a quart of milk. There's not even an antique shop. The old bar at the lake is now a restaurant called Locavore; you don't see many cars outside, and when that goes under, I'll be the only employer in town.

For me personally, it's all good. It was my company that turned the Lakeside Lounge into Locavore with barn board and copper countertops; we built a writing studio in the mystery lady's barn; when a guy whose company makes drones for the military bought the sweet little Federal house next to the town hall, we dismantled it, numbered everything and put it back together for him in the middle of the hundred acres he owns on Charrington Hill. But I feel like I got in just under the wire. Last fall a real-estate agent from Pittsfield called me with an offer of four-fifty for my house, which I'd bought for a buck and a quarter. I hadn't put it on the market—somebody from New York had just driven by while leaf peeping on the back roads. It's like I'm finally one of the locals myself: if I were young and starting out again, I couldn't afford to live here.

A couple of years ago, an investment banker bought the dairy farm where Mike used to work, and he comes up here for a couple months in the summer. His caretaker lives in Mike's old cabin, which we moved out of sight of the main house. The Holsteins are long gone; now there's a herd of shaggy longhorns grazing on his side hill among a flock of twisting metal sculptures. (It was Johnny who dug down with the backhoe and poured the concrete.) The guy also bought Billy Sibley's little ranch house, just to tear it down so he wouldn't have to see it when he turned onto his road. *That* got the locals' attention.

Billy worked for me maybe fifteen years; before that he had a roofing business, and he built that little house with his own hands. Amber called him Uncle Bill; actually, he would've been her great-uncle. Billy never got married. He built the house for his sweetheart when he came home from Vietnam in '66—he'd put in his years and he saw where shit was heading—but she broke their engagement and left town, and that was it as far as Billy and females. The banker offered him twice what the place was worth, then three times, and finally Billy grabbed his chance to retire in style. His younger brother was already down in Florida. We got the contract to tear the house down; if we hadn't, somebody would have. I would've put Billy on something else while this was going on, but he said no, he wanted to do the job himself. Mostly he supervised, since his back was getting worse from sleeping on what he called a few-ton. Still, Jesse let him run the dozer when it came time to fill in the cellar hole.

Billy stayed with his nephew for the time being; the nephew, Amber's father, was a drunk whose wife had quit her job and walked out leaving him hard up for money, so he charged Billy fifty dollars a month. Amber got on the Internet and found Billy a bunch of Florida listings, but he didn't like any of them, and when she dropped out of school and moved back up to live with her boyfriend over in Egdon, he got an efficiency in the senior housing complex there. He'd quit working by then, put the house money into CDs that didn't pay shit—I *told* him not to—and started collecting Social Security. The first good day in spring he'd always be on the lake in his aluminum motorboat; Amber's got a picture on her phone of him holding a largemouth bass that measured sixteen inches. He and Jesse used to go deer hunting—Jesse was a vet too; he'd been at Hamburger Hill in '69—but when they went out last December Billy had so much trouble walking that they had to turn back after an hour. In February, Amber told me he was in the VA hospital down in Northampton, and they didn't expect him to go home.

When I came into his room they had him sitting up in the chair next to his bed, in a white gown that showed his hairless shins. He had a few days of stubble.

"Hey, bub," I said. "How you feelin'? You *look* pretty good."

"Is that so."

"What are the doctors saying?"

"Well, they don't dance all around the mulberry bush like they used to. Get my affairs in order, that's the quotation. Amber's been helping me out on that."

"Jesus, Billy. I'm sorry."

"Not any sorrier than me, I'll tell you that."

"There anything I can do for you?" I said. "I bring you anything?"

"Not a thing." Shook his head again. "Nope, I'm all set here."

"How about music?" Billy would always have his heavy-duty Makita radio going while he was on a job. How many times in his life had he heard "Layla" and "Hot Blooded" and "Alison"? They weren't even songs he grew up with.

"I don't care about it. Amber asked me did I want to borrow her iPod, iPad I guess she's got. *Borrow.* I don't know why that tickled me." He lifted his chin at the television that had women's basketball on mute. "You ever watch these gals?" He ran a hand over his face "Come to think of it. It's a funny thing to ask a man, but I got my razor in that drawer, and I don't like these nurses fussing with me."

I found a towel to put around his neck and when I was soaping up his face his stubble felt just like mine. He had the same problem place I do, the corners of the mouth, and I told him to stick his tongue up under. "*Now* you look handsome," I said.

"Sure, handsome enough to go right into the box. What kind of a day is it out?"

"Cold. They're calling for another six to ten inches overnight. And we got to start tearing out a house on Miller Brook Road where the guy let his pipes freeze. Boy, you want to see some water damage."

"Then I guess you'll have quite a time of it. I tell you Jesse was by? Said I better straighten up and fly right so we could get back in the woods. Nobody knows *what* the hell to say. He had his mind set on getting a minister to come around."

"You think you might want that?"

"*Those* birds? What I *should've* done, I should've just taken myself out in the goddamn woods. You want to think you'll make up your mind to it tomorrow, and pretty soon they got you in this goddamn place. Guess I'll know the next time."

The lady I'd started seeing when Billy got sick taught at the community college in Greenfield. Amber had taken her for composition and said she was a bitch on wheels. This was before I ever met Kristin, but I can see how she might have come off like that. Back in the nineties she was studying to get her Ph.D. at BU when she got pregnant; she married the guy, which she said was the mistake of her life, moved with him to Stanford, where he'd landed some big teaching job, and now here she was in what she liked to call The Land Time Forgot, grading papers while her eighteen-year-old was bumming his way around Europe. I met her at a bar in Greenfield where I'd gone after freezing my ass all day at Miller Brook Road. I went over to her because she wasn't so young that she would've blown me off from the get-go. I had a few years on her but I was in decent shape from working. She must have let me keep talking to her because she couldn't quite figure me out—a guy in the construction business that wasn't a Republican? She said she'd *never* asked a man home with her that she'd just met. It turned out she liked to play rough in bed, and of course I was up for that. I think both of us knew the deal, but we started hanging out and pretty soon it had turned into a thing where I was pretending that she needed to finish this book she was supposedly working on and she was pretending that I needed to get back to playing the guitar. She was a good drinker, and we were both tired of not having anybody in our lives.

Kristin didn't know the people who worked for me—I doubt she would have remembered Amber—and that was how I liked to keep it. I'd see her two or three times a week, and other nights I'd go out drinking with Johnny, who was usually having trouble with his old lady. We'd ask Jesse along sometimes—his wife had given it a try up here, then went to live with her sister down in Queens—but we'd had a couple incidents. One night in North Adams, at a bar we should've known to stay out of, Johnny and I had to go over and straighten out some asshole and his buddy, Johnny lost his shit on the guy, I got into it, Jesse tried to pull Johnny away and old as he was *he* ended up getting into it. We spent overnight in jail because Johnny had put one of them in the hospital. So sometimes I'd just have him and Jesse come to my house, and Billy before he got sick. Billy could drink too—he had a saying, "Good for what ails ya, and if nothin' ails ya, it's good for that." We'd sit around the kitchen table playing hearts and I'd put on music I thought they could tolerate. One thing, nobody had to worry about a DUI getting home, because the staties never patrolled up this way and the town constable knew our vehicles. Johnny said he wished he was me—pussy on demand and nobody waiting up. So when was he going to meet this lady?

Amber wanted to know about the new girlfriend too. When she realized who it was, she said I had to be fucking kidding, that Kristin was a stuck-up cunt who was probably just after me for whatever she could get, which wasn't too flattering. But of course you had to know Amber. Her father was always broke and she'd never been any farther than Northampton to visit Billy, so she didn't have much of a framework for anything. Whatever Kristin might have wanted from me, it wasn't anything along the lines of houses, cars, vacations—what Amber would have thought of as the good life. Amber's boyfriend was getting heavier into drugs and she was always talking about moving out. I said I'd help her anytime, but you could see it was one of those dramas that was just going to go on and on. She could have stayed at my house until she got shit figured out—I had all these rooms I wasn't using—but that would have been misunderstood, by everybody. Amber, Johnny, Billy dying in the hospital, Myron with his chainsaw act, Asscrack Harrys coming and going: none of this was anything Kristin needed to be around.

So when she offered to come with me to Billy's funeral, I said I'd be fine and nobody'd be expecting her to show up anyway. She said in that case she'd go to Boston for a few days; she could cancel her Monday and Tuesday classes, and she might see me Tuesday night. I couldn't tell if she was bent out of shape or just glad she wouldn't have to meet these characters. This was the end of March; the old-timers were sugaring, and the rich people were skiing up at Killington, or maybe tanning in the Caribbean. The snow had begun to melt, but it was supposed to turn cold again next week and the ground was still hard, so Jesse would have to hold off on going in with the backhoe to dig the grave. Amber said it was Billy's wish to get buried here in town instead of the veterans' cemetery down in Agawam.

The service was at ten o'clock Saturday morning, at the funeral home down in Martin's Falls. I got there early and found Johnny, Jesse and Amber out in Johnny's new Pathfinder, parked next to Amber's Chevy Cobalt that had the one primered quarter, with the heater and the radio going, passing a bottle. Johnny's wife was nowhere to be seen, so they must have been fighting again. I climbed in the backseat with Jesse, who took a pull, wiped the mouth of the bottle with the lapel of his suit jacket and offered it to me. "Looks like this is going to be a long day," I said.

Johnny watched me tip it up. "Pussy. You need to do better than *that* if you want to run with the big dogs."

"Don't think I won't."

"*Hey,*" Amber said, and reached out her hand. She took a pretty good pull too—maybe not the best idea because she couldn't have gone more than one-ten, which made her a standout around here. "So listen, how this works? The minister said they're going to have a time for people to get up and talk if they want."

"Fuck, I will if anybody else does," Johnny said. "Let me have that bad boy."

"I should do it," I said. "Would your father want to?"

"He probably hasn't even woke up," Amber said. "He said he hates funerals. Like who doesn't? Fucker."

Johnny took another slug and passed me the bottle. There wasn't much left. "I guess I could say how he ran the grill and shit. When the firemen used to have the chicken barbecues."

Jesse gave him a look. *"Billy* did?"

"I *think* it was Billy. Shit, maybe I better not. Jesse, man, you were closer to him than anybody."

"I'll get up," Jesse said.

"Maybe I could tell about the bird that time?" Amber said. "Where he put it in the shoe box in the office for its wing to get better and then it flew into the window? I can leave out the window part."

I looked at my watch. "We need to get in there."

Johnny said, "We need to *finish* this," and passed the bottle to Amber.

They'd set up the casket in front of the rows of folding chairs, with a flag draped over it and the top half open like a Dutch door. You could see what looked like a statue of Billy inside, displayed not quite flat on its back and turned a little toward the audience.

"Jesus fuckin' Christ," Johnny said to Amber. "You didn't tell me about *this* shit." The organ was going—probably organ music on tape—but Johnny was loud enough that a couple people looked up from where they were sitting. There couldn't have been more than a dozen in all, ladies in flowered dresses, men with too-tight suit jackets. I saw Myron in the back row, in his sport coat and a plaid shirt; he got up and headed my way. "Johnny okay to be here?" Then he must have smelled it on me. "Ho boy."

We sidestepped into the third row of chairs, Johnny taking Amber's arm to guide her in after Jesse and me. "Hey, wait," Amber said. "Don't we have to like go up and pay our respect?"

"I'm as close as *I* fuckin' need to be," Johnny said. A lady in front turned, Amber stuck her tongue out and the lady whipped her head back around and leaned to whisper to what must have been her husband. Amber got up, worked herself past Johnny and fell in behind some old guy with a four-footed cane, probably some friend of Billy's from back in the day. He nodded at Billy like he was passing him on the street, then shuffled back to his chair. Amber stopped in front of the casket, reached in, then came back and squeezed in over Johnny.

"I touched his *arm*," she said. "I was going to touch his hand, but it looked like it had foundation all over it. Face *definitely* did."

"I don't want to fuckin' hear about it," Johnny said.

Somebody behind us said, "You mind keeping it down?"

Amber turned and gave the finger and I looked around: it was Junior Copley, chief of the volunteer fire department.

"Hey Junior?" Johnny said. "Whyn't you go fuck yourself?"

"Okay," I told Johnny. "Let's just chill."

"*This* motherfucker needs to chill," Johnny said. I noticed somebody behind us—it could have been Myron—getting up and walking back toward the double doors.

"How come we can't talk?" Amber said. "I'm his only next of kin."

A pair of heavyset guys in cheap black suits and hair buzzed down to nothing came up and stopped beside Johnny's chair, and the fatter one of the two bent down to whisper. "Sir? Can we see you for a minute? Ma'am, if you want to come too." The other one stood there with his arms folded like Mr. Clean.

"Bullshit," Amber said, good and loud.

"Hey, Johnny?" I said. "Let's not make this into a thing." I had no idea who the guys were—they looked like small-time mafia out of Chicopee. The funeral director was head-to-head with the minister up by the casket, looking like they wanted to get this show on the road.

I stood up, then Amber, then Johnny; Jesse looked over at us but stayed in his chair. The fat one led the three of us back to the double doors, the Mr. Clean guy behind us, and out into the vestibule.

"Look," the fat one said, "these things are heavy for everybody, you know what I'm saying? What we don't want is—"

"Yeah, okay, you did your job," I said. "We're cool."

"If you haven't signed the visitors' thing, it's over there." The Mr. Clean one nodded at a book sitting open on an oak lectern.

"Right," I said. "Let's get that done and we'll go back in."

"So you're with *them* now?" Amber said.

"Sir?" The fat one touched Johnny's elbow to guide him over to the lectern, which he shouldn't have done, and Johnny shoved him against the wall and then the other guy was on him, twisting his arm up behind his back. Johnny broke away, swung at him, and both guys took him down. Amber went for them, but I pulled her back—that was my excuse.

"You think we're playing now?" The fat one was panting and sweating. He took Johnny by the hair and slammed his face against the floor. The other one had his cellphone out. "Okay, you," the fat one said to me. "I'm giving you a break, right? Get the lady out of here and we'll call it good."

"Where's he going to be?" I said.

"What, you want to come with? He'll get his phone call. You and this lady better scoot before I change my mind."

I had to get Amber under the arm and march her out to my truck— I told her she could pick up her car later. She wouldn't speak to me, but once we got clear of Martin's Falls she made me pull over, got out, stumbled into the dead grass, went to her knees and vomited. I let her have her privacy while traffic whipped past, then found paper towels behind the seat and did my best to clean her face with some old snow. "You okay to stand up?" I said.

"We have to go back."

"I don't think so," I said.

"What happened to Johnny?"

"Let's just get you home. You think you can walk?"

"I can walk. Why couldn't I walk?" She shook her head. "I fucked up, didn't I?"

I helped her back toward the truck and she sat down in the dirt with her back against the front wheel. "I think I have to again," she said.

"Just let it go," I said. If a cop pulled over to check us out, I might pass the Breathalyzer and I might not. She turned her head and coughed out some more. I took another paper towel and dabbed at her lips. "When did you start drinking?"

"Over at Johnny's," she said. "Before he went to pick up Jesse."

"So pretty early is what you're saying."

"Pretty early," she said.

"Is it going to work if we try to get going? You're going to catch cold sitting here."

"Fuck, where's my *coat*?"

"We'll find it. Best thing now is just get you home." I reached down; she took my hands and let me pull her up and help her into the cab. I got in my side and buckled her up.

After a couple of miles she said, "Where are we going?"

"Like I said. Taking you home. You have anything to eat this morning? Might do you good. We could stop off at the Hob Nob."

"Gross, no *way*. I don't know, maybe."

"See how you feel when we get there. You want music?"

"I don't care, if it isn't something shitty."

"Check in there." I pointed to the glove box.

She looked through the CDs and shut it again. "That must be the kind of shit what's-her-name likes. You know what we used to call her? Bitch on wheels."

"Yeah, you said."

She looked down at her long fake nails; I guess she'd painted them black for the occasion. "You're like not into me at *all*, are you? Because I don't think I'm really probably into you."

"I'd say you're a little on the young side," I said. "Like about thirty years?"

"Thirty-seven. I looked up your Social one time. So how old is *she*?"

"She's appropriate." We were coming into Crowsfield, so I set the cruise at thirty to be extra sure. There's usually one of them parked beside the convenience store. "You've seen her."

"Yeah, that's what I want to look like when *I* get old. *Not*."

"Look," I said, "we better get some food into you. Then you can go home and sleep."

"You don't even know I was at Johnny's last night."

"That wouldn't be my business." The past week I'd thought Johnny was hanging out at her desk too much. I'd seen her touching his chest when she was making a point; she was always touching somebody. But no, I didn't even know. "So where was his wife?"

"I don't know, Johnny said she went to Foxwoods."

"What about your boyfriend?"

"Everybody gets to do what they want," she said. "Anyways, *you're* not going to tell, and Johnny's not."

"Perfect. What could possibly go wrong?"

"Shit," she said. "That was real attractive, me puking and everything."

I'd never seen where Amber lived—someplace in Egdon, that's all I knew. It was mostly A-frames, double-wides and unpainted farmhouses; when the old town hall burned down in the fifties they'd put up a Quonset hut. There was still a commune left over from the hippie days, and you could smell their goats half a mile away. Amber pointed me to the shortcut off the Bozrah road, which turned to dirt and then back to pavement and came out by the Egdon Tavern. "What do I do here?"

"Left at the stop. Then just keep going till I tell you."

We passed a swamp with cattails, a falling-down barn with no house nearby—I'd have to find out who the owner was—next to a cornfield that nobody'd gotten around to harvesting last fall.

"He left me his all money," she said. "He didn't want my dad or any of them getting it. I'm going to be a rich-bitch like *her*."

"I would doubt she's rich. You know what she probably makes a year? It's not like she's teaching at Harvard."

"Yeah, well she sure lets you know it. Okay, so fine, it's this school for fuckin' losers. She was always looking at my nails and shit—and even like the way she said my name. It's a fucking porno name, okay? Well, my moms thought it was beautiful. You know what I'm going to do? Go somewhere."

"Where were you thinking?"

"Where the fuck ever. Away from *this* shit place."

"So am I going to be losing you?"

"Well, I don't have it yet. It's got to go through probation—no, what is it, probate. Shit, and I didn't even get the fucking *flag*. Just up here on the right. You think they'll still let me have it?"

We turned into a dirt drive, with a two-legged wooden sign reading Nagirreb Estates. Right, I remembered: a developer from Holyoke named Tony Berrigan started putting up crappo town houses in the middle of a field and then got sent away for tax fraud. I don't know why he wanted to make it sound like someplace on the West Bank, but maybe Egdon had enough Sunnyhursts and Bonnie Braes.

"That one there." She pointed to a two-family with aluminum siding and a three-foot-square overhang above the door. The path to it was just footprints, and somebody'd parked a rusted-out Buick Regal on the muddy lawn, next to a lamppost with the numbers 5-7 on it. "You better just go."

"You still be in Monday? Or you need some time off?"

"I don't not show up for work," she said. "I sort of don't want to see Johnny, though."

"You might not."

"He's going to be pissed at *you*," she said. "Just saying."

T-Mobile doesn't work at my house, so I still have a landline and an answering machine. I thought it would be blinking when I came in— who else would Johnny call? But I made coffee, ate some cereal and still no word. From Kristin either; she was doing whatever you do in Boston. I turned on the radio, forgetting that Saturday afternoon was the opera. I tried to stick with it for a few minutes, then turned it off. My parents used to listen when I was little, and this man with a cultured voice would give the plot beforehand, which I could never follow— actually, I remember his name, too. Milton Cross. He must be dead by now. I remember our house smelled like mothballs, and the women singers would be shrieking away and the men singers bellowing, and I always thought my parents were just pretending to themselves that it was beautiful. I mean, I can recognize it as beautiful now—I've studied enough theory since then—but it's not a beauty I can make myself rise up to all that often. Kristin was going to take me. She went down to the Met when she could afford it; she said supertitles made all the difference. Watching on DVD was good, but not the same thing. And she wasn't even an opera buff per se—just a regular educated person, and this was part of life to her. I wasn't that anymore, and I wasn't completely the other thing either—Amber spotted that the second she opened my glove box, not that she didn't know already. Nights when I don't go out, I'll read books because I can't stand how a television *sounds,* no matter what they have on, which means half the shit people talk about is lost on me. Hey, this is where I live. When Obama ran the second time, I looked up the local returns the morning after, and Bozrah went for Romney 178 to 51. Jesse refuses to vote, even though he sent Obama a hundred dollars, so the one would've been me. The locals just know me as basically a good guy, kind of an oddball sometimes, and of course the new people wouldn't think to have me over for cocktails. I'm their fucking contractor.

Johnny didn't call till five o'clock, from the lockup in Greenfield. They were charging him with assault and battery, disturbing the peace, drunk and disorderly, they'd probably towed his car, they hadn't set bail and could I get somebody down there. I tried the lawyer who'd handled that bullshit in North Adams, but all I could do was leave a message, so I drove down myself and there was nobody to talk to but the cop at the desk, who wouldn't let me in to see him. Johnny had to stay in till Monday when he could finally get in front of a judge and the lawyer got everything knocked down to disturbing the peace. I handed over my debit card to pay the fine, wrote a check to the lawyer and told Johnny I'd run him back up to Martin's Falls—turned out they hadn't towed him after all. He said he'd found out about the suits: one of them worked at the funeral home as an usher and did the heavy lifting, and the other was an off-duty cop picking up extra change. They'd both been in Afghanistan.

He got in the truck, shot the finger at the courthouse and said, "How's my face?" I turned the mirror toward him. "Fuck," he said. "Good job."

"They knew some tricks," I said. "I felt bad I didn't get your back."

"Hey, they had a few years on you. No offense. Tell you the truth, I think *I* might be getting a little old for this shit. Fuck, man, ten years ago? *Five* years ago. I owe you money."

"Forget it. I can probably write off the lawyer as legal fees. Buy us lunch if you want."

"You mean drinkies too, right? That was a long couple days, man."

"I guess I wouldn't say no."

"*I* ought to," he said.

We drove over to Buster's, where they've got wooden booths and old metal signs on the walls and they keep it dark in the middle of the day and the waitresses will flirt back with you up to a point. We got a young one whose white apron was tight across her breasts and we both ordered Jack on the rocks. Johnny looked at her chest and said, "I want mine *double*." She said, "I could've guessed."

"Hey, I might not be that old after all," he said when she went off to the bar. "We don't have anything this afternoon, do we?"

"Miller Brook. Jesse and Myron are over there."

"Well hell then."

"I'm going to need you tomorrow."

"Tomorrow, man. My favorite day. Thank you, sweetheart." The waitress set our drinks down. "And how about a couple of menus?"

"No problem," she said.

"You don't have to hurry," he said. "Not that we don't like your company."

We raised glasses, and he downed about half of his and said, "Hal-a-fuckin'-looyah." I guess I downed half of mine too. "So Amber get home okay?" As he said it, he looked up at an old Kelly Tires sign.

"Well," I said, "she got home."

"How about Jesse?"

"He probably caught a ride with Myron."

"See that?" he said. "I fuckin' *love* Jesse. Because he knows how to fuckin' carry himself. I don't give a shit if he's black or what he is. Now me, couple of drinks and I'm liable to get right into it with you."

The waitress put menus in front of us. "Can I tell you about our specials?"

"Sweetheart," Johnny said, "you make *everything* special. Why don't you come sit down with us?"

"You could bring us another round," I said. On her way to the bar, she whispered something to an older waitress.

"Goddamn right," Johnny said. "Let's be assholes. So okay, you took her home and then what? She say anything to you?"

"She was pretty hammered," I said. "I kind of let it all go in one ear."

"Shit," he said. "Yeah, I don't know, fuck it. Arlene hates my ass anyway." He downed the rest of his drink. "Hey, she's got all that bullshit with her boyfriend, plus Billy and dealing with all that, so we're having some drinks, sitting on the couch—I'm not gonna fuckin' send her home. She *is* hot. You know this."

"So did Arlene find out?"

"I been off the *grid* for three days, man. They probably had it on the fuckin' *View*. That's what she watches."

"Amber said she was off somewhere."

"Well *yeah*. Else it wouldn't of fuckin' happened."

"So maybe you dodged the bullet."

He counted on his fingers. "You, me, Amber, the motherfuckers next door—they had to see her car there in the morning. I mean *you're* not going to be telling Arlene, right? Because you already fucked me once. I had *your* back that time."

"Johnny. Different situation. You moved on the guy."

"Nah, come on, I'm just fuckin' with you. *Maybe* I'm fuckin' with you."

The other waitress put our drinks down. "You gentlemen make up your minds?"

"What happened to your friend?" Johnny said.

"She went on break. What can I get you?"

"Cheeseburger well," I said. "With fries? And a cup of clam chowder."

"You?" she said to Johnny.

"I am such a fuckin' fuckup," Johnny said. "Just one more of these bad boys and bring me the check."

"I'll have those right out for you." She headed for the kitchen.

"Listen," he said, "they don't stop you in the middle of the day, right?"

"Probably not if you color between the lines."

"Fuck, man, and Arlene's probably home by now. She doesn't go in till tonight. I'm thinking just get in the car and *go*. Fuck *all* these crazy bitches."

"You'll get through it," I said.

"Easy for you, right? I been working for you how long? Well one of these days you ain't gonna see me."

The house on Miller Brook Road belonged to the Web designer, Steven Holtzman. He took his wife to Aruba for three weeks, didn't drain his pipes, the power went out, everything froze, then we had a thaw and you can imagine what they came back to. Great old house too. When the insurance adjuster came out with me to look over the damage, he said a good clean fire would've been better. We gutted the whole house back in February, right down to the studs, wearing coveralls and masks; we kept heaters going, but they didn't do much. We filled two dumpsters, the mold-remediation guys came in and did their thing and now the wife wanted everything back just like it was; she still had pictures on the computer. It was going to end up at least a three-hundred-thousand-dollar job. Holtzman was sick about it, and ashamed of himself—it really *had* been a dumb-ass move—so I had to do some hand-holding. I told him probably July; I knew in order to make that I'd have to hire on extra people. There's never a shortage of guys out of work; the trick is finding anybody that knows what they're doing. I had my big three, because Myron had done his cutting over the fall and winter, and I'd be pitching in myself, but we had some smaller jobs coming up, plus the lawns and landscaping right around the corner.

When I got to the site Tuesday morning, Jesse and Myron were already out in the yard sanding the twelve-inch hemlock floorboards we'd managed to dry out, the legs of the sawhorses in the mud and old snow. A pair of Asscrack Harrys were humping sheets of drywall into the front room, where Jesse'd gotten plywood down, and the radio was going. Billy's old radio, which Amber had passed on to Jesse.

Johnny still hadn't showed by ten o'clock, so I called his cell and his house, then tried Amber at the office; she hadn't seen or heard from him. "Anything else shaking?" I said.

"Some guy called about the ad. And somebody else, but they hung up."

Jesse and I started hanging drywall in the upstairs while Myron stayed with the floorboards. That was a waste of him but I didn't trust the Asscracks not to leave marks with the sanders; they both looked about sixteen, though the one with the tattoos running up his neck had finished high school. I put him to work stapling rolled insulation between the studs in the dining room and sent the bodybuilder one over to Security Supply in North Adams, where I had an account, to pick up toilets for the half baths, rolls of PEX and a list of other stuff; the toilet in the master bath, with the wooden tank up top, had been ruined too, but that I'd had to special order. This afternoon I'd get him started cleaning up everything we'd taken out and stored in the shed— the claw-foot bathtub, the antique sinks with the brass fixtures, the wood-burning Glenwood kitchen stove that Holtzman's wife actually cooked on once in a while. She claimed you could taste the difference.

When the noon whistle blew down at the town hall, the guys brought out their lunches—Myron's wife always packed something hot for him in a zippered bag—and I got in my truck to go by Johnny's house. It was getting colder and starting to cloud over. His Pathfinder wasn't there, so I sent him a text—*Where U?*—then drove to the office and found Amber on the Internet as usual.

"What stinks in here?" I said.

"Coffee was tasting like shit, so I ran some white vinegar through the coffeemaker to get all that scunge out. I was just about to vacuum. This place is going to be a disaster area after I'm gone. You better get somebody good in."

"So no word? I stopped by his place."

"I told you he'd be pissed."

"He'll probably turn up." I looked in the mini-fridge and found a single peach yogurt. "This yours?"

"You can have it. So how come you're mad at me?"

"Who said?"

"I call bullshit."

"I'm not too happy with *Johnny*."

"You just wished it would've been you," she said.

I peeled back the foil and found a plastic spoon in my drawer. "I'm good with who I'm with."

"Well, if you want to know, it wasn't exactly epic."

"I don't need details." I ate a spoonful of the yogurt, then pushed it away. "Here, you want the rest of this? I better get back."

"So is everybody thinking bad about me?" she said.

"I would doubt anybody knows. Jesse might. He wouldn't judge you."

"Shit," she said. "I am so out of here."

Jesse and Myron were sitting on lawn chairs in the Holtzmans' front room when I got back, still finishing their lunches. "How's our young lady?" Jesse said.

"She's holding up," I said. "How *you* doing?"

"I don't think they should've put her out like that," he said. "She was just upset like anybody else. We did have a little to drink. I would've followed y'all out, but I had to make sure and say a word for Billy."

"I wish I'd got to hear you."

"It wasn't much. I just said he was my friend, and he was a good man and he loved all of them, which I don't know he always did, but I *am* pretty sure he wanted to. He was more of a Christian than he let on."

"You had *me* pretty near to crying," Myron said.

"Now is Johnny all right?" Jesse said. "I expected he'd be out here."

"He might still roll in this afternoon," I said. "If we can get the rest of the drywall up in the next couple days, I'll call the guy in Conway to come up and do the taping and we'll be able to get the plumber in and start on the woodwork."

"Be good to have Johnny." He looked over at the tattooed kid, who was chucking a Red Bull can into the dumpster. "Those two, I don't know."

"We might have to think about them. Hell, *we* used to be kids."

"Now you're trying to hurt me," Jesse said.

A cold rain started about one o'clock and Myron put a tarp over the floorboards and came in to help with the drywall. I got out my phone and called the guy who'd answered the ad; he sounded like I'd woken him up. I told him to come around to the office tomorrow morning, eight o'clock sharp. He said he'd try. So probably cross *him* off. The rain had turned to snow by the time the bodybuilder got back with the stuff from North Adams; he said cars were slipping off the road at the top of Route 2, so after he and his buddy got the truck unloaded I sent them home. Finally, about four o'clock, I got a text back from Johnny reading *Fuck U*.

Kristin was due back from Boston sometime today, and I remembered her saying something about maybe getting together. I hadn't had time to stop by and feed the stove during the day, so the house was cold when I got in, even though I block off most of it in the winter—all I use is the living room, kitchen and one upstairs bedroom. The one time my father ever came up after my wife left, he said I should sell the place so some family could have it.

The snow hadn't amounted to much, but the thermometer in the window said it was down to fifteen. I opened the draft and the damper, poked up the embers, put in some good birch logs and watched the bark flame up, then turned on the public station from Amherst and got their daily dose of Iraq and Syria and Israel and Gaza. All names as far I'm concerned, though you didn't want to tell Kristin this; she said you couldn't just ignore what was happening in the world. Every time they had another school shooting somewhere, she was all set to—and that's the point, right? Set to do what? Of course look at where she worked. One thing about Bozrah, *we'll* never have a school shooting.

If it had been up to me, I would've broken out the Jack Daniel's while the house was warming up, cooked myself some pasta, then turned in early and read myself to sleep; I'd been working my way through *The Duke Ellington Reader,* which Kristin ordered for me off Amazon. No particular occasion, just that she'd heard me mention Duke Ellington. Actually, I was afraid it might have been our one-month anniversary until I looked back at my calendar. But I knew I should check in with her before pulling the phone.

"Perfect timing," she said when I got her on her cell. "I'm like ten minutes out of Greenfield. Why don't you start down? I'll make us some dinner and you can stay over. Or we could go out."

"I think I better pass," I said. "I got some guy coming around to interview first thing in the morning."

"So how about if I come up? Since I'm already on the road. I don't have class till tomorrow afternoon. Is there any food in the house?"

"You must be whipped, though."

"I'm buzzed, actually—I stopped at a Starbucks. So did the thing go all right? Your friend?"

"It wasn't my favorite day. How was Boston?"

"Fine, except I missed you. I'll stop and pick us up something."

"I don't know how the roads are going to be. It's cold as hell up here."

"Oh, pish tush," she said. "Nothing can daunt a Subaru girl."

By the time I saw her headlights coming up the drive, I'd brought in wood for the night, I had the Jack Daniel's rolling and I'd dropped a blue pill and could feel my face starting to get red. I didn't always take one, but I was fifty-nine and she was forty-four, I'd worked all day, had plenty on my mind and I had to admit I was pissed that she hadn't wanted to hear me when I was giving her hint after hint, not *pissed* pissed but annoyed. When she got out of the car I saw her breath smoking. I went out onto the porch; she stuck her tongue in my mouth and I took the canvas grocery bag and her suitcase.

"Nice and toasty in *here,*" she said when I shut the door behind us. She tossed her coat down and she was on me again. "See, I did miss you. So I brought scallops. And chives, and ginger. I know you have rice. I'm going to make us something healthy. If I know you, you've been eating crap all weekend. What are we drinking?"

"Just having my usual," I said.

"Is that vodka still there? I'll get it, I have to go make my preparatory preparations."

I picked up her coat off the floor and hung it on the coat tree, then sat on the sofa. "You need to get a gas stove," she called from the kitchen. "How can you cook on this thing? And a decent refrigerator." She came back with a glass of vodka and ice, put her knees over the arm of the sofa and rested her head in my lap. I smoothed her bangs away from her wide forehead; her face looked strange upside down.

"You seem like you had a good time," I said.

"It's always a little painful to go back." She raised her head to take a sip, then eased it down again. "But I got to see a couple of people, and they were showing *Out of the Past* at the Brattle. Have you seen that? You have to *see* it. Oh, and I went and revisited the Monet haystack— I know, I'm such a cliché. Anyway, thanks for letting me come up. I really didn't want to go back to the hellhole tonight." Her apartment in Greenfield was in a turn-of-the-century building on Main Street, above the stationery store. She'd fixed it up with white particle-board cubes for bookcases and good rugs and painted the walls sky blue and hung a Star of Texas quilt over her bed. But yes.

"I thought it was all about *me*," I said.

"Oh, it will be. Do you want to get fed before or after? Or before *and* after?"

"You mean you want after."

"Oh, my." She leaned her head farther back to look upside down in my eyes. "Is it that effortful?"

"It's been a shitty few days," I said. "I'm losing people."

"Who are you losing? Not me."

"At work."

"Ah," she said. "Construction and its discontents."

"One of them used to take class with you. Amber Sibley?"

"Oh God, all the Ambers and Crystals and Tiffanys. She probably hates me, right? I don't mean to be a terrible person. I just feel they're all so *sunk*. Like, *submerged*. You want to weep. There isn't any *light* there." She took another sip, a bigger one. "They're the same age as Everett, some of them." This was the son who was in Europe, living in fucking hostels. I guess he *could* have been some shining spirit and not just another privileged twerp. Like me at that age.

"So maybe you shouldn't be teaching them," I said.

"I *try* to like my life," she said. "I really do." I heard the ice cubes knock against her teeth. "So are you going to be able to find other people?"

"I don't want to worry about it now." With her head in my lap and the blue pill starting to work, I could feel myself growing. I liked that her jeans were tight on her thighs and I wormed my hand down between where it was warm. She clamped my hand down harder and I thought I'd be able to get the job done. "You want to have the next one upstairs? I don't know how warm it is up there."

"Then you must have a short memory," she said. She went into the kitchen for refills, switching her ass like she was making fun of me. I put more wood in the stove and followed her up the stairs, my four fingers between where the thighs met, squeezing, my thumb poking where her butthole would be. She stopped, eased back into it and said, "I like the way you think."

I shoved her into the bedroom, making her spill her drink; she tossed down what was left and sat on the bed. I drank mine in one gulp, pushed her onto her back and she bounced up again and slapped me, which was how we generally got started. But I felt my hard-on going away. *Construction and its discontents*—she just had to be snotty. I watched her unzip her jeans and begin working them off and I noticed welts along her big white thighs from the seams. I yanked them off the rest of the way, socks inside, and got my mouth down where her underpants were already wet. She tasted sour. She twisted out from under and tried to get at the top button of my jeans and I pushed her away and slapped her good. "No," she said. "I want that."

If she'd just let me go down on her I might be able to get it back, or else she might come a couple times and maybe I'd be off the hook. I grabbed at the underpants and she clawed my arms, still within the rules, but instead of wrestling her down or whatever I was supposed to do, I got up off the bed and just stood there. "Fine," I said. "Knock yourself out."

I let her unzip me, she slid her hand down in, then looked up at me. She did have that pretty face. "Poor baby," she said. "Okay, I know how to fix this. Get those off and lie back down."

This time I hit her hard.

"What the fuck are you *doing?*" She put a hand to her jaw. "That's not cool. I think you hurt me."

"I *am* going to hurt you," I said.

"Okay, stop. This is scaring me a little."

"Maybe you better get out."

She got up, took my arm and kissed where she'd scratched me. I pushed her back down. "What's going on with you?" she said.

"I don't know," I said. "I'm just not into it."

"You mean tonight? Or anymore?"

"Christ," I said. "Is it going to be *that* conversation?"

"Oh. Wow. Then I guess there's my answer. So how long—no, actually I don't need to know." She found her socks, pulled them on and stood up to get into her jeans. "Here's one thing about me, I make a clean exit. You don't have to worry about hysterical phone calls."

"Wait," I said. "We're really doing this?"

"Apparently there *isn't* any 'we,'" she said. "Why have I not learned this by now?"

I finally had to take a couple of Advil PMs on top of the Jack Daniel's to get myself to sleep, and when I made it down to the kitchen in the morning I dry heaved at the smell of the scallops, which were still out on the counter. It was cold downstairs, but there wasn't time to load the stove or make coffee—Amber would have some on, in the newly clean coffeemaker—or to shower or shave. If this guy did show up for an interview, it wouldn't hurt for him to see me looking like a hard-ass. I stuck a PowerBar in my jacket pocket, put on my gloves and went out to start the truck and scrape frost off the windshield. Thermometer said three above. This would probably be the last cold snap, and then everybody's fucking lawns would start greening up.

Amber poured me coffee and got milk out of the fridge. "I thought it was supposed to be *spring*," she said. "You look like shit, by the way. She wearing you out or something?"

"Something."

"You should've had *my* morning. I go to brush my teeth and there's his fucking outfit in the sink. I didn't even want to *handle* it."

"Jesus," I said. "You didn't tell me he was slamming. Okay, you need to get out. Like *today*. Is he selling?"

"Well, it's not like there's people coming to the house. Anyways, I decided the place I'm going. Venice, California. It's right by L.A. and they have the beach there." She sat back down at the computer. "You want to see pictures?"

"Amber."

"I know, I know, I know. Everybody says. It's not going to be all that much longer."

"You could even— Shit, okay, you're going to do what you do. Can I get on that for a second?"

I had three messages, a Canadian pharmacy that got through the spam filter, an ad from Lowe's and an email from a guy I hadn't been in touch with for years, with the subject line *Look at this!* Nothing from Kristin. I looked through the headlines in the *Times* but nobody good had died. I checked Renovator's Supply for deals, then couldn't think of where else to go.

"Okay," I said, "I better roll. I knew that asshole wouldn't show up. He gets here before nine, give him directions over to Miller Brook, okay? No, actually, tell him fuck it. Nothing from Johnny, huh? We're in *great* fucking shape here."

Over at the site, Myron was back outside with the floorboards, wearing gloves and brown coveralls; the sawhorses were frozen into the mud. Jesse was upstairs hanging drywall and the two kids were in the living room standing around a heater with their thumbs up their asses. I sent the one with the tats up so Jesse could maybe start teaching him and put the bodybuilder to work insulating the rest of the downstairs; the other kid hadn't made much progress yesterday. We should have had the plumber in already, to run PEX on top of the plywood—Holtzman had decided that while we were at it he wanted radiant heat under the floors—but that couldn't happen until we got the fucking walls squared away. I never should have said July. This was what my life was.

I'd thought that Dana—the woman I'd been married to—didn't come into this story, but she saw it all those years ago. Nobody would anymore: the people I deal with now see only what I show them. She and I had a big thing in high school; then I went off to Berklee and she got into RISD. I used to go down to visit her in Providence until she hooked up with somebody there. Which is part of why I went with that stupid band. Then, ten years later, when my mother died, I came down to Darien and she was visiting her parents because it was Christmas. She had a job as a graphic designer in New York, still living with that same guy. But she said he was cheating on her—it actually might've gone both ways—and she was talking in terms of just chucking every-thing, maybe going off somewhere to raise vegetables and write chil-dren's books. Not to suspect her, but she already knew, because my father had been bragging, that I'd bought a big house and my business was making good money. So long story short. I think she was remem-bering me like I used to be.

Today she'd probably tell you I dragged her up here, but I remem-ber how pumped she was when I had Jesse come over with the tractor to plow out a garden patch and she found an arrowhead; she thought she might write a book about a Mohawk Indian girl. But she couldn't really talk with the locals—at first I didn't blame her; it had taken me a while—and she found out the new people and weekenders had their own world that you couldn't cross into. Jesse had the same problem with his wife—even worse, naturally, because people were always looking at her. Don't think they didn't look at Dana too, but for a whole other reason, which also got to be a problem. I was gone all day, and I guess when I got home I didn't want to talk about much but what we'd done on the job today and what we were going to do tomorrow. She said she couldn't believe I didn't care about anything anymore. I said I couldn't believe she had nothing to do up here—what about this, what about that. It made me sick to hear myself. Maybe she'd be glad now if she knew my little empire was falling to shit. I mean glad for me.

When we broke for lunch, I waited until Myron went into the Portosan, then took Jesse out to my truck and started the engine so we could warm up. He started taking stuff out of a paper bag. A bologna sandwich in waxed paper—like his mother had packed it for him. I bit the wrapper off my PowerBar.

"That's your lunch?" he said. "Gonna make yourself sick. You want my orange? You better eat it first or it's going to taste sour."

"I'm good. How's he working out?"

"Who, Gene? He'll learn, he's a good kid. That *other* one, though."

"We might need all the help we can get," I said.

"I wouldn't give up on Johnny just yet. He might be trying to figure some stuff out. He *needs* to."

"This is a fucking train wreck," I said.

"Man? No, we got this. You're tired, is all. Look at you. I tell you what. Me and Myron can hold things together for a week or two. And that girl—don't sell *her* short. Why don't you take your lady someplace warm?" He took a bite of his sandwich.

"I'm in a lot deeper shit than you know," I said.

"Is it a money thing?"

"Jesse, can I just ask you? How the fuck do you stand it here?"

He put his sandwich down. "You mean as a black man."

"Yeah, okay, that," I said. "But Louise is gone, you go to the firehouse one night a week, go to church and that's your life. Understand, I'm not criticizing you."

"Black people can't like peace and quiet? *You* go live in Hartford for a while. Vietnam. Which is the same goddamn place. How come *you're* here? You're a man with an education. Look, Louise gave me my choice. She was crying when she went out the door." He picked up his sandwich again. "I better finish up." He took a bite, swallowed hard. "I'm going to miss Billy, though. He never let on to me, but I know why that girl wouldn't marry him. You see a lot of things in the military. I know I did. I was eighteen when I went in. Now you probably want the war stories too."

"Not unless you want to tell me."

"There's a reason I don't go down to the VFW," he said. "I don't want to tell anybody shit. That's how come *I'm* here. You didn't say about you."

"I didn't go through what you did."

"Then don't be a fool. Take your lady someplace nice. You keep her with you. Me and Myron can look after all this." He took a last bite and unscrewed his thermos. "I ever got to where I couldn't work any-more— But hey, all of us are going to get there."

The bodybuilder kid had finished insulating the dining room, so I started with him on the walls; I had him hold up the panels while I drove the screws. I felt so lightheaded that I had to steady the driver with two hands, got a screw started crooked, chewed out the head trying to drive it in and then I couldn't back it out, so I ended up tak-ing a hammer to it. The mud would cover up the mess, but the kid was watching. "You and your friend can handle the rest of this," I said. "Now that I showed you how not to do it."

"He's my brother," the kid said.

"Okay," I said. "Better still."

Jesse was in the living room, cutting a triangle from a piece of dry-wall to go in the stairwell. "Coming right along," he said.

"I got some business over at the office," I told him. "I might not be back."

"We're making progress here. Rest up and book yourself some tick-ets. You know where's a good place? Hawaii."

"Never been," I said.

"My unit stopped off there. *Some* of us did. You got the money. Spend it while you still can."

Amber must have heard me come in, but she didn't look up from the screen; her lips were tight together and she was tapping her nails on the desk. I stood and watched her. Finally she moved the mouse and sat back. "You ever play chess?"

"When I was a kid. My father used to let me win."

"They say if you're good with numbers, so I'm trying to teach myself. It's *hard*. The computer just comes in and destroys you every time. I might be better with a person. If it was somebody stupid enough. I'm not really fucking off, okay? It's slow this afternoon."

"Any calls?"

"Oh, shit! Yes! The *lawyer*. That I found for Uncle Bill? I have to see him next week, but you know what he says? Rough figures? Like two hundred and fifty thousand dollars. Mostly from the house, but he saved a lot. What the *fuck*, right? I mean I'd give it all to have him back and everything."

"Don't let that asshole know about this."

"I'm not. I'm not going to even tell my friends."

"Don't." I sat down in my swivel chair, at the rolltop desk I used to think was cool. "Listen, what would get you to stay?"

"With *him*?"

"With me."

"And be stuck *here*? It's not like you can't get some other girl to answer the phone and shit."

"But they wouldn't be you. Listen, what if I made you a partner? Maybe you and Jesse. I don't mean put *your* money into it."

"I don't even get what you're saying. Is this some fucked-up way of trying to get into my pants or something? Just because I got drunk and fucked an old guy one time—you're even older than him. Anyway, you *got* your rich-bitch."

"I just don't want anything to change," I said. My stomach heaved and I pulled the wastebasket over and retched into it. There was nothing to come up.

She came and put a hand on my shoulder. "Are you okay? Are you having like an episode? You want me to call somebody?"

"Like who? Just give me a minute. Then I'm going to go home and have a drink."

"I don't think that's a real great idea."

"You remember what Billy used to say—'If nothin' ails ya, it's good for that.'"

"I never heard that one. What does that even mean?"

"Think about it," I said. "You might as well take the afternoon. I won't be needing you for anything."

I was all over the road, and when I made it to my house I stayed in the truck running the heater to put off going in. The last time I'd fed the stove must have been before I'd gone upstairs with Kristin the night before, and I could see frost starting on the insides of the windows. You won't believe this, given what I do for living, but I hadn't touched the place since I bought it, not even blown in insulation so the house would hold heat. Dana used to get on my case about that, along with everything else. It had belonged to an old farmer named Clarence Johnson, who couldn't keep it up anymore after his wife died and who went to live with his son in North Adams. Inside, it was the real deal: not the real deal circa 1803, when the place was built, but the *real* real deal: I'm a bigger purist than any of my clients. Flowered wallpaper that had turned sepia, flowered curtains that didn't go with the wallpaper, rag rugs, linoleum in the kitchen, Depression-era cabinets with Bakelite handles, a pink electric range from the fifties—this must have been Mrs. Johnson's call—and an old single-door Kelvinator with a foot-square aluminum freezer compartment. The cast-iron woodstove in the living room had a nickel-plated finial on top in the shape of an urn; the stovepipe, with its old-fashioned damper, ran through the wall and into the chimney with a tin collar against the wallboard. It felt as cold inside as it was out. Thermometer said fourteen. I sat on the sofa with my jacket on and the bottle of Jack Daniel's. I'd polished off half of it last night, but there was still that vodka out in the kitchen if need be. The days had been getting longer since December, but the sun was already down behind the hill.

I sipped for a while, thinking the thing through, ate some cereal to have something in my stomach because it wouldn't do to vomit, then drank more while I went around opening windows, except the ones at the front of the house that somebody might see from the road. I brought the bottle upstairs—I could feel it was starting to get the job done—and ran a hot bath. I had a claw-foot tub like the Holtzmans', but somebody (I bet Mrs. Johnson again) had dolled up the outside with pink house paint. I counted out six Advil PMs. Any more and I might puke up everything and be back to square one. I stripped down to my boxers and got in the tub. It seemed wrong to get them wet, but I didn't want anybody to have to see the whole deal and then not be able to get it out of their head. I had the bottle right there next to me. Eventually the water would get cooler—I thought I could already feel it—and then cold, but I'd be asleep by then. I got a ridiculous image of a man in a block of ice shaped like a bathtub, which told me I was going down. When the pipes and toilets froze up and burst, somebody would end up with a good-paying job: whatever rich person got the house would want everything brought back to 1803 and they'd have themselves a showplace. I could just see it.

Of course it was the dumb-ass move of all time. I don't think the water was even fully cold when Jesse hauled me out, though I can't remember much about those minutes. Amber had called him to stop by and check on me when he got off work. He got hold of Junior Copley, who was just sitting down to supper, and Junior came around with the EMS van and they got me down to Greenfield for an overnight in the hospital. The doctor wanted me to go into counseling; I was back hanging drywall Friday afternoon. Junior and Jesse both said they'd keep it quiet, but things like that get around in a town this size. Then after a while, they just fade into the background of what people know about you.

Johnny ended up coming back to work for me. He'd driven all the way down to Daytona Beach and Arlene was pissed as hell, but he says they're getting along better now. So I've got my big three together again. Myron's talking about retiring, but Jesse, they'll have to carry him out feet-first. I figured out I'm worth a million dollars; that's on paper, though, and a million's not as much as it used to be. Amber didn't go to California; she moved to South Carolina, bought a little condo and got into veterinary school. I don't think that's right for her; she should be working with people. I'll hear from her a couple times a year. She'll send me pictures of pit bulls she's rescued, but never one of herself. She's got a website called forpittiessake.com, which she thought up herself. She's going to get married someday, I know that about her.

You always like to say that if you were young and starting out again you'd do this or you'd do that, but I don't think anybody seriously means it and it's not going to happen anyway. I took myself out of the world early on, and looking back now I don't think I ever got close to anybody, and of course you get judged for that. *Apparently there isn't any "we"*—like I had something lacking. But what everybody needs to understand, you get to a point where you can't do anything about who you are anymore. And the same applies to other people, so that's who you're dealing with. And then the best you can hope for is not to do anybody damage, and good luck with that. I don't know, maybe I'm just talking to myself here: Who made *me* the big authority on what everybody needs to understand? It could be that I never got the memo, and that it's all about love, so-called, but am I the only one? You'd hate to think so.

Monsalvat

||||||

Back during the summer, a mockingbird had perched in the ginkgo tree in front of their building and kept at it all night. Paige would lie there while Richard slept, trying to count how many different songs it knew, but by the third or fourth she'd forget the first: it had been her summer of having just a hit or two of dope before bed, sticking her head out the bathroom window before she lit the pipe. Richard said the songs weren't music, strictly speaking, but sounds meant to warn predators away from the young, and he did know music if nothing else; in that, her father was wrong about him.

Now, in October, the mockingbird was a long-gone daddy and ginkgo nuts lay all over the sidewalk, looking like evil white grapes, smelling like vomit. She and Richard were both back teaching, and she'd added a little bump of speed in the morning to her drug regimen: just a bump—one—in each nostril while running water in the bathroom sink. On Tuesday and Thursday mornings, higher than a motherfucker, she'd come out of the building with that god-awful salty taste still in her throat and step around the ginkgo nuts so the Ten O'Clock Scholars wouldn't think they were smelling vomit on her shoes. The other mornings, after she and Richard moved the cars, she could actually work again on her book, without which she would always be an adjunct and whose title she had now changed to *Merrill, Mirabell and the Mystical Moment*, though sooner or later she'd have to admit to herself that the alliteration was tacky. She hid her really very modest stash in her plastic makeup bag, along with the silver salt spoon, once her grandmother's, its tiny bowl fluted like a scallop shell, the lighter and the wooden hippie pipe that was the least depressing one she could find in the head shop on Eighth Street. She kept the makeup bag in her underwear drawer on top of her diaphragm.

Paige just happened to know that she and Richard last had sex on May 24, the day after her fortieth birthday. He'd taken her to Café Loup, and he drank so much that when they got into bed and she reached into his boxers he asked for a rain check. He honored it the next morning, or, rather, she did. Then she found out about Mary Beth. He swore never again, and the never again turned out to extend to Paige as well. Nowadays Richard would wake up first, stretch and stretch, then hop out of bed: get down there, soldier, and give me twenty. He kept himself in such nice shape that she hated to watch. But. Then he'd go out to the kitchen to make their coffee while she woke up by reading a poem or two in her father's first book, which she didn't want to admit was his best; she'd begun keeping it on the night table. And sometimes she put her hand in her pants and did the supposedly necessary.

On a Thursday in the middle of October, he brought in coffee and said, "I need to tell you something."

"What can *this* be?" she said.

"Nothing you don't know," he said. "It's just—this is all really confusing to me. And I thought I might just go take some time to think."

"If what?"

"I don't follow you."

"You said you *thought* you might," she said. "You might if what?"

"Okay," he said. "This is an excellent example of why."

She closed her eyes, shook her head. "I've been awake for like two *minutes*," she said.

"Sorry," he said. "I guess I shouldn't have jumped you first thing." *Jumped you?* He must already have been wishing he'd rephrased that.

"Actually, I don't think I really want to talk," she said. "Why don't you just go."

But you know? It turned out to be a good morning. Because she was totally jazzed to teach. For her Ten O'Clock Scholars she detangled

"Aire and Angels," "The Sunne Rising," "The Good-Morrow" and "The Extasie." (She'd xeroxed from an edition in the original spelling, so as not to soften the alienness.) Then she cabbed it down to the World Café to meet Sally. You could count on Sally to be late, so she nursed a cup of coffee while prepping for her two o'clock class, Dante for Dummies. (Only Richard knew these nicknames. It was unfair that he should still know them.)

Sally came puffing in, wriggled out of the silk-thin leather jacket she'd gotten when the movies bought her book, handed a manila envelope across the table and said, "Here's your care package." Paige stuck it in her backpack and took out her wallet; Sally held up a hand. Silver rings on each finger, thumb included. "My treat," she said. "Tomorrow's the first day of principal shooting. I am *so* in the money."

Paige had meant to tough it out, but when Sally asked how Richard was she sort of had to tell. Sally shook her head at the right places, then said she'd never told anyone this but as a matter of fact *her* Richard—how weird was it that they'd both married guys named Richard?—had also left for a while, taking a cab over the bridge every night to sleep at the Fort Lee Best Western. A week of that, she said, had brought him to the bargaining table.

"Right," Paige said. "I guess I'm not sure what to wish for."

"What about a couple of sturdy twenty-four-year-olds?"

"What about them?"

"They're a good thing, twenty-four-year-olds, I can tell you that," Sally said. "I mean, I know you run more to fifty-five-year-olds."

Richard was in fact fifty-three.

"I doubt I'll be running to anybody," Paige said.

"Yeah, well, give it time," Sally said. "You too might come to the bargaining table."

When Paige got home, his suitcases were gone. He'd left the bookshelves gap-toothed, and his depredations showed among the CDs. She decided to break her rule this one time and opened Sally's envelope. Wowzer: now there was a generous friend. She did a couple of bumps just sitting there on the sofa big as life. Then she put on *Time-*

less: Hank Williams Tribute, her new good thing, which Richard had not taken—he considered it, quote, fourth-rate—and got busy shoving books together and fine-tuning the alphabetizing. After that she moved the bed back from the windows, as she'd been wanting to, and did what that necessitated in terms of the dressers and the floor lamp going where. In the bathroom, she scrubbed his soap scum off the walls of the shower stall. With this very, very good product called Zep.

She began marking up the Ten O'Clock Scholars' first set of papers, comparing Sonnet 34 (greatly underrated) with the "Full Fathom Five" song. It touched her to see them pretending they had a preference. She got through five of them—four and a half—then took a break with Merrill's essay in *The Poets' Dante,* which might be crucial to this one chapter of her book. But she hit the wall, as always, when she got to the part about how Dante's universe was a "cosmological solution of Einstein's equations in general relativity theory":

Let who can, experience for themselves the full complexity and symmetry of the resulting figure. Roughly, two spheres are joined *at every point* through their "equator," itself a third sphere of sheer connectivity, and the whole suspended within a fourth dimension. The figure has finite volume but no boundary: "every point is interior."

She could *not* experience this. Because it was insane.

She reshelved the book and called her father.

"Well of course, kitten," he said. "We'd be delighted. Honored. We'll be in bed, but you know where we keep the key. Don't say it on the phone. So just you? Sans Rick-hard?" The first time Richard had met her father, he'd gotten drunk and gone into his rap about how Bayreuth in effect was Monsalvat; the phrase "sacramental spaces" had been the deal breaker.

He coughed. "Well, we'll just have to bear up, won't we? I'll have Abigail make up the bed off my study. You've got the tube-o-lator in there, DVDs, stay up all night if you want. We won't hear a thing."

"The *tube-o-lator?*"

"It's a young person's expression," he said. "I've decided to be young from now on. The old-person thing simply wasn't working. Anyway. Manifold options in there. Books, even, if you're feeling earnest."

"Heaven itself," she said. "I'm a fool for options."

Her Cavalier was parked around the corner on Eighty-Third. Only yesterday morning she and Richard had done their routine of moving both cars, then sitting together in his Saab until eleven sharp, drinking coffee and sharing the *Times,* Paige trying not to snuffle. Richard called the Saab "the Roundhead"—wasn't that good? Didn't you have to give it up for him? Mary Beth had. Not a student but an ex-student, which made it ethical. He'd taken her for drives in the Roundhead, Paige had gotten that much out of him. To where, he'd refused to tell. That refusal, too, was ethical.

She got off the Thruway at New Paltz and found a dark place to pull over and have her nightly couple of tokes. As she came up her father's driveway, the Islamic moon was about to touch the pointy hemlock. As in Wordsworth, where the moon goes down behind the cottage and he thinks, *Dum dum dum and dum dum dum if Lucy should be dead.* Not *Ah my foes and oh my friends*—that was Edna St. Vincent Millay burning her candle at both ends—but something to the tune of that. (She'd only taught this about a million times.) What about *Holy shit and holy fuck if Lucy should be dead*? Okay, getting too silly now.

She crept up the flagstone walk, smelling the metallic, bloodlike stink of the boxwoods. A white envelope was taped to the door, with WELCOME! in girlish handwriting. Paige pulled it free: empty. The key must still be hidden underneath the bronze turtle. How offensive was it that Abigail was bidding her welcome? Then again, Paige had never lived in this house. She'd have to consider this when she was straight. And when might that be?

In the morning she did just a single bump, since here she was in the healthy countryside. But what if in doing just the left nostril she'd activated only the left brain? If she could remember whether that was the rational side or the emotive-intuitive, she could monitor herself for a possible imbalance. She went out to the kitchen for water, saw a strip of duct tape across the sink like the international NO and stepped out onto the porch, where she found Abigail sitting sidesaddle in one of the Adirondack chairs. A hot autumn day, trees already past the peak, wasps crawling on the posts where the sunlight hit. In daylight Paige could see that the boxwoods had suckers sticking up. Must "topiary" and "topology" not have the same root? Something to do with surfaces?

"Hi, welcome." Abigail stood up. Bare feet, piggies painted pink. "Let me get you some coffee. How do you take it?"

"I often wonder," Paige said. "Actually, I can get it."

"No, no, sit."

Paige watched her go: dirty heels, rising to show white insteps. You couldn't not look at her ass. Abigail played tennis, yes, but this had to be gym related. She was four years older than Paige.

She set a mug on the arm of Paige's chair. "Charles is still sleeping. I think he was up most of the night. At some point I got up to go to the bathroom, and he was in there with his laptop. I don't ask anymore."

The coffee tasted foul because of that salty chemical shit still in the back of her throat, but actually pretty great. "I didn't hear any of this. I thought you guys were like early to bed, early to rise."

"Well, sort of yes and no," Abigail said.

Paige had never been able to discern whether or not this woman was stupid. She did have a Ph.D. On the other hand, Charles Eckhaus had chaired her committee. "So what's up with the sink?"

"Oh, it's such a pain. Charles called the plumber a week ago, they were coming right over—this is what it's like up here."

"So you still miss the city."

"Yeah, no shit." Abigail started to cry. "Oh God. Too early in the fucking day for this." She got up and went inside, a hand before her like a blind person. Paige heard a door shut somewhere. Probably that bathroom off the kitchen. Two people and three bathrooms: What could he have been thinking? Right, well, if you knew *that*.

———

Back in the study, Paige checked the Wordsworth poem—it was "'O mercy!' to myself I cried"—and felt a headache sneaking in. She got up to look for aspirin and met her father coming down the stairs: black shorts and a regrettable white alligator shirt, his calves still muscled. He hugged her, then took a step back, his hands cupping her shoulders. "Terrific."

"Looking good yourself," she said. Well, he did have a tan.

"Actually," he said—and she knew what was coming—"there's this extremely horrifying portrait of me up in the attic." She tried to give him a smile; her mouth did something but her eyebrows wouldn't go up.

She followed him out onto the porch. She didn't want to do the exact same scene over again, though she couldn't not sit down in her same chair.

"You sleep all right, kitten?" He coughed.

"Fine," she said. "It's so quiet up here."

"It is that," he said. And as if to demonstrate.

Paige listened awhile. Then she said, "Did Abigail go back to bed?"

"Yep." He coughed again. A barking cough. "I don't think she got much sleep."

"She was telling me *you* didn't get much sleep."

"Aha," he said. "And how did she know? You see the pathology. Well, 'pathology' is too strong a word." Coughed again.

"How long have you had *that*?"

"What, the cough? Dah—not worth discussing. Now, how are you?"

"Oh. You know."

"Mm," he said. "I'm not quite getting a reading here."

"No, I'm fine," she said. "It's just nice to be away, you know. From all of it."

"All of it, eh?" he said. "No, you certainly won't find *that* here. So what shall we do to amuse you?"

"Put me to work? You want me to finish your hedge for you?"

"Ah. Thereby hangs a tale. I was merrily trimming away with the hedge trimmer—before cocktails, I'll have you know—and I some-how managed to cut through the cord. You'd think one would see an orange cord. I assume this is why they *make* them orange. I'm just not a country boy, kitten." Cough.

"Well, I could splice the cord," Paige said. "You have electrical tape?"

"Alas," he said. "But there's a True Value in town." He looked sky-ward. "God knows I've tried to find it. Well? Don't we laugh?"

In the room where she'd slept, she got her car keys out of her jacket and considered: she'd meant to do the supposedly necessary this morning and had forgotten. But having to face her father afterward—no. When she came back to the porch, he stood up, stretched and coughed, and she followed him down between the boxwoods, then to her car.

"Now in the city," he said, "we'd be sitting somewhere reading the *Times* and drinking Bloody Marys."

"Do you ever think about moving back?"

"Well, of course Abigail would do it in a heartbeat." Cough. "For all I know, I'm just hanging on here because she hates it."

She opened the passenger door for him, then got behind the wheel. Another cough. "Did I tell you I bought this Eminem record? CD, I should say."

"Why on earth?" She was having trouble getting into reverse.

"I'm quite taken with it. He just *vents*. And he's not without self-irony, you know."

"Lucky him," she said. Damn this thing. There.

"Abigail, of course, loathes it with all her middlebrow soul."

She stopped at the end of the drive and looked both ways.

"Watch for people coming around that curve," he said. "I always feel safer at night. At least you can see the lights. Does it sound to you as if everything I'm saying is a metaphor?"

She popped the clutch and got them safely out there. "Don't go by me. I'm sort of having echoes myself."

"Echoes! Excellent. Well, this is a grim subject for a beautiful day." He coughed. "May I open your sunroof?" He pointed upward with his thumb and started fiddling with the catch.

"So why did you marry somebody you think has a middlebrow soul?"

"You've heard of oral sex, yes?" he said. "Big deal in my day." The sunroof slid open, and she thought she felt the warm air in the car whoosh up and back.

"Ah," he said. "Delightful." He stuck a hand up through the roof and wiggled his fingers.

"So where do I go?" she said.

"Just go straight at the light," he said. "There I go *again*. Stop! Stop!"

She hit the brake. "What?"

"No, no, I meant me. So listen, what would you say to getting me out of here?" She looked at him. "Quite serious. Well, you know. Quasi."

She pulled up in front of the hardware store and cut the engine. "How badly are you not getting along?"

"Get me out of here and I'll tell you everything." He coughed. He was tapping his knee with his index finger, fast, like a telegrapher. He'd trimmed his white beard so nicely, shaving his neck below the beard line and the upper part of his cheeks. She pitied the way his glasses cut into his temple, bit into the bridge of his nose. He was still a beautiful man. Objectively.

"You should see a doctor about that cough," she said.

"I have. Shall I come in with you so you can keep an eye on me?"

"No, I'm not that into drama," Paige said. "Otherwise I'd still be in the city."

"Oh?" he said.

"Oh," she said.

She looked for electrical tape with the electrical stuff—silly girl—and found it instead over with the tape. Had this been *her* hardware store, she would have put a portion of her inventory of electrical tape in each place. Cross-referencing.

Back in the car, she closed her eyes for a second just to slow things down, though she wasn't crazy about the light show going on in there. She heard her father cough, then say, "Are you going to take me seriously? What I asked you?"

"Daddy," she said. "I mean—come on. Am I supposed to abduct you or something?" She started the engine. "Where would we go?"

"That's the spirit. You just carry on as the dutiful daughter and listen for your cue."

"Why are you being so cloak-and-dagger-y?"

"You'll enjoy it," he said. "The intrigue. I know a *little* something about my girl."

When they came up the driveway, there was Abigail sitting on the porch again. This day didn't seem to be, like, progressing. In the garage, Paige took down the hedge clipper and the severed cord, found a sheetrock knife among the tools and brought everything back to the porch.

"And I've learned that his real name is Marshall Mathers," her father was saying. He had a glass in his hand; a glass for her sat on the arm of her chair. "Apparently no relation to the Beaver."

Paige picked up her glass and tasted: vodka tonic.

"He's become quite the authority," Abigail said. She reached into her glass, fished out the lime slice and bit out the inside part without even wincing.

"Hardly that," her father said. "Shall I get you a little more, dear?" Cough. "You look like you're still able to sit up straight."

"Appearances are deceiving. But I don't have to tell *you* that." She stood up. "Does anybody care for some lunch? We have, let me see. We have lunch meat."

"I don't believe Paige understands your humor, dear. Why don't you let me do this."

"I am *fine*." Abigail went to the door. "You can carry on with the tutorial." She turned to Paige. "You don't know how refreshing it is. Marry an aging poet and they throw in a young person to sweeten the deal."

Paige put down her glass and watched a gray squirrel creeping on the flagstones, in little freeze-frame movements. She heard the screen door close. "This is what it's like?" she said.

"Give or take."

"So why do you not leave?" She picked up the severed plug end of the cord and started slicing plastic away from one of the ragged copper wires.

"And who takes care of me when I get cancer?"

"Your doctor," she said. "You're not planning to give yourself cancer, I hope."

"Give myself cancer? How sixties. What's that line? 'Canker is a disease of plants, cancer one of animals.'" He coughed again.

Paige got an inch of copper bared on a red-clad wire and started on the matching red wire in the other part of the cord.

Abigail opened the door. "The bread has *mold*," she said. "It's *horrible*. I've got to go into town."

"Why don't we just all go to the Cup and Saucer?" he said. "You'll be amused, kitten. They've got a blackboard with the pies du jour. Oh, sweetheart? I meant to tell you, after lunch? Paige would like me to drive down to the city with her to visit Ken. In the hospital."

Paige stopped carving at the wire.

"And who is *Ken*?" Abigail said.

"Old, old friend of mine and Catherine's. I've told you about Ken. He and his wife used to watch Paige—their daughter went to Saint Ann's, too. At any rate, Paige tells me he's in Sloan Kettering. And I gather he's not doing well."

"Oh, of course," Abigail said. "Any friend of yours and Catherine's. I'm sorry the man's ill. Were you asking my permission?"

"Sweetheart—"

"Were *you*?" she said to Paige. "Christ, you both disgust me. Oh, and thank you for the gracious invitation. But I think I'll just eat shit."

"Daddy," Paige said as she drove them toward town. "Next time brief me a little?"

"Next time? You're a worse pessimist than *I* am. No, your silence was golden. I love you very dearly, kitten, but you are *not* the world's best liar. Remember the time you took a puff off my cigarette and tried to—"

"I was four years old."

"You said, 'The wind did it.'"

"I know, Daddy. I remember." This might, in fact, be Paige's earliest memory. Sun on the stoop, Remsen Street, early spring, forsythia. He'd put his cigarette down on the edge of the brownstone step; it sat there, smoke streaming up from where the ash met the paper. She'd thought it was a clever lie: You sucked air through a cigarette, so why couldn't the wind have gone through on its own? For a four-year-old, wasn't this a lie of genius?

She said, "I'm glad you gave up smoking."

"Well. I'm glad you're glad." He coughed.

She checked her mirror: there was a car behind them, so close she couldn't see its grille.

"I'm just going to let this asshole go by." She slowed down, pulled over, heard her tires crushing fallen leaves; the car roared past and she gave it the finger.

"Temper temper," her father said. "We're not in any hurry. How does it go? 'We'll sit here like birds i' the cage. They'll talk and we'll talk with 'em—who's up, who's down, and fire us forth like foxes.'" Cough. "God, I'm missing whole chunks."

She shifted to second and pulled back onto the road. "So where are we going?"

"Well, here's a thought," he said. "What would you say to Cape Cod? You remember that song? *Cape Cod girls they have no bones*—or, rather, they have no combs. *They comb their hair with codfish bones.* You know, it may well be that the Indians actually did that. Must have smelled to high heaven."

"Well, isn't the smell the whole point?" Paige said. "Girls and fish smell? Or am I being too feminist?"

"Ah well, see now, there we come to a whole discussion that fathers and daughters probably ought not to be having," he said. "Even in these enlightened days."

"Daddy, you need to be back writing."

"What, keep rearranging the bric-a-brac? No, I've been to the mountaintop. I'm perfectly content at this point to leave the field to Mr. Mathers."

Just before the Thruway entrance, she pulled into a gas station and put the car in neutral. "So?" she said.

"I'm quite serious about the Cape," he said. "And I do know someone we could impose on."

"Who's that?"

He coughed. "Old friend of mine. Former student, actually."

"Somebody *else* who used to babysit me?"

"Now, I thought that sounded very plausible. No, you never knew this person."

"I never knew the other person, Daddy. Ted?"

"Ken," he said. "As in, beyond our ken. A little more than Ken but less than kind. No, this is actually a real person. Let me get out and see if I can maybe raise her on the phone."

"Use mine?" Paige said. She reached behind his seat for her backpack.

He held up a hand. "No, we don't want brain cancer on top of everything else."

"So who *is* this real person?"

"Louisa Philips?" he said. "You've heard me mention her."

"An old *friend*?" This was the one who'd broken up his second marriage. Okay, the one he'd used to break up his second marriage.

"Well, now she is. She's in North Truro, I believe. With her husband. To whom I gather she's very happily married."

"I'm thrilled for her," Paige said.

"You're not going to have an attitude, kitten?"

"What attitude would you like me not to have?"

"Look, I promise you, kitten, it will be a mindless good time. Pleasant people? Lovely old house? The ocean? Abigail and I have stayed with them. On a couple of occasions. And it's never been the *least* bit." He opened his door and put one leg out. "You know, we don't need to do this."

"All my stuff's back at the house," Paige said. "I don't even have a toothbrush."

"Nor do I," he said. "But the Lord has spoken to me of Walmarts in the wilderness."

He walked to the pay phone and she watched him poking at the numbers as if counting heads. Why had she not understood until now that this had been a done deal?

"Well," he said as he fastened his seat belt. "*She's* there at any rate. He, apparently, is in Tokyo. Telling the boys at the Nikkei what's what. Or that's my understanding. She says she'd be delighted to have some company."

"Won't I be a third wheel?" Paige said.

"Dear heart," he said, "you make it *possible*. So." He pointed out the window. "Follow the pillar of smoke."

"Tell me one thing, okay?" she said. "When did you *really* call her?"

"What do you mean, kitten? Just now." And anybody would have believed him.

The map showed that there was no decent route to Cape Cod. They didn't even hit Hartford until the sun was glaring and flashing in her rearview mirror, and at Manchester they had to choose between 44 and 6; each seemed hopeless. So 44: this dreary two-lane with the occasional white colonial. The sun went down, the morning bump had long since worn off and now, in the half dark, hearing the white noise of the road, she started having moments where she'd jerk awake realizing that she was driving.

"I need to stop and close my eyes for a minute," she said. "That or we're going to die."

"Stark choices," her father said. He coughed. "You sure you don't want me to take over?"

"You said you weren't used to standard anymore," she said.

"That was a metaphor." He coughed. "Don't we laugh?"

A picnic area appeared: Could she possibly be dreaming it? But he was pointing. She parked under an evergreen, let the seatback down and closed her eyes, feeling her father to her right as a luminous presence.

She woke up to the sound of him snoring. He'd let his seatback down too; they seemed to be side by side in a space capsule. She unfolded the map as quietly as she could. By holding it right up to her face, she saw that at Putnam you could pick up this 395 and go north and then eventually you'd have to end up in, what, New Hampshire probably. The White Mountains. When he came to, she could maybe amuse and mollify him by saying they were now en route to Bretton Woods, for the world conference on what to do about their lives.

As they came into Worcester, her father began rolling his head back and forth on the seatback like *No no no.* He woke up coughing.

"Are you okay?" she said.

"Bad dream. Where are we, anyway?"

"I'm really worried about that cough, Daddy."

"It's being dealt with," he said. "I'm going in for more tests next week."

"Wait—*more* tests?"

"Too tedious to go into. Abigail, by the by, knows none of this. Now, where are we?"

"We're sort of taking a detour. Daddy, how long—"

"What detour?" He touched his watch and its face lit up blue. "We should be almost—"

"I just thought this would be a better thing for us," she said.

He looked over at her. "Kitten," he said. "You're not having a psychotic break?"

"I'm not?" she said. "Good to know."

"Well," he said. "Hmm. I've clearly missed some excitement. Now, we're where again?"

"I don't know. Worcester. I'm sorry, Daddy. We could still—"

"Good God. You know, kitten, if this was a problem for you, you might have said so. Instead of—" He stretched forth a palm at the lights of what must be Worcester. *"Now* what to do. Louisa is probably— Oh well. I guess I won't be inviting myself back *there* in a hurry."

"Now I feel terrible," Paige said. "Maybe you should call her?" She reached back to unzip her pack and felt around for her cell.

"Don't feel terrible, kitten. Nothing's worth that. Where's the inside light? Now there I go again."

At the front desk of the Holiday Inn, a young blonde with three rings in each earlobe gave them a very-much-not-my-business smile. Her father asked for a room with two queens and signed them in as Charles Eckhaus and Paige Eckhaus. "And where would be a good place to eat?"

"A *good* place to eat?" The girl put a finger to her lower lip and pretended to be puzzled. "Maybe New York?"

"Now, what if I were a secret agent from the Greater Worcester Chamber of Commerce?" he said. "Let me rephrase. Where will they not poison us?" Paige saw him give his head that little twist to the side. Once, drunk, he'd let it slip to her that he knew which was his better profile.

"You could try Hot Biscuit Slim. It's just down—I don't know, I think three lights? On the left? At least they don't overcook the pasta."

"Well," her father said, "I must say we've lucked out in meeting *you.* And do your gifts extend beyond food criticism?"

"You might be surprised," she said, then gave Paige such a look: eyes full-on, then dropped as if demurely. Only rarely had Paige thought about other women. But this was a fetching girl. "Enjoy your dinner," she said.

"What on earth was *that?*" her father said as Paige unlocked the passenger door.

"Every man's fantasy, apparently," Paige said. "She's probably making up her own key card as we speak."

"Ah, I doubt that. I'm old enough to be her father. Old enough to be *your* father."

Hot Biscuit Slim turned out to have white tablecloths and a pink tulip on each table. The one objectionable thing was Old Glory push-pinned to the wall. That and the line on the menu about roast beef "in its own au jus." And to be really bitchy, had one not heard enough of *Kind of Blue*?

The waitress set their drinks down, and her father made Paige clink her Jack Daniel's to his martini. "Ah," he said. "This and this alone." He tapped a finger on the menu. "Have you made up your mind?"

"You *are* being double-edged," she said. "Have you?"

"Well, one couldn't come to Hot Biscuit Slim and not have the pasta. I wonder if they'd do just a simple olive oil and garlic. What about you, kitten?"

"Ooh," she said. "It all just looks so good I can't decide." She made what felt to her like a Betty Boop mouth.

"Oh come now," he said. "It's not that bad. Remind me to call Abigail, will you?"

"Here." She took out her phone. "If she star-sixty-nines you, you won't have to explain why you're shacked up at a Holiday Inn in Worcester."

"You're always thrusting that *thing* at me. Anyway, I doubt Abigail is that high-tech a person."

"Don't say I didn't warn you," Paige said. She put the phone away and got out her makeup kit. "I have to hit the little girls'."

"*That's* not very nice, kitten," he said. "Hitting little girls? If you see our waitress, hit her too."

In the toilet stall, Paige sat, peed for form's sake, took out her speed and her pretty salt spoon. Even in here, she could still hear John Coltrane reeling off those angry coils of notes. Another of Richard's big favorites: all these men who went on and on and on. God, this stuff took hold in a hurry—like, how could molecules get to the brain so fast? Unless they penetrated right through like rays, without bothering to take the bloodstream? So embarrassing, though. If somebody heard her snorting away in here, they'd think she was doing coke like some spoiled little Eurotwat.

Back at the table, she raised her glass to her father and took another sip. What the fuck? This wasn't Jack Daniel's. She vibed the waitress until she *made* the bitch turn and look.

Driving back to the Holiday Inn, she spied a liquor store and pointed.

"Great minds," her father said. "Still open, do you think?"

"Great minds are *always* open," she said. "It's their what-do-you-call-it. Hallmark." She actually better not get much higher. "You know, we could just drive on from here to your friend's," she said. "I don't really *want* to, necessarily."

"If I call her again, she'll think I have Alzheimer's." He coughed. "Would you get me a pint of, I don't know, Tanqueray? No, actually, pints are for rumdums. How about a fifth? I can't believe I even *know* the term 'pint.' That in itself is a bad sign." He thrust three twenties at her. "This should be enough to get us each a little something."

She plucked one. "We'll go Dutch," she said. "Speaking of Alzheimer's. Actually, you know what I love? In *Variety,* when they say 'prexy'? Like, 'So and so, Sony Pictures prexy'?" She shook her head. "Whew. And with that."

Lying on their beds, each propped up with two pillows, they watched *Eyes Wide Shut* on the pay-movie channel. Paige sipping Jack, her father sipping gin, the plastic ice bucket on the night table between them. The beauty of the ice cubes went to her heart: each cube with a tunnel going through and about ten colors clashing around and adding up to not any color at all. The beauty of the ice bucket too, let's contemplate that: marbleized plastic, pinks and grays swirling, done very honorably.

Just as canker was a disease of plants and cancer one of animals, so methamphetamine was—well, something like "a vice of the lower classes," but Paige couldn't get the phrase to turn. She'd gone out to the car, supposedly to get her CDs, but in fact to sit in the passenger seat and have her really very modest two or three little hits of pot, which she might as well make half a dozen tonight. And good pot too, what Sally called "better living through hydroponics." But wouldn't her father smell it on her clothes? No, because she'd hung the hand holding the pipe out the car window and breathed the smoke out there too, into earth's atmosphere. True, someone else might have happened by and smelled her at it. But the atmosphere was so vast. It was like, parts per million.

"Why on earth would you be reading *Variety*?" her father said. Nicole Kidman was pretending to be stoned by looking sleepy and speaking slowly.

Paige had to spit her ice cube into her palm to answer. "What are you talking about?" Cold. This was why they called them ice cubes.

"You said you'd seen something in *Variety*."

"I did?"

"Well, I'm not imagining this. I hope."

She dropped the ice cube back into her glass and wiped her palm on the weirdly smooth synthetic blanket that wetness didn't seem to penetrate. "Oh. Oh oh oh. Sally? My friend Sally? She sold her book to the movies, and she emailed everybody this thing about it in *Variety*, and it had all these words like 'prexy.' Prexy. I mean, it's hilarious, right?"

"Ah. See, I was imagining something quite different." He poured more gin, and Paige heard his ice cubes snap, even with Nicole Kidman going on and on. This was the worst performance, bar none, she had ever seen, unless it was pretty good.

"Like what were you imagining?"

He coughed. "I had this nightmare vision of you turning into one of these pop-culture—whatever they call them. Cultural media studies."

"I don't think I'm turning into anything," she said. "I'm just *watching* this, you know?"

"I'm sorry, kitten. And I interrupted. Why don't we— Well, I guess we can't wind it back." He meant the movie.

Eyes Wide Shut might ordinarily have been depressing, since it was about sex. But the jeweled mask on the pillow: that was so genius. It was totally totally Richard. Though let's be fair: totally totally her too. A suspicion made itself known in the upper left front of her mind that if she wasn't high she would think it was heavy-handed.

When she saw her father had fallen asleep, with the plastic glass of ice cubes on his—whatever you called it between chest and stomach—she reached for the remote and sneaked the volume down, got up and turned off his light, then lifted the glass away.

The phone rang. As Paige brought it to her chin, she had time to see her father raise his head, time to hear him say "What's—" and time to understand that it must be Abigail.

"Hello?" She said it deeper and softer than her real voice, her tongue up and back to roll the *l*s.

"Who is this?" Abigail said.

"Well, who is *this*?" Paige said, in the same happy-birthday-Mr.-President voice.

"Who is it?" her father said.

"They hung up," Paige said.

On the screen, people were silently interrogating silent Tom Hanks. Tom Cruise, rather.

The phone rang again. Paige picked it up and said, in the same voice, "Hello?"

"Who the hell keeps *calling*?" Her father coughed and rolled on his side, his back to her.

She pinched the little tab on the phone plug and pulled out the cord, the last thing linking them to earth, and snapped off the remote. Let him sleep. She would be their sentinel tonight, her eyes drilling into the dark.

A Hand Reached Down to Guide Me

|||||||

The name Paul Thompson won't mean any more to you than mine would, but if you'd been around the bluegrass scene in New York some thirty years ago, you would've heard the stories. Jimmy Martin had wanted to make him a Sunny Mountain Boy, but he'd refused to cut his hair. He'd turned Kenny Baker on to pot at Bean Blossom and played a show with Tony Trischka while tripping on acid. Easy to believe such bullshit back then. The first time I actually saw him he was onstage, wearing a full-length plaster cast on his—give me a second to visualize this—on his left leg, a crutch in each armpit, playing mandolin with only his forearms moving; someone had Magic-Markered the bottom of the cast to look like an elephantine tooled-leather cowboy boot. This was at an outdoor contest in Roxbury, Connecticut, in 1977, the summer I turned eighteen. The band I'd come with had finished its two numbers, and we were behind the stage putting instruments back in cases when Paul kicked off "Rawhide." I heard our mandolin player say, "Okay, we're fucked."

His band—older longhairs, except the fiddle player, a scary guy with a Marine buzz cut—won first prize, as they had the year before. But we placed second, and he lurched over to me on his crutches and said he'd liked how I'd sung "Over in the Gloryland." It was *Paul Thompson* saying this. I suppose I was a good singer for a kid just out of high school; I thought of Christian songs simply as genre pieces in those days, but I had the accent down. I said, "Thanks, man," and refrained from embarrassing myself by complimenting him back. We ended up singing a few songs together out by the cars—I remember him braced up against somebody's fender—and I think it surprised him that I knew so much Louvin Brothers stuff: "Too Late," "Here Today and Gone Tomorrow," "Are You Afraid to Die?" I let him sing Ira's tenor parts; now that he'd stopped smoking, he said, he could get up there in the real keys. He was taller than me, and his cheekbones made him look like a hard-luck refugee in a Dust Bowl photograph; he had white hairs in his sideburns, though he must only have been in his thirties. He told me he'd broken the leg playing squash; naturally, I thought it was a joke.

We'd both come up from the city that afternoon, me in a van with my banjo player and his wife and kids, Paul driven by his girlfriend. He asked me how I was getting back and could I drive stick. The girlfriend was pissed at him, he said, and had gone off on the back of somebody's motorcycle, and now he was up here in East Buttfuck, Connecticut, with no idea how to get home. His car, an old TR6, had so much clutter behind the seats we had to tie my guitar to the luggage rack with bungee cords; all the way back to New York he played the Stanley Brothers on ninety-minute cassettes he'd dubbed from his LP collection. We didn't talk much—I had to wake him up to ask directions once we hit the West Side Highway—but I did note that he said *mand*olin, not mand*olin,* and I've taken care to say *mand*olin ever since.

He lived in a big old building on West End around Eighty-Sixth; because it was Saturday night I had no trouble finding a space on his block. He said he'd figure out what to do with the car on Monday. Did I want to come up, have a few more tunes, smoke some dope? He hadn't given *that* up. But it was late to be taking my guitar on the subway, and I already had enough of a Paul Thompson story to tell.

Most of us were just weekend pickers, and only little by little did you learn about other people's real lives. Our banjo player taught calculus at Brooklyn College; the fiddler in Paul's band (the one native southerner I ever ran across in New York) managed a fuel-oil business in Bay Ridge; another guy you saw around, good dobro player, was a public defender. I was working in a bookstore that summer before starting NYU, where I planned to major in English. And Paul Thompson turned out to be a science writer at *U.S. News & World Report*. One day I saw him in the subway at Rockefeller Center, and I had to think a minute to remember where I knew him from: he was wearing a blue oxford shirt and a seersucker blazer, with jeans and cowboy boots. Somebody told me he'd published a novel when he was in his twenties, which you could still find at the Strand.

A couple of years later, Paul brought me into his band when their lead singer moved to California, and we also played some coffeehouses as a duet, calling ourselves the Twofer Brothers. I went to the University of Connecticut for graduate school but drove down to the city a couple of times a month, and every so often Paul would put the band back together for some party where they'd pile hay bales around the room. After these gigs we'd go up to his place, get high and listen to music, or drink and talk books. He told me he loved "Jimmy Hank," and gave me a copy of *The Ambassadors* from his collection of pristine old Signet paperbacks; it had a price of fifty cents. By then I'd decided to specialize in the nineteenth century, and I resented Jimmy Hank for his review of *Our Mutual Friend*—"poor with the poverty not of momentary embarrassment, but of permanent exhaustion." I've still got that book: the cover illustration shows a top-hatted gent seen from behind in a café chair, with wineglass and cane. I suppose it'll be on my shelves, still unread, when I die.

While I was finishing my dissertation, I got married to the first woman I'd ever lasted with for more than a month. Diane, I might as well admit, was my student when I was a TA, and why bother trying to extenuate it, all these years later, by telling you that we started sleeping together only after the semester was over? Or that in our History of Us conversations, we could never decide who'd made the first move? She'd go to festivals and parties with me to be the cool girlfriend with the cutoff jeans, and we promised each other that once we got out of married-student housing we'd live in the country somewhere, in a house full of books, no TV, and raise our own food.

I'd grown up in Park Slope, but my father was an old folkie—he used to hang around Washington Square in the fifties—and when I was twelve or thirteen I began listening to his LPs and fixating on the photos of ruined grampaws on their falling-down porches; even the mean, sad bluegrass guys in business suits and Stetsons, holding thousands of dollars' worth of Martins and Gibsons, had been posed by abandoned shacks in the mountains. Everybody in our little scene thought of himself as a secret country boy. My old banjo player, the one I rode up to Roxbury with, quit his teaching job and moved to the Northeast Kingdom, where I hear he makes B-string benders in his machine shop and plays pedal steel in a country band. Our bass player left the East Village for Toast, North Carolina, to sit at the feet of Tommy Jarrell. Even my father, in his bourgie-folkie fashion. He was an engineer at Con Edison for thirty years; when he retired, he and my mother built a solar house up near Woodstock.

I found a teaching job at a small college in New Hampshire, and Diane got accepted at the New England Culinary Institute. We bought a fixer-upper farmhouse on a dirt road, with a woodstove, a barn and twenty acres, equally inconvenient to my school and hers. I put a metal roof on the old henhouse—Diane had always wanted to keep chickens—rototilled our garden patch every spring and bought a chainsaw and a splitter, as well as a rusty Ford 8N, the pretext being that we needed to keep the fields from growing back to brush. Our neighbor, a man in his seventies, kept the thing going for me; he liked us because I was so helpless and Diane was so pretty. In the spring he and I would work up the next winter's wood together, sharing my splitter and running his buzz saw off the tractor's PTO. I don't know how I did all this while teaching three and three and working on my book; when the old man finally went into a home I started buying cordwood. My parents drove up a couple of times a year, and my father always brought his single-O Martin, the guitar on which he taught me my first chords. He and I would sit around playing the half-dozen fingerpicking songs—"Lewis Collins," "Spike Driver's Moan"—that he'd never cared to get beyond. They seldom stayed more than a day or two. The woodstove didn't keep the guest room warm enough in fall or winter, and my mother got bitten to death by mosquitoes in the summer.

Every July Diane and I threw an outdoor music party and pig roast; she'd cook the whole week before, and her friends from Boston and my friends from New York brought tents and sleeping bags and tried to dance to the ad hoc bands that formed in the corners of the field behind the house. Paul Thompson always turned up with his mandolin, some good weed and a younger woman, never the same one twice.

For a few years, he'd drive that summer's woman to catch a bus in White River Junction and stay on until Tuesday or Wednesday. Diane liked him—what woman didn't, at first?—and he was no trouble to have around. He took walks in the woods by himself, spent hours reading in the hammock on the porch and didn't mind when we went up to bed and left him downstairs with his weed and his headphones. "A man could die happy up here," he used to say. He told me he liked hearing the rooster at first light, because it made him feel safe to go back to sleep. When he finally got up, he'd go out to the henhouse, gather eggs and cook his own breakfast—and clean up afterward. Diane usually picked eggs early in the morning, but she'd leave a couple for him to find. Once, when he'd been out there for what seemed like a long time, I went to check and saw him through the window, squatting on his hams, his cowboy boots the only part of him touching the floor. He was talking and nodding to himself, or to the hens, who came right up to him as they never did for me. I sneaked back to the house and I didn't think he heard me.

But most of the time, Paul wasn't anybody I thought about much, though I know now that he was thinking about me.

For whatever reason, I never wanted children. Not a crime against humanity—arguably quite the opposite—but of course this became an issue when Diane turned thirty. That and suspicions about me and my students, which I should've seen coming as well, and about one student in particular. (The wrong one, as it happened.)

Diane and I lasted ten years, and after she left I drank myself to sleep every night for a month. She's remarried now, has her own catering business, and her older daughter's applying to colleges—better schools than the one where I teach. We're on good enough terms these days that she sends me pictures. At the time of the divorce, though, she held out for money in return for her share in the house, and I had no prospect of a better-paying job. My book, *Cathy's Caliban: Sex, Race and the Sublime in "Wuthering Heights"*—a rewrite of my dissertation—got only one notice, in *Victorian Studies,* whose reviewer (from some other no-name college, in Missouri) called it "by turns perverse and pedestrian." The book got me tenure, since nobody else in the department had published a word in the past ten years, but only a two-thousand-dollar raise. So I went back to working up my own wood until— God, must we? Until I was able to sell my father's house.

Diane had already left the last time he came up, the fall after my mother died. He had his Martin with him, as usual, but didn't feel like playing. Could he leave it with me? The strings felt stiff, so maybe I could take it to the guy who worked on my guitar. It didn't feel any different to me, but I told him I'd see if Brad could bring the action down a little. Hell, I thought, he's seventy-eight, his fingers might not be as strong as they used to be.

I set the chessboard up on the wooden factory spool Diane and I had used for a coffee table—he mostly kicked my ass—and poured glasses of the Bushmills he always brought. While I was considering whether or not to move a rook, he picked up a photo from the table beside the sofa: Diane and I sitting at a café in Lisbon, the one time we went to Europe.

"What are you, running a museum?" he said. "Look, I liked Diane. Your mother had her opinion, fine. Me, I think you were crazy to let her go. But you made your choice, right?"

"You *could* call it that."

"And you still got all her hair shit in there." He flipped his thumb in the direction of the bathroom, where Diane had left behind half-empty bottles of conditioners, moisturizers and lotions.

"Don't think I don't see what you're up to."

"What, throw you off your game? You fucked yourself two moves back." I looked the board over again, then got up and put another couple of logs in the stove.

"What I'd do?" he said. "Find some sucker who wants to be—who'm I trying to think of? Thoreau. Then buy yourself a nice little place in town where you don't have to do *that* nine months a year. You want to be living like this when you're my age?"

"I seem to recall you couldn't wait to get out of the city."

"Not to live like a sharecropper. You even get cable up here?"

"We don't have a TV." I sat down again and took another look at the board.

"Interesting," he said. "And who's the 'we'?"

"Yeah, okay. I get it."

"Anyway, now your mother's gone and I'm staring at trees all day. You could have a life. You meeting anybody?"

I laid my king on its side. "Pop. It's been a month."

"That's my point." He looked out the window. "These trees are gonna kill you."

By the time Janna moved in, I'd been living in New Hampshire for longer than I had in the city, though I still wasn't fooling the locals any. You could see another house by then: an A-frame up on the rise catty-corner across the road. Diane and I could have bought that parcel along with the land on this side, but we hadn't been able to come up with the extra ten thousand dollars. I hated to look over there.

Janna worked at Century 21, near my college in the old downtown. Yes, I met her at the bar where I'd started going after classes. She'd gotten her job just by walking in and asking for it, and her boss liked the tricks she'd picked up on some website: putting bowls of lemons and Granny Smith apples on kitchen counters, fanning out copies of *Country Journal* on coffee tables. I thought she was too bright to have ended up here: she had an M.A. in political science from Tufts. But she said she'd found her place in the world. I suppose I had too.

She told me right from the beginning that she didn't want to be the Second Wife, and she'd put a bumper sticker on her Land Cruiser reading COPULATE DON'T POPULATE.

Her apartment had track lighting, Turkish rugs and a gas fireplace, but she seemed to feel at home in my house. Aside from repainting the living room—a yellow she said would feel warmer than the white Diane and I had gone with—all she did was move the sofa over to where the armchair had been and find us a pine blanket chest for a coffee table. She was fine with dial-up and no TV—she'd let corporate media waste too much of her time already, she said—and she even claimed the rooster didn't wake her, though she refused to go into the henhouse herself. After five years, we still had sex more days than not: I'd made peace with her chubby knees, as she'd presumably made peace with my loose belly and my too-small hands.

Janna played guitar—another point in her favor—and we sang together once in a while. I'd back her up on her songs—Ani DiFranco, Michelle Shocked, the Indigo Girls, some of it not as bad as you might think—and she knew "Silver Threads and Golden Needles" and the usual stuff by Emmylou Harris. I tried to teach her a couple of Porter and Dolly songs, though she didn't have much of a range and we could never hit on the right key for her. It was Janna, in fact, who talked me into having the music parties again. She hated to cook, so we'd lay in beer and whiskey and chips and tell people to bring whatever. She hung back most of the time and let the bluegrass guys do their inside-baseball thing—"Yeah, 'Rank Strangers.' Who's gonna do Ralph's part?"—but late at night I could sometimes get her to step into a circle of pickers and sing "Sin City."

"We could probably make this work," she'd told me when we'd been together for a month. "If neither of us turns into an asshole."

"How likely is that?" I said.

"Well," she said, "if people aren't willing to change. I mean when things call for it."

"But you're happy *now*."

"You would've heard," she said.

———

When I sent the notice out for the party that last summer—we were
having it early, since we were going to Yorkshire in July, to see the
Brontë country—Paul emailed back that he'd taken a buyout from *U.S.
News* and was "living on Uneasy Street" but would try to make it. He
was working on a book proposal, he said, about mountaintop removal.
It should get him some time in eastern Kentucky, where maybe he'd
be able to play some music too, if he didn't show up in a car with New
York plates.

The Friday night of the party, he rolled into the dooryard just after
dark, in a Jeep Wrangler, with a woman at the wheel. She looked to
be Janna's age and not quite up to Paul's standards—maybe too much
nose and too little chin—but with a slender body and straight, dyed-
black hair down to her shoulders. He got out, stretched and looked off
at the hills. "Shee-*it!*" he said to the woman. "Just smell the air. I ever
tell you? This is my favorite place in the world."

"Several times," she said.

"I want y'all to meet Simone," he said. He always talked more south-
ern when he was around the music. "My last and best."

"Until the rest of the ass parade comes around the corner."

"Never happen," Paul said. He looked even lankier than usual, and
when he turned to me I saw dark pouches pulling his eyelids down,
exposing some red below his eyeballs. "Hey, listen, we gotta do 'Hit
Parade of Love.' But first off—what do you say?" He opened his mandolin case and took out a pipe and a plastic bag of buds.

After one hit, I knew I'd had plenty, and that a beer might help and
might not; even Paul stopped at three. He kicked off "Hit Parade of
Love," and somehow I found myself singing the first verse, whose
words I thought until the last instant wouldn't come to me—*From
what I been a-hearin', dear, you really got it made*—but when we got to the
chorus, with the tenor part, his voice cracked on the word "top," and
he asked if we could take it down to A. Well, hell, he had to be what,
pushing seventy by now? If I was fifty-one?

He gave up before midnight—he said the drive had done him in—

and we put him and Simone in the big guest room at the far end of the hall. When the music petered out around two thirty and people retired to their tents and RVs, Janna and I came upstairs and saw their light was still on; Janna thought she heard him coughing. The rooster woke me for a few seconds as the windows began to show gray, and I hoped that if Paul was hearing it too he'd fall back safe asleep.

In the morning I put on one of the knee-length white aprons Diane had left behind, cooked up enough scrambled eggs, along with kale from the garden, to fill the turkey-roasting pan, set out paper plates and plastic forks and clanged the triangle she'd always used to get the party guests in. Paul and Simone didn't come down until the others were finishing up. "You sleep okay?" I said.

"Never better," he said. The pouches under his eyes looked darker in daylight. "Once I got my *nightly obligations* taken care of." He put a hand on Simone's ass and squeezed. "This is the one that's gonna be the death of me."

"You'll scandalize your friend," she said. "Look how he's blushing."

Paul reached down, lifted the hem of my apron and peeked under. "What's fer breakfast, Ma?"

They took plates onto the porch, and when I came out after a preliminary cleanup, I found Janna sitting next to him while Simone was on the lawn trying to get up into a headstand, her black hair splashed out on the grass. He hadn't touched his eggs. "Hey, the Iron Chef," he said. "Listen, did I tell you I'm playing bass in a rock band? Like one of those daddy bands? I fuckin' love it—we missed so much shit being hillbillies." He speared a forkful of egg but set it down. "I might have to quit, though."

"What's going on with the book?"

"Yeah, well, that too. Story for another time." Simone had gotten both feet in the air, muscled legs straight, toes pointed. Paul clapped his hands and called "Brava!" He turned back to me. "I can't believe I finally got it right," he said. "In the bottom of the ninth. Check her the fuck out."

"She seems great," I said. The legs of Simone's shorts had fallen just enough to expose black lacy underwear.

"Listen, I might call you pretty soon to ask you a favor," he said. "I *might*. It would be a *big* favor." He looked at Janna. "From both of you."

"*You're* being mysterious," she said.

"Sure," I said. "Whatever whenever."

"I appreciate it." He stood up and called to Simone. "You going to stay like that all day, babe? Come on, I want to show you the gals."

He took her hand and led her along the path to the henhouse. He was limping worse than usual—that broken leg had never healed properly—and I noticed he was wearing Nikes instead of boots.

Janna touched my arm. "I don't think he's okay."

"He's just in love," I said.

"I could see that little display wasn't lost on you." I was thinking of how to deny it, but she put a finger to my lips. "I mean, you know him better than I do," she said, "but *I* think she's got a situation on her hands."

That summer was the first time Janna and I had traveled together. The Brontë Trail turned out to be a five-hour trudge through British badlands—"No wonder the brother was an alcoholic," Janna said—and back in Haworth we found our rental car had a yellow metal clamp on the front wheel. At Whitby it was too cold to swim, and neither of us had any interest in joining the fossil hunters at low tide or taking the Dracula tour. When we got home, I found a package Janna had sent me from Amazon—she'd found an Internet café in Whitby—with a book of Doré's illustrations of *The Divine Comedy* and a note reading *It's time we got you interested in writers from Tuscany.*

A week later, I got the email.

This is Simone, Paul's friend. I hope you remember me from your party. He doesn't know I'm writing this (truly), but I was afraid he never would ask you. I'm sure you must have seen that he wasn't well, and the truth is that he's been diagnosed with liver cancer, stage 4, though he still seems like his old self most days. Anyway, I know that his wish is, and I apologize if this is just too much to ask, that you could let him be in your home for the very last part of this—he says he will know when. He has always told me your home was his favorite place ever to be. I can take care of all the arrangements, home hospice and etc. (truth is, I've already made some calls to places in your area). Not really knowing you, I hope I've explained all this in the right way. Do you think you could possibly do this for him?

"What?" Janna said. We were propped up together on the bed. One thing I'd learned from being married to Diane was not to be furtive about email.

"Here." I turned the screen toward her. "I guess you called it."

I watched her face as she read, but Janna didn't give much away. "He put her up to it," she said.

"She says not."

"Well of course," she said. "That's the tell."

"I just have no idea what to say to something like this."

"He's your friend," she said. "What time is it?"

"So you're saying I should call?"

"I don't even know the man," she said. "But I'd do this with you."

They came late on a Sunday afternoon in October. Simone helped him out of the Jeep, then reached behind the seat and handed Janna a gallon of cider, just as she might have done if they'd been normal lovers up for a country weekend. The label showed it was the catchpenny orchard on the state highway, where kids could feed donkeys with pellets from dispensing machines at a quarter a handful. Paul had let his beard grow in, entirely white; he looked like the last pictures of Ezra Pound. "And here he is," he said. "Appearing for a limited time only."

"He rehearses his lines," Simone said.

Janna put him on the sofa with the afghan over him while Simone and I went back out to get his stuff. "It's just a few clothes," she said, "and a couple of pictures he wanted to be able to look at. He didn't want to take up your space. I think he's planning to give you this." She held up the mandolin case.

"That's crazy," I said. "It's got to be worth a fortune." Paul's F-5 wasn't a Lloyd Loar, but I remembered that it was from the thirties.

"He tried to leave *me* his apartment," she said. "He's turned into the Bill and Melinda Gates Foundation. I have to get with his brother tomorrow in the city and figure out what to do. Paul won't talk to him."

"You're not driving down again tonight?"

"Breakfast, eight a.m. The brother's a freak too."

"But you're coming back."

"And you've known Paul for how long? I mean, I wanted to. He's got it all plotted out, like each of us with our own little jobs—I mean, not that yours is little. He's just putting everybody away, away, away. Fuck *him,* you know? I was a good girlfriend."

"Would you like us to disappear for a while? We do need to go to the store at some point."

"No, it's fine. He already got the last sweet blow job. Under this fucking apple tree—sorry. I just feel like *somebody* should know. And all the way up here, he keeps finding these sports-talk stations. Did you know that the World Series begins next week? It's going to be quite a matchup."

We found him sitting up on the sofa, propped up by pillows under his back, looking at *The New York Review of Books.* "So," he said, "did she tell you what a dick I'm being to her?"

"I can imagine how hard this must be for both of you," I said.

"Ah, still the slick-fielding shortstop," he said. "But we're into serious October baseball here."

"Can you just *stop*?" Simone said.

"Isn't that the whole idea?" he said.

Janna came downstairs with her arms full of sheets and blankets. "We're going to put you guys in the den tonight," she said. "I thought it would be easier than having to do stairs."

"She has to go back," I said.

"You know," Paul said. "Stuff to do with the, ah, e, s, t, a, t, e."

Simone turned to me. "They said they'd be coming with the bed tomorrow morning. And the nurse should be here. You have my information, right?"

Paul shook his finger at her. "Now *that* should have been said sotto voce."

"Let me make you some coffee," Janna said. "I don't know if anything's open between here and the interstate."

"She'll be cool," Paul said. "My guy brought over some Adderall before we left. He gets the *real* stuff. Made from adders."

I walked Simone out to the car. She opened the driver's door, then turned back and came into my arms, taking deep breaths. "He's been lucky to have you," I said.

"And now he's lucky to have you," she said. "There's just no end to his luck."

In bed that night, I said to Janna, "Can we really do this?"

"What's our choice at *this* point?" We were lying on our backs, and she rolled over, her breasts against my arm. "Did you two talk at all?"

"I don't want to, you know, press him." I worked my arm over her shoulder and pulled her closer. Her belly into my hip. She sighed and moved her palm up my thigh.

"Why didn't he ever, you know, find somebody?" she said. I felt myself beginning to get hard—could we really do *this*? "That woman loves him."

"He never had any trouble *finding* them," I said.

"Do you ever wish you were like him?"

"What, you mean dying?"

She jerked away and rolled onto her back again. "I hate when you pretend to be stupid."

"No," I said. "Who would ever want a life *that* lonely?"

"It's even more obnoxious when you try to figure out the right thing to say."

I shoved a pillow against the headboard and sat up. "Are we fighting?" I said. "Because this is a hell of a time for it."

"For the record, I don't blame you for getting us into this. I just hope it gets over with quickly. Is that horrible to say?"

"No, it's actually the *kindest* thing you could say."

"But would you say it about me? If *I* were in the situation?"

"Come on," I said. "Nobody can ever—"

"Okay, I need to go to sleep," she said. "Obviously I'm not going to get laid tonight. Why don't you go down and check on your friend and see if he's still breathing. Then you can get yourself a drink and forget all about it."

I put my legs over the side and got to my feet. "I bring you one?"

"I'll be asleep," she said. "You don't even listen anymore."

The rooster woke me at six. I heard Janna breathing away and couldn't get back to sleep. But when I came downstairs Paul had already dressed himself—except for shoes and socks; he'd told us it hurt to bend down—and had managed to get from the den, where Janna had made up the fold-out, to the living-room sofa, and was stretched out listening to something through earbuds. He flicked them out when he saw me.

"How are you?" I said. "You hurting? I can get you another Vicodin."

"Just took a couple. They're coming with the real shit this morning, right?"

"They should be here by ten," I said.

"What we like to hear. Listen, did I even thank you for this?"

"You'd do it for me."

"*There's* a hypothetical we won't be putting to the test. Man, I have been such a shit. To everybody in my life."

"You were never a shit to me," I said.

"You weren't *in* my life. Well, who the fuck was. Not to be grim. How did I get onto this? That Vicodin must work better than I thought. Your lady still asleep?"

"She was."

He nodded. "She's going to need it."

I was in the kitchen cutting up a pineapple when I heard Janna come downstairs. She must have smelled the coffee brewing. "You boys are up bright and early," she said.

"Only way to live a long and healthy life," Paul said. "Get up, do the chores, plow the north forty—I don't mean anything sexual by that."

"No, I'm sure that's the *last* thing you'd think of." She came into the kitchen and put a hand on my arm. "Did you get enough sleep? I'm sorry I was being . . . whatever I was."

I set the knife down and put an arm around her. "I think you get a free pass, considering."

"I hope I was just getting it out of my system early." She poured a cup of coffee and put in milk for me. "Will you be okay with him if I go in for a while? I should get some stuff done while I can."

"Hey," Paul yelled out. "Why's everybody talking behind the patient's back?"

"Shut up, we're having sex," she called back. She poured a cup for herself. "He seems pretty chipper this morning."

"Yeah, I don't know what to hope for," I said. "Quality, I guess. And then not too much quantity."

A little after nine they came with the hospital bed, and the guy helped me move the sofa into the corner so we could set the bed up in the living room, by the window looking out at the hills. Janna and I would take the fold-out in the den when it became clear that we had to be nearby. Paul watched us from the armchair, his bare feet on a footstool, his earbuds back in, his eyes on us. When the guy left, he turned the iPod off, plucked out the earbuds and said, "Why am I reminded of 'In the Penal Colony'?"

The FedEx truck delivered a cardboard box with the drugs, then the nurse from the hospice showed up. She had thick black hair, going gray, down her back in a single braid, and hoop earrings—not what you'd expect with the white uniform. Her name was Heather. I brought her a mug of herbal tea—she wasn't a coffee drinker, she said—and she showed me the spreadsheet-looking printed forms on which we were to record dosage and time, then opened the FedEx box, picked up her clipboard and took inventory. She wrote down Paul's temperature and blood pressure, listened to his heart. "So, Paul," she said, "how would you say your pain is right now?"

"One to ten? Let's give it a seven. Good beat and you can dance to it."

"We can improve on that," she said.

"Can you do less than zero?"

"That's going to be up to you. And your caregivers. I'm a believer that you keep on top of the pain. This shouldn't be about you being in any discomfort." She got up and put on her jacket—wool, with a Navajo design. "I'll be by tomorrow, but if you have any concerns or questions, any emergency, someone's always there."

I took my jacket off the coatrack. "Here, I'll walk you out. I've got to feed the hens."

"Smooth," Paul said. "Jesus Christ, why don't you just ask her how long?"

"I knew I was going to like you," she said to him. "I'll be seeing you tomorrow—that much I think we can count on."

I followed her to her car. "I'm not asking you to make a prediction," I said. "But just from your experience."

"Okay, based on nothing? I think he'll move fast."

When I came back in he was sitting on the edge of the hospital bed, bare feet dangling, pushing the button and making it go up and down. "So, we gonna break out the good stuff?"

"Should you wait till what she gave you kicks in?"

"Don't start *that*," he said. "You heard the lady." He lay back, stuck out his tongue and pointed at it.

He dozed—call it that—until the middle of the afternoon while I sat in the armchair, checking from time to time to make sure his chest was rising and falling and making notes in my new paperback copy of *Middlemarch;* the covers had finally come off the old one. If Janna could hold the fort tomorrow while I went in to campus, that's what I'd be teaching.

"Let's go for a ride." I looked up: Paul's eyes were open. "I want to see some trees, man. And can we bring some music? I got weed."

"If you're up to it," I said. "Stanley Brothers? You remember driving back from Roxbury that time?"

"Not really," he said. "Did I have that fucked-up Triumph?"

"Yeah. Whatever became of that?"

"Whatever became of anything? I should've kept a journal. Fucking *years* of fucking lost days."

The truck had a handle above the door frame that you could grab to pull yourself up onto the seat; Paul used both hands, but I still had to take his legs and hoist. I could feel the bones.

We took back roads, dirt roads when I could find them. Cornfields with ranks of tubular stubble, broken-back barns with Holsteins standing outside in the mud. Hunting season had started—that morning I'd heard gunshots in the woods—and we passed a double-wide where a buck hung from a kids' swing set, one front hoof scraping the ground.

"My kind of place," he said. "You know, when they say you're dead meat—like isn't meat dead by definition?" He snapped the buck a salute. "Shit, *I* should've settled up here. Come to think of it, I *have* settled up here."

"I always thought *you'd* get a place out of the city. At least for weekends."

"I think that would've ruined it," he said. "I was really just into the songs. Hey, can we have the Stanleys?"

"I just want to say," I said. "I admire how you're dealing with this."

"Yeah, wait till the screaming starts."

I put in a Stanley Brothers CD—*Can't you hear the night bird crying?*—and he began packing a bowl. He blew out the first cloud of skunky smoke, then held it out to me. I put up my hand and opened my window.

"You mind cracking yours just a little?" I said. "If this is that shit you had last summer . . ."

"That? That was fucking ditchweed." He exhaled again. "Yeah, actually I wouldn't advise you." He closed his eyes. "Okay. Better. I haven't heard this for fucking ever."

After a few miles, he packed the bowl again. "What's so weird," he said, "I can't tell if something's beautiful anymore. Like, is *that* beautiful?" He pointed at the CD player: the Stanley Brothers were singing "My Sinful Past," where the harmony comes in on *A hand reached down to guide me.*

"Well," I said, "I'm not always in the mood myself."

"Okay, you don't want to talk absolutes," he said. "Can't blame you there."

I stopped at the convenience store outside of West Rumney—we'd run out of milk. "Anything I can get you?" I said.

"I'm disappointing you," he said. "You want to know what it's like."

"Not unless you want to tell me," I said. "This isn't about me."

"See, that's my point," he said. "Listen, would they have eggnog this early? I mean in the year?"

"That's a thought."

"Yes it is," he said. "Good for me, right? Could you leave the thing on?" We'd switched over to the King recordings; the Stanley Brothers were singing "A Few More Years."

But when I came out with the milk and a half gallon of eggnog, already with holly wreath and red ribbon on the carton, he was sitting in silence. "I didn't want to run down your battery," he said. Could he have been crying? His eyes had looked red all day. Though of course he'd been smoking. I had to help him get the eggnog open and hold the carton up so he could sip. "How did Bob Cratchit drink this shit?" he said. "Guess I can cross this off too."

Back at the house, he lay on the sofa for a while, then got up, bent over, groaned and picked up the mandolin case. "You know, I haven't played since your million-dollar bash," he said. "I want you to have this."

"Come on, no way. I could never play mandolin for shit. There must be somebody who could really—"

"Fuck *somebody*," he said.

Just two days later, he'd gotten so weak that Heather brought him a walker, which he used to get back and forth to the armchair and the bathroom. Then he stopped making *that* trip, so she brought in a commode; he could get his legs over the side of the bed, and if you'd bring the walker over he could get to his feet, go the two steps by himself, turn and sit, in his open-backed hospital johnny. And then Janna had to help him; he wouldn't let me. And then the bedpan. And then the day Heather came to catheterize him. He said to Janna, "Here goes our last chance." That was the same day Heather hooked him up to the morphine. "Think of this as the baseline," she told us, "and then you give him more by mouth. This is in your hands. You understand what I'm saying?"

After our car ride, he never wanted music again, and he had no interest in hearing the World Series. He'd brought pictures in stand-up Plexiglas frames: a photo of Simone, a postcard reproduction of Scipione Pulzone's *The Lamentation* (1591)—I looked at the back—and a snapshot of the two of us standing in front of my house. I set them up on the table by his bed, but I never saw him look at them.

He screamed when we turned him to prevent bedsores—it took me and Janna together—but still insisted on being turned, until he didn't. When he could no longer drink, we swabbed the inside of his mouth with supposedly mint-flavored sponges the size of sugar cubes, on plastic sticks. At first he'd made faces at the taste of the morphine; then he was sucking at the dropper.

One day, the day before the last day, he motioned me to bend down and whispered, "Why will you not just *do* it? They're not gonna say shit to you. *She* knows."

"Buddy," I said, "you know I can't." Which *she* did he mean? He'd gotten to a point where he was conflating Heather and Janna.

"I'm not your buddy," he said. "You cocksucker."

On his last night, we both slept in the living room with him, though I guess "slept" isn't the word—Janna on the sofa, me on the floor—and took turns getting up every half hour to dose him again. I'd stopped drawing the morphine up to the exact line on the dropper: just squirted in as much as it would hold, then watched the tip of his tongue touch at the green crust on his lips. I'd write down the time and "20 mg," hoping they wouldn't check my chart too carefully against what drugs would be left. When the light finally started turning gray outside, I switched on his bedside lamp—I saw his eyelids tighten—and gave him the next dropper, ten minutes early, then another one for good measure. In a while, the moaning quieted down; I turned the lamp off, went to the window and saw pink above the mountains. I pulled my fleece over my sweatshirt and went out to feed the hens. Frost on the grass, a faint quarter moon still high.

Walking back to the house, I saw the light go on in the living room. Janna was standing over his bed and holding his hand, the one with the needle taped to it. "Where *were* you?" she said. "He was asking for you."

I leaned over him; he was still breathing, but with shallow breaths. "Should we call them?" I said.

His eyes came open and he said, "I've never been *here* before."

"Don't be afraid," Janna told him.

He rolled his head an inch to one side, an inch to the other. "I don't know how to do this."

"You can just let go," she said.

"Oh, fuck," he said. "You are one stupid twat."

Janna's head jerked back, but she kept hold of his hand.

"Is there anything you want us to do?" I said.

He closed his eyes. "You won't." He began drawing harder, deeper breaths. "I keep being mean," he said.

"Rest," I said. I took his other hand.

He rolled his head again. "I need to get this right."

Janna put her other hand on his, over where the needle went in.

"We both love you," she said. "It's okay to go."

"I don't know," he said.

We watched him breathe. It took longer and longer for the next one to come, and then there wasn't a next one.

I looked at Janna. She pointed back at him. You could see it: there was nobody in there anymore.

I let go of the hand. "I better call them."

"Can't you take a *minute*?" she said. "This is what he came to give you."

After Heather left, and the guy from the funeral home took the body away in the back of his black Escalade, I drove Janna into town for breakfast. It was still only ten in the morning. There was a family in the next booth, so it must have been Saturday. Or Sunday. One of the kids was playing games on his phone or whatever; I could hear the little beeps and the snatches of metallic music. How could this not be driving the parents crazy? Janna ordered a grapefruit that she didn't eat; I had pancakes and no coffee. They were supposed to pick up the bed around noon, and I planned to sleep away the rest of the day.

"How are you holding up?" I said.

"He was absolutely on the money," she said. "I *am* a stupid twat. At least you kept your mouth shut. *We love you we love you we love you it's all right to go.* I'm going to be hearing that the rest of my life."

"He didn't know what he was saying. We did right by him."

"So that's what you'd want? Somebody *doing right* by you?"

"You're beating yourself up," I said. "We're both exhausted."

"This has to change." She pushed the grapefruit away and waved to get the waitress. "Can you take me back to the house so I can get my car? Shit's been piling up at the office."

"They can spare you for one more day."

"You don't get what I'm telling you," she said. "I'm not spending another night there. You can do what you want. Wear her fucking aprons, feed her fucking chickens. Sing your dead-people songs, whatever. Read your dead-people books. You're going to kill yourself one of these days, making that drive in the winter. Look, this is my fault— I should've helped you. But you don't even know who I am."

These days the summer parties happen in other people's fields, behind other people's farmhouses. So far this year I've been to one near Ludlow, Vermont, and another one an hour south of Albany. It's always the same people, give or take, and the same songs, said to be timeless. Our crowd isn't old enough yet to be dying off; they don't even seem to age that much year by year. But their kids, whose names I never remember, keep getting older, until you don't see them anymore.

When I go, I go alone: Janna says if she has to hear a banjo one more time she'll shoot herself, and I'm grateful to her for saying so. I've given Paul's mandolin to the son of that banjo player who was in my band all those years ago. He's nineteen or twenty, the son, loves the music and has the gift; he'd been playing some hopeless Gibson knockoff. You still see one or two like him. He makes it to some of the parties and we'll do a song or two, I hope not just because he feels obliged. I suppose I'm getting too old to be standing out in a field on a summer night as the dew makes the strings slick, but I can still sing; having some age on me, maybe I sound more like the real thing.

It only took Janna two months to sell the old house on the dirt road. She got us our asking price, enough to buy a three-bedroom Craftsman-style bungalow—an office for her, a study for me—ten blocks from campus, four blocks from the health-food store. I walk to class, except on the coldest days, and Janna rides her bicycle to work. I play squash once a week with my department chair. We've bought a flat-screen television, forty-six inches, high definition, for my ball games and her shows. I'm making notes toward a second book. If I can ever finish, it could get me invited to a conference or two; despite that trip to the Brontë country, Janna says she wants to travel with me. You see all this as a defeat, I know. I would have. But I can't begin to tell you.

Acknowledgments

My thanks to those who have published and edited these stories over the years: Amy Bloom, Michael Hainey, Yuka Igarashi, Field Maloney, Sigrid Rausing, Rob Spillman, Lorin Stein and Deborah Treisman.

To Molly Atlas for her diligence in placing them.

To Ruthie Reisner, for her patience in guiding me through the process of publication.

To Amy Ryan, for her vigilant copyediting.

To Alethea Black, Kevin Canty, Amy Hempel, Lee Johnson, Tom Piazza, Amanda Robb and Alison Weaver, for their advice, encouragement, support and friendship.

And to Gary Fisketjon and Amanda Urban, once again, for everything.

A Note About the Author

David Gates lives in Missoula, Montana, and Granville, New York. He teaches at the University of Montana and in the Bennington Writing Seminars, and was a writer and editor at *Newsweek*, where he specialized in music and books.

A Note on the Type

This book was set in Monotype Dante, a typeface designed by Giovanni Mardersteig (1892–1977). Modeled on the Aldine type used for Pietro Cardinal Bembo's treatise *De Aetna* in 1495, Dante is a modern interpretation of the venerable face.

Typeset by Scribe, Philadelphia, Pennsylvania

Printed and bound by R.R. Donnelley, Harrisonburg, Virginia

Designed by M. Kristen Bearse